Shifting into Shadows

by

Zanna Archer

The Shapesisters, Book Two

Dedication

To Chuck and Evita
with love

Acknowledgements

I would like to thank everyone who has played a role in bringing this book to print. Once again, my editor, Callie Lynn Wolfe, has provided swift, thoughtful guidance and patient feedback with making this book the best it could be. Debbie Taylor has designed another beautiful cover. Amanda Barnett, the senior editor for paranormal romance; and Rhonda Mosher Penders and RJ Morris, the hearts of The Wild Rose Press, were always available to cope with any unresolved problems.

With this novel, our writers' group became more than a good critique group. Everyone commented on the first "final" manuscript. When I decided to make significant revisions, they read a second complete version, with more useful comments and without a single complaint. Double thanks to Colleen Driscoll, R. Gene Turchin, Lindsey Minardi, Pepper E. Hedden, Nancy Hall, and Joanie Raisovich!

Finally, I'd like to thank everyone who read the first book in the series, Shiftless in Sheboygan—especially those of you who have been waiting patiently for Book Two! I hope that all readers, new and returning, will enjoy shifting into shadows with Libby and Dash.

Chapter 1

Familiar chimes in the darkened bedroom. *Ellyn? At this hour?* Hair rising on the nape of her neck, Libby Anbruzzen sat up and grabbed her phone. On the screen, her Mentor's eyes were wide, her usually sedate curls like silver spikes guarding her skull. "Has something happened to Steffi or Dayzee?"

"Your sisters are fine."

Good. Libby's breath resumed its normal human rhythm.

"Dumire is running!"

Libby grimaced. *Just what I need.*

"I thought you should know since—"

"Since I helped catch him. Didn't OASIS give him X-Ting?" A dose of the drug should have extinguished the rogue shifter's shapeshifting ability and substantially lowered his IQ.

"Something must have gone wrong."

"No kidding." Libby nipped her tongue. No need to be snarky. "Thanks for the warning."

Returning her phone to the nightstand, Libby glanced at the undisturbed side of the queen-sized bed and sighed. What had begun as a celebration of Tommy's promotion at Kingston, Inc., had degenerated into another round of The Argument. Disgusted by her refusal to trade her detective badge for marriage and family, her Simple Human lover had bedded on the sofa.

1

"Lib, come here." A quivering voice unlike Tommy's usual husky one penetrated the flimsy door that separated the bedroom from the rest of the condo. A strangled sob punctuated his "Please!"

Libby's chest tightened. Dumire hadn't wasted any time. She punched the emergency button on her phone to summon OASIS. "I'm on my way," she called in her brightest voice. Her bare feet hit the carpet. She pulled on her robe and retrieved her gun from the nightstand drawer. Taking a deep breath, she opened the door and froze.

Summerhaven University T-shirt hanging on his lanky frame, Tommy stood beneath the overhead lights in the space that separated living and dining areas. Behind him lurked a burly figure who held the blade of a knife close to Tommy's neck. "Hey, Detective Maitland. Long time no see."

Libby tapped one toe and looked at a far corner of the room. "Not long enough."

"Is that any way to greet a fellow shifter?"

"Fellow...what the—" Tommy started to turn his head.

Libby's gaze snapped back to her lover.

"Shut it." When the knife pressed harder, Tommy's lips clamped together. He looked like a rabbit caught in a trap.

Poor guy.

Dumire bared his teeth. "Put that gun down nice and easy, and nobody will get hurt."

Not yet. Keeping her eyes on the knife, Libby complied.

"Now kick it over here."

When she hesitated, Dumire snarled. She gave a

weak kick in his direction.

"So Lover Boy doesn't know about you." A nasty chuckle crawled out of Dumire's mouth.

"Let him go. I'm the one you want."

"First, let's have some fun." Dumire's lips split in a fiendish grin. "Show him what you are." She shook her head. *Not like this*.

Another snarl. "Shift. Or Lover Boy dies."

When Tommy whimpered, Libby's heart twisted. Gaze fixed on the knife, she took off her robe and dropped it on the floor.

"Keep your eyes open, buddy. You don't want to miss this."

Libby removed her nightgown and stood naked on the rug.

"No predators, or he's dead. Got it?"

"Yes." At least, Dumire couldn't predict the shape she would take. No more than four feet between them. *Size. Speed. Venom!* Closing her eyes, she visualized her black mamba.

Scales popped out on her skin. Her shrunken organs relocated. Her head, torso, and legs united in a sinuous tube the length of her human five-foot six.

The horror and disbelief in Tommy's eyes chilled her awareness.

She flicked her tongue. *Target Dumire*. He had a distinctive scent and vibrations that made her quiver.

She coiled and struck, her fangs finding food, which moved. Something hit her. A second vibration roared through her.

She struck again. Hot, salty liquid pulsed into her mouth. Something tore her off, but her fangs held a piece of the food. She struck something and slid until she rested on a level surface. *Be human. Be Libby.* Spitting out the flesh in her mouth, Libby returned to her naked human form, drenched in blood.

On the floor in front of her, Dumire lay, with his hands against his throat. Blood everywhere.

Libby clapped a hand to her human mouth. Mouthwash might remove the foul taste of his blood, but nothing would remove the shock of the moment. *I killed.*

Backing away from her, Tommy tripped over Dumire's body, grabbed the knife, and scrambled to his feet. For a heartbeat, they were eye to eye, and she peered into a well of terror.

Her hammering heart threatened to burst her human frame. "Tommy, it's me. Libby."

He waved the knife. "Get out! Now!" When she grabbed her gun, he stepped back.

"I need to clean up." *By then OASIS should be here.* Holding the gun, she backed into the dark bedroom and locked the door behind her. Alone, she shuddered. *I had to. He would have killed us both.* She drew several slow breaths. *Poor Tommy. Now he knows…*

Beneath a steaming shower in the adjoining bathroom, she scrubbed so hard she almost peeled off her human skin. Half a bottle of mouthwash and fanatical toothbrushing removed the remains of the snack her snake had relished, but the memories made her stomach heave.

She pulled on underwear, jeans, and the first T-shirt she could find. Then she tossed additional clothes and necessities into her suitcase. *I'll get everything else while he's working.* Her clean body yearned to return to the nearby bed. *Not here. Not now.* Gun at the ready, she eased the door open.

Instead of lurking with the knife near the bedroom, Tommy sat in a dining room chair on the far side of the dining area. The knife lay on the table in front of him. His dark hair stuck out in different directions, and he stared at Dumire's body as if he'd never…he probably never had seen a corpse.

She'd seen more than her share. *But not on my living room rug and not one I…* Blood-covered hands at the ghoulish wound on his neck. *Carotid artery.*

"What are you staring at?"

Her eyes met Tommy's cool gaze. "I killed him."

"You're a cop. That's your job."

"Not usually." She nudged her stronger foot forward.

"Stop!" Stumbling to his feet, Tommy brandished the knife.

She obeyed and kept her gun at her side. She gestured at the sofa against the opposite wall. "Mind if I sit there?" With the emotional impact of the kill piled onto the physical stress of the shift, she felt ready to collapse.

Tommy's chin dipped in a reluctant nod. His shoulders were so stiff someone might have stuck a steel rod through them. He sat and stared at the table.

Libby settled on the edge of a sofa cushion.

"Tommy, I—"

His head snapped up. "What are you?"

She flinched. He was angry. *Understandable.* "A Shapeshifter." No reason not to tell him. When OASIS finished the mind-wipe, he wouldn't remember any of this.

"Like movie monsters?" He grabbed his elbows and drew his shoulders closer as if warding off an attack.

5

"But if you're—then, they're not made up. They're real. Like Crispin Alexandros says."

Libby frowned at his reference to the man who'd become a public figure by insisting that Shapeshifters were not only real but also threats to Simple Humans.

"What about your sisters? Are they like you? Or are they normal?"

His last word made her wince. "Like me."

"Snakes."

"Yes." Other known Shapeshifters inherited their ability and belonged to a single animal family. Products of a genetic mishap to their Simple Human parents, she and her sisters could take any animal shape. Tommy didn't need to know that.

She rubbed her elbow and eyed the bloody spot on the wall. *Dumire threw me.* "I know this is a shock." The image of Tommy's face during her shift flashed in her mind.

Tommy snorted. "Shapeshifters. Shadow people. Waiting for the opportunity to seize power."

"Don't believe that Alexandros crap." Libby picked up a pillow. An hour ago, she would have thrown it at him. A tussle would have ended with making love. An hour ago. It felt like a lifetime.

She returned the pillow to the sofa. "We Shapeshifters want what you humans want: to live and let live."

Tommy pointed at the corpse. "He didn't." He touched his throat.

"Some Shapeshifters are criminals. Just like humans."

"You should have told me."

"I know. I'm sorry. I kept waiting for the right time,

but it never…I never…" She put her healthy elbow on the arm of the sofa and rested her forehead in her hand.

"Let me get this straight." Tommy stood and leaned on the table as he speared her with his gaze. "You've been lying to me since the day we met, but *you* don't trust *me*. Unbelievable!" If she were still a snake, the vibration of his bitter laugh could have ripped the scales from her skin.

"It's not that. I wasn't…ready."

"Well, the cat's out…or snake's out of its hole." He bared his teeth. Then his face lit up. "I could write about this. Tell the world how it feels to live with a Shapeshifter. Crispin Alexandros might help me publish it. I bet he'd take me on tour with him." He looked around. "Where's my phone?"

Although it took most of her remaining energy, Libby seized the phone he'd left near the sofa. "That's not going to happen."

"Come on, Lib." Tommy turned on his Gosh-let's-make-up-I'm-a-good-guy smile. "I should get something good out of this god-awful mess."

"You're alive." Libby glanced at Dumire's corpse. The doorbell buzzed. *About time*. Libby walked to the intercom and hit the respond button that unlocked the downstairs door. "Come on up."

When the crew entered, most of the group headed straight for the corpse, but a tall, slender woman approached the dining table.

Tommy blinked. "You don't look like cops."

"We're from the Organization to Assist, Support, and Inform Shapeshifters." The woman spoke in a low, melodious voice. "Don't you worry. We'll take care of everything."

Including your memory. When Tommy awoke in the morning, Dumire and all traces of this horrible incident would be gone from this apartment, from his life, from his mind. The mind-wiper would also plant the false memory of an argument that ended with Libby leaving.

****

What now? Libby stared through the windshield of her used hybrid sedan parked in the lot adjoining the condos. *Where—* She pulled her phone from a pocket in her jacket.

Ellyn picked up on the second ring. "Libby?"

"Sorry to wake you, but…can I stay with you for a while?"

Ellyn hesitated.

She's afraid. "Dumire's dead. Tommy and I are…over."

The other woman released a breath. "I have room. Once a Mentor, always a Mentor."

Twenty minutes later, Libby parked in the empty space in front of a tidy brick home at the end of a paved road lined with elegant old houses. Ellyn answered the doorbell and regarded her in the light of the streetlamp. "You've had a rough night." She stepped back and admitted Libby to the small foyer. "When you were younger, tea and cookies helped. I suspect tonight calls for something stronger."

Libby rubbed her forehead. *When I close my eyes, what will I see? Those flat eyes? That open mouth? All that blood? Or Tommy's face?* "Good idea." Leaving her suitcase by the stair, she followed her Mentor into the small dining room.

While Libby sat at the round table, Ellyn plugged a phone into the speakers on the top of her gleaming wooden sideboard, and a dreamy melody filled the room. "Talk if you like, or let the music quiet your inner turmoil."

The gentle chords soothed Libby's jangled nerves. "You always know the right thing to do."

Ellyn pushed the edge of a protruding napkin into an open drawer near the top of the sideboard, which she shut. Then she extracted a bottle from the liquor cabinet in the sideboard base. "I've had years of practice."

Libby smiled. "And an old-fashioned Southern lady for a mother."

Ellyn offered a glass filled with a generous blend of Scotch and soda. When the smoky heat slipped down Libby's throat, the knots in her shoulder muscles loosened. "This is just what I needed. Thanks."

"You're welcome. What time do you report in tomorrow?"

For the first time in hours, Libby's lips twitched in a near-smile. "I'm off for the next three days. I can take you out for a long, leisurely breakfast."

"Not tomorrow. I'm working at the homeless shelter." Ellyn took a drink. "What happened with Dumire?"

As Libby briefly described the deadly encounter, the older woman sat forward and listened. When Libby finished, Ellyn cried, "Good job!"

Libby shook her head. "I keep thinking there should have been another way."

"Nonsense." Her Mentor patted her shoulder. "You did what you had to do."

"I suppose. And that was the high point of the evening." Libby took another sip. "I think I've known for a while that what Tommy and I had wasn't working, but I kept hoping things would improve. Tonight, everything came crashing down." She lifted her glass. "Thanks to Oliver Edward Dumire." She drank, set her empty glass on the woven coaster, and yawned. "Perfect anesthetic."

Ellyn guided her up the stairs to the small study. "Sleep well."

Libby turned to give her Mentor a quick hug, but Ellyn was already gone. The sheets on the futon held a faint lavender scent. As soon as she closed her eyes, Libby was out.

Chapter 2

"Let me make myself clear." Dash Honeycutt sat forward in the small office chair across from Jack Weatherby's weathered wooden desk. "We need a security specialist, not some...Special Ops. Sounds like a discount store."

"Let me assure you Detective Maitland is top of the line. She graduated with distinction from our police academy. She and her recently retired partner earned numerous commendations for outstanding work. She's also the youngest to reach detective rank."

She? Honeycutt maintained his neutral expression. *Great! Some hot-shot female using us for a career boost.* And if anybody on his team got the hots for her... *Nothing but trouble.*

Stacking his hands over his chest, Jack Weatherby piled on the praise with words like "meticulous" and "precise." "I'm not saying she's perfect. Who is? Libby can be stubborn."

Alexandros would enjoy that.

"She's also the first to tackle any new challenges and to volunteer for dangerous assignments."

Honeycutt chuckled. "You make her sound like Joan of Arc."

Weatherby's broad face creased in a smile. "Libby Maitland would have given Joan a run for her money. She will be an excellent liaison between your group and the Summerhaven PD." When his phone rang, his smile disappeared. "Excuse me."

****

Libby woke to sunlight spilling in her window. She sat up and checked the time on her phone before remembering she had the day off. Neatly stacked towels and washcloth sat on the desk. *Thank you, Ellyn's oldfashioned Southern mother.*

Several paperback books and pamphlets on the desk caught Libby's eye. Her hand hovered above the author's name. Why would Ellyn read Crispin Alexandros?

After a quick shower, she dressed, texted her family about breaking up with Tommy, and went downstairs.

"Good morning!" Wearing a simple pair of gray slacks and a long-sleeved blouse, Ellyn stood in the dining room. She gestured for Libby to turn. "New dress?"

"Last thing I stuffed in my suitcase. It's probably silly for apartment-hunting, but after last night, I need something bright." The floral print on the full skirt and the pink toenails peeking out of her sandals made her feel like a new woman.

"Did you sleep well?"

"Better than I thought I would."

"There's coffee and cereal in the kitchen. Please help yourself."

When Libby returned with her breakfast, Ellyn pointed to pieces of the *Summerhaven Herald* on the table. "You can check for rentals."

Libby sipped her coffee. "Don't worry. I'll be out of your hair ASAP."

"Take your time. It's good to have company." Ellyn checked her watch. "But I should go."

"Before you do, can I ask you something?"

Ellyn folded her arms. "Make it quick."

"Why do you have all that Crispin Alexandros junk on your desk?"

"You know what Mel says." She placed her hands on her hips, puffed out her chest, and lifted her finger in imitation of the Director of OASIS. "Know your enemy."

Libby laughed. "That's one of the first things you taught me."

"If trouble comes, I want to be prepared." Ellyn wiggled the wrist with her watch. "Now, I really must run." She paused in the arch between the living and dining rooms. "Happy apartment hunting! See you this evening."

After finishing her breakfast, Libby made a second cup of coffee and drank it. Scanning the ads for a place to live felt strange. *Of course, it does.*

After graduating from high school in Montana, she'd moved across the country to live in Summerhaven with her recently widowed grandmother.

Recalling the evening she'd run into Tommy while she was out with her fellow officers, Libby smiled. First time they'd seen each other since that deadly university psych class, and they'd talked until closing time. When Tommy said good night, magic filled the air. Friendship soon became something more. He was so sweet with Gran when she became ill, so comforting at the end. When he suggested that Libby move in with him, it felt right. *I thought I loved him, but… Twenty-seven years old and on my own for the first time.*

Libby put the paper aside. Excitement and a finger of fear wrapped around her spine.

Captain Weatherby's ring tone boomed on her phone.

"Maitland here."

"I know this is your off time, Detective, but we have a ten six seven at the Mark Five, and I need you there. Room One Four One Zero."

Dead body at the newest, most expensive hotel in town? *I'm Special Ops, not Homicide.* "One Four One Zero." She echoed the room number and brushed the skirt of her dress. *No time to change.* "On my way, sir."

Chapter 3

Nearing the entrance of the Mark V, Libby slowed her car. The massive façade of the new hotel dwarfed the other, more historic structures that occupied Mount Vernon Place in the heart of downtown Summerhaven. The imposing structure could have been an ancient tomb. *Fitting.*

Usually a crime scene meant patrol cars, at least one ambulance, often with lights flashing, and sometimes cameras and microphones. This morning, the hotel driveway was empty. *Must have chased us away so we don't scare the guests.* The owners had the money and the clout to do that. In front of the doors, Libby shut off her engine.

A gray-haired bellman appeared. "Sorry, miss, you can't—" When she flashed her badge, he didn't miss a beat and signaled a younger associate.

Valet parking. That explained the absence of patrol cars. She wrapped the tip around the keys she gave the skinny bellboy.

The registration area of the hotel was bigger than a football field and packed with many Simple Humans who had one thing in common: money. Men in tailored suits and silk foulard ties. Women in asymmetrical skirts, boldly mixed patterns, and enough gold jewelry to fill Fort Knox. No vacationing families with flip-flops, tank tops, sagging cut-offs, or dripping ice cream cones. No college kids on break. No interlopers who made the hair on the back of her neck stand up.

The thick carpet on the fourteenth floor muffled her footsteps and emphasized the eerie silence. In a room at the far corner of one hall, the door stood ajar. Someone was examining the locks. *Touch nothing*. Libby stuffed her hands in her jacket pockets.

The specialist gestured at Libby's floral skirt. "You sure you're in the right place?"

"Very funny, Pru. This was my first day off. Didn't have time to change when I got the call. I was planning to go apartment hunting."

"No kidding?" The other woman paused in taking photos. "My brother and his husband closed on a house and are looking for someone to take over their place in the Hamilton area. Old carriage house renovated into a one-bedroom above a garage. Some furniture, too."

Libby's heart gave a cheerful bounce. "Sounds promising."

Her colleague scrawled something on a blank piece of paper and handed it to Libby. "Here's his info."

"Thanks." Libby pocketed the lead and returned her hand to her pocket. She'd call after she finished here. The sitting room was crawling with specialists, yet another indication that this was not your typical homicide. "What have we got?"

"White male. Midthirties." Pru tilted her head to the left. "Bedroom."

"Maitland."

The deep voice that made her turn belonged to a husky African American man in a tailored gray suit. Deputy Inspector Ken Jansen. Head troubleshooter for the chief of police. He must be the one who'd locked everything down.

She glanced toward the open door of the bedroom. White male. Midthirties. A politician who died with a hooker or boy toy in the bed? Wouldn't be the first time. They wouldn't need all the forensics workups for that. *And why would they call me?*

"Why am I here, Ken? I haven't worked Homicide since Mike and I transferred to Special Ops."

"All I know is we have a nasty situation, and the chief wants you. Vic checked in two days ago under the name Sam Poe. ID in his wallet is for Schuyler Pope. He worked for Crispin Alexandros."

A chill crept down her spine. *The creep who wants to brand me and make sure I get a rabies shot.*

"Looks like he might have been scouting locations for the Alexandros presentation."

"Slow down. Crispin Alexandros is coming to Summerhaven?" Although she kept her voice steady, she bit her inner lip. "I thought he liked crowds." Jansen shrugged. "He's headed our way." "Lucky us." Libby wrinkled her nose.

"The chief agrees." Jansen either misunderstood or ignored Libby's lack of enthusiasm. "Wherever he goes, Alexandros attracts a crowd, and crowds mean money. He could be a bigger draw than SU sports or Harrier baseball."

When Jansen opened his hands as if bills were raining down, Libby nodded.

"The chief wants to keep a lid on the details so we don't spook Alexandros and his followers. In addition, the vic's a hometown boy." Libby stared at him.

"Hal Miller ran track with him in high school." He indicated the bedroom. "He's taking this pretty hard."

"If the vic's from Summerhaven, why was he staying here instead of with his family?"

"I'm sure we'll find out at some point. Right now, the basic story is hometown boy, sudden death, hearts and prayers with family, and ongoing investigation."

Libby pressed her lips together. Everyone in the sitting room was working with their usual precision, but whenever they glanced toward the bedroom, they clenched their jaws. Murder was an ugly business, but there must be something more about this one. "How bad is it?"

"See for yourself." Jansen led her toward the bedroom where everyone was measuring, dusting, or photographing. As she stood on the threshold, for the second time in twenty-four hours, Libby scented blood. The body lay at the foot of the bed on the charcoal carpet no doubt purchased because it wouldn't show spills and stains. The interior designers hadn't planned on a rug soaked with human blood. *Like Dumire.*

Jansen spoke. "Looks like the killer cleaned up in the bathroom. Towels are missing. They've already done a clean sweep of the suite to pick up any traces of hair or skin. We're checking security tapes for the back entrances and exits, along with the hotel parking lot. Uniforms are digging through the trash bins."

Libby turned her attention to the victim. White male. About six feet tall. Stocky build. Dark hair. Her gaze traveled farther. "Dear God." Most of her homicide cases involved guns, blunt objects, or knives. The deep, irregular wounds that shredded Schuyler Pope's business shirt and ripped open his torso looked as if they could have come from the claws of a giant bear. Bile burned her throat.

Aside from brief responses to her questions, the investigators focused on their tasks. Their pressed lips, tight jaws, and tense shoulders suggested they were doing their best to keep from breaking down.

Libby studied the gruesome wounds. Had someone killed the vic to scare Alexandros away? From everything she'd read and seen, Alexandros would gladly find a way to turn this murder into an attack on Shapeshifters.

"Schuyler Pope." A deep voice rumbled in her ear. Startled, Libby turned and nearly broke her nose when it collided with what felt like a cement block. Not a block. A shoulder. Someone behind her gasped.

Libby's eyes moved from the shoulder-boulder to the corded neck and up, up, up. Tommy had played basketball, but looking up at him had never made her head spin like looking at this guy did. Strong chin, chiseled cheekbones, and deep blue eyes. He could have been a bigger, blonder version of the Norse god Thor. All he needed was the hammer. He looked over Libby's shoulder and regarded the corpse with an expression of detached interest.

Kneeling by the body, the medical examiner looked up. "Who are you?"

"Dash Honeycutt." He already had his ID in his hand, had no doubt showed it to Jansen, who stood behind him.

Dash? Libby stifled her laugh. What kind of a name was that for a guy who looked as if he'd been carved from a chunk of the Grand Canyon?

"I'm with Alexandros security."

The laughter in Libby's throat died. She turned to the ME. "What can you tell?"

19

The ME tore her eyes away from the newcomer to answer. "He was alive when the killer started slicing." She held up a glass enshrouded in plastic. "Probably drunk or drugged." *Let's hope.*

Dash Honeycutt spoke to Jansen. "Any suspects?"

"Not yet. But Mayor Dawson wants you to assure Dr. Alexandros that everything will be taken care of before he arrives."

First the chief, now the mayor. Who next? "And when would that be?"

Honeycutt glanced at her. "Three weeks from tonight."

Libby lifted an eyebrow. With no weapon, no witnesses, and no suspects, he thought Homicide would find the killer in three weeks? *Watches too many cop shows.*

Returning to the front room, she approached the tech at the entrance. "Any signs of forced entry?" Pru shook her graying head.

"So he may have known the killer."

"Maybe not." Dash Honeycutt now stood by her shoulder. "The nature of the wounds suggests a Shapeshifter." When one of the officers in the sitting room sniggered, Honeycutt pounced. "Don't laugh. Those shadow creatures walk among us. They can be anywhere. Anyone."

Beneath a gaze as cold as blue steel, Libby froze.

"Dr. Pope could have hooked up with the killer and brought him or her back to the room. Maybe they got into an argument. The killer shifted, attacked, then returned to the human shape and escaped."

Omit the Shapeshifter part, and Honeycutt could be describing many of the homicides she'd covered. Libby focused on the door. No forced entry. The victim let him in. Or her. Or them. A woman could dope a drink as easily as a man could. The victim might have been more willing to drink it, too, if a woman—or any potential sexual partner—offered. Of course, shifters had to strip before transforming, but since Pope was killed in the bedroom, he and the killer—dear God, even she was starting to get sucked in by this Alexandros propaganda!

"The killer could have taken a shape that let him sneak in and out without anyone noticing. Could have been a bug in the ventilation. Memorized a map of the hotel and waited up there for the right time to strike." One of Honeycutt's big hands gestured toward a vent near the ceiling.

He sounded so confident that Libby wanted to shake him until his brain rattled, but Alexandros had already damaged him enough. Hands in pockets, she focused on the geometric pattern of the rug. Accustomed to instantaneous horror-movie creatures, Simple Humans didn't understand how much physical and mental energy shapeshifting required. Not to mention the problem of proportion. For even a large cockroach, the journey through the Mark V system would have been like a human hiking the Great Wall of China. More important, even the largest members of that insect family were not large enough or savage enough to eviscerate a human. Once in the room, a cockroach could have returned to his human base but would have been vulnerable during the human shift and the necessary recovery time.

Honeycutt watched the vent as if the killer lurked behind it. "Could have escaped the same way once he was finished."

And shut the vent behind him? Clever cockroach!

21

He turned to one of the techs. "Better check up there for blood traces."

An expert on Shapeshifters and on homicide investigations! No doubt picked up his valuable store of misinformation from Alexandros himself. Libby would have scoffed, but that would have been disrespectful to the victim. Everyone else in the team seemed to hang on this idiot's every word. No doubt the other women liked looking at him. What woman wouldn't? Until he opened that mouth and spouted nonsense. Libby tore her gaze away. *Elizabeth Irene Anbruzzen, you just broke up with one guy. Stop ogling this one. If he looks too good to be true, he probably is.*

While the medical staff carried out the body bag containing the victim, everyone stood in silent respect. *RIP Schuyler Pope. In the wrong place at the wrong time.* Wrong was the right word for this case in more ways than one. Shifters learned, early on, never to harm Simple Humans. Rogues who broke that rule, like Dumire, seldom attacked in a way that drew attention. If this killer was indeed a shifter—and Libby wasn't willing to concede that—he or she had killed in a dramatic manner. It didn't make sense.

If the killer were a rogue shifter, the autopsy should find traces of fur, claws, and saliva. Al Prince, a shifter who worked in the medical examiner's office, would edit the report and forward all the evidence to OASIS, which would identify the criminal and send an APB to all shifters in law enforcement.

"Anything useful on his phone?" The deep Honeycutt voice rolled in her ear, but he was talking to Hal Miller from Homicide.

"Looks like the killer may have taken it." "That's

one huge cockroach," Libby muttered.

Those nearby chuckled, but a scowl bisected Honeycutt's broad forehead.

Libby looked down to hide her smile.

"Too bad." Honeycutt grunted. "He might have marked his contacts to indicate suspected shifters."

"Is that something else you learned from Crispin Alexandros?" When Libby uttered the name, her stomach did a queasy roll.

"It's a procedure we all follow." He spoke in a matter-of-fact voice. "You're a skeptic."

She met his cool blue gaze. "A realist. This Shapeshifter notion strikes me as too obvious. I think the killer wants to send a message. I'm not sure what it is."

"Who knows?" Huge shoulders rose and fell in a shrug. "Shapeshifters are unpredictable. They spend so much time in animal minds that they don't think like us."

"You don't say!" Libby feigned curiosity with a blink. When an emphatic nod threatened to loosen a wave of golden hair across Honeycutt's forehead, her fingers itched to brush it back. She clenched her fists in her jacket pockets and focused on his ear. Was there any part of this guy that didn't have a pleasing shape? *His Alexandros-molded mind.*

"The Alexandros Foundation has published numerous studies on Shapeshifter psychology. Give me your address, and they'll send you some."

"No thanks." Alexandros "research" no doubt supported his antishifter lies. With a curt nod at Dash Honeycutt, she returned to Jansen. "Who found the body?"

"One of the hotel security people." He checked his notes. "Bill Simpson. Concierge sent him up. Manager called it in." Another look at his notes. "They're all downstairs waiting for interviews."

"I'll do it." When she and Mike worked Homicide, she'd often gone back to the crime scene after everyone else had finished. Her rat shape had a sharper sense of smell and sometimes discovered details that escaped the humans. Glancing toward the bedroom, Libby's nose twitched. *Later...*

Chapter 4

As Honeycutt walked down the hall behind Detective Maitland, he kept a comfortable distance. From Jack Weatherby's description, he'd expected a strapping Valkyrie, complete with shield and helmet. How wrong he'd been!

Her mammoth shoulder bag and business-like navy blazer clashed with the bright flowers on a dress that accented curves in all the right places. The full skirt ended with a little ruffle that flattered shapely calves. Sling-back sandals undercut her crisp, no-nonsense stride. The pale nail polish on the finger that pushed the Down arrow of the elevator contrasted with the bright pink toenails peeking out of the sandals. Did Summerhaven's Joan of Arc have a wild side?

She stood for a moment facing the elevator. Her shoulders tensed, and her chin lifted. Sliding one hand beneath her jacket, she turned. The tip of her head rose slightly above his shoulder, and she would have collided with him again if he hadn't touched her arm. *Solid biceps. Must work out.* He lifted both hands. "Don't shoot. I'm on your side."

"That remains to be seen." She removed her hand from her holster.

In the hotel room, Schuyler Pope's mutilated body had commanded his attention. Now, Honeycutt studied the face shaped like a Valentine's Day heart, the determined pink mouth, the sassy nose with its slightly tilted tip, and the gold sparks in her big brown eyes.

"Why are you following me?"

The reason for those sparks! "You're Detective Maitland, right? Special Ops? Sorry we weren't properly introduced. I'm Dash—" When he extended his hand, she looked at it as if she expected him to crush her bones.

"Honeycutt. I heard it the first time."

"Call me Dash, please."

She glanced at the lights above the elevator doors. "I don't have time to socialize, Mr. Honeycutt." She patted her shoulder bag. "I'm working."

"I know." He gave an emphatic nod. "Since we're going to be working together—"

"What?" Her forehead creased in the hint of a frown.

Interior alarms buzzed. Not all the women he'd worked with had greeted the news with delight, but most didn't look as if he'd poured lemon juice down their throats. "You're our liaison for the Alexandros presentation."

Her sleek eyebrows lifted. "That's news to me. Where did you hear it?"

"Jack Weatherby."

Her lips gathered in a moue.

"I was in his office when he got the call on this." Honeycutt gestured toward Pope's suite. "Decided to come here since it involves one of ours. I'll have to report to Alexandros."

She lifted a finger. "No details, Mr. Honeycutt. Nothing leaves the department except the victim's name. Is that understood?"

"Yes, Detective." She looked ready to nail him to the wall with that finger if he refused. "I also thought it would be an opportunity to meet you."

"We've met." The elevator door opened. "Now, if you don't mind—" She stepped into the car.

When he followed her, she turned and placed her hands on her hips. "Mr. Honeycutt, I understand that you and your employer have an interest in this case, and if permitted, I will share anything I learn that may be relevant to you. But I see no reason for you to accompany me on these interviews."

He pushed the Lobby button and stood against the opposite wall. "I do."

The floor lights flashed. Under other circumstances, her pout would have been sexy. *Stubborn and sullen.* A beatable combination.

"Your people don't know this yet, Detective, but Schuyler Pope was a senior scientist in the Alexandros research lab. His death could mean that we have a serious security breach. I handle travel security for Alexandros. And I'm coming with you." He took out his phone. "If you like, I'll get permission from Jack—your supervisor."

"Please try to be unobtrusive."

When her gaze traveled from his head to his feet, he could almost hear her thinking "Fat chance." *After this, I'll call Jack.* Instead of making his job easier, Detective Maitland was making him fight for every inch. The sooner he and his team had a more congenial liaison, the happier everyone would be, present company included.

The elevator door opened, and they exited side by side.

Crossing the lobby, he smiled at the women who smiled at him. Any of them would be a better companion than the dour detective, who seemed to be keeping a mental score of his encounters. Exchanging smiles with pretty women still wasn't a crime, thank God.

Their first two interviews, in the small meeting room in the corridor off the main desk, went quickly. The hotel security agent, a wiry man in his forties, was still shaken by what he'd discovered in Room 1410. The manager had little to offer.

"Who's next?" Honeycutt asked.

Detective Maitland reviewed her list. "Peter Barnett. The concierge who sent security to the victim's room."

A tall, thin young man with dark eyes and golden skin stood in the doorway. "You wanted to see me?"

She stood and showed her badge. "Mr. Barnett, I'm Detective Libby Maitland with the Summerhaven PD, and this is…my associate. Mr. Honeycutt."

They'd agreed on the introduction. Although her jaw no longer stiffened when she called him her

"associate," it still sounded unnatural.

"I understand your shift ended a few hours ago, Mr. Barnett, so thank you for waiting. Please take a seat." She smiled as she indicated the chair.

Same smile she'd given the others, and every time, it lit up her face. *How could I get a smile like that?*

"I won't keep you long."

Peter Barnett took his seat with the comfortable precision of someone who'd studied martial arts. "I'm happy to be of service, ma'am. Detective." He stroked his tie. "That's my job. Not as important as your service, of course."

"I understand that you sent Bill Simpson up to Room 1410."

"Yes."

"Is that part of your job? Sending security up to the

guest rooms?"

"No, ma'am."

Detective Maitland opened her mouth, then pressed her lips together.

"We handle special services. Group tours. Theater tickets. I also give directions to guests who don't trust their GPS. Sometimes they want advice. Like where to get the best Italian food at the best price.

"Sometimes they report a disturbance. Like a loud party. Guests call me when the front desk is busy. I alert the front desk, and they handle the problem."

When Detective Maitland leaned forward, her butterscotch-colored hair brushed her cheek, and she flicked it back. "What led you to ask Bill Simpson to go to 1410?"

"I got this phone call."

"Do you remember when you received the call?" she asked.

"We keep contact records." The young man took out a tablet and pointed to an entry. "Around four this morning."

"Did the caller identify himself?"

"She—it sounded like a woman—didn't give a name."

Honeycutt leaned toward the smaller man, who flinched. *Good.* "Do you have any information that could help identify the caller?"

The concierge tapped his tablet. "Phone number."

"Why was this person talking to you instead of the front desk?" Honeycutt asked.

The younger man swallowed. "They transferred her to me. She said she was worried about the guest in 1410. Said they planned to meet, but he hadn't shown up. Said she'd been trying to contact him. Left messages everywhere, but still hadn't heard from him. She sounded really upset. Asked me to check on him."

He tugged at his tie and shot a conspiratorial smile that Honeycutt didn't return. "With all those on-line dating sites, I get calls like that sometimes." Now on familiar territory, he spoke more smoothly. "People agree to get together. Then somebody gets cold feet. Leaves the other person waiting. I thought that was what happened here, and I tried to let the caller down easy, but she wouldn't let go. Said I was her last hope before she called the police. So, I told her I'd check. Last thing we need is the police—no offense, Detective, but police presence can disturb guests."

"None taken. Please continue."

He sat back and rubbed his arms. "I wasn't going to do anything, but she was so upset…I asked Bill to go up to the room. Then we got busy. That's how it goes. Nothing and then a million and one things that need immediate attention." He shook his head. "I forgot all about her call. Until you showed up." He looked from Honeycutt to Detective Maitland. "Did something happen to the man in 1410?"

Detective Maitland nodded.

"Oh, no!" The concierge glanced at his phone.

"Somebody should let the caller know." "Somebody will," she assured him.

Honeycutt said, "We want that number."

Detective Maitland spoke up. "I'll take it." She copied the information before Honeycutt could see it. "Thanks."

When the concierge glanced toward the exit, Honeycutt shifted position. "Right now, Mr. Barnett, this

30

case is under investigation. If we hear anyone has been leaking information, we'll know where to look." When he pointed at the slim concierge, the younger man drew back. "Is that clear?"

The concierge kept his eyes on Honeycutt's finger. "Yes, sir."

"Good." Honeycutt dropped his hand. "Don't leave town."

"No—that is, yes—sir."

"Mr. Barnett, thank you for your help." Detective Maitland spoke in a voice that would have tempted a jumper to come in from the ledge. "If you remember anything else—no matter how small—please call me." She gave him her card.

The concierge stared at the card as if he'd never seen one before. "1410. I never even saw him."

They both watched the young man return to his station near the hotel entrance. He gave them a furtive glance and moved behind the matronly woman who stood at the big desk.

"He's upset," Detective Maitland murmured.

"Wants to provide good service. Must think he failed."

When Detective Maitland took a deep breath, the corners of her mouth softened. Her face lit. She crossed the lobby, found the young man at the concierge desk, and locked onto his gaze. When she finished speaking, her listener rewarded her with a weak smile. They shook hands, and she exited the hotel.

Honeycutt joined her in the line of people waiting for their cars. "Mr. Barnett looked happier. What did you tell him?"

"Not much." She kept her gaze on the driveway. "I

said that what he did served the guest in 1410 much more than he knows."

"Nice."

When she looked at him, gold flashed in her dark eyes. "I don't need your approval, Mr. Honeycutt."

If she had a whip, she would have snapped it. He opened both hands. "I wasn't—I didn't—I'm impressed, Detective." Her jaw relaxed. "You went out of your way to do something kind. Lots of people wouldn't have bothered. This business has probably been eating at that kid for hours. A few words from you, and he felt better."

Chapter 5

Libby blinked. *Did Mr. I-Hate-Shapeshifters compliment me?* She opened her mouth, but before she could thank him, he spoke again.

"You should have someone watch that guy." Honeycutt nodded toward the concierge desk.

Libby's gratitude dropped to the pit of her stomach. "That's not necessary. You scared him enough to keep him from talking to the press."

Honeycutt's jaw stiffened. "He's a Shapeshifter."

"Really?" Libby swallowed a laugh. "What makes you think so?"

"Physical traits. Posture. Tells."

Libby touched her twitching nose. *Temper, temper.* She silently counted the cars in the parking lot. "You seem to know a lot about shifters." *Or think you do.*

"I've attended many Alexandros workshops and seminars. It's a free education."

And worth every cent you've paid. "Want to check his nails for blood or skin fragments?"

"No." Honeycutt's crisp response suggested she'd wasted her sarcasm. "He has an alibi. He was on duty." He scratched his chin. "Guess he could have stepped away from his desk."

"Homicide is reviewing the cameras in the lobby."

"Something about him doesn't feel right."

"How many homicides have you worked?"

"None." He looked down and rubbed the back of his neck. "I defer to your experience."

"I've learned not to take anything for granted. Sometimes, a case is open and shut. You have a victim, a weapon, and a killer all in the same room. Sometimes, it's someone you'd never suspect. Like Mr. Barnett."

"I don't really think he's your guy. But he might lead you to the killer." Leaning toward her, he lowered his voice. "They stick together. Shifters."

The image made her laugh. She'd never be able to keep a straight face working with these Alexandrites. *Alexandrwrongs*.

The parking attendant delivered Honeycutt's car first. Before getting in, he turned to her. "I'm picking the rest of my crew up at the airport around six. Would you like to join us for dinner?"

So you can feed me more so-called facts about Shapeshifters? "Thanks, but I'm busy." She fingered the paper in her pocket. *Hope this place is as nice as Pru made it sound.* "Next time we meet, tell me what you want from us, and I'll find out what we can provide. With budget cuts and staff shortages…"

"We'll work it out."

His knock-your-socks-off smile hit her like a burst of sunshine after a thunderstorm. Lifting her gaze to those deep blue eyes didn't help. From staring into the sun to diving into Summerhaven Lake. *Breathe!*

"Tomorrow morning at eight-thirty, we'll be at the convention center."

So much for days off. Libby entered the appointment on her phone. "See you there." She gave a half-hearted nod that Honeycutt didn't acknowledge.

Watching his SUV pull away, she frowned. What

Shifting into Shadows

had Captain Weatherby been thinking when he chose her for this? Under normal circumstances, the prospect of spending time with a guy who looked like Dash Honeycutt would have stirred a whirlpool of delight in any woman's belly, but Alexandros had shrunk the brain beneath that golden mane. What a shame!

Jansen's comments made it clear that anything connected with this Alexandros appearance was a big deal. If she asked Captain Weatherby to take her off the assignment, he might interpret the request as an indication that she couldn't handle important jobs. That would put a bad mark on her record.

A few minutes later, her car arrived, and a soft voice uttered her name.

Libby glanced over her shoulder. The shadows of the entry almost hid the slim concierge. "I'll be right back," she told the parking attendant. She approached Mr. Barnett. "What is it?"

His eyes shifted from side to side. Then, he leaned forward and spoke in a near-whisper. "That man. Honeycutt. Here yesterday. In the lobby."

When Schuyler Pope was alive. Libby's pulse raced.

"Are you sure? You said it was busy."

"Oh, yes. He's so big you can't miss him."

When Libby's gaze slid from the concierge's timid face to the lobby, she envisioned Dash Honeycutt's broad-shouldered figure towering above other, punier Simple Humans. She'd have to interview whoever was working at the front desk. If Dash Honeycutt had inquired about Schuyler Pope—

"Slow down, Hotshot." Her retired partner's

cautious voice pulled her back from the brink of speculation. Pope registered as Sam Poe. How could Honeycutt have known that? Honeycutt might have a legitimate reason for being at the hotel, a reason that had nothing to do with Schuyler Pope. Yet he was so determined to pin the murder on a Shapeshifter. The questions in Libby's brain multiplied until the top of her head felt ready to erupt. When the concierge gripped her arm, she almost jumped into the driveway.

"You won't tell him, will you?"

"No." She pried his sweaty hand loose. Trying to ignore the gnawing suspicion, she got into her car and drove away.

****

Before he pulled out of the hotel drive, Honeycutt had taken one last look at Libby Maitland in his rearview mirror. They'd gotten off to a rough start, but the witness interviews had gone smoothly. She was good at her job. She was good with people—she'd gone out of her way to comfort that concierge.

She was also good to look at. Except for that slight crease between her eyebrows whenever the topic of Shapeshifters came up. Then, she almost sprouted porcupine quills. He chuckled at the image. A lot could happen in three weeks. He might not convince her Shapeshifters were real. *But I'll have fun trying.*

After parking his car in the lot adjoining the hotel where he and his crew were registered, he took out his phone and eyed the screen. At least, Libby Maitland was honest. He, on the other hand… *I have a job to do.* "Call Alexandros."

"Hi, Dash." Julianna purred in his ear.

"Hey, Jules, I need to talk to The Boss."

"He's not in the office." The pretty, red-haired assistant would be looking over her shoulder to double-

Shifting into Shadows

check—as if a man who looked like Santa on steroids could sneak in. "He's been working on his presentation, and you know how he gets."

"Pacing new patterns in the carpet?"

Julianna's laugh warmed him. Nice to talk with a woman who didn't sound ready to tie you up in an interrogation room. Of course, being tied up by Detective Maitland might not be so bad. He smiled.

"I'll buzz him."

"Thanks."

"Honeycutt! I just got off the phone with the Summerhaven Police."

Honeycutt swore silently. *Should have called from the Mark V.*

"They wanted information on Schuyler Pope's next of kin. What's going on?"

Honeycutt hesitated. "He's dead. That's all I know, sir." By now, lies came with the ease of breaths. "The police aren't going public with anything pending notification of family."

"I have to say something to his colleagues. I'll tell them it was unexpected." When Alexandros paused, Honeycutt imagined his gloved fingers stroking his heavy jaw. "I was going to call you about Pope. He took some files when he left. Proprietary information. I want it back."

Honeycutt mentally revisited the crime scene. The hotel room had contained a small suitcase with Pope's clothing, but no computer or files. The killer must have taken more than the phone. News of the missing files might trigger another terrible cockroach joke from Libby Maitland. Wiping away his smile, he cleared his throat. "I'll see what I can do, sir."

"Make it happen, Honeycutt."

"Yes, sir."

"And stay on top of this investigation. I don't want anything interfering with my presentation."

"Yes, sir." Honeycutt swallowed. "It's not too late to change location."

"Nonsense. Summerhaven will draw a substantial audience from three major metropolitan areas. More important, Crispin Alexandros does not bow to bullies." *Takes one to know one.*

"I presume everything else is going well. The authorities are helpful?"

"Yes, sir." *Except for our liaison.*

A grunt. "Given the boost to their economy, I would hope so. And your local contact?"

"Detective Maitland has earned numerous commendations. She's very professional." *But can't have dinner with us because she's busy. Doing what? Where? Who with?* Was she dumping that boxy jacket, adjusting her neckline so it showed off the tantalizing curve of her breasts, and wiggling those hot pink toenails?

"I look forward to meeting her."

Imagining the encounter, Honeycutt smiled. "I should warn you, sir, she is a skeptic when it comes to Shapeshifters."

"I love a challenge." Alexandros guffawed. "In no time, I'll have your Miss Maitland eating out of my hand."

Honeycutt nearly snorted. If Alexandros wasn't careful, he might come away from his encounter with Detective Maitland a few fingers short.

Chapter 6

With the concierge's remarks churning in her brain, Libby returned to Ellyn's house, where she exchanged her dress and sandals for clothes more suitable for Captain Weatherby's office. Before leaving, she called the number Pru had given her. When an automated voice picked up, she left a message. *Please, please get back to me.* If no one returned the call, she could try again later. She could also begin working her way through the possibilities from the morning paper. She tucked the pages in her bag, put on her jacket, and returned the front-door key to its hiding place.

During her drive to headquarters, thoughts of Dash Honeycutt interfered with her efforts to review her encounters with the hotel staff. He had behaved well and hadn't gotten in her way. He'd asked some good questions. Even said something nice. Too bad he immediately undercut the compliment with Shapeshifter nonsense. But for his Alexandros fixations, he'd be good to work with.

Of course, he was no Mike Schrader. Who was? She smiled. Her retired partner claimed he'd been born carrying a badge and reaching for a gun. When she'd asked if he would miss them, he'd laughed and said, "Fishing is like a stake-out...but wetter. And you get to eat what you catch." Her smile deepened. *Taught me so much. And made it fun even when it was the scariest.*

Especially when it was scary. The vision of Schuyler Pope's mangled body replaced the memory of Mike's wild white hair waving in the wind, and Libby's stomach roiled.

Mike, be with me.

The squad room hummed like a human beehive with detectives moving in all directions as, like good worker bees, they prepared for their next venture into the unknown. Unlike the bees, which retrieved golden pollen from the hearts of beautiful flowers, she and her colleagues returned to this hive carrying darkness from the Summerhaven crime pits.

When she entered, the big room grew so quiet the smack of her solid heels against the wooden floor rang in her ears like castanets. Everyone seemed to be watching her. *Get a grip*. She was projecting her own anxiety about this new assignment.

Seated at his desk closest to the entrance, Jared Jamieson was working on what looked like a missing persons case, while his partner, brawny Bill Howard, circulated between desks. Bill was probably trying to start a new office pool. On the far side of the big, open room, Robin Calvert sipped coffee and scribbled notes while conducting a phone interview. She greeted Libby with a quick wave. Today, her hair was a magenta shade not found in nature. She wore a skirt and sat at an angle to her desk. Still showing off that Bahamas tan. *Wish I had legs that long*. The desk opposite Robin was empty, but papers cluttered the desktop. Seated closest to the captain's office, Emily Blackburn and Chad Gray, AKA Tweedledee and Tweedledum ever since their disastrous performance at the annual talent show, conferred over photographs from what looked like a store fire. Outside

Captain Weatherby's office, Libby stopped and turned. Everyone except Blackburn and Gray returned to their work. They pretended to work, but T-

Dee kept an ear tipped and T-Dum slid sidewise glances.

"I need to see the captain," Libby told Weatherby's clerk, who relayed the request on the speakerphone.

"Send her in."

When she entered the office, Captain Weatherby looked up from the spreadsheet that covered most of his desktop. "Make it fast, Detective. I've got a budget meeting."

"I'd like you to clarify something." Clasping her hands, Libby planted her feet in front of his desk. "This morning, a man named Dash Honeycutt who works for Crispin Alexandros told me I was going to be working with him."

The captain ran a hand through thinning hair that matched his tobacco-colored suit. "I was planning to tell you about the assignment when you came back on duty, but things moved faster than I expected. Yes, you will be handling local security for the Alexandros event. That will include the mayor's welcome reception as well as the actual presentation."

"I haven't worked much security, sir."

Captain Weatherby tapped a pen against his phone. "You're Special Ops, Detective. You work where you're assigned."

Libby blinked. "Sir?"

"You are experienced. You are a fast learner. You have an outstanding record. You are also the only detective in this unit without a partner."

"What about the Pope case—the Mark V

homicide?" She'd planned to track down the dead man's mysterious caller.

"Homicide has it. Since it's connected with Alexandros, do what you can, but the Alexandros presentation takes priority. I've got everyone from the mayor down clawing at my back to make sure everything goes right. That means you've got everyone from the mayor down, plus me." Libby flinched.

The beefy man sat back. "Is that clear?"

"Yes, sir. So I should meet Honeycutt and his people at the convention center tomorrow morning?"

"If that's the plan, yes." He paused. "Cheer up, Detective. Do a good job, and you'll have a nice bump next time you put in for promotion."

Screw up, and that bump could become a knock-out punch. "I'll do my best, sir. Thank you for your time." With a grunt, he returned to the spreadsheets.

****

Ellyn answered Libby's knock on the front door. "You're late." Her gaze traveled down Libby's torso. "What happened to that pretty dress?"

"Crazy day. I had to work." Libby clasped her Mentor's hands. "I also found my apartment."

"Already? You have been busy."

"I know." Libby followed the older woman into the parlor. "I wanted to take you out to dinner, but I've barely had time to turn around." She sank into one of the armchairs and rubbed her chin. "One of the guys who was living in the apartment showed me the place. Reasonable rent, great location, and the perfect size!" She hugged herself. "Then we talked to the landlady, who had final approval. Turns out her late husband was Summerhaven PD, so she is delighted to have me as a

tenant. I signed the papers and handed over my check."
Standing, Libby held up three keys on a chain. "Meet the
new resident of 2701 Lovegrove Lane."

Ellyn applauded. "We have guys at the shelter who
can handle heavy lifting, so if you need help moving, let
me know."

"I'll keep your offer in mind. Fortunately, Mitch and
his husband wanted new furniture for their new house,
so they sold me some stuff they left behind—table,
chairs, and queen-sized bed. And the landlady supplied
a sofa, an easy chair, and a dresser. They've all seen
better days. But it's a start."

"I look forward to visiting when you're ready for
company."

Libby wrapped an arm around her friend's thin
shoulders. "You're at the top of my list."

Ellyn eased away. "With so much to do, have you
eaten?"

Libby scratched her head. "I've been so busy I don't
remember."

Ellyn guided her toward the dining room. "I'll reheat
my pot roast if you'd like."

"That sounds great."

When Ellyn returned from the kitchen, she set a
bottle of red wine and two glasses in the middle of the
table. "While waiting for your supper, let's toast your
new apartment." She poured wine into both glasses and
offered one to Libby.

They touched glasses and drank.

"Tomorrow I'll pick up the rest of my stuff at
Tommy's." She rolled the wine around in her mouth
before she swallowed.

A beep summoned Ellyn to the kitchen, and she

returned with a platter on which vegetables surrounded shredded beef. "Careful." She set the dish in front of Libby. "Hot."

"It looks wonderful. Smells great, too." Enticing aromas swam in Libby's head and awakened the hunger in her stomach. Relishing every bite, she devoured the meal without talking or drinking. When she finished, she sat back and smiled at the woman sitting across from her. "That was delicious! Thanks." She sipped her wine. "Tomorrow night, I am taking you out to dinner."

"Don't worry about it." Ellyn frowned. "I thought you had the day off. What happened?"

The image of Schuyler Pope's body flashed in Libby's mind. "I got called in." She stretched. "I may have to come to you for Crispin Alexandros background."

Ellyn lifted an eyebrow.

"He has an event here in three weeks. I'm the liaison between our department and the Alexandros people."

"Sounds like a big responsibility."

"It is." Libby swirled her wine and drank. "I don't understand why he's coming here. Whenever I've seen him on the news, he's in a big city with a big crowd."

A twinkle lit Ellyn's eyes. "Maybe he wants to check out the demon portal."

Libby sputtered a few drops of wine on her white shirt. She dabbed at the stain with her napkin. "You know that's a crock."

The older woman sat back with a smile. "I don't know. I read the original Caulfield land grant posted in the historical society. To keep their property, the Caulfields had to satisfy a number of conditions, one of which was careful surveillance and prompt maintenance—those were the exact words—of the demon portal."

"That was…when? The 1700s?" Libby scoffed. "People believed all sorts of superstitions in those days."

A corner of Ellyn's mouth quirked. "Don't dismiss those beliefs so easily. Simple Humans executed witches. They also slaughtered some of my ancestors and those of other traditional Shapeshifters." She rested a hand on her heart. "As Anomalies, you and your sisters don't share our history."

"True." Libby looked down at the table. "But a demon portal in Summerhaven?"

Smiling, Ellyn poured herself another glass of wine. "Why are you smiling?"

"Force of habit." Ellyn's smile dimmed. "OASIS trained us always to smile in the presence of you and your sisters. They didn't want us to risk upsetting you because no one knew what would happen if you responded by shifting to something destructive." "Like Steffi's first dragon." Libby laughed.

"Exactly." Ellyn leaned forward. "Now, tell me about this new apartment."

Chapter 7

While the rest of the team poured coffee and devoured pastries arrayed on the other side of the office, Austin Crenshaw, the dapper, white-haired director of the Summerhaven Convention Center, introduced Honeycutt to the svelte woman at his side.

"Zoe handles our legal matters," Crenshaw informed him. "Would you like to review our standard contract before the presentation?"

Honeycutt shook his head. "First, we need to decide if this will be our location." He turned to the attractive attorney. "Even then, our legal staff handles contracts. Tony, our tech leader, can set up a conference call."

"That sounds—Libby!" Crenshaw approached the new arrival.

Honeycutt checked his watch. *Late!*

This morning, a gray pantsuit had replaced the sexy dress, and polished black shoes hid the bright toenails. Except for the knit, off-white top that clung nicely to her upper body beneath her jacket, she could've had "strictly business" tattooed on her forehead. She returned Crenshaw's smile with one that warmed the room.

"Wonderful to see you, dear!"

She tilted her head and regarded him with concern. "It's been a while. How are you?"

He released her hands. "Reasonably well." Smile fading, he drew her toward Honeycutt and the attorney.

She greeted the attorney and nodded at Honeycutt.
"Mr. Honeycutt."

"Detective Maitland."

"I was about to give Mr. Honeycutt and his team an overview of our facility." The director indicated a small meeting room adjacent to his office. A screen on the back wall bore the message "Welcome to the Summerhaven Convention Center!"

Detective Maitland scanned the office in which they stood. "Where's Ivy?" "Personal leave." Her eyebrows lifted.

Honeycutt glanced at the director. He must be doing work he usually delegated.

"How can I help?"

"Everything's under control, Lib—Detective. You know I'm delighted that Mr. Honeycutt and his people are considering the convention center for their meeting. Most organizations that anticipate large crowds use the university stadium or the Harriers' Nest."

"We considered those venues." Standing beside Detective Maitland, Honeycutt caught the faint scent of roses. "But they have problems. Both are open to the weather. Because the stadium is part of the university, it would be hard to control access. Most important, those facilities are designed for entertainment. Dr. Alexandros has a serious message."

The detective clapped a hand over her mouth, looked down at the indoor-outdoor carpet, and coughed.

Crenshaw regarded the others in the room. "Does anyone know the Heimlich maneuver?"

Honeycutt ditched his coffee cup and started to shed his jacket.

"No, no!" Detective Maitland lifted her head. Her

cheeks were flushed, and tears welled at the corners of her eyes. "I'm not choking. Swallowed...wrong." She drew a deep breath. "See? Fine." She dabbed at her eyes with a tissue.

"Good." Honeycutt adjusted his jacket, retrieved his coffee, and took a drink. "Been a while since any of us practiced." His colleagues muttered their agreement.

"Let's get down to business." When Crenshaw rested bony fingers on the detective's shoulder, she didn't flinch. She seemed to like that Crenshaw character. She patted his hand on her shoulder when she could have rolled it off. He might be—he was old—and wearing a wedding ring at that, but he could still have the hots for a pretty woman. Not any pretty woman, either. That attorney looked like she'd stepped out of a fashion magazine. "Would you like a cup of coffee and something to nibble on?"

Detective Maitland smiled at him, not as delighted as that first smile, more accommodating. "I'll get a drink from the water fountain. Why don't you begin?" She patted his hand and eased it off her shoulder.

Take the hint, Crenshaw. Paws off.

When she hurried out of the office, Crenshaw's gaze flowed from her to the attorney. "Zoe, if you have other work you'd like to do, you can use my office until we finish the presentation."

"Thanks. I'll take the tour with you so I can note any suggested modifications to our standard contract." With the hint of a smile, she withdrew.

Crenshaw gestured at the presentation room. "Gentlemen, please make yourselves comfortable."

Honeycutt let the others sit in the front of the room but squeezed himself into a conference chair built for smaller humans near the back. Not for the first time, he wished he could shrink as well as expand.

Gripping the remote as if he feared it might leap out of his hand and escape, Crenshaw stood near the screen. "Welcome to the Summerhaven Convention Center."

Honeycutt swallowed a groan. *Please don't read the slides!*

Pride and pleasure evident in every rehearsed word, Austin Crenshaw provided the history and layout of the convention center in excruciating detail. *Must not have much of a life.*

At some point, the door behind Honeycutt opened slightly, and Detective Maitland slipped into the chair beside him. As the director did everything but count the bolts and nails, Honeycutt leaned toward her. "If he starts dancing," he whispered, "I'm out of here."

Casting a cautious eye on the director, she leaned toward Honeycutt and touched her throat. "Don't make me laugh."

Her breath made his ear tingle.

"And there you have it." The screen went dark, and the lights came up. "Questions?"

Honeycutt stood. "Thank you for showing us your impressive facility." The director's chest swelled slightly. "Our primary concerns are utility and safety. Prior to the event, we will screen problem areas. We need a space large enough to accommodate several hundred people and technologically equipped for Dr. Alexandros's presentation. We also need to get him in and out safely, control access, and neutralize any potential disruptors—we always have a few."

Crenshaw tugged at his bow tie. "You'll have no problems here."

"If we do, I'll let you know so you and Detective Maitland can find a prompt solution."

The director gave a half-hearted laugh. "Of course." Although his mouth smiled again, his pale eyes were wary. He must have a lot riding on this event. "If you like, pick up more coffee and another pastry on your way out, and we will begin our tour."

As his associates moved past, Honeycutt turned to the woman standing beside him. "You were late." Flickers of gold sparked in her dark eyes. *Temper, temper, Detective.*

"Accident on the ring road. Had to detour through downtown at rush hour."

Although they explored the entire building, and the director seemed determined to comment on every inch, Honeycutt and his group soon narrowed their interest to two possible meeting rooms.

Detective Maitland joined Honeycutt in one corner of the large auditorium. "Give me a number, and the department will assign uniforms at all the entrances." Honeycutt made a note on his phone.

Crenshaw and the attorney joined them. "Don't forget, Libby. We have our own security."

Honeycutt regarded the older man. "I'm sure they're adequate for daily activities. But for something this large, we need professional law enforcement." Detective Maitland didn't return his smile, and he addressed the attorney. "We will occupy the whole facility for two full days: the day before the presentation and the day of the presentation. All floors must be locked down twenty-four hours prior to Dr. Alexandros's arrival."

Crenshaw checked a large calendar on the wall. "We can do that."

The attorney also made a note. "You do understand that the cost will reflect how much the center stands to lose by closing the facility in that manner?"

"Not a problem."

Detective Maitland spoke up. "If you want manageable access, restrooms are outside the auditorium. If you use the Exhibit Hall, restrooms are one level up, so people will need to use the elevators or stairs."

Honeycutt surveyed the auditorium. "This would work."

"Dash!" Jeff Dearborn, the youngest member of his crew, spoke with a slight whine. "That Exhibit Hall holds more people. You know how much The Boss likes a crowd."

Honeycutt faced the speaker. "True. But this room has a permanent stage. In the Exhibit Hall, we'll have to set one up."

The director joined them. "Our maintenance people can erect a portable stage in the Exhibit Hall." While Honeycutt considered the offer, Crenshaw gestured at the auditorium. "In here, you'll need someone to help with lights, curtains, and sound system."

Honeycutt gestured at his tech guy, whose latest hairpiece resembled a dead raccoon. "What do you think, Tony?"

Tony regarded Crenshaw. "My people and I will need an orientation three days before the actual meeting. We'll do a walk-through without The Boss two days before and a full-dress rehearsal the day before."

The center director smiled. "No problem."

Although facing the auditorium, Honeycutt itemized problems with the Exhibit Hall on his fingers. "It will take more people and preparation to set up the room, and Dr. Alexandros doesn't like the look of those temporary stages. The restrooms are inconvenient and harder to monitor." He glanced at the director. "The Exhibit Hall also has loading docks and a rear entrance, right?"

Crenshaw gave him a faint smile. "Right, Mr. Honeycutt. As you may have already noticed, the entrances to the auditorium here are all along one side." He made a sweeping gesture. "Easily monitored. Outside the auditorium, we do have stairs and a few public elevators to watch, but the space is open. A private elevator adjoins the VIP room so Dr. Alexandros can come and go without much fuss."

"He likes to mix with his followers," Honeycutt observed. "Shake hands, sign programs, books."

"The space outside the auditorium is ideal for tables offering publications and other merchandise. And we can broadcast the presentation live on big screens mounted on all exterior sides of our building so anyone who wasn't able to get in will be able to see it. And, of course, local media will be here as well."

Detective Maitland looked as if she might be sick.

Tony beamed. "The Boss will like that."

Honeycutt turned to the director. "We will sweep the center and the surrounding area at least twenty-four hours before Dr. Alexandros speaks."

"Hold on." Detective Maitland consulted her phone. "The Harriers have a game the night before your event, and the ball park's a few blocks away."

"So?"

"Good point, Libby." When his gaze met Honeycutt's, Crenshaw's smile withered. "After the games, the nearby streets always fill up. Troublemakers could easily wander down to our loading docks without anyone noticing. You may want to schedule your first sweep for after the game."

Harry, who handled crowd control, cracked his knuckles. "Instead of waiting until the game ends, we can station folks on the loading dock during the game."

Honeycutt made a note. "What's that mean for you?"

Harry made some calculations on his phone. "Double the number."

Honeycutt glanced at Detective Maitland. "We'll want uniformed police, too."

Her mouth softened, but she didn't smile at him the way she'd smiled at the old guy. "Of course." She made a note on her phone.

"Good." Honeycutt opened his arms. Although he looked ready to embrace the entire convention center, he itched for open space. "We'll make this place so tight not even a shadow can get in without a ticket."

****

Over lunch, Libby tried to keep up when Honeycutt introduced his associates. Tony Benson, the guy with the ghastly hair mat, was his technology expert. *Toupee + Tech = Tony Two-T*. Harry Kramer, the knuckle-cracker, handled crowd management. *Cracker Kramer Crowd*.

Jeff Dearborn, who looked as if he'd been sent to the principal's office, coordinated with Crispin Alexandros's personal security. *Boy Jeff*. Ben Turner, who seemed to have muscles on his muscles, would monitor everything outside the auditorium. *Big Ben, like that clock*.

Honeycutt waved his fork at her. "Detective Maitland is our link to the Summerhaven Police

Department, and you will listen to her the same way you listen to me. Got it?" His crew responded with dubious grunts and nods, and the three older men looked skeptical. "Anyone who crosses Detective Maitland will answer to me." When Honeycutt thumped his broad chest, his quartet straightened up.

After eating, Honeycutt and his team prepared to disperse, each with an assignment. "We'll meet tomorrow morning. Eight-thirty. Sharp." He turned to Libby. "Your captain said we could have a conference room with plenty of wall space and good technology. Can you handle the setup?"

She saluted and eyed the team. "We supply endless coffee but bring your own doughnuts." When she started to leave, Honeycutt touched her arm. She should have shaken off his firm yet gentle grasp but didn't. Austin Cramer touched because he wanted connections after his wife's death. Honeycutt projected strength and something else. Safety? *From a murder suspect? No way*.

"The mayor is holding a reception for Dr. Alexandros the evening before he speaks. We'll need the details on that venue."

"I'll have them. See you all tomorrow." Libby swept out of the restaurant. Before the day ended, she could at least call the medical examiner's office, stop at the Mark V, and pick up her stuff at Tommy's. Drop off the key, too.

Chapter 8

Libby approached the Mark V registration desk. "Good afternoon. I'm with the Summerhaven PD. Detective Elizabeth Maitland." She flashed her badge at a young woman with skin the color of polished mahogany. "I'd like to talk with whoever was working the desk two days ago at this time."

"That would be me." The woman's professional smile dimmed. "But I can't talk now." She gestured at a traveler standing behind Libby.

A man with a bald dome that looked freshly waxed materialized behind the woman. His piercing gaze flew from Libby's badge to the clerk's face. "Do you have a problem, Bella?"

The woman behind the desk stiffened. "No, sir."

Libby read the woman's name tag. "I'd like to talk with Ms. Kilgallen about what she might have seen when she was on duty two days ago."

"Officer, we've had a remarkably busy week. I'm sure she didn't see much."

"I didn't see anything."

The bald man eyed the growing line of restless travelers waiting to check in.

"I need to speak with Ms. Kilgallen regarding the incident that occurred in Room 1410." Libby tried a soft, persuasive voice. "If we talk here, she'll be back on duty in a few minutes." She squared her shoulders and lifted her chin. Time for Tough Cop. "Otherwise, I will have to take her down to the station and interview her there. Which will take more time and might lead to your guests asking questions you don't want to answer. The choice is yours."

"Very well." The manager spoke to the clerk. "Use Meeting Room B." Pasting on a smile, he turned to the first person in line. "Welcome to the Mark V, sir."

In the same room where she'd conducted the other interviews, Libby chose the same table. "Sorry to interrupt your day."

"We're short-staffed." Sitting across from her, Ms. Kilgallen positioned a curl behind one ear. "One planned vacation and two unplanned sick kids. Plus, we're the main hotel for a national convention that starts tomorrow."

"Let's make this quick. I'm interested in someone who may have been here two days ago. Late morning or the afternoon."

The clerk opened her hands. "I was so busy I didn't see anything."

Libby took out her phone and showed the photo of Honeycutt and his crew she'd taken during the convention center tour. "What about these people? Did you see any of them?"

Ms. Kilgallen gave an embarrassed laugh and pointed at Dash Honeycutt. "He's hard to miss."

No. Honeycutt wasn't hard to miss. He was impossible to miss. Libby glanced toward the lobby. When he'd been standing out there, Schuyler Pope had been in his room. Alive. Libby breathed a quick "thanks." She started to put her phone away, but the other woman reached for it.

"He wasn't alone. With this man." She indicated a figure on the edge of the frame.

Boy Jeff! Libby drew in a sharp breath. *Not one, but two members of the Alexandros team...* "Are you sure about this?"

"Yes. They wanted to see the penthouse suite Crispin Alexandros reserved."

Libby rested her phone in her lap and put her hand over the shot of Honeycutt standing in the convention center auditorium. His smile pierced her heart like a laser. "Did you show them the suite?"

"I confirmed the reservation but called Security to take them up. I don't remember who they sent, but Security can tell you." Her words tumbled out.

"Thanks, Ms. Kilgallen." Libby stood. When the clerk joined her, Libby turned. "One more thing." She held up the photo. "Did either of these men ask about whether anyone connected to Crispin Alexandros was staying here?" Silly question. Schuyler Pope had checked in as Sam Poe, hadn't provided any employment info. But he might have let something slip.

"No." A wrinkle appeared between the young woman's eyebrows. "And we don't disclose information about our guests except, of course, if the police..." She gestured at Libby.

"I understand. Thanks again."

A quick check with hotel security disclosed that the officer in question had left town on vacation. When Libby requested his phone number, the supervisor said, "Lots of luck." The officer had taken a family trip to the Green Bank Observatory, a National Radio Quiet Zone, so his kids could practice surviving without cell phones.

Libby thrummed her fingers with impatience. Green

Bank was over four hours away by car. Saddled with the Alexandros team, she was stuck in Summerhaven unless... *As a bird, I could fly back in time for the morning meeting.*

She rolled her shoulders. Even with good winds, flying was work. If she wanted to talk with the vacationing officer, she'd have to bring clothes. The mere thought of flapping her wings for several hundred miles with the weight of an extra pack made her bones ache. She'd barely be able to keep her eyes open when she returned to Summerhaven, let alone cope with Honeycutt and his team. She'd have to wait to interview the officer. A few more days wouldn't matter. Schuyler Pope wasn't going to get any deader.

Instead of leaving the hotel, she strolled toward the elevators. Yesterday, she'd hoped to visit the crime scene after the investigators finished, but Honeycutt stuck like a tick. Like a killer. A killer would want to know everything the police knew. *Pope worked for Alexandros, and so does Honeycutt. Of course, he's interested.*

If she revisited the crime scene, she might find something everyone else had missed, perhaps even something that exonerated Honeycutt. The hotel would reopen the room ASAP. Best look now.

Minutes later, Libby used a room card provided by a desk clerk and slipped into the empty room. A thoughtful examination disclosed nothing her human senses hadn't already experienced. She wrinkled her nose. Her rat occupied a different world. In the bathroom, she stripped and left a neat pile of clothing on the closed toilet seat. Then she closed her eyes and visualized her rat. Dark ears, inquisitive eyes, long whiskers surrounding a powerful sniffer, useful teeth, and sharp claws. She'd taken this shape so often that the transformation occurred almost instantaneously.

In the bedroom, the stench of old blood and a drug on the carpet assaulted her rat's nose. Human scents. Whiskers sweeping side to side, she explored the darkened closet. Nothing. Everything gathered and sent to the labs.

She scooted under the bed. Clean carpet here, too. The trace of Pope's odor drew her to the inner edge of the bed. Her whiskers probed a small space between mattress and frame. Gnawing on the wooden frame, her teeth exposed a small rectangular object. *A few more bites—*

Noise in the outer room! Beneath the bed, Libby's nose twitched. *Hide!* Her human would have chosen the closet. Terrible idea. Simple Humans always searched closets first. *Bathroom. Clothes and gun.*

She scurried into the bathroom.

Honeycutt opened the door to Schuyler Pope's suite and stepped inside. The bedroom door stood open. When another door closed inside the bedroom, he smiled. Detective Maitland must not want to be found here. She might appear if she thought he'd gone. He closed the door to the suite. Maybe they could toss the place together. His smile deepened at the prospect.

While waiting for her to emerge, he'd search for the stolen files in the sitting room. Tables, shelves, and counters all had clean, bare surfaces. No papers attached to their undersides. Cabinets and drawers of the small kitchen held nothing except basic equipment. Honeycutt searched the spaces between chair cushions and arms. A penny here. Popcorn kernels there. No papers anywhere.

He tilted each of the easy chairs and examined the bases and the carpet. Mark V housekeeping and the Summerhaven PD hadn't missed an inch.

Removing the sofa cushions exposed a mattress, which he unfolded. Nothing but fabric, padding, and springs. He refolded the bed. Bending his knees in front of the sofa, he flipped it on its back but held it steady with one hand so it didn't hit the rug. Underneath, bed frames and freshly cleaned rug. He set the sofa down gently and returned the cushions.

He entered the bedroom as the bathroom door eased open. When Detective Maitland stepped out, his smile vanished. "Whoa!" He held up both his hands. "Like I told you yesterday, I am one of the good guys."

"So you say." Her tone was light, but her pretty mouth was set in a straight line.

"Didn't they teach you at the academy not to draw a weapon unless you plan to use it?"

"They also taught us to be careful about what's on the other side of a door." She returned her gun to its holster. "Why are you here?"

"I could ask you the same question."

"You could." She placed her hands on her nice, round hips. "But I don't answer to you. Whereas—" She tapped her badge. "How did you get in here?"

"I told the front desk I was looking for some lost files. They gave me a key and mentioned you were here. They must think we're working together." He hadn't corrected their misapprehension. He scanned the room.

"Find anything interesting?"

"No."

Her denial came too quickly. His muscles tensed. *You're lying.* "Schuyler Pope got time off because he claimed someone in his family was sick. After he left, the lab supervisor found that he'd cleaned out his desk. He also took some files. Alexandros wants them."

"That material would be in Evidence. Check there."

"I did. It's not. The information in those files belongs to Alexandros, so if you've found—"

"Nope." Her nose twitched, and her gaze seemed to drill into his jaw.

When he stepped toward her, an odd undertone lurked beneath the rose fragrance. Something dark, mysterious, and not quite…human. *Who are you, Libby Maitland?* He regarded her through narrowed eyes. She didn't look any different than she had earlier in the day.

"You're welcome to look around." She made a sweeping gesture.

"Nothing in the sitting room. If you didn't find anything in here, I probably won't either. We can lock up and go."

She scratched her nose. "I want to do one last sweep in here."

"Let's do it together."

"Fine. Why don't you start on that side?" She indicated the doorway to the sitting room. "I'll start over here by the bathroom, and we can work toward the middle. Not—I mean—" She looked away from the bed, but not quickly enough to hide the very human flush that colored her cheeks.

"Of course not." Honeycutt suppressed his chuckle. "Though I suppose it would be an unusual place for an assignation."

"Unusual…and unpleasant." Blush deepening, she began a deliberate search in her area, and he followed her lead. On his own, he would have finished by lifting the

62

bed and examining it as he had the sofa bed in the outer room. That didn't seem like a good idea with Libby Maitland around, so he got down on his knees and peered under the bed.

When his gaze locked on the detective's, she gasped and drew back. "You surprised me."

He played the light of his small flashlight around the underside of the bed, the legs, and the floor. Unlike the pristine living room carpet, this one contained a tiny pile of...wood bits? Fresh, too. *What the...* When he eased the light up from the pile to the bed, he drew in a breath. *Eureka!* Turning off the light, he stood.

A moment or two later, Detective Maitland got to her feet on the other side of the bed. "I guess it was time well spent." The corners of her mouth turned up, but she looked down. She stuffed her hands in the pockets of her jacket.

Honeycutt gave a slow nod. "I think you have what I'm looking for."

She lifted her eyebrows and parted her lips. "What?"

"Nice try, but I saw something stuck under the bed, too." He moved to her side of the bed and reached down to find the spot where he'd seen the contours of a flash drive. Empty. "I believe you put it in your pocket."

She clapped one hand on the pocket. "Schuyler Pope hid it. It could be important. It's evidence."

"You don't know if it's of any use to you. Even if it is, don't you have to establish...what's it called...some sort of evidence chain? You don't even know if Dr. Pope put the drive there."

"You seem to think he did. Isn't that why you want it?"

He scratched his jaw. "Pope stole proprietary

information. I want it because Alexandros ordered me to get it."

"Tell him the police were faster. We'll check the contents. If these files aren't connected to the crime, we'll return his property."

"Alexandros doesn't want outsiders accessing his research."

"Too bad." She patted her pocket.

"You win. This round."

"Will you get into trouble for losing?" When she reached into her pocket, he could almost see her fingering the flash drive.

"He'll chew me out for not getting here first. Never pleasant. Then, he'll pressure the Summerhaven police to release his property. You could eliminate all those extra steps and simply give me the drive."

"True. But everyone else makes it too easy for Crispin Alexandros." She uttered the syllables of his name as if her lips were knives.

"You really hate him, don't you?"

Her eyebrows drew together. "I hate what he does, what he says, what he stands for. Simple…simply put, humans…we people…are often afraid of what we don't know. Alexandros could use his research and his meetings to create understanding about

Shapeshifters…if, of course, Shapeshifters really existed."

"Of course," Honeycutt echoed. *Nonhuman scent…those marks on the wooden frame…teeth?*

"Instead of understanding, he creates division and hatred. That never ends well."

"I understand your point, but when people feel threatened…"

"That's just it. He has created a threat where none exists."

"You seem awfully sure of that."

"I've studied enough history to know how demagogues work."

Honeycutt glanced at his watch. "It's getting late. Any chance we can put our Alexandros differences aside for a while…get something to eat?" She hesitated.

"What's wrong?"

"I think it's best to keep a clear line between personal and professional activities."

"So you don't ever go out with your colleagues?"

"Sure, I do. But that's different."

He leaned against the bedroom doorjamb. "Since we're going to be working together, don't you think it would be a good idea to get to know each other better?"

"Maybe." She spoke as if he'd had to wring the concession out of her.

What was he thinking? She might have a date. "If you have other plans—"

"Not exactly, but I'm moving, and I have to bring stuff from my old apartment to my new one."

He felt as if she'd handed him a medal. "Now, that's something I'm good at!" He rubbed his hands together. "I've moved two brothers and two sisters, along with myself."

"I don't have that much…"

"One thing I've learned is that people always have more than they think they do."

"Mr. Honeycutt—"

"Call me Dash, please."

Her mouth twisted. "It's nice of you to offer, but I neither need nor want your help."

"I've seen your car, Detective. If you fill more than three boxes, you'll either mash something or make several trips. My rental has lots of space."

When she moved toward the front room, he followed her and blocked the door to the suite. She seemed so sure of herself he itched to take her down a peg. "Tell you what. I'll trail you over to your old place. If you really can't use any help, I'll leave and see you tomorrow morning. But if the project's more than you expected, I'll give you a hand. At the very least, it will cut your moving time in half, and we'll both work up a good appetite for dinner. How does that sound?"

A reluctant smile teased the corners of her full lips, but she kept a hand on one pocket. "You drive a hard bargain."

Chapter 9

Coming down the hill into Thorne Valley, Honeycutt's SUV almost kissed the rear bumper of Libby's sedan. *Tailgater!* If she tried to shake him, the cocky bastard would no doubt stick even closer and give her a hard time once they reached the condo. More important, if she let Honeycutt help her, she might have a chance to question him about being at the Mark V with Boy Jeff. *But if he...killed...* Shapeshifting to something big and fierce would take too long, and she'd be vulnerable during the process. *Best stay human.* She patted her holstered gun. *Nothing I can't handle.*

She'd pack more rapidly than Honeycutt predicted. While she handled Gran's dishes, Honeycutt could stack her books in boxes. It might even be good to have someone else on hand if Tommy came home early. And Dash Honeycutt was a big someone else.

He claimed they would work better together once they got to know each other, but some things he didn't need to know. *Quick in, quick out, no chatter. Let him strut a while. Then, when he's feeling good about himself, spring the question. Why were you at the Mark V the day before Schuyler Pope died?*

She parked in the visitors' lot nearest to the big, angular building but groaned when Honeycutt chose Tommy's favorite spot close to the doors. She hurried to his SUV and tapped on his window before he cut off the engine.

The glass slid halfway down.

"You can't park here." She gestured at the sign. "It's reserved."

He looked around. "Nobody here now. If we're fast—"

"The people who live here can be very… possessive…about parking spots. Anyone who's watching can call and have you towed."

Honeycutt swore. "So I should park out in the boonies with you?"

"Yes." She stepped back. "Please." While he pulled into the visitors' lot, she opened her trunk and retrieved a stack of flattened boxes, her empty suitcase, and a pile of old newspapers. Sliding her hand through the open core of a duct-tape roll, she juggled the packaging and started to walk—more like a waddle—toward the entrance. *If I were a duck, I'd be quacking.*

When Honeycutt joined her, he scooped up the boxes and the newspapers.

"Do you know how to pack dishes?" she asked.

Honeycutt grunted. "My sisters pack. I haul."

Figures. "You can take care of my books while I handle the dishes. Then, you can carry the dishes out while I get the rest of my clothes and grab my laptop."

"Looks like you found something for me to do, after all."

Great grin! "Since you're here, you might as well be useful." She surveyed the almost-empty parking lot.

"The sooner we're done, the better."

She put her key—the key—in the lock and froze.

Honeycutt stood at her shoulder. "Problem?"

She swallowed. "It feels…this is the first time I've

been back since…" Had Dumire's attack occurred only two days ago? It felt like a lifetime. She forced her hand to turn the key. Walking into the apartment, she shivered.

The front rooms looked as if she'd never left. *How did OASIS get those stains out of the carpet?* She checked the clock on the wall. Time to see what's in the fridge for dinner.

Honeycutt surveyed the room from the doorway. "Nice place."

When you didn't have a corpse lying in a sea of blood. "It's all right. Windows don't open. As you may have noticed, the air's not so great in this part of town because of the chemical plants."

She walked to the bookcases near the sofa and rested one hand on the third shelf from the top. "My books go from here to the bottom. My laptop's there, too, but I'll take it separately."

Picking up a few boxes and the newspapers, she moved to the kitchen cabinets. As she wrapped Gran's fine china with the delicate floral pattern in newspaper, Libby could almost feel her grandmother standing beside her. Gran liked Tommy. She'd have disapproved of their living together, but she'd have been disappointed about the breakup. *Sorry, Gran.*

She was almost finished with the dinner service when Honeycutt announced, "Books are ready."

Libby looked at her helper and frowned. Something about him looked different. Bigger? *Get real.* Maybe he was bigger than she'd originally thought. Or maybe he was simply flexing his muscles to impress her. When he stooped to pick up three stacked boxes, Libby held up a hand. "Wait. You shouldn't lift that much."

A smile flickered across his face. "Guess you're

right." He hefted the top box.

"Are you sure you can manage that?"

He juggled the box. "I'm good."

"Do it your way, but if you pull a muscle, don't come crying to me." He didn't look as though he was straining. "Be careful. Take a break if you need to, and you can take books out to lighten the load."

"Yes, ma'am." A strange twinkle danced in his blue eyes, and then he was gone.

Minutes later, he returned for the second box. By then, she had sealed the dish boxes and begun to pack platters, bowls, cups, and odd pieces. She also counted the silverware in the wooden chest.

"Pretty." Standing at her shoulder, Honeycutt's gaze moved from her to the gravy boat in her hand.

"My grandmother's good dishes." Libby caressed the graceful porcelain lines. "She kept them in a cupboard in her dining room. Took them out every Thanksgiving when the whole family assembled." She settled the piece in the box as if she were snuggling an infant in its cradle. "This is the last box. The others are ready." She looked deep into Honeycutt's eyes. "Please be careful."

He put a hand to his heart. "I'll treat them as if they were my own…well, my mother's."

Libby laughed. "Even better."

She was in the bedroom packing her clothes and personal items when Honeycutt stood in the doorway. "Anything else?" He glanced toward the outer room. "TV? Speakers? DVDs? CDs?"

"No." Libby's eyes moved from the crown of his head to his big feet. He looked…as normal as someone his size could look, but no bigger. Must have been a trick of the afternoon light. She indicated the boxes that littered the floor. Footwear, coats, jackets, and clothes that didn't fit in the suitcase. "This is it." *Two years of my life boxed and sealed.* Her filled suitcase lay open on the bed. She closed it and drew a breath that reached to her toes. "I'm done." She turned away from the bed she and Tommy had shared. *Let it go.*

Honeycutt lifted the remaining boxes and led the way. Despite everything he'd carried, he still moved as if he had energy to spare.

Walking through the apartment for the last time, Libby waited to feel sadness or regret. Instead, relief rolled through her. She left the key on the dining room table. That same table where she and Tommy had entertained. The same table where Tommy sat so stunned after... *This is the right thing to do.* She walked away from the table. *I made a mistake. I will learn from it and move on.* She flipped the lock and closed the door behind her.

Honeycutt was waiting by the cars. "What took you so long?"

"I had to leave the key and lock the door."

"Goodbyes are never easy."

He must have endured his share of breakups. Libby slid him a sidewise glance. Who would break up with him? He wasn't simply gorgeous. He was nice. Too bad he was also an Alexandrite. *And a murder suspect.*

Fingering the flash drive in her pocket, she worried a wood sliver stuck between her teeth. *Rats.*

Honeycutt leaned against his vehicle, packed with more of Detective Maitland's earthly possessions than she'd anticipated. "What next?"

She didn't reply for a minute, but when she looked

up at him, her pretty mouth moved from a neutral position to a take-charge smile. "We could drop everything off at my apartment" —she emphasized the "my" slightly— "and then eat. Or we could eat first and then move in my stuff."

And maybe stick around for…no. That was stupid.

She'd just split up with someone. The last thing she needed was… *She wants me to decide.* Honeycutt brushed his hands together. "Let's go to your place first and then eat. That way we'll work up more of an appetite." *For food. Only food.*

"Sounds good."

Did she look relieved? She got in her car, and Honeycutt followed her past the chemical plants, up the winding road that led to the center of Summerhaven. A few blocks past the university, she turned into an alley and pulled up in front of what looked like a carriage house. He stopped behind her.

Getting out of her car, she stepped back to survey the small building. The glow in her face was as warm as the late afternoon sun. "This is it." She pointed the opener at the garage door, which slid up. "I can park my car in here, and you can pull in there—" She gestured at a narrow lane that intersected the alley. "—or park in front of the garage."

Carrying a box of her dishes, he joined her in the garage. She'd opened a side door that revealed the start of a narrow stairway leading straight up. She wrestled a box from her trunk and set it on the floor beside her car. "Leave everything here. I'll take it up to the apartment when I get back from dinner."

Still holding the heavy box, Honeycutt eyed the stairway. "I'll do it."

"You don't have to—"

"Even the dishes are heavy, so you'll have to unpack almost everything before you can carry anything. You'll be going up and down those stairs for hours. If I—"

One corner of Libby's mouth curled. "I know you're strong. But I can use the exercise. And I don't have to do it all at once."

Stubborn—like Weatherby said. "Do you really want to have a lot of half-empty boxes sitting around the garage?"

Her hesitation spoke more loudly than words. "I'll go up and open the door to the apartment. The landlady and her husband originally planned to put a second apartment down here." She gestured at the garage.

"Lucky for you they changed their minds."

Her laughter was like the moment before sunrise. She grabbed her suitcase from her car and disappeared up the stairs. Her voice rang out. "All clear!"

He carried the first of her boxes up the narrow stairs—she'd have had an awful time—and into a combined living-dining space with worn inside-outside carpet, a shabby sofa, and a small but serviceable dining room set. Built-in bookcases framed big windows that faced the alley. Tiny kitchen. To his right, a narrow hallway with one doorway on the inside wall and another at the end of the hall. Small but comfortable.

She looked as if she were welcoming him into her throne room. "You can leave everything here." She gestured at the front room. "I'll sort it out later." She carried her suitcase into the room at the end of the hall.

After bringing up a few of the lighter boxes, she stayed in the apartment while he delivered the rest. "The end." Honeycutt set the last box of dishes on the solid table.

"Thank you so much." She eyed the boxes that almost filled the room. "You were right. This would have taken me hours if you hadn't…" She tapped her collarbone. "Dinner is on me."

"Now, Detective—"

"I'm not on duty, and you've done me a big favor." She extended her hand. "Please call me Libby."

Wrapping his fingers around her hand, he felt as if she'd given him a birthday present. "Sure. If you'll call me Dash."

"It's a deal, Dash." She pulled away. "What would you like to eat?"

Honeycutt laughed. "I don't care as long as it's good and there's lots of it. Any Irish pubs?"

Libby snapped her fingers. "Whiskers!"

Chapter 10

Honeycutt drank in the subdued tempo of the restaurant along with the rich mixture of caramel and coffee in his stout. "Funny name, but nice place." Libby's smile didn't reach her eyes.

Something's bugging her. "You come here often?"

"More than I should. My grandmother loved Whiskers."

He savored a piece of grilled flounder. "You're from Summerhaven?"

She shook her head. "Montana. Moved here after high school."

"Montana to Summerhaven—that's a long haul."

"My mother grew up near here. She met my father while they were working in Greenbelt. Scientific research. Very hush-hush." She brought a finger to her lips. When she spoke again, she seemed to weigh each word. "They moved West after Steffi—my older sister—was born. Wanted more room to raise a family."

Honeycutt chuckled. "They didn't have to go that far. My folks raised five of us in northern Pennsylvania."

"You must have had a full house. Are they all like you? I mean, you're a big guy."

He grinned at the blush that bloomed on her cheeks. "We're a solid bunch. How big a brood did your folks have in Montana?"

Libby held up three fingers. "Steffi's the Brain.

Dayzee's the Beauty. I'm in the middle."

"The Peacekeeper."

"That's how my interest in law enforcement started." Once again, she seemed to measure what she shared. "Steffi's the oldest. She and her husband live in Canada. They have twins."

Twins. Honeycutt clenched his jaw.

Libby leaned toward him. "What's wrong?" "I have a twin sister. Haven't seen her in a while." *Too long*. He took another drink. "What's your younger sister doing?"

Libby's laugh made him want to kick up his heels. "Dayzee's a law unto herself. For example, Mom and Dad named her Marguerite, but when she found out that Marguerite means daisy in French, she didn't just change her name. She also came up with her own spelling. She's in Los Angeles."

"Good place for a drama queen."

"That's what she believed when she went to Hollywood right after high school. She's been in some movies and TV shows. She's also done stunt work. Lately, she's gotten interested in filmmaking. What about your family?"

He drained his glass and signaled for another. "My parents are doing well. My brothers all seem happy. My baby sister Kinsey—"

"Unusual name."

"Not when your mom loves mysteries."

"Oh!" Libby clapped and brought her hands together at her lower lip. "That's why you—I thought maybe Dash was a nickname because you were a runner, but your name is Dashiell." She grinned. "As in Hammett. I've never read any of his books, but I love the movies."

"Who doesn't? As names go—"

"Could have been worse." Libby gave the server her credit card. "You could have gotten stuck with Sherlock. Or Hercule."

"Dad would have stepped in before Mom got too carried away. According to him, he voted for Christie as my twin's name. They both agreed on Travis for my middle brother, but Mom chose Wolfe for the youngest." He smiled at Libby. "Feels good to talk about something other than work." *Especially with someone who looks like you.* That sweet face with a hint of fire in the eyes.

When the server returned, Libby signed the bill and returned her card to her wallet. Then she threw back her shoulders. The light in her face dimmed, and her sensuous lips became a rigid line. "Before this goes any farther, there is something I need to know."

So much for a pleasant evening. Honeycutt drained his glass. "This is too nice a place for a serious conversation." He stood. "Let's take it outside."

****

In the brightly lit parking lot, Honeycutt's shadow loomed over Libby's hybrid. "What's up?"

Tell him. This is what you've been waiting for, isn't it?

"Well?"

Libby drew a deep breath. "Why were you at the Mark V hotel two days ago?"

"What? How did you—oh, it was that little weasel of a concierge, wasn't it?" Honeycutt laughed. "I saw him all curled up near the door. Thought he was getting up the nerve to ask you out."

Libby rolled her eyes. "He's a kid."

"But he looked at you like an adoring puppy."

Libby scowled. "Stop trying to change the subject.

You were at the Mark V, but you didn't tell anyone." His big shoulders rose and fell. "No one asked."

"I am." She leaned against her front fender and waited. At this point, in the interrogation room, suspects sometimes babbled. Honeycutt remained silent. Was he going to lawyer up?

"Since you ask—"

When Honeycutt spoke, Libby's shoulder muscles relaxed.

"Alexandros reserved two penthouse suites in Summerhaven, and he delegated Jeff Dearborn and me to see which of the two would best meet his needs. We started at the Caulfield Arms and finished at the Mark V."

"What time were you there?"

"We spent the morning at the Caulfield Arms, went to the Mark V after lunch. I talked to the clerk on duty. She might be able to confirm—" "She remembered you." *Who doesn't?*

"Then you know someone from hotel security took us to the penthouse. He was with us the whole time."

Libby nodded. "How long did your inspection take?"

"We had to get back to our hotel for a three o'clock conference call. After walking through the penthouse, we sat down, compared our scores for the Mark V, looked at our numbers for the other hotel, and decided on our recommendation."

"Was hotel security with you all that time?"

"Yes…I mean, no. He left us in the lobby, where we went over our lists. Good thing he didn't stick around, or we wouldn't have gotten anything done. He was excited about Alexandros coming to town."

"Did he mention that someone else connected to Alexandros was staying at the hotel?"

"I don't think so, but I tuned out most of what he said." Honeycutt's frown was like a lance aimed straight for her forehead. "You think that he told us...and that Jeff and I...Schuyler Pope."

"I don't think anything yet." Libby's hand moved closer to her holster. "But you were in the Mark V before Pope died."

"I can assure you—"

"I don't want assurances. I want information." *And an alibi if you have one. Please have one!* "When did you leave the Mark V, and where did you go from there?"

"Like I said, we had that conference call, so we were gone before three. After the call, Jeff and I prowled around the university football stadium and the baseball field. Talked to some people in charge who might remember us. Then, we had dinner together at our hotel."

"You weren't staying at the Mark V?"

"No. We'll move there shortly before Alexandros arrives." Beneath the parking lot lights, Honeycutt's eyes glittered like icy blue marbles. "You don't seriously think that Jeff and I—"

"I'm trying to get an idea of who was doing what and where."

He stiffened at the implication. "The hostess at the hotel restaurant saw us."

A woman. She'll remember you.

"The server for our table...and the hotel record. It should be easy enough for you to verify."

I'll make time for the interviews tomorrow. "Where are you staying now?"

"A hotel on the other side of the university from you.

Summerhaven Heights."

"What did you do after dinner?"

"Had a couple drinks at the bar. Stared at whatever was on TV. Went back to my room. You can check that with the bartender."

"Was Jeff Dearborn with you?"

"No."

"Did you see him?"

Honeycutt's lips twitched. "Did I lead him into the elevator, walk him to his room, and tuck him in? No."

"So you don't know where he went after...what time did you finish dinner?"

"About seven—wait a minute. You don't seriously think Jeff Dearborn—No way!" Honeycutt shook with laughter.

"He's on the personal security squad."

"Dearborn has a job title, but little responsibility. His parents are major Alexandros contributors. When their baby got kicked out of school for something their megabucks couldn't fix, Alexandros agreed to hire him."

"What did he do...to get kicked out?"

"I'm in charge of travel security. How should I know?" When Honeycutt extended his arms, they seemed to go on forever. "Definitely no physical violence. Might muss his hair."

Libby tapped her chin. How could she get hold of Dearborn's juvenile record? "You saw him around seven that evening. When did you see him next?"

"I don't...I had an early breakfast because I was meeting Jack Weatherby. Then I ended up..." He gestured at Libby.

"So Jeff Dearborn could have gone back to the Mark V after dinner."

"I'm telling you—"

"I know you think he's not involved, but he had Opportunity." Libby held up her index finger.

"Why in the world would he have…"

"I don't know about Motive." She lifted a second finger. "But he works for Alexandros. So did Schuyler Pope."

Although Honeycutt rested his big—huge! —hands on her shoulders, they didn't feel heavy. If anything, he seemed to think he was steadying her. Her shoulders tightened. *Don't let him grab the gun.*

"A lot of people work for Alexandros."

Don't look at me like I'm some five-year-old on the first day of kindergarten. I'm doing my job. Why didn't you and he spend the evening watching sports in the bar?

"That may be." Libby shrugged off Dash's hands. "But Jeff Dearborn, Schuyler Pope, and you are the only three who were at the Mark V."

"Jeff Dearborn—that's a real stretch. If you really want to find the killer, you should focus on whatever Schuyler Pope did that riled a shifter."

"He riled someone." When she injected a note of lightness into her voice, Honeycutt smiled. "But not a shifter."

The smile vanished. "Who says?"

"The medical examiner's office. No trace of organic matter in the wounds—no fur, no animal skin, no bits of claw. Cuts are clean. Like knife slices. They think the killer may have weaponized a hand cultivator." Libby held up one hand and flexed her fingers around her palm. "Welded knives to the metal fingers." The tips of her fingers tingled. "The killer is a Sim…simply human."

"Wait a minute. You're accepting everything your

contact told you. For all you know, he—or she—might be a shifter who wants to cover things up."

"Really, Mr. Honeycutt?" Libby put her hands on her hips. "Al Prince has excellent credentials. He's won awards for his work here and received national recognition for his thoroughness and integrity." He was also the fierce wildcat alpha of Ellyn's feline pack and the prime link for relaying rogue shifters from the Summerhaven PD to OASIS.

"Dearborn doesn't have the organizational skills."

"So he couldn't have acted on his own. But if he were following orders?"

"He's lousy at that, too."

"What does he do…for work?"

"Stays close to Alexandros, so he gets his picture in the papers and makes Mom and Dad happy."

"That's horrible."

Honeycutt opened his hands. "Minimizes damage and keeps the donations coming."

"So Dearborn is a definite no."

"With a capital N. And you know what I was doing."

"Until you left the bar."

He recoiled as if she'd struck him.

"You could have gone back to the Mark V."

"You can't be serious."

She swallowed. "You really want those Alexandros files. You have a motive."

"I didn't know about the files until after…but I guess you think I could be lying about that." Honeycutt scratched his jaw.

"You could have gone to Schuyler Pope's room and had a drink with him. When your attempt to persuade him failed, you could have drugged him, ransacked the room while he was out. If he came to, and you still hadn't found what you were looking for, you might have been feeling frustrated—"

"Stop right there. That's a cute little story you're spinning, but first, I didn't know Schuyler Pope was in that room until your captain told me of his death. Second, I didn't know about the missing information until I spoke to Alexandros. Again, after Dr. Pope's death. Even if I had known and had gone to talk to him…that weapon wasn't something handy like a lamp. The killer came primed to… Do you really believe that I—"

The image of Honeycutt's handsome face with its dropped jaw and horizontal lines above his lifted eyebrows burned into her brain. "Of course not. But good people sometimes do…bad…things. Dash—"

"Since you're accusing me of premeditated butchery, we should return to a more formal basis, Detective Maitland. How could you bear to sit and talk…for even five minutes in the company of such…evil?"

"I'm not accusing—"

"You're getting damn close to it."

When he leaned toward her, the breath caught in Libby's throat. She rested her hand on her holster.

"I know you've got a gun. I'd be foolish to even think of hurting you. Of course, desperate people…" The flash of wildness left his eyes. "Who am I kidding? I was born to help, not harm." He took out his phone and called a ride service. Then he turned to Libby. "I'll have the driver verify where I was between the time I left here and the time I picked up my car in front of your apartment."

"That's not necessary. I'm sorry. I never thought that you—I was—"

"Doing your job. We both are. Thanks for the dinner." He turned and walked back to the restaurant.

As she got into her car, Libby pondered the resignation in his tone. He spouted Alexandros nonsense about shifters like a true believer. Did a secret Dash lurk beneath that exterior? One who programmed Jeff Dearborn to kill Schuyler Pope? *Don't be ridiculous. He doesn't trust Dearborn enough to use him. And he's not…he can't be…he's right about the killer being a monster…and I don't believe he is.*

But he had been looking for the stolen files. Libby touched the pocket that held the flash drive. This might be the key to everything.

Entering her new apartment, she surveyed the boxes in the front room. When Dash—Honeycutt—had helped her earlier, energy, movement, and conversation had filled the air. Now, silence surrounded her. *Even after Gran's funeral, family stayed with me at the house. This is my first night alone. On my own.* She walked from the front room to the bedroom and back. Creepy. But exciting.

When she hung up her jacket, she bumped the pocket that held the flash drive. *Wonder if I can get anything out of this.* She opened her laptop on the dining table and turned it on. Holding her breath, she fitted the drive into a USB port and waited. She smacked the table so hard the boxes with the dishes vibrated. *Hope I didn't break anything.* "Password."

With a litany of swear words, she pulled the uncooperative device from the port. What now? She rolled the drive between her fingers and returned to the closet where she'd left her jacket. *Tomorrow, I'll pass it on to Homicide.*

Then she stretched. *Missed tai chi class.* She made a circuit of the large room. Everywhere she looked, boxes. *It would have taken me weeks to get everything up here, but Honeycutt ...agile for such a big guy. Didn't even stop to wipe the sweat off his forehead.*

Recalling his slightly flushed face, she stopped by the built-in bookcase. *He wasn't sweating. He hauled all these boxes from the apartment to the cars, packed everything, unloaded the boxes, then carried them up here. Not even breathing hard when he finished.* She'd almost had to force him to take a drink of water. *When he took the glass from me, it was so funny. His hand is so big he nearly covered mine.* She clasped her hand.

Libby opened a box. *Better get started. Will you look at that?* He could have tossed books into the box as he pulled them off the shelves. Instead, he'd maximized space—and the weight—by fitting the books into the boxes like pieces of a 3-D puzzle.

After unpacking one box and putting the books on the shelves, she moved on to the next packed box. *We're working together.* One shelf full. On to the next. *He'll have to talk to me.* Of course, their on-the-job exchanges would lack the pleasant comfort of their dinner conversation. *Until I wrecked it. But I had to.* She put down the book she was holding. *If I'd told Homicide, they would have assigned someone else...someone who doesn't know him...like I... I do like him...the more I know...but I don't really know him.* And how often had surprised neighbors or coworkers proclaimed a killer "a really nice guy"?

Dash was right about her having no evidence aside from his presence at the Mark V the day before the killing. She could interview hotel staff who'd been on duty in the early evening. If Dash had been there, someone would remember him. *I could search his room, too, and if I found nothing... Tomorrow, while he's at breakfast, I could shift...but I need to get to the station early to set up the meeting room. So I'll have to search while he's there...check Dearborn, too. I'll need a warrant.*

Libby closed the book box, went to her computer, and began to type.

Chapter 11

The next morning, she arrived at the station well before the Alexandros team and headed for the reserved conference room. From the way Dash—*Honeycutt*—and his colleagues had stood in the convention center, they liked elbow room. She arranged the chairs around the long table with ample space between them.

When she placed Honeycutt's seat at the head of the table, her fingers lingered on the backrest. Had a good night's sleep mellowed him? *Doesn't matter. He's still a suspect. Nothing I can do about that, but once I've cleared him, maybe we can be friends.*

She set up the computer and made sure it communicated with the video screen. The technology for this meeting was simple, but she'd sit near the door so she could quickly summon their computer brain in case anything did go wrong. After programming the coffee maker, she took the stairs down to her office. Although Robin was at her desk, her partner was in court, testifying.

"Hey there."

When Robin looked up, Libby stepped back before the breeze from her colleague's industrial strength eyelashes could knock her over. "Anything buzzing yet with the Honey-man?"

"That's the last thing I need." No need to mention the bounce in her belly whenever he dazzled her with that smile or the pleasant evening she'd wrecked with her after-dinner interrogation. "He and his team are meeting in our conference room."

"Maybe I'll drop by to say hello."

When Robin caressed her purple upper lip with the tip of her tongue, Libby suppressed a gag. "Know if anyone has ID'd the woman who called Schuyler Pope?"

"I thought you were off the case."

"Technically, yes." Libby tried to sound indifferent. "But since it's connected to Alexandros, I'm still…involved."

"Homicide pulled Zeke and me for some of the searches. Let me see." Robin accessed a folder on her computer. "Name's Nadine Victor. She and Pope were in med school together."

Libby's pulse quickened. A long-time friend might be able to guess Pope's password. And a doctor could translate technical jargon.

Robin closed the file. "Teaches immunology and does research at the Patterson School of Public Health in Baltimore."

About an hour's drive. "Have you interviewed her?"

Robin shook her head. "She's in the hospital. According to the office manager in her unit, she brought a nasty bug back from a conference in Colombia. Yesterday, in the office, she complained of a headache. This morning, she went straight to the ER, and they put her in the ICU."

"Sounds serious."

"She's quarantined. No visitors." Libby opened her mouth to swear.

A red-faced Captain Weatherby flung open his office door. "Maitland! My office! Now!"

"Uh-ho." Robin dived back into her paperwork.

Careful not to further aggravate her supervisor by brushing him, Libby squeezed her arms close to her ribs and eased into the office.

The captain slammed the office door so hard the window rattled. "Sit."

Choosing the chair farthest from the desk, Libby rested her hands in her lap and prepared for a royal reaming. *Honeycutt must have complained.*

"I just got a call from Judge Olsen's office." The captain hovered above her like the eye of a hurricane. "You requested search warrants for Dash Honeycutt and Jeff Dearborn's hotel rooms? Have you lost your mind?"

Libby fixed her gaze on a stink bug wandering across the carpet. If the captain saw the invader, his shoe would crush it. *Poor bug!* She looked up. "No, sir. Honeycutt and Dearborn were both in the Mark V the day before Schuyler Pope died. When I interviewed Honeycutt yesterday, he said they inspected the Mark V penthouse suite, which Alexandros had reserved. They were together until they finished their dinner at their hotel that evening. They didn't see each other until the next day. During that period—when the Pope homicide occurred—either of them could have returned to the Mark V and...killed...Schuyler Pope. A search of their rooms might find significant evidence. Or the weapon."

"When did you interview Dearborn?" Captain Weatherby's voice sliced into her bone marrow.

"I didn't. I didn't want to alert him."

"Do you have any evidence that either of these men returned to the Mark V after that first visit?"

"No, sir." Answering the question, she felt a quick

rush of hope.

"Do you have any evidence that either Honeycutt or Dearborn even knew the victim was at the Mark V?"

"No, sir."

The captain moved to stand behind his desk. "According to the ME's office, the weapon suggests premeditation. That means the killer knew the victim was at the hotel and went to his room intending to murder." Putting both hands on the desk, the big man leaned forward. "Why would Honeycutt or Dearborn do that?"

The captain looked ready to leap across the desk and throttle her if he didn't like her answer. Libby hugged her elbows as if that would protect her. "I don't know. Yet. I do know that Pope requested personal leave but cleaned out his desk. He also took some files that Alexandros wants back." The flash drive seemed to burn a hole in her jacket pocket. "If Alexandros thought the victim was going to expose—"

Weatherby shut her down by lifting his hand. He could have had a big red STOP sign tattooed on his palm. "Maitland, you were chosen for this assignment because of your strong organizational skills and your attention to detail. You also work well with people. You and Mike did, that is."

Me and Mike. Libby bit her lower lip.

"You've been on this assignment for two days, and it's clear that you are having problems. Instead of working with the Alexandros security team to provide smooth sailing for the Alexandros appearance, you're floating a conspiracy theory that could involve Alexandros and his people in a murder." He hammered the word "Alexandros" as if she could possibly overlook it. "Homicide is reviewing videotapes from the Mark V. Have you talked to them?"

"No, sir. But I was going back to the hotel."

"You should have done that before applying for the warrant."

Libby gazed at her hands. "Yes, sir." *I didn't want to see Dash Honeycutt in the lobby that evening.*

The captain sat down. Although the desk separated them, he looked as if he might erupt at any moment. "Crispin Alexandros is giving Summerhaven a chance to shine in the national spotlight. But you—you're ready to embarrass the police department, the mayor's office—the whole town."

Libby drew herself up and set her feet firmly on the floor. Ready, set…

"What's worse is that Schuyler Pope is one of us. He took one of my cousins to the junior prom. He comes from a good family, and the last thing they need is a media circus." When he pointed at her, Libby flinched. "As of this moment, you are on two weeks personal leave. When you come back, you'll spend some time with O'Malley."

O'Malley? Libby coughed. *Might as well be writing parking tickets.*

The captain snarled. If he were a Shapeshifter, he'd have been halfway to a bear. "You can appeal to the union, of course, but it won't come to anything since everyone in the department, including your rep, knows how important this Alexandros visit is." He stood once again. "Badge and gun."

Placing the items on his desk blotter felt like ripping them out of her gut.

"Two weeks. Stay away from Alexandros and his

people. You're good, Maitland. Get your act together."

"Yes, sir."

When Libby exited the captain's office, the Tweedles straightened up and shot her sidewise glances. With desks closest to Weatherby's office, they no doubt heard almost every word. With a jaunty wave, Libby headed out.

Behind her, Captain Weatherby bellowed, "Calvert!"

Robin will enjoy working with Dash. At least my disaster will reward someone. If Libby walked fast enough, she might escape from the station before the gossip metastasized. Chewed out by Weatherby, the most even-tempered captain in the district! Two weeks leave! Stuck with O'Malley!

Keeping her head down, Libby aimed for the front door.

And ran straight into a wall.

Not a wall. Dash Honeycutt's chest. As solid as a Ponderosa pine. Smelled like one, too, but the aroma of the soap didn't mask his own musky masculine scent.

Hands gripped her elbows.

Honeycutt's glare silenced his crew's sniggers. He dropped his hands to his sides. "Are you okay?" Detective Maitland's turned-up nose wasn't bleeding.

"I'm fine." She moved her head up and down like one of those bobble-headed dolls. "Sorry to bump into you. Everything's ready for your meeting." She turned and gestured. "Check in at the front desk."

Honeycutt glanced at his team. "Go on." He returned to Detective Maitland. "Where are you headed?"

"Out."

Before Honeycutt could protest, she scurried past.

He turned as she zipped through the big automatic doors. *What the ... ? She's in such a hurry ... Does she still think I could have ... Given her hate for Alexandros, I guess her suspicions are reasonable ... but still insulting.*

Absorbed in his thoughts, Honeycutt automatically checked in and would have walked past the conference room if a tall, slender woman with outrageous purple hair hadn't cried, "Ah, there you are!" and held out her hand. "I'm Detective Robin Calvert. My partner Zeke Pritchard and I will be serving as your new liaisons. Zeke's in court this morning but should be here after lunch. It's a pleasure to meet you, Mr. Honeycutt." When she smiled, glistening white teeth flashed, and the corners of her eyes crinkled. Real smile. Real pleasure.

He took her hand. Soft but bigger than Libby's. "Good to meet you, too, Detective."

She gave a husky little laugh and fluttered amazing eyelashes. "Oh, please! Call me Robin."

He touched his chest. "Dash." This Robin was going to be easier to work with, but what had happened to Libby? She'd looked upset. Where was she going? He had a job to do. Why did he care? "Did Detective Maitland get called out on a case?" Maybe they'd found the Pope killer.

"Things weren't working out." Robin leaned toward him and spoke in a near-whisper. "That's the Official version."

And the Unofficial?

Resting a hand on his jacket sleeve, Robin drew him into the room where his colleagues were getting coffee, arguing over the doughnuts they'd brought, and finding name cards by their chairs. Robin's come-hither perfume was a trifle heavy, but she didn't seem to suspect him of murder.

Tony took his place at the head of the table by the computer. "What took you so long getting here?"

Honeycutt ignored the question. "Are we ready to go?"

Tony nodded at Robin. "Nice setup."

Robin's purple lips curved slightly. "Libby did it earlier."

Honeycutt's gaze roamed from Tony and the computer to the comfortable spacing at the table. *She must have done that, too.* Honeycutt surveyed his team.

"Let's begin. I assume you've all met Detective Calvert." When he gestured at Robin, she leaned forward as if she might pounce. "We use whiteboards for preliminary planning. We'll put our final decisions up on the screen. At the end of the meeting, I want hard copies of everything we discussed for everyone here as well as you and your partner." Honeycutt met Robin's gaze. *How long did it take her to plaster that stuff on her eyes?*

She beamed at him as if he'd said something wonderful. "Will do."

The morning meeting went smoothly, which was good because Honeycutt's thoughts kept wandering. *Who decided things weren't working out? What things?*

Although he and his team had planned so many public presentations that they could almost do the job in their sleep, every venue was different, and they approached every presentation as if it were the first and only one. Carelessness caused problems. Alexandros hated problems almost as much as he hated

Shapeshifters.

Robin joined them for lunch at a small diner within

walking distance of police headquarters. Although she basked in the attention from the other members of his team, she claimed the spot by Honeycutt's shoulder and seized every opportunity to chat with him. After the meal, she followed the team out of the diner while Honeycutt settled the bill.

When he stepped outside, Robin was waiting. "That took a while."

"Since we're going to be here for a few weeks and probably eat at this place a lot, I wanted to get to know the proprietor. You didn't have to wait for me."

She twirled a strand of purple hair. "You're new in town, and I don't want to lose you."

"We're not far from your headquarters." Honeycutt touched his jacket pocket. "And I have my phone." He set a brisk pace, but Robin kept up.

"I'm sorry, Dash. I didn't mean to imply you'd get lost. I thought it would be nice to have some time to…get to know you."

He stopped and looked at Robin. "This is a professional arrangement. Nothing more." He resumed his pace. "We have all the information we need for the conference center, but we do need a layout of the mayor's house. Entrances, exits, the area where the reception's being held. Any weapons on the site and how they're secured."

"Do you want me to do that while you're meeting this afternoon or tomorrow before we meet?"

"The sooner, the better."

"I'll have it for you before you leave."

"Thanks." *Much easier to work with, but no Libby. What really happened?* When he slowed down, Robin followed his lead. "Detective Maitland was doing a good job for us."

Robin smiled. "I'm sure she was."

"I know you said things weren't working out." He opened his palms to the sky.

"That's what the captain told me this morning."

So she didn't choose to leave. "He's the Official Version?"

Robin chuckled. "Always."

"What about the Unofficial?"

"You didn't hear it from me"—Robin rested one hand on her well-endowed bosom— "but the office gossips overheard snatches of his tirade. Something about search warrants."

Honeycutt came to a full stop. "Search...warrants." He uttered the words as if he were practicing a foreign language. *She wants to search my room? If she'd asked, I've have taken her there last night...could have gotten real interesting.* "That's crazy."

"But totally Libby." Robin's husky laugh rubbed against his ear like sandpaper. "She's not even on the case, but she can't let go. That's how she's always been."

Stubborn. Honeycutt resumed his walk.

"Committed to her work."

Robin fell in step beside him. "Obsessed. Mike Schrader was her partner until he retired a few weeks ago. He'd been on the job a long time, worked strictly by the book, but Libby—she takes a more creative approach. Drove him up the wall."

Also earned him a boatload of awards, according to Jack Weatherby. Sounds like he was coasting till Libby came along. She made him a better cop.

"Since you and I are going to be working together, I'd like to learn more about you." When Robin moved closer, Honeycutt picked up his pace. She kept up even though she breathed more heavily. "Like…how long…have you…been…with…Alexandros?"

"A few years." By the time he turned the corner of the block occupied by police headquarters, he was nearly jogging. "Here we are!" He eyed the big clock set above the entrance. *If I check before supper, I might catch Libby tossing my room.* He smiled.

"With time to spare!" Robin cried.

Honeycutt removed the hand she'd dropped on his arm and walked up the steps.

Chapter 12

The front doors to the station closed behind her, and Libby peered through one of the big windows. As Honeycutt walked away from her and approached the front desk, his powerful shoulders seemed to slump. *When I told him, he looked surprised. Disappointed? If he learns about the search warrants, he'll be dancing in the streets.* She turned toward the parking lot. *I should have smiled at him.* She scoffed. *Why? I've got nothing to smile about.*

During the drive back to her new apartment, the scene with Captain Weatherby replayed in her brain, but no redeeming possibilities emerged. When she entered the front room, she dropped onto the lumpy sofa and took out her phone. "Call Steffi."

Three rings later, her sister's face lit up the screen. "Hi, Lib!"

"I need to talk." Steffi's glow faded.

"Have you got a minute?"

"You're in luck. Twins are napping."

"It's been ages since I've seen them. How are they?"

"Busy. Four wolf-pup legs are faster than two small human ones. Of course, they've also learned that being human has advantages." Smiling, she held up her free hand and rotated her thumb. "Nothing beats the opposable thumb. But enough about them." Steffi curled up in a big armchair. "Talk to me." Her voice was as soothing as the cream Mom used on skinned knees.

By the time Libby finished her recitation, the inner tips of Steffi's dark eyebrows almost touched. "I caught a broadcast of an Alexandros speech last year." Steffi's mouth tightened like a steel line. "When he finished, the audience looked ready to light torches and hunt us down. Like the bad old days. How could you work for that man?"

Libby lifted her hands. "I didn't volunteer, I was assigned. It could have been a big career boost. But I blew it. Big time." She stood. "What really bugs me is that I'm a professional. I thought I could do an excellent job, but right from the start when Dash"—the vibration of his name in her mouth teased a smile— "started spouting Alexandros propaganda—"

"Whoa!" Steffi waved. "Who's this Dash? Your new partner?"

For the first time that day, Libby laughed. "No way!"

"Wow!"

Libby froze. "What's that mean?"

Steffi's eyes sparkled. "Like the queen in *Hamlet*, you may protest too much."

Huh? Trust Steffi to come up with an academic reference. "I didn't...I wasn't...he's not..."

"Keep going, Gertrude."

Libby sat up straighter. "Dash Honeycutt handles Alexandros travel security. Nice guy. Looks like Thor." *Bigger and blonder.* "Yesterday, we got to know each other over a pleasant dinner." *That I wrecked with the interrogation.*

Steffi leaned into the phone. "Are you telling me
Shifting into Shadows

you just broke up with the guy you've been living with for two years, and you're already dating Super-Thor?" Steffi's hand touched her temple. "From Dayzee, I expect this, but *you*—"

"It isn't like that. Tommy and I were having problems for a while. And Dash isn't Super-Thor. He's…just a good-looking guy." *Who looked bigger lifting all those book boxes*. "When he helped me move, he missed dinner with his crew, so it seemed only fair that I feed him."

"Only fair." Steffi repeated the words with an ironic twist. "Hope you took him someplace nice."

"Yes, Mother." Libby focused her phone on the front room. A tour might distract Steffi. "Let me show you my new apartment."

"Don't try to change the subject. Ooh! I love those bookshelves!"

Libby laughed. *I knew it!* With her phone, she scanned the hall and the bedroom.

"You're going to need a bigger bed if—"

"This one's fine." Libby patted the queen-sized mattress. Steffi lifted an eyebrow.

As Libby returned to the front room, Steffi said, "So tell me more about this Super…this Dash. Why is a guy like that working for—"

"I've been asking myself the same thing." Libby paced. "He doesn't simply work for Alexandros. He buys the whole Evil Shapeshifter Package." She showed her sister the kitchen. "Trying to nudge him in the right direction is like talking to Granite Peak." She regarded her sister. "Why are you looking so smug?"

"There's something…interesting…in your voice

when you talk about him."

Libby squared her shoulders. "He's good to look at, and he's good company. But he works for Alexandros."

"Maybe you could convince your captain to give you the assignment back and work on him some more."

"No. Captain Weatherby's right. I let my personal feelings cloud my professional judgment." She eyed her sister. "Soon, Alexandros will be gone, and I'll win back my captain's trust. In the meantime, I'll get the apartment in shape. Maybe get a massage, too." Libby rubbed her neck. "That always makes me feel good."

Steffi smiled. "I bet Super-Thor gives a dynamite massage."

You and me both! Libby scoffed. "I'm never going to see Dash Honeycutt again." She spread her fingers over an aching spot in her chest.

"Never is a long time." Steffi's smile deepened. "And you never know." A cry pierced the quiet, and she pushed herself out of the big chair. "Time to check on the Daring Duo."

"Send videos!"

"I will." Steffi rolled her shoulders.

"Thanks for listening. I always feel better after I talk with you."

"That's what sisters are for, eh? Next time, I want the whole Tommy story." Steffi leaned into the screen. "And keep me posted on Super-Thor."

Super-Thor indeed! Libby blew her sister a kiss and ended the call.

Chapter 13

Libby unpacked her possessions and found places for them in the new apartment. Every box triggered memories of Dash Honeycutt's big hands and broad shoulders, not to mention that amazing smile.

When she finished, she surveyed the front room and hugged herself. Then, she folded the empty boxes and stored them in the back of the garage. She opened the downstairs door in front of the stairs, stepped into Lovegrove Lane, and stretched. The scent of lilacs in a nearby garden reached out. So much sweeter than the chemical aromas near the place she and Tommy...

Tommy's condo. She rubbed her hands against her jeans. *I should walk.*

The new neighborhood contained old houses with massive trees, a big brick elementary school, and a sprinkling of small shops. The primary street—an avenue—led straight to the downtown historic district, where Libby stopped in front of the Mark V. *Might as well tie up loose ends.*

At the concierge's desk, Peter Barnett almost spilled his coffee. "Hi there, Detective." He looked around. "Working alone today?"

"Yes." Dash was right. Barnett did look goofy when she was nice. *Use it.* "I have one more question for you." "Happy to oblige."

"And I can't tell you how much I appreciate it." She

moved closer and dropped her voice. "Other people who were on duty the day before the incident in 1410 confirmed that they saw Mr. Honeycutt—" She held her hand about a foot above her head. "You remember him?"

"Oh, yes!"

"So I know he was here that afternoon, and he was with me the following morning." Another nod.

"What I'm wondering is…were you working that evening…after dinner?"

"I pulled a double shift because somebody was out sick."

"I want you to think about this very carefully. I know you saw Mr. Honeycutt in the afternoon. Did you see him here again…that evening?"

The young man scratched his chin and screwed up his eyes as if he could peer into the past. "No. No. I don't think I did."

The tense knot between Libby's shoulders disappeared. *All clear*. For Dash, at least. As far as his associate was concerned… *Dash doesn't think Dearborn is smart enough, and that's good enough for me.* Libby turned her smile up a notch. "Thanks so much, Mr. Barnett."

"Happy to help, Detective. Anytime." The young concierge swiped a trace of sweat from his forehead. He picked up a pen. "Here's my number."

When she took the note, he looked ready to melt on the spot. "Thanks again." Libby almost danced to the exit.

Returning to the traffic-filled street from the luxurious hotel was like awakening from a happy dream into gritty reality. *If I'd checked here first, I wouldn't*

Shifting into Shadows

have requested the warrant. We might still be… No. I wouldn't be working with Dash. I'd be helping Crispin Alexandros. And Alexandros might still be involved with the murder. What's on that flash drive? Something worth killing for?

On her walk back to the apartment, she bought a take-out chicken dinner and a bottle of apple juice at a local market. After setting the small dining table with Gran's dishes, she found some of her favorite rhythm and blues on her phone, scooped the dinner from its containers onto her plate, and sat down. "Should have bought wine." She filled a small glass with apple juice and lifted the glass. "Here's to my first night—to my first *meal* on Lovegrove Lane." *Last night was really my first night…after Whiskers…with Dash.*

She itched to share her final Mark V interview with him, to let him know… *He already knows he's in the clear. He told me the truth. He thought I should trust him. I wanted to, but…*

She chewed a tasty chicken chunk and stared at the green beans. *Tomorrow, I'll shop.*

On a notepad, she made a list. Between bites, she entered items ranging from coffee maker to salt. When she finished her meal, she scanned the list. Who would have guessed that a single person needed so much stuff? *I'll try that big-box store in the shopping center.*

She stacked her dishes in the sink. Fortunately, the former tenants had left dish soap. When she finished cleaning up, she eyed her phone. *Might as well check on Nadine Victor.*

Standing at the table, she speed-dialed Homicide. Victor still in ICU. And Homicide still waiting for lab results. Overloaded and understaffed, facilities in the state capital were slow, and Homicide always had plenty of cases. *They'll talk to her as soon as she recovers...if she recovers.*

Libby set her phone on the table and rocked on her heels. The day before Dr. Victor checked into the hospital, she'd returned to the Patterson School of Public Health. Why not start there? Maybe she'd left a record of her contact with Schuyler Pope in her office.

A quick online tour disclosed that anyone entering the urban campus had to pass through security. *Where did I stash my undercover clothes?*

She opened her closet door but stopped. Whenever she'd gone undercover for the department, she'd worn a disguise. But on her own... *I'll shift. Let's see now...college girls...* She searched online until she saw an appealing young woman in California. As she focused on the image, her body changed. A shorter figure, rounder face, big green eyes, bouncy blonde hair. When she finished, she eyed the reflection in the mirror. Her jeans were too long and too snug in the hips. Buttons strained to contain the blouse, and her bra was too tight.

Looser, shorter pants. Knit top. And she already had a fake student ID for a blonde.

Chapter 14

The next morning, while eating breakfast at a restaurant near Dr. Victor's school, Libby—now Lizzie Lemont—mentally reviewed the building layout she'd found online. Dr. Victor spent most of her time in the Crowley Wing.

In front of the massive stone building, Libby attached herself to a flow of Simple Human students. She passed through the metal detector without setting off alarms, sent her backpack through the screening device, and flashed her ID at one of the male guards. It didn't hurt that she gave him a good opportunity to look down her scoop-necked top. *So far, so good.* She marched toward the Crowley Wing.

Moments later, official-looking yellow tape barred her way.

Closed!

The huge, bold print slammed like a fist between her ribs.

"Looking for something?" The speaker, a grayhaired man in a suit, looked like an administrator.

Libby gestured at the sign. "I was wondering what happened."

One corner of his thin mouth quirked. "Don't you read the newsletter?"

"I don't have time." She batted her false eyelashes. "I've been too busy with my studies."

The man's gaze probed. "Someone brought an infection back from South America. Health Department doesn't want it to spread."

"Good thinking. Oh, my!" Libby glanced at her watch. "I should go." Turning away, she swore silently. Not even a badge would have gotten her into the Crowley Wing. Shapeshifting could get her into Nadine Victor's office, but she'd have to return to her human base to search. She'd have to risk catching Dr. Victor's nasty bug. *No thanks.*

Libby headed for the main exit. Nadine Victor and Schuyler Pope had gone to med school together. Their relationship might be personal as well as professional. *She might have notes at her home.*

An online search located Dr. Victor's house in Odenton, near the BWI Thurgood Marshall Airport. *Short drive from here. I could go.* Libby eyed the short skirt and blue crop top she'd squeezed this body into, along with the stylish athletic sneakers into which she'd jammed her toes. A student wouldn't go to Nadine Victor's house. But a colleague might.

I'll need a more professional appearance, wear the red wig so anyone seeing me will remember the hair. I'll have to go home to change. An hour's drive. She checked her watch. Noon. Home by one. *Ready by two. Reach the Victor house around three.*

In her apartment, she took a deep breath before returning to her human base. She chose a sleek red wig and more subdued makeup than her student shape had worn. A sedate navy pantsuit replaced her collegiate attire. She also packed a mask, gloves, and protective gear for her body. After coffee and a blueberry muffin from the local sandwich shop, she got in her car and set a new course.

****

Like the entrance to Dr. Victor's academic world, the front door of her two-story house, which sat back from the paved neighborhood road, had warning tapes. Libby parked on the street slightly past the house and prepared to slip into her protective covering when someone shouted.

"Don't go there!"

Libby looked out her car window at the small, plump woman standing in front of the large ranch house on the opposite side of the street. Her white hair matched the fluffy fur of the Persian cat perched on her shoulder.

Libby got out of her car and crossed the street. "I work with Nadine Victor." The lie slid out like silk. "She asked me to stop by and bring something to the hospital." Libby gestured at the tape. "What's going on?"

"Health Department people said Deenie was in the hospital, but they didn't tell me which one. I called the county—"

Libby supplied the name of the city hospital. "I'll tell her you asked about her." Libby indicated the Victor house. "The Health Department was here?"

The other woman's white head bobbed. "They said Deenie caught some kind of virus, and we should all stay away so we didn't get it, too. That's why they put those warnings up. They don't want anybody getting sick." *Or getting in.*

The plump woman extended her hand. "I'm Tina Patrick."

"Nice to meet you."

The woman indicated the front door of her house. "Why don't you come on in, sit down, and tell me how

Deenie is doing?"

The neighbor's picture window had a clear view of the street and the Victor house. *Bet she sees everything.*

Libby accepted the invitation.

In the living room, Libby surveyed the five cats who surrounded them. "Quite a clowder you have here."

"This is Ajax, Muffin, Calypso, Peewee, and—" Tina Patrick stroked the Persian. "—Queen Savannah. You like cats?"

"My grandmother always had at least one." Libby reached out to the calico, who drew back and regarded her with narrowed eyes that showed more than feline awareness. *Shapeshifter. What are you doing here?*

Libby returned her hand to her lap and dipped her chin in recognition. The calico sniffed and sauntered off, tail held high. She knew an imposter when she saw one.

"They keep turning up on my doorstep." The other woman gestured at the departing cat. "Like Calypso. She was near the garden a few weeks ago. Looked like she'd been in a fight, so I wrapped her up and took her to the vet. Now she races me to the door."

"Maybe she has another home." *Ellyn will know about missing Felidae.*

When Mrs. Patrick waved a finger at another cat, Libby glimpsed a wedding ring. "Now, Ajax, stop picking on Muffin. Shoo!" She turned back to Libby. "Would you like some tea or coffee? A little shortbread?"

"No, thanks. As I said, I'm here to pick up something Deenie wants."

"You work with her?"

"I started a few months ago."

"She's a good neighbor…helps me get my cats to

the vet's…taught me how to order their food and litter on the computer. I can't carry those heavy bags, and the little ones are more expensive and don't last, you know?" Libby nodded.

"How is Deenie? Have you been to see her?"

"She's in intensive care."

The older woman pressed a fist against her red lips. "Oh, no!"

"They're keeping her in quarantine until they can figure out what she has."

"But you saw her? Talked to her?"

"I stopped by on my lunch-hour today and sent in a message. That's when she asked me to bring her stuff."

"One of those Health Department people probably got it for her."

"They went into the house?"

"One did." Mrs. Patrick poured herself a cup of tea, added cream and honey, and stirred slowly as if she could see Libby's impatience building. "Two men from the Health Department."

"What did they look like?"

"Government types. You know." The neighbor gave a little wave. "Dark suits. Ties. One was young and skinny. Reminded me of a boy on my son Pete's high school basketball team. The other one was older, short, and a little heavy. Kind of bald."

"Did you see any identification?"

When the neighbor pursed her lips, she looked even more like the haughty Persian now occupying her lap. "They showed me some badges. I didn't look too—" Her hazel eyes got bigger and rounder. "Do you think they weren't real?"

"I don't know. I'm curious." Libby petted the

nearest cat, a big mackerel tabby that rolled over and purred. "Did you notice what kind of vehicle they had?"

"Big black car."

She wouldn't have noticed the license plate. "Did it have any writing on it?"

"Oh, no. Like I said, it was—now, Dave Mason across the street—he knows all about cars." She snapped her fingers. "But he was at work when they came. Everybody on the block was except for the Cabots. They're camping in their RV. Haven't been home for more than two weeks since they retired." Her lips curved. "Must be nice."

"You said one of the Health Department people went into the house?"

The neighbor scratched the Persian's whiskers. "The skinny guy put on one of those space suit getups and carried some empty boxes in. When he came out, they looked full, and he wobbled a little.

"When they showed me their badges, they said they were looking for something of Deenie's that might have information they could use to help her get better." She looked at Libby. "Do you think I should have called someone?"

Libby thought of Schuyler Pope's mutilated body and Nadine Victor's convenient illness. With the neighborhood all but deserted, it would have been easy to knock an old lady under the car if she got in the way. "I think you did fine, Mrs. Patrick." She checked her watch. "I should be going."

"I sure hope Deenie's gonna get better."

"Me, too." Libby stood. "I want to look around the house before I go. Maybe there's a way I could get in and find what Deenie wants."

"You really shouldn't—"

"Don't worry. I brought a mask and one of those space suit things. I'll be fine."

While Libby pulled on her hazard gear in her car, Tina Patrick maintained her vantage point from her front window. The rest of the street looked deserted. Libby approached the rear of the Victor house. Door keys under a fake rock. Might as well hang an invitation for thieves. *A doctor should be smarter*. Libby entered the empty house.

Immaculate kitchen. Nothing out of place in the living room or the bedrooms. Spotless bathroom. Libby swore. Unless Nadine Victor had obsessive-compulsive disorder, the intruder had made a clean sweep.

The study contained no calendars. Nothing on the desk. Although she doubted she'd find any, Libby did a quick dust for prints. Half-hoping to locate an e-mail or a file with Pope's name or initials, she switched on the computer. Nothing. The fake Health Department must have wiped the hard drive.

Libby examined the desk itself. Nothing in the drawers, which had easily opened locks. She checked under the drawers in case Nadine Victor had hidden something there. The more substantially locked filing cabinets didn't look as if anyone had touched them, but Libby noted several empty sections.

"Come on, Doc." Libby eyed the barren desk. "Give me something. Anything." But the room, like the woman who lived there, remained silent. Libby left the house, stuck her protective gear in the trunk of her car, and waved to the neighbor, who was still watching. *She doesn't miss much*. Libby pulled away from the Victor house. *Should have rented a car*.

For the next few days, Libby buried her frustration in housework and distractions. Shopping. Cleaning. Baking Gran's bread for herself and the Mission. Practicing tai chi. By Saturday, she'd seen all the good movies and a few of the stinkers, mangled a beginner's knitting class, and run so much her shin splints should have developed shin splints. In quiet moments, she tried not to wonder what Dash Honeycutt was doing...with Robin, who wouldn't have wasted any time.

An item popped out from the obituary pages of the Sunday *Summerhaven Herald.* Schuyler Samuel Pope,

38, had unexpectedly been summoned Home to Heaven, where he would find Eternal Peace. *Eternal peace?* When the image of Pope's mangled body flashed across her mind, Libby almost threw up her coffee. She pushed her home-cooked pancakes away.

Memorial service Tuesday. She circled the event. She was no longer on the Pope case, but she could pay her respects. *And if Nadine Victor has recovered by then, who knows?*

Chapter 15

Leading the Alexandros entourage, Dash Honeycutt stopped on the threshold of the chapel designated for the Schuyler Pope memorial service. Accommodations would be tight for Alexandros, his personal guard, and the media people who'd followed them from the airport.

Honeycutt lifted his hand, and a tall, pale man in a solemn black suit—the funeral director—left his position beside a burly man who looked lost and a small, white-haired woman.

Honeycutt stepped to the side.

When Crispin Alexandros entered the room, many of the mourners shot out of their seats, and excited whispers erupted. No weapons unless someone planned to clobber Alexandros with a phone. Even Jeff Dearborn could handle that.

"Welcome, Mr. Alexandros. I'm Ted Stewart." Extending his hand, the funeral director spoke above the looming chaos. "Meeting you would be a pleasure…under different circumstances." He indicated the big man and the short woman. "Schuyler's parents and I…we were touched when we learned that you cared enough…please, please allow me to introduce you to them."

One of Alexandros's small hands gripped the funeral director's hand. As always, Alexandros wore thin leather gloves that purportedly helped him avoid "disturbing" touches. "I would be honored." The deep Alexandros baritone rolled, and he pressed his free hand to his chest, a gesture he often used to demonstrate intense emotion belied by the cold glitter in his deep-set gray eyes.

Overwhelming the recorded strains of "Amazing Grace," the arrival of their group turned the dignified service into a public spectacle. Two personal guards marched in front of Alexandros and the funeral director. Another pair brought up the rear. On the right, Jeff Dearborn scanned the gathering and kept one hand on the holster at his hip. On the left, Robin Calvert still looked as amazed as she had when Alexandros entered the private airport—like a kid who'd seen Santa Claus on Christmas Eve.

Honeycutt smoothed his tie. Alexandros's fullbodied frame, white mane, and slightly rounded face enhanced the Santa Claus image…if you ignored the practiced smile on the greedy mouth.

As Alexandros and company moved toward Pope's family, assertive mourners pressed forward. In this state, plenty of people didn't leave home without a pistol in their pocket, but no one appeared to be carrying.

When his personal guard moved toward the admirers, Alexandros stopped and lifted his hands. "Please, please, return to your seats. I will be happy to speak with you all individually…after I have met poor Schuyler's grieving family." He faked a sniffle and pressed a white handkerchief to the corner of one dry eye.

Honeycutt took his position at the wall by the entrance. A good place to stop intruders and to check out everyone who'd come to pay their respects.

The younger members of the Pope family greeted Alexandros as if he'd flown in from Paradise Central, but the parents showed more restraint. "My dear friends" — he grasped their hands— "I am so sorry for your loss."

When Pope's parents showed him the tribute that lined the front of the room, Alexandros uttered appropriate comments for every image of the dead man with his parents, siblings, other family members, and friends. The montage ended with a simple urn adorned with flowers. In the front of the urn was one large photograph of a smiling, young Schuyler Pope standing on the steps of an impressive institution. Wearing a white lab coat with a stethoscope dangling from his neck, he looked ready to take on the world.

So many tomorrows... When the image of the mutilated body he'd seen replaced the optimistic young doctor, Honeycutt frowned. *What a loss! Hope they catch the killer.*

Dr. Pope's father lingered by the montage as if he hoped those happier images might replace his last look at his son, the formal identification at the morgue. Or maybe these photos simply reminded him of better days. His wife rested a hand on his arm and whispered in his ear, but the miserable man looked frozen. One of the younger Popes pushed through the mourners who were converging on Alexandros and persuaded Dr. Pope's father to walk with them to his seat.

As he'd promised, Alexandros spent time with each admirer. Although he seemed to listen more than he talked, he seized every opportunity to hand out cards with the date and place of his Summerhaven presentation. When the flood of conversation and selfies slowed to a trickle, he finally lifted his hands. "Please,

please, this is enough…more than enough. Let us not forget why we are here. To honor the memory of a fine man, Dr. Schuyler Pope." He regarded the funeral director, who stood with downcast eyes by Pope's parents. "Please return to your seats, and let the service begin."

While two of Pope's young relatives played piano and violin, the funeral director escorted Alexandros and his guards to newly placed upholstered seats near the immediate family—no metal folding chairs like the ones crammed into the back of the room on which other late arrivals—

Hello! The sight of Detective Maitland brought Honeycutt to full alert. Had she come out of respect, or was she hoping the murderer would make an

appearance? Did she still think that he…

As if she could read his mind, her mouth blossomed into a smile. Prettier than he remembered. Honeycutt winked. She frowned.

Oops. Definitely not appropriate. Still, it felt great to be off the hot seat. *Alexandros wants to thank her for her work. I'll have to tell him she's here.*

Detective Maitland looked down at her program. Trying to hide a blush? Too bad she was too far away for him to see it. *Back off, Honeycutt. You're on duty.*

He glanced at the narrow corridor outside the room. No activity. The musicians returned to their seats. A minister came to the front and asked everyone to stand.

The attendants sang "How Great Thou Art" and returned to their seats. After several short prayers, the minister surveyed the assembly. "Now, I am honored to yield the floor to a very special speaker."

When Alexandros stood, Honeycutt watched the

mourners and the media. Hands reaching into pockets or purses, this time for phones instead of tissues. Honeycutt relaxed.

"...how his early life shaped the Schuyler Pope I knew." Instead of impassioned oratory, Alexandros used a conversational tone appropriate to the occasion. His words cast the usual spell. Except for immediate family members, whose sobs punctuated the eulogy.

When Alexandros praised the dead man's loyalty to the Alexandros Foundation, Honeycutt covered a laugh with a cough. In describing Pope's theft of Alexandros property, the big man had used more colorful terms, none suitable for polite company. Honeycutt glanced at Detective Maitland. *What has she done with that jump drive?*

Casting a mournful eye on the portrait mounted by the urn, Alexandros leaned forward, a movement that usually preceded a dramatic finish. "Schuyler Pope was a dedicated scientist. A good man taken well before his time." Alexandros's calculating gaze took in the transfixed audience—well, mostly transfixed. Libby's eyes narrowed. "I fear that his dedication and determination may have led to his untimely demise."

In her seat, Libby stiffened. Expecting an attack on Shapeshifters?

"Although I understand the police are still investigating the cause of his death, as one who knew the nature of Schuyler's research, I am certain his findings must have threatened the Shadow People, who

undoubtedly retaliated."

Many listeners leaned forward, but Libby grabbed the edge of her seat with both hands as if preparing to jump up in protest. *Stay cool.* For his full-throated attack on Shapeshifters, Alexandros required a paying audience.

"Schuyler Pope was a good man, a fine scientist, and he will be missed." Alexandros planted his hands on his chest and dipped his chin. "May he rest in peace."

As everyone else murmured, "Amen," Alexandros started to return to his seat, but the funeral director stepped in front of the lectern.

"Thank you for those kind words, Mr. Alexandros." When people began to move, he lifted a hand. "Please stay where you are for a moment. We have refreshments in another room."

What room? Where? Leaving the chapel, Dash strode down the hallway and found the large reception room with catering staff and a small buffet set out. By the time he finished in the adjoining kitchen—more caterers, one unsecured exit—the funeral director was leading Mr. and Mrs. Pope and the rest of the family toward the buffet.

Behind them, people swarmed toward the room with the food and tried, unsuccessfully, to get close to Alexandros. Jeff Dearborn kept his post on the right hand, and Robin Calvert stood as if glued to the man's left side. Now that she'd met the real power, she'd redirected her come-hither looks. Honeycutt tapped one of the other guards on the shoulder. "Tell The Boss Detective Maitland is here."

As the crowd leaving the chapel thinned, Libby appeared, but instead of following the others, she turned in the opposite direction, toward the exit.

Honeycutt brushed past a few other departing mourners. "Lib—Detective Maitland, wait. Please."

At the sound of Dash Honeycutt's deep voice, Libby

froze. *Oh, no. What do you want?*

He stood behind her shoulder. "You're not going to the reception?"

What's it to you? She turned. Instead of looking up at Honeycutt's face, she focused on the knot of his tie. Dark blue. Like his eyes. "No. I'm leaving." In case he couldn't see the exit, she indicated the door behind her.

"Haven't seen you around."

The concern in his voice made her look up. When a smile lit his features, the tension in her jaw eased, and she felt herself smiling like an idiot. "I'll be back on duty next Monday...unless I'm seen with your boss." She gestured at Alexandros, who was ignoring admirers and shrugging off Robin Calvert as if she were a pesky fly. "Then I could get fired."

Honeycutt shuffled his feet as a sonorous voice declared, "So this must be Detective Maitland." Crispin Alexandros edged Honeycutt aside and faced Libby.

Libby clamped her arms to her sides. "Mr. Alexandros."

He clapped Honeycutt on the shoulder. "Honeycutt spoke so highly of you that I've been wanting to meet you. Sorry it had to be under such circumstances."

When he extended a gloved hand, she stared at it as if he held a viper.

"Allergies." His lips curved, but his gaze remained cool. "It is a pleasure to meet you." He grasped her hand.

Libby swallowed a gasp, and every nerve in her body seemed to shout. The paper-thin leather of the glove Alexandros wore had once been the skin of a Shapeshifter in doe form. Not a clean kill. Terror and suffering struck like a blow to her solar plexus. Libby took a slow, steady breath.

"Thank you, sir." She shook the small hand. Instead of releasing her, Alexandros covered their joined hands with his free one. Absorbing a double dose of pain, her muscles twitched in sympathy with the lost shifter. Her gaze fixed on that of Alexandros. As cold as steel chips, his eyes betrayed no awareness of her discomfort. *Good.*

"I was sorry to learn that you were no longer working with my team."

She freed her hand and gestured at Robin, who was scowling. "You're in excellent hands with Detectives Calvert and Pritchard." She dropped the hand he'd shaken to her side. Instead of cuddling it in a pocket, she rested the palm against her hip. *Nothing to see here.*

Alexandros turned back toward the room with the refreshments.

Libby kept a measured pace to the exit. In the open air, when she relaxed her guard, her hand trembled uncontrollably. Once safely away from the funeral home, she stopped, rubbed the hand against her skirt. Rounding the next corner, she headed toward the parking spot she'd found on a nearby street.

"Libby—" Honeycutt was on her heels. For a big guy, he was fast. Of course, he also had incredibly long legs.

What did he want? Fishing for her keys in her small purse, Libby stopped by her car.

Honeycutt halted beside her. "Alexandros said you looked upset. He sent me to check on you."

Libby eyed the big guy's earnest face. Super-Thor? More like Super-Flunky. He didn't care about her, and neither did Crispin Alexandros. Libby wiped her palm against her skirt. *I kept eye contact, and my hand was steady until...* When the trembling resumed, she stuck the hand in a pocket. "I'm fine. I get emotional at funerals." As she opened the car door, the scratchy sounds of a police scanner filled the air.

Honeycutt gestured at the device. "You listen to that when you're not working?"

"Sure. You never—" The broadcast information slapped her. Blood turning to ice, she squeezed the edge of the door with her hand and tilted her head toward the alert.

Honeycutt hovered by her shoulder. "What's wrong?"

Holding up her free hand, she silenced him. "A body...friend's...house." Ellyn's name stuck in her throat. "You better stand back. I may be...sick." When she fumbled with her keys, Honeycutt caught them.

"You're too upset to drive." He guided her to the passenger side. "I'll take you. Get in."

"What about—?" Libby pointed toward the funeral home.

"No problem." He eased Libby into the passenger seat and fastened her seat belt. "He has his full personal guard, along with Robin. He doesn't need me." He took out his phone. "I should check." Crossing in front of her car, he made a brief call. Then he got in the car and pushed the driver's seat as far back as it would go. "Tight squeeze."

"You don't have to—"

"You're in no shape to drive." He started the car.

"Where are we headed?"

"Caulfield's Ridge. It's about fifteen—"

"I know how to get there. Give me directions to the house when we're closer."

"This can't be happening." Libby pressed a hand

against her forehead. "I can't believe anyone would… Oh, God. Not Ellyn." Grabbing her knees, she rocked back and forth. "Thank you for doing this. I can't…I don't…Homicide won't let me in, but I have to know…"

When Honeycutt patted one of her hands—the one that—she started to pull away but stopped. The touch of Honeycutt's calloused palm seemed to soothe that toxic Alexandros grip.

"Let's not worry about getting in until we get there. I'm sure we'll think of something."

He sounded so steady, so dependable. *We*. She'd never really been a "we" with anyone except her sisters—not even Mike or Tommy. But with Dash Honeycutt, "we" felt right.

Chapter 16

During the drive to Caulfield's Ridge, Honeycutt could almost see the emotional tempest swirling around the hunched figure beside him. This Ellyn person really mattered to Libby. Maybe she'd misunderstood the dispatch, or the dispatcher had scrambled the information. With any luck, her friend was alive and well, and they'd share a good laugh.

"Next light, go right." Without taking her eyes off the road, Libby issued the directions as if she were biting off each word. "At the four-way stop, go left." Libby sat up and uttered a moan that tore at Honeycutt's heart. She jammed a fist against her mouth. Police cars and a windowless white van were parked in front of the small house at the end of the street.

Honeycutt pulled up behind the van. He ached to comfort Libby, but before he came to a full stop, she threw open the door.

"Wait."

She sprang from the vehicle and raced to the front porch, where a young, uniformed officer stood.

"Let me in!" Libby cried.

Speaking in a lower voice, the officer blocked the entrance.

"Please!"

When Honeycutt joined her on the porch, the patrolman clenched his jaw but stayed put.

"I'm Detective Libby Maitland. Special Ops." Libby's dark eyes drilled into the other cop. She slapped her hand against her jacket. She pointed at the door. "Ask anyone from Homicide. They know me."

"What's going—Libby!" A striking brunette appeared in the doorway. Her pantsuit emphasized a slim figure, more angles than curves. She held up her phone. "I was getting ready to text you."

When the dark-haired woman shifted position to face Honeycutt, her crimson lips parted. "And you must be Dash Honeycutt. I've heard a lot about you." Her hazel eyes traveled up his torso as if she were measuring him inch by inch. She must have approved because when she met his gaze, she offered her hand. "Sergeant Gina Gilbert. Homicide."

When he grasped her hand, she caught her breath as if she might faint. No, not faint. Swoon. All she needed was a fluttering fan and a fancy sofa. "Pleased to meet you." Her crisp voice became breathy.

"Same here, Sergeant."

Libby tapped her foot, and a hint of fire blazed in her eyes. Jealousy? More likely impatience. "Why were you texting?" She drew in a deep breath. "The dispatcher said a body…"

The dark-haired woman held up a weather-beaten leather notebook. "You're in Ellyn Broderick's appointment book. A lot."

"We're…Ellyn's like family. I've known her since I was a baby." She glanced at the young patrolman who stood in her way. "I need to know… Please let me in, Gina."

"She's good, Joe." With a nod at the patrolman, the homicide detective stepped back to admit Libby. "We're almost done." When Honeycutt entered, Sergeant Gilbert moved to his side. "You should wait outside." "Oh, for heaven's sake, Gina, he's not an idiot."

One corner of Honeycutt's mouth curled. *Gee, thanks.*

"He won't get in the way or touch anything."

Sergeant Gilbert gave him another of those crownto-toe surveys. Her eyes locked on his. "Keep your hands in your pockets."

"Yes, ma'am…Sergeant." Honeycutt started to salute but stuck his hands in his pockets.

When Libby lifted her chin, threw back her shoulders, and scanned the foyer, Detective Maitland replaced Libby Maitland, distraught friend. She marched through the small room. Honeycutt followed her into a solid, middle-class living room.

Beside him, Sergeant Gilbert asked, "You work for Crispin Alexandros, right?"

"Yes."

"What's it like?"

He shrugged. "It's a job. Nowhere near as hard as yours."

In the living room, Libby's quick glances suggested she saw nothing missing or out of place. Clearly, she knew this house.

At the next doorway, she stopped.

"What are you doing here, Maitland?" Homicide detective Hal Miller blocked the entrance.

"Listening to my scanner."

Sergeant Gilbert joined Libby and held up the appointment book. "She's a friend of Ellyn Broderick."

"Good." When Detective Miller glowered at Libby,

Honeycutt's fingers curled into fists.

Libby's lower lip quivered. "The dispatcher...a body..."

Detective Miller stepped back so everyone could see into the small room. A round dining table and several chairs had been moved to one side. Investigators surrounded a tall figure lying face up on the carpet. The dead man stared at the ceiling with his mouth open as if death had taken him by surprise. He looked to be in his forties. A mat of grizzled hair soaked up blood from the exit wound of the bullet that had entered his forehead. The skin of his face stretched tight over his bones and contrasted with his meaty frame. A crimson splash on the front of his white shirt marked a second bullet hole. Frayed shirt collar. Chipped buttons. Chinos with worn fabric at the knees. Scuffed shoes. Dirty trench coat.

"You know this guy?"

"No. Where's Ellyn?"

"In the wind."

"Burglar?" Honeycutt asked.

"Maybe. But no sign of forced entry, and most burglars don't operate in broad daylight, especially when the owner's car is in the garage."

Libby looked from Detective Miller to Sergeant Gilbert. "It must have been...self-defense."

"That's how it looks. He had this in his right hand." Detective Miller held up an object in a plastic bag.

When Libby gasped, Honeycutt reached out to steady her, but Sergeant Gilbert growled, "Hands in pockets."

"That's the—" Libby's blinking eyes registered surprise and a trace of fear.

Honeycutt studied what looked like a weaponized

gardening tool. A dark substance—dried blood? — covered small, sharp blades welded onto the extended metal fingers. His gaze took in the other police as well as Libby. "Looks like what you were expecting."

Libby nodded and returned to the dead man. "Any ID?"

"Nothing but three new C-notes in his coat pocket."

"Ellyn doesn't keep that kind of money lying around."

"He got it somewhere," Detective Miller observed.

"We took his prints, but his teeth are—" Sergeant Gilbert's upper lip curled. "Doesn't look like he's ever seen a dentist. Rossiter's taking a photo to those camps by the railroad tunnels. Maybe one of those guys can ID."

Libby said, "You should check with the university center that helps the homeless. Ellyn's done some work with them."

Detective Miller indicated the dead man. "You think she knows him?"

"She's often hired guys from the homeless project to do work around the house." She glanced at the body. "This time, something must have gone wrong." Libby rocked back and forth on her heels.

Honeycutt dug his hands into his jacket pockets.

"I'll say." Detective Miller handled the evidence bag with the deadly hand cultivator. "Or somebody might have paid him to do a job." He looked at Libby.

"Any reason someone would want to kill her?"

Libby swallowed. "No."

Honeycutt frowned. *What's she hiding?*

Detective Miller stretched. "We're putting out a bolo, so if you hear from her—"

Libby's head came up. "I'll tell her you want to talk to her. If I see her, I'll bring her downtown myself. I'm so...relieved she's not..."

"We'll have to wait on confirmation from Ballistics, but we found this in the back yard." Sergeant Gilbert held up a bagged pistol. "Recently fired."

Libby studied the weapon. "Looks like Ellyn's. I helped her pick it out and took her to the firing range a few times."

Honeycutt glanced at the corpse. Perfect shots. No evidence of hesitation. *Either she's done a lot of practicing, or that's not her first gun.*

"We found this, too, on one of the other benches." When Gina held up the neatly stacked clothing, Libby suppressed her smile. *Ellyn's still here! Must have shifted.* "The clothes are Ellyn's." She wanted to bounce on the balls of her feet.

"Why were they outside? She wouldn't run off naked." Gina looked skeptical; Honeycutt, mildly amused.

"That would make her easier to find." Honeycutt chuckled. When Libby scowled at him, his smile vanished.

"One reason Ellyn bought this house is that she likes sunbathing, and the yard's so private she can soak up rays whenever she wants." Libby indicated the sliding door in the back of the kitchen. "She always takes clothes outside in case a visitor shows up. That way she can throw something on and answer the door. It's very efficient."

Gina lifted an eyebrow. "If you say so. But all anyone would need is a robe or a muumuu."

"Ellen grew up in a very formal home. She wouldn't

answer her front door unless she was fully dressed." Libby eyed the garments left in the garden. *Did you think no one would find them? Dumb move.* "You're putting that in Evidence?" Gina nodded.

"There's a good possibility those clothes have been sitting outside for weeks. Ellyn doesn't have the greatest memory. Sometimes, she brings clothing out but forgets it." Libby lifted her hands. "Do whatever floats your boat. Not like we don't have enough bags in Evidence."

Gina laughed. "You got that right." Instead of relinquishing the clothing, she tightened her grip. "Still...you never know what might be useful."

"True." *She must be outside. Waiting for everyone to leave? What can she do then? If she becomes human, one of her neighbors will surely notice lights or movement. If I can find her, I might be able...* Libby moved toward the back door. "May I sit outside for a few minutes and think? Everybody Ellyn and I both know is probably already in her appointment book, but maybe..."

"No problem. We'll use any help we can get." Gina accompanied her into Ellyn's outdoor retreat, and Honeycutt stayed close behind. "Maybe you could come up with some of the places she might be."

"I'll try."

"We found the pistol over there." Gina indicated a marked spot near one of the stone benches. "Looked like she dropped it." Gina's gleaming white teeth disappeared when Honeycutt looked away from her and surveyed the yard.

"Seems pretty straightforward." Standing by her shoulder, he could have been reading Libby's mind. "Intruder broke in, threatened your friend. She shot him, panicked, and took off."

Shifters avoid Simple Human authorities.

Gina added, "Her car's still in the garage, and none of the neighbors saw her leave."

Libby stopped scanning the shrubs that rose against the stone walls. "How did you get the call? Did a neighbor hear the shots?"

Gina shook her head. "The front door was wide open. The woman who lives next door came over, rang the bell, went in…"

"If Ellyn was too shocked to drive, she might have walked out and left the door open…and then called a ride service…from wherever she was standing."

"We haven't talked to all the neighbors yet, but we haven't found anyone who saw her leave." Gina approached the closed gate at the back of the garden. "If she's in good shape, she could have hiked down the hill to Locust Avenue and called a ride from there."

Libby eyed the terrain. "That's a steep hill. I can't imagine Ellyn…of course, I can't imagine…she must have been stunned."

Something stirred in the bushes. A low cry almost like a baby's.

Libby reined in her racing pulse.

"Well, will you look at that!" Grinning, Honeycutt reached into the leaves to be rewarded with a loud hiss as a ball of gray and white fur shot into view and stopped in front of Libby, who squatted and extended a hand.

"Hey there, puss." The cat rubbed her head against Libby's palm.

Behind her, Honeycutt's big frame blocked the afternoon sun. "Looks like you've found a friend."

Libby's head whipped around to regard him. His

grin betrayed nothing but delight. She managed a smile.

"Guess so." She started to pick up the cat.

"Be careful, Lib."

Libby rolled her eyes at the Homicide sergeant. "Planning to stuff her in an Evidence bag?"

"Of course not." When Gina stiffened, all the soft, sexy energy she'd been directing at Honeycutt disappeared. "We should call animal control." She took out her phone and gestured at the cat. "He could be feral."

Libby scooped the cat up in one arm. Leveling a sniff at Gina, the cat snuggled into the curve of Libby's arm. "Doesn't seem wild. Must be one of Ellyn's strays."

"It likes you," Honeycutt observed.

If you only knew... But, of course, he couldn't. Not ever.

Gina spoke up. "He might need shots. I'll drop him at the shelter—"

"No!" Libby held the cat close.

"Careful." Honeycutt's voice warmed Libby.

"You'll scare it back into the shrubs."

"Don't worry." Libby glanced at the cat's butt and hugged her. "She's not going anywhere, are you, kitty?" When she stroked the cat under the chin, Ellyn's wise eyes regarded her. Libby hoisted the cat to her shoulder and turned to Honeycutt. "Let's go."

Gina lingered. "If you hear from your friend—"

"You want to talk to her, and she has nothing to be afraid of." Libby stroked the cat's soft fur. "Good luck with the investigation." She started toward the walkway that ran along one side of the house.

Behind her, Gina made one last pitch for

Honeycutt's attention. "Nice meeting you, Mr. Honeycutt." Would her drawl anchor him to the spot?

"Libby!" Once again, Honeycutt was on her heels.

She stopped beside her car. "Don't worry. I wasn't going to leave you behind…although I'm sure that Gina would be delighted to give you a lift back to your hotel."

Honeycutt scoffed. "You'd have a hard time leaving." He leaned one elbow on the roof of the car and reached into his jacket pocket. Her dangling car keys reflected the sparkle in his blue eyes. When she reached for the keys, he pointed at the cat. "You've got your hands full. I'll drive."

Neither of them spoke until the car was moving away from Ellyn's house.

"Looks like you may have caught a break in the Pope case."

Libby took in Honeycutt's cleanly sculpted profile. "I don't know about that."

"It's a unique weapon…and the dead man may have tried to use it on a second victim."

"True." At the thought of Ellyn facing the same fate as Schuyler Pope, Libby shuddered.

"It's a big case. I think you would be happier."

Libby rocked in her seat. Honeycutt was right. Where was the relief that swept through her whenever a case reached a satisfying conclusion? "I'm sure everyone will celebrate, but…"

"But what?"

She focused on the cat in her lap. "It's not my case anymore—it never really was—but some things still don't feel right. The victim…I can't believe they'd even let him inside the Mark V, let alone that he wouldn't

133

attract attention."

"Maybe he was wearing a disguise today."

"It's possible." Libby rubbed her chin.

"Did you see anybody who looked like him when you checked the security tapes?"

"I haven't seen the tapes. Everyone I spoke with confirmed what you already told me. I'm sure Homicide will look for this victim."

"Good thing your friend had a gun."

"I'll say." When she considered Ellyn's narrow escape, a chill slithered down Libby's spine. She hugged the cat.

"You did good." Honeycutt's approval was like a breath of spring. "We can stop and pick up what you'll need to get your new pet settled."

"Please! She's not mine." Libby stroked the cat's fur. "And you've already done more for me than—I mean, you helped me move in...and you spent a big chunk of today driving me around. Why don't you drive to wherever you're meeting your crew? I can get home from there."

"I don't think so." Honeycutt kept his eyes on the road. "Driving with a loose animal in the car isn't safe. As far as work's concerned, meeting Alexandros at the airport and hanging out at the funeral home wrecked my day. The crew members will give me progress reports tonight. I can call a ride from your apartment or get someone to pick me up in our rental."

The cat meowed. Libby sat back. When Honeycutt left the ring road at the university exit, she sat up. "You should get in the left lane."

"On our way out, I noticed a shopping center. We can stop for cat supplies."

Libby's pulse pounded in her ears. "I've already told you I'll take care of it." She cuddled the cat. "Right now, we need to be…home."

Chapter 17

"This is insane." Libby indicated the last set of boxes and bags Dash Honeycutt had deposited on the floor near the other cat paraphernalia that occupied at least half of her combined living-dining room. On the plus side, he'd taken off his jacket and rolled up his sleeves, which provided a dynamite view of his arm muscles. "I never should have let you go into that pet store alone."

"Relax."

When he rolled down his sleeves and covered those gorgeous arms, Libby suppressed a sigh.

"You had to stay in the car with your cat." Dash held up his phone. "I called my mother to make sure I got everything."

"Like two litter boxes? For one cat?"

"According to Mom, you should have one more box than you have cats. We had five." He opened one hand and lifted his thumb on the other. "Six boxes."

"I hope you invested in kitty litter." Libby pointed at the tall cardboard box. "What's that?"

"Cat tree. Set it up by the big front window, and she'll climb and scratch to her heart's content without mauling your furniture. If you like, I can stop by tomorrow evening to help you put it together."

Another chance to see you, but...not a good idea. Libby shook her head. "You have enough to do. By this time tomorrow…"

Dash cocked his head. He looked as if he were waiting for a major revelation. "You were saying…?"

Libby brushed her hands. "The cat will scratch anything she can. The sofa's already so beat up I don't think she can do much damage. If Ellyn turns up…I'll take her to the police station for an interview."

Dash scratched his chin. Even his stubble held a trace of gold. "I know that's what you tell people, but the situation's not that simple. This Ellyn may be your friend, but she killed a man."

Killed. The word hammered Libby's heart with extra intensity. She lifted her chin. "It was self-defense." She'd been repeating the idea to herself as if repetition would automatically make it true. "They won't keep her."

"She ran away. I'm not a cop, but if I were, I wouldn't risk her giving me the slip again." He looked around. "Where'd that cat go?"

Libby waved toward the open door at the end of the short hall. "Probably hiding under the bed. I'll fish her out later."

"I can help you set things up."

"You don't have to…"

But Dash had already picked up both litter boxes with one big hand and hefted the bag of litter with the other. "Where's your bathroom?"

"Down the hall. First door on the left. I don't think more than one litter box will fit."

Dash moved with quick precision, and Libby eyed his broad shoulders.

"I'd offer to help, but it's too crowded for both of us." She put her dress heels on the shoe rack that hung on the back of the apartment door and padded down the hall to the bedroom. "While you're doing that, I want to get out of these funeral clothes." She closed the bedroom door behind her and knelt beside her bed. "Look what you've gotten me into," she whispered.

The feline beneath the bed lifted her head.

"I'll get Dash out of here as soon as I can and leave some clothes on the bed for you."

The cat dropped her head onto her paws and curled back up.

Libby stood. She carefully removed her stockings and replaced her black dress with a pair of khakis and a cream-colored V-necked top with aqua bursts. Then she laid out a few loose garments that would fit her Mentor.

When she opened the door, water was running in the bathroom.

Dash dried his hands and stepped into the hall.

Libby eyed the litter-filled boxes. "Nice job. Thanks." She checked her watch. "It's getting late. Your people must be wondering where you are."

"I called them from the pet store." Dash straightened his shirt. "I figured that since you've had a rough afternoon…after you got the…cat… settled…"

Libby blinked. *Why did he say it that way…like he suspects something?*

"…maybe even eat."

Libby rubbed her forehead. "I'm sorry. I didn't catch all of that."

Dash's blue gaze locked on hers. "I thought you might want to get something to eat. Lots of restaurants in this area."

"Usually crammed with hungry university students." *I need to get him out of here.*

Dash leaned against the doorjamb. "Aren't they on vacation now?"

"Some are. But plenty have summer school." She faked a yawn. "It's been a long day, and I am tired."

He straightened up. "Hungry, too, I bet. I haven't eaten since breakfast, and neither of us ate at the funeral home."

Libby glanced toward the bedroom.

"We won't be gone that long. Your friend...ly cat will be fine."

Another hint. Does he think I'll fold that fast?

He tapped his chest. "I'm buying."

"You're not going to give up, are you?"

He grinned. "I was taught if at first you don't succeed...you know how it goes."

"You win. This time. Let me get my jacket." Their first dinner had gone well... *Until I ruined it. Maybe tonight...* Her stomach growled. *If I'm this hungry, he must be ready to eat a cow.*

After dinner, she'd wrestle the pet store bill out of his grip. Shimmies skipped down her spine at the thought of Dash's long, muscular arms pinning her to the carpet. *In your dreams.* "Let's go."

****

The warm lighting of the Italian restaurant brought out golden glints in Libby's hair and the soft rose of her lips. She sipped her wine. "This place is much nicer without the students." A crease appeared at the bridge of her nose. "What are you staring at?"

Honeycutt sat back. "This is the first time I've seen you relax."

"That's not true. At Whiskers—"

"You spent the whole meal preparing to grill me."

139

"No, I didn't." She put down her glass. "I knew I had to ask…but everything else felt good. Sorry they don't have stout."

"I'll survive." He tasted the wine. Fruity but not too sweet.

"Thanks for coming with me today. I still can't believe Ellyn…she mentored me and my sisters, taught me…so much. She was someone I could always count on, but now…my world feels upside down."

The server arrived with their meals, and Libby devoured her eggplant parmesan.

Savoring the scents of garlic and basil, Honeycutt ate slowly. "I think I understand why you stick up for Shapeshifters."

Libby's fork paused midway to her mouth.

"Your friend is one, isn't she?"

Libby's fork clattered to the plate. "Why in the world would you think that?"

"You didn't want to buy anything for the cat. Is that because you know she'll soon be human?"

"You've got it all wrong." She tucked a strand of hair behind one ear, and roses bloomed on her cheeks. "My problems with Alexandros aren't simply about Shapeshifters."

"Really?"

"Yes! I'm worried by how he arouses human emotions…especially hatred. I've studied enough history to know bad things happen when humans focus negative energy on a specific group. Persecution. Genocide."

He shifted position and looked deep into her dark eyes. "You think that will happen to Shapeshifters?"

"Of course not." She gave a quick laugh.

"Shapeshifters aren't real."

"Libby—"

"But Alexandros can endanger anyone he identifies as a Shapeshifter."

"Shapeshifters do exist." He leaned toward her. "My sister Christie fell in love with one. A wolf."

One of Libby's eyebrows rose. "Did you ever see him shift?"

"No."

"So you have no evidence that he was a Shapeshifter."

How could someone with such a soft smile be so stubborn? Dash saluted her with his wineglass. "You're so good at cross-examination that you'd be a great prosecutor. You should go to law school."

Libby shook her head. "My sister Steffi is the scholar, not me."

"Christie told me Josh was a shifter. That's good enough for me." Dash finished another glass of wine. "When she brought him home, I thought he was like all the other guys she dated. Nice enough, and he seemed to care about her." He shook his head. "Christie looked at him as if he made the sun rise and set with a wave of his hand."

"She's your twin, right?"

Her question tugged at Honeycutt's heart. *Now and forever.* "Yes, but she didn't tell me everything until she got pregnant, and he disappeared." Honeycutt's hand hit the table. The dishes bounced.

Libby sat bolt upright and pressed her fingers to her lips. "How awful!"

She's got sisters. She understands. "It was." He toyed with the remains of his pasta. Christie made great pasta. "We got into a huge argument."

Libby reached out. "Easy."

When she touched his arm, Honeycutt drew a deep breath and covered her hand. *Warm. Steadying.* "Sorry. After all this time…you'd think that I could…talk…without…"

"She means a lot to you."

Libby's soft words caressed his ears. He patted her hand, and she took it back slowly. "I wanted her to come home with me and tell Mom and Dad, but she refused. Said she didn't want to worry them." He scoffed. "Like we weren't already worried about her. Next thing I know, I get this message that she's heading West to meet Josh's folks.

"That was four years ago. We texted until she reached Wyoming. When her connection went dead, I quit my job. Tracked her as far as the Lolo Trail." Standing there on the edge of the Clearwater River with that stupid checkered shirt she'd left at the rest stop. "Lots of wolves out there, but no Shapeshifters. More important, no Christie."

Libby leaned forward, hanging on every word.

"That's when I went to work for Alexandros."

Libby breathed a soft "oh."

"Since he's trying to locate Shapeshifter populations, I figured I could use their resources to find Christie. If she's still with the wolf, and she's happy, so be it." He brought his hands together. "If not—" His fingers bent, and he made a ripping motion. "—I will tear him to pieces." He sat back with a groan. "Sorry. I haven't talked to anybody about this since…actually, I've never told anybody else. Alexandros knows I'm looking for a missing sister but not the details." He leaned toward her. "You're a good listener."

"I do my best." She shifted position. "Thanks for telling me. Now, I understand... My sister Steffi lives in western Canada, and Dayzee's in California. They might be able to ask around..."

"Not likely they'll find anything."

"It won't hurt to ask. Does this wolf have a name?"

"Josh Savant."

"Do you have any photos of him and your sister?"

"I have some of her." He took his wallet from his jacket pocket. "This one's old, but..." When he showed Libby the photo of the two of them standing face to face in their graduation robes, the brilliance of Christie's smile struck him like a knife wound. *My sister who ran off with the wolf.*

With her phone, Libby took a picture of the photo.

He flipped the wallet shut and stuffed it back in his pocket. He drew a deep breath, and his jaw softened. He signaled for the server. "We should go."

"You're right." Libby looked at her watch. "It's getting late."

****

They didn't speak again until they'd left the restaurant and started walking. "I don't like the idea of you alone in your apartment with that..."

"Dash!" Libby stopped. Her head drew back, and her fingers spread across her chest. "It's sweet of you to be concerned, but I'm in no danger." She resumed walking.

Dash kept pace. "What if you find out that cat is not what it seems?"

Libby sighed. "Let's say you're right, that Shapeshifters do exist and the cat does turn out to be

Ellyn. She's my friend."

Dash stopped on the pavement and regarded her.

"Who shot a man."

"In self-defense."

"Even if she did, won't you get in trouble if you let her stay with you?"

Libby scoffed. "I'd get her to come down to the station with me." She resumed walking.

Dash was by her side. "If it was self-defense, she could have turned herself in at her house. Instead, she became a cat and used you to get away from the other detectives."

"She used you." I never thought of it that way. What if...don't be silly. "I know Ellyn. She's not a violent person. She must have been terrified."

Dash scratched his jaw. "I don't know much about Shapeshifters, but everything I've read and heard—"

"From Alexandros?" Libby's words dripped with scorn.

Dash grimaced. When she opened her mouth, he lifted his hand. "Hear me out."

Libby pressed her lips together. *What now?*

"A little cat like the one you brought home could turn into a bigger cat...a lion...or a saber-toothed tiger."

"They're extinct."

"The minute you walk in the door, she could attack you."

Libby laughed.

Dash dropped his hands to her shoulders. "This is no laughing matter."

Standing beneath the streetlight, Libby's laughter died, and her fingers itched to smooth the wrinkles from Dash's brow. "Please stop worrying. I've known Ellyn for ages. And Ellyn knows—she knows me." *My gorilla. My dragon.* Libby eased out of his warm, protective grip. "I'll be fine."

Dash gestured at the shoulder where she carried her holster. "You're not even armed."

Libby's gaze moved off his face to something over his shoulder. "We haven't had dessert yet." She pointed. "La Patisserie. Right there on the corner. Graduates of the culinary arts school started it a few years ago."

One of Dash's thick eyebrows rose. "I thought you wanted to get home to check on the cat."

"Yes, but…they make amazing French pastry."

Dash twirled an invisible mustache. "Ooh-la-la!"

Libby laughed. "They also have homemade ice cream and fruit tarts to die for. You can call your ride from here."

"That sounds like a plan."

When Dash returned her smile, her heart did a little somersault. Pastry, ice cream, and fresh fruit arranged like a work of art. And an amazing work of human art to share it with. Who could ask for anything more?

Chapter 18

"Wow!" Libby stopped and pointed at the big SUV crammed into the alley that intersected Lovegrove Lane.

"Your whole crew showed up."

"Must have gotten bored with the hotel bar."

Libby shot him a sidewise glance. "Or they want to save you from my anti-Alexandros influence."

Dash chuckled. "More likely they want to see me entrapped by your seductive wiles."

The heat rising in her cheeks threatened to blow off the top of her head. Libby swallowed hard. "What?"

He grinned. "I seldom spend time alone with our local liaisons."

Libby's face heated. "I didn't realize…you've been a terrific help. I hope I haven't caused you trouble."

He gave a dismissive wave. "Good-natured teasing. And I've enjoyed getting to know you…especially since I'm no longer a suspect."

Libby's cheeks warmed. "You're never going to let me forget that, are you?"

"Probably not. When you blush, it destroys your tough-cop image."

"I'll keep that in mind." She swallowed. "Thanks again for helping me this afternoon. Good night." Turning, she didn't open the garage door, but put her key in the lock of the street door that opened directly into the stairway.

Dash rested his hand on hers. "I'm coming up with you."

The warmth of his palm relaxed her tense fingers. "Your people are waiting."

"It won't take long. I want to make sure you're safe."

"That's not necessary." She rested one hand on the lapel of his jacket. "I'll text you from the apartment to let you know everything is good. If you don't get my message, feel free to break down the door."

"Hey, Dash!" Someone bellowed from the vehicle. "Kiss the girl and let's roll!"

The girl? Libby's shoulders stiffened.

Dash slapped a hand over his eyes. "I haven't been this embarrassed since the sophomore Spring Fling. Sorry about that."

"Big Ben must be a perpetual sophomore." She gritted her teeth. "Girl!"

"I'm sure he didn't mean it as an insult. They all like you."

"If you want to keep them off your back, go ahead." She looked up into those midnight blue eyes. "I won't bite."

His gaze traveled to a point over her shoulder. "No."

Libby's smile dimmed at his brisk, emphatic rejection. "Good night." She unlocked the door and started to open it.

"Wait." Dash touched her shoulder. "You don't understand."

She turned. Beneath the light above the door, longing and anxiety battled across Dash's features.

"Kissing you…I wouldn't do it for…I mean, they're good guys, but sometimes they go too far. What I do want I can't…" He shifted position. "Let me put it this way. A first kiss is an invitation, you know? Like at a dance. You ask someone, you step out when the music starts, and you wonder…what will happen next. But we've barely said hello and it's already…"

"Time for goodbye." *Unfortunately.* She glanced at the SUV. "If you want, we can give them a little show. We're standing in a nice tight corner. I'll move in closer to you." She snuggled against his shoulder near the door. "If you pretend to hug me and bend over, they can imagine we're tangling tonsils."

Dash's lips curved in a wry smile. "And I thought you were a hopeless romantic."

"You don't know the half of it." *And you'll never have the chance to find out.* His hot breath gliding across her lips erased all other awareness. They were so close. Too close. Another second and—

"Woo-hoo!" "Wowie!" Shouts, whistles, and a beeping car horn jolted her back to Planet Earth.

She met Dash's gaze. "Get those guys out of here before my neighbors call the cops." She opened her door.

Dash pointed at her. "Text me."

"Do I have your number?"

"Jack Weatherby gave me yours." He pulled out his phone. "I'll text you in three minutes. You get back to me in five."

With a salute, Libby closed the door behind her.

****

Behind the wheel of the SUV, Tony Benson tweaked his toupee.

Honeycutt opened the back door and stood for a minute looking at his phone. Libby's message appeared. *—All is well. Thanks again for a pleasant dinner.*

Hope you find your sister! L.—

He slid into the backseat.

Tony backed out of the alley and into the narrow street. As they passed the converted carriage house, Honeycutt looked up at the large window where Libby stood framed by the inside light. She lifted her hand in a slight wave that he returned. Then he surveyed the occupants in the car. "Where's Jeff?"

Beside him, Harry Kramer spoke up. "At the hotel."

"Sulking," Ben Turner boomed from the shotgun seat. "He's pissed that he had to take care of The Boss."

Honeycutt grunted. "That's his job. All he had to do was get him on the plane."

"Yeah, but you took off with Luscious Libby!" When Tony chortled, Ben contributed an assortment of lip-smacking sounds.

Fighting the urge to shake his friends, Honeycutt returned his phone to his jacket pocket. "The Boss wanted me to keep an eye on her."

"Looked like you were keeping a few other things on her, too. Took long enough." Harry fidgeted. Even in rental cars, the company No Smoking policy drove him up the wall.

"Yeah." Honeycutt could hear Ben's smirk. "If we hadn't gotten here when we did, you'd probably be putting it—"

"Come on, guys. You sound like a bunch of horny teenagers."

"Easy for you to say, Dash." Tony stopped for a red light and fiddled with his hair.

"Yeah," Ben agreed, "you're the guy the girls have the hots for."

Honeycutt shifted position. He could point out Ben

might have more success if he stopped calling grown women "girls," but why bother? Ben wasn't going to change. "The Boss fly out?"

"Eventually." Tony pulled into the hotel garage.

"They had a weather delay." Harry pulled a pack of cigarettes from his shirt pocket and sniffed them.

"He called us," Ben said. "We dragged all our work to the airport so he could look it over while he was waiting."

Look it over? I've sent him everything except today's... if I'd been there to talk with him... "I'm sorry, guys."

"No problem," Tony said.

When Ben turned, his muscular frame blocked the passenger's side window. "After he reviewed what we did today, he wanted to see the convention center."

"Oh, no." Honeycutt rubbed his forehead. *We sent him enough pictures to wallpaper his office.*

Beside him, Harry shrugged. "You know how he is." *Always second-guessing.*

Tony laughed. "Fortunately, the pilot convinced him to stay put because they didn't know when they'd be cleared to fly." He parked near the elevator.

Harry leaped out and headed for the smokers' spot.

Honeycutt fell into step beside Tony. "I didn't get a chance to send him what you did today. Did he approve it?"

"A few tweaks here. A few tweaks there." Tony feathered his toupee close to his forehead.

"He did treat us to dinner in the private lounge." Ben smacked his lips together. "Though I don't suppose you have any regrets."

Honeycutt stopped and regarded his colleague. "I'm

glad you all got some reward for the extra effort. If I'd known…" *Who am I kidding? If I'd known, I'd still have stayed with Libby. She needed…maybe not me, but someone.*

Later, in his room, he stared out the window while images drifted in and out of his awareness.

Libby's panic-tightened features relaxing the instant she saw the victim and knew her friend was alive.

When his bones began to stretch, Honeycutt eased out of his jacket and hung it in the closet.

Libby's face lighting up when she saw that cat. The exasperated twitch in her lips when she'd seen his shopping cart stuffed with cat supplies.

The fabric of Honeycutt's shirt pulled against his shoulder muscles.

The sympathetic intensity of her gaze when he'd told her about Christie.

The cuffs of his trousers tightened at his ankles.

The pink tip of Libby's tongue stealing out to lick ice cream from her upper lip.

His waistband expanded.

Amusement shining in her eyes as she offered her mouth in response to the crew's teasing. And that last moment, standing so close by the door surrounded by the scents of roses, oranges, and something distinctively Libby. She'd felt so comfortable against him. Luscious Libby indeed.

His arousal occupied every available space in his trousers.

It had taken every ounce of restraint to keep from kicking open the door, carrying her up the stairs, and—

When his head almost bumped the ceiling and his body nearly split the special fabric of his shirt and trousers, Honeycutt took a deep breath. *Slow down. Get smaller*. Focused on his breathing, he stood in the middle of the room until the fit of his garments loosened. The erection remained, but he could move without destroying anything. He regarded his human-sized reflection in the mirror. *Good night. Goodbye*. "You should have kissed her."

****

Libby leaned against one of the bookcases. The sound of the SUV as it left the alley still roared in her ears.

Dash had been right, of course. A fantastic first kiss…and she had no doubt that, despite the teasing, it would have been fantastic…but she'd have come away longing for all the other kisses they'd never… She sank into the old armchair.

She and Dash were like two diagonal lines on a graph that intersected at one point but separated, never to meet again. Dash had his work with Alexandros and his search for his sister. And she had to get her job…her life…back on track. She also had—

"Ellyn." Pulse pounding in her throat, Libby took slow, silent steps down the short hallway.

She stopped outside the closed bedroom door and brought her hand to the spot on her shoulder that usually held her holster. *It's in the bedroom closet with… No badge. No gun.* As Dash's warnings echoed in her brain, Libby rubbed her face. *This is Ellyn.* She lifted her hand, but before she knocked, the door opened.

Ellyn's silver hair was rumpled. Without the makeup that smoothed away wrinkles, evened skin tones, and erased age spots, she looked older and frail. The way Libby's A-line dress hung on Ellyn's body didn't help.

The questions crowding Libby's mind streamed out. "Are you hurt? What happened at your house? Do you know that man? Why didn't you call—"

"Libby, dear" —Ellyn's hand patted her shoulder— "please slow down."

Libby dropped her hands to her waist and swallowed. "Sorry. I've been worried sick about you."

"Silly girl." The other woman laughed. "I'm fine." She fanned her throat like a true Southern belle.

We need to go to the police station.

Ellyn slid one hand down the skirt of the knit dress. "I left my clothes in the yard when I shifted." She tilted her head. "I suppose I wasn't thinking clearly."

"Someone in Homicide took it all for Evidence. Sorry."

Ellyn dismissed the apology with a wave. "I rather liked that skirt."

You killed someone, but you're worried about a skirt?

Ellyn tilted her head. "Why are you frowning, dear?"

"Once everything is settled, I'm sure you'll get your skirt back." Libby eyed her friend. "After spending so much time as a cat, you must be hungry." She entered the small kitchen. A plate, glass, and utensils sat in the dish drainer. "Oh! You've already—"

"Hope you don't mind." Ellyn stood by the dinner table. "I didn't fancy cat food...even premium canned." Libby laughed.

Ellyn sank onto the sofa. "It's been a long day."

And about to get longer. Libby's chest tightened as she eyed the older woman's slumped frame. She went to her front door and pulled a pair of sandals off her shoe rack. "Try these. I think they'll fit you."

Ellyn's gaze went from the shoes to Libby's face.

"We need to go to the police station." Libby pulled out her phone. "The detectives need to talk—"

Suddenly erect, Ellyn sat up and planted both feet on the rug. A light blazed in her eyes. "Elizabeth. Stop."

The quiet command pierced the layers of adult and adolescent memory to awaken the child within. Libby froze.

"Good girl." Her Mentor stood and gestured at the phone. "Enter your access code."

Libby pushed her finger against the phone screen.

Her Mentor extended her hand. "Now please give me your phone."

Libby held out her device.

"Good girl." Ellyn pointed at one of the chairs by the dining table. "Why don't you sit down over there?" It was more of a command than a request.

The adult in Libby hesitated. "What are you going to do?"

"Elizabeth. Sit." Her Mentor waited until Libby complied. "Good girl. I'm calling my attorney." She entered a number. "I would have done it earlier, but I had no phone."

Libby's Mentor lifted a finger and listened. "Nigel, dear! It's Ellyn. Sorry to call so late, but something has— on the news, already?" She rubbed her throat. "Then you know—yes." She pointed at Libby. "What is your address, dear?"

"2701 Lovegrove Lane."

Her Mentor repeated the information. She listened again and then snickered. "Nigel says it sounds like a brothel." She returned to the call. "What's that? Yes. Thank you." She put the phone on the table, and her thin lips curved. "Someone will be here soon."

Libby tensed. "Who?"

"Don't worry, dear. Just sit. And wait. All will be well."

"All I want…if you…a few questions and you could…don't you want to go home?"

"Of course I do, dear." "Then come with me."

"Oh, Elizabeth. My poor dear girl." Her Mentor uttered a tiny, mirthless laugh. "You've worked among Simple Humans too long. You've forgotten the First Rule: We take care of our own."

"But…but…self-defense. Even in a Simple Human court, it wouldn't go to trial."

With another small laugh, her Mentor patted Libby's cheek. "Why go to all that trouble?" Her fingers brushed Libby's forehead. "Elizabeth."

The syllables caressed Libby's child.

"Look into my eyes."

When Libby's adult failed to obey, her Mentor's terse "Now" had the strength of steel. "Look!"

Something swirling in the depth of her Mentor's irises pulled her in and held her fast.

"You've had a very hard day. You must be tired." Her Mentor's whisper brushed her child's ear. "Very tired. Very…very…tired."

"Very…very…tired." Libby echoed the phrase. Muscles melting to jelly, she yawned.

"Lie down for a bit." Her Mentor's arm dropped across Libby's shoulders like a concrete bar. "Close your eyes. Rest."

"No." Libby tried to pull away, but the struggle

added to her fatigue. "I should stay…stay awake…alert." Her inner child giggled at the funny word. Why was that so important?

Her Mentor smiled. "Elizabeth." This time the power felt softer, more like a blanket than a girder. "You've always been so stubborn. I could reason with Steffi. I could flatter Dayzee. But not Elizabeth. You never gave an inch. If you don't want to lie down, fine." She stroked Libby's forearm. Hand moving slowly. Up and down. Up and down. Barely touching Libby's skin, but her Mentor's power penetrated to her bones.

"I know…I know…what you…want."

"I want you to relax, dear. That's all. You've had a long, long day. A long, hard day. And you're tired. So very tired. You must be exhausted. Come sit with me on the sofa."

With you? Libby's "no" emerged as a squeak.

"As you wish." The other woman's strokes continued. "Sit at one end of the sofa, and I'll sit at the other. We don't have to touch. We don't have to talk. All we need to do is sit…and wait. Soon, very soon, all will be well." Crossing her arms, Libby settled into her corner. *Stay awake. Stay alert.* Ignoring the orders of her brain, her body melted into the lumpy cushions. Nowhere near as enjoyable as snuggling in the doorway with Dash. *Daring Dash. Darling Dash. I should have told him…*

Libby touched her mouth. *Should have kissed…*

Chapter 19

Libby's phone rang. "Unknown caller."

Unlike the fog that crept in on little cat feet in the poem young Libby learned, the morning fog in her adult brain thundered like buffalo hooves across Montana terrain. She lifted her arm to block the daylight that seared her eyes through the bedroom window. What time was it? What day? She fumbled for her phone. *Am I late for work?*

The audio trill assaulting her ears, she inched her way to a seated position. With every movement, tiny daggers dug into her brain. *One glass of wine at dinner. Where did I get this horrible headache? Last thing I remember...Dash. I watched the car...saw him leave... He wanted to come up, but I...did I invite...did he...* Libby sat straight up. *Have I been roofied?*

Her hands covered her open mouth. When she eased her legs over the edge of the bed, those mean mental knives struck again. She mumbled something into the phone.

"Good morning!" Dash Honeycutt sounded indecently happy.

"What...you...?"

"I wanted to make sure you—you sound different."

She rested her thumbs on her cheekbones and pressed her fingers to her skull to keep her head from exploding. "Hangover."

"I didn't think you had that much wine."

"Neither did I."

"How's the cat?"

Libby glanced at the window, and the memory played out with incredibly crisp details. "Gone."

"What?"

"Yesterday, when I came into the bedroom to change my clothes, I opened the window and forgot to close it. I didn't notice the little hole in the screen. But the cat did. Scratched her way out while I was gone." Libby approached the big hole and touched the strands of cat fur caught on the edges.

She ended the call and deposited her phone gently on the nightstand.

Head throbbing, Libby sat on the side of her bed. *Work.* She covered her eyes. On the best of days, O'Malley was loud. This morning, his voice would split her skull, and pieces of her brain would drip all over the floor. When she checked her phone again, a laugh scratched across her dry mouth.

Four more days on leave. By then, she might feel human again. Why had Dash called? Trying to be nice…or feeling guilty?

Drug test? She rested her head in her hands and spoke to the ache in her heart. "I like Dash. He's been honest with me. He's given me no reason to distrust him." She grabbed her phone and found his response to her message.

—*Stay safe.* —

"The last thing I remember…watching him leave. Would he have come up here and raped me with his colleagues waiting in the car? I don't think so."

She returned to the window screen. *That cat felt like*

Ellyn, probably because I was upset. By now, the runaway was back on Caulfield's Ridge. *Ellyn is fine.*

Libby staggered into the bathroom. Last night's eggplant parmesan and delectable desserts made a vile tasting return. She sat on the floor, with her back against the side of the tub, and waited for her stomach to settle. Tomorrow, she would dump the unused kitty litter and toss the untouched food. Picky cat.

"Like Ellyn." She uttered a strangled laugh.

Standing, she lifted a cup of mouthwash to her lips and rinsed her bottom-of-the-birdcage mouth. After a shower, she returned to the bedroom and pulled on some jeans and a T-shirt. Then, she edged along the wall from the bathroom to her kitchen area. No glasses in the sink or in the drainer. *No drug evidence.*

From the cupboard above the sink, she pulled jars of thyme and rosemary. She rubbed the herbs between her palms until the scents crept into her head. Her fingers skimmed her forehead and the sides of her nose. The aromas soothed her aches.

Sitting in the chair on the far side of her dining table, she studied the sofa that occupied the opposite wall. *Something happened, but I can't... If it wasn't a drug, what could make me feel so...disoriented?*

She spoke into her phone. "Call Steffi."

"Hi, Lib." Her sister shooed two frisky wolf pups from the room. "Go play, you two." She returned to the screen and leaned in. "You look awful!"

Libby lowered the volume to keep her sister's voice from hammering her eardrums.

"Hearty partying with Summerhaven's finest?"
Who—Special Ops! "No. Dinner with Dash Honeycutt."

Her sister's smile lit up the screen. "Twice in two weeks. You're not wasting any time."

"It was a friendly meal. Then we said goodbye."

"Libby!"

She covered her ears. "Please don't shout."

Steffi looked chastened. "Sorry."

"Can I talk to Sawyer?"

"I'll get him." Steffi moved away for a moment and returned to the screen. "He'll be here in a minute." Her face lit up. "He's playing with the pups."

"I can call back later if you'd like."

"No, he's meeting with the architect later. We're building a guest house. We thought this place would be big enough to accommodate both our families, but it's not."

"Hi, Lib!" Steffi's tall, dark-haired mate appeared with a volume that made Libby's brain threaten to explode. The first time she'd seen him, he'd been wearing a cotton dress shirt stained with Steffi's blood. Today's scruffy gray T-shirt was a definite improvement.

Steffi pressed a finger to his lips. "Softer, please." Sawyer kissed his wife's finger and leaned in. "What's wrong?"

Libby touched her cheekbone. What was he looking at? "I'm feeling weird. Something happened yesterday. At Ellyn's."

Steffi joined her husband. "What do you mean?"

"It looks like a man got into her house, and she...shot him."

Steffi covered her mouth. Sawyer draped an arm across her shoulders.

"How is she?" Sawyer asked.

160

"Gone. But...for some reason I feel sure...she's...fine."

"Ellyn's always been super competent," Steffi observed.

Sawyer's gray eyes narrowed.

"I suppose. But running away..." Libby massaged her temples. "I found a cat in her garden and brought it back to my apartment because I thought it was Ellyn." She gave a rueful laugh. "I woke up with no cat and this horrible fog in my brain."

"What's the last thing you remember?" Sawyer asked.

"Coming upstairs...after saying goodbye to Dash...and watching from my front window as his car left. I think something...important... happened. But when I try to remember, my head hurts."

Steffi looked ready to leap out of the screen at her. "Call the Lassiter Clinic and get tested. This Dash character could have drugged you."

"That's possible...but...I have no reason to believe he would do such a thing. In fact, he's given me every reason to trust him. This morning, he called to check on me."

"Feeling guilty?"

"More like concern. Last night he suspected the cat was Ellyn, and he was worried that as a human, she might hurt me."

"He thought Ellyn was a shifter?" Sawyer scratched his jaw. "Interesting insight for a Simple Human."

"He's had a bad family experience involving shifters. I was planning to call you to ask—"

Sawyer cleared his throat. "Let's take care of you first." He rested his big hand on top of his wife's. "The date-rape drug is a possibility, but it could also have been a mind-wipe."

Libby's jaw dropped.

Steffi regarded Sawyer. "I thought OASIS restricted mind-wiping to Simple Humans."

"In principle, yes, and certainly while an agent is active with OASIS. But agents who have learned the procedure take it with them when they leave or retire."

Libby scoffed. "I'm surprised OASIS doesn't mindwipe them."

Sawyer chuckled. "I'm guessing they tried and failed. Erasing embedded skills may be harder than deleting recent memories." He gestured at Libby. "If it is a mind-wipe, you'll never really know, so stop trying to fill in the blank spots. Take something for the headache. The mental fuzziness should disappear, and you'll feel like yourself again."

"Except for the holes in my memory."

"Whoever did it should have supplied alternative memories."

Like they did with Tommy. Libby snapped her fingers. "The window! I remember opening it before I changed my clothes. Which is strange because I was getting ready to leave. In the middle of all my mental fuzz, that image is so sharp…"

"Just like a planted memory."

Relief relaxed her neck and shoulders. "You have no idea…I mean, I know Dash could have…but I don't think he's…"

"You like him." Steffi spoke in her soft Mom voice.

"Yes." *Even though I'll never see him again.* "More important, I trust him. Mind-wiping makes more sense. Thanks, Sawyer."

He tipped a finger to his forehead. "Happy to be of service to one of law enforcement's finest."

"Please! This time next week, I may not even have a job."

Steffi's eyebrows lifted.

"If you ever get tired of working with Simple Humans, I bet OASIS would hire you in a heartbeat." Sawyer leaned in. "In fact, they recently lost their Alexandros watcher."

Libby's breath froze in her throat. "Schuyler Pope? But...he...Simple Human."

"And a shifter friend."

Libby pulled the flash drive from her jacket pocket. "I found this in his hotel room. Alexandros wants it. If I send it to you, will you pass it along?" "Of course." Someone screeched.

Steffi stood. "I'm being paged. Love you, Lib." She disappeared.

Libby regarded her brother-in-law. "I know you guys are busy, but I have one more thing. Dash's sister Christie disappeared, presumably to join a wolf named Josh Savant. Doesn't one of your sisters know a lot of the packs in the Vancouver area?"

"From Victoria to Kispiox."

"Do you think she could locate them?"

"If he's in the area, Lucie and her mate will find him. What do you know about the sister?"

"She's done ecological work. And I'll send you a picture. She and Dash are twins. She's tall, like him, and has blue eyes." *Incredible blue eyes.* "Her hair is close to my shade."

Sawyer scratched his chin. "So we're looking for Josh Savant and tall, dark-blonde ecologist Christie

163

Honeycutt?"

"I don't know what names they're using. They may have a kid. About four years old."

"Even better. I'll make some calls."

"Thanks."

"Call Dayzee, too. Lots of shifters in the movie business."

Chapter 20

Libby eyed Schuyler Pope's flash drive. If Pope had found something dangerous, all the more reason for Alexandros to want him dead. If Homicide had ID'd the dead man at Ellyn's house, they might have found a connection to Alexandros. But why bother? The higher-ups wanted this case closed, and a dead killer neatly did the job.

Packing the drive for its trip to Sawyer, Libby frowned. How long would OASIS take to access the files? Nadine Victor and Schuyler Pope had been friends since med school. She might know his password. If the information threatened Shapeshifters, the sooner OASIS had the knowledge, the better.

Libby picked up her phone. Homicide might not provide any current info on Nadine Victor's condition. Trying to get information from the hospital would be fruitless without a badge, which she wouldn't have until Monday. By then, she'd have too much work to drive to Baltimore.

Work! Gripping her phone, she searched for the Patterson School of Public Health and entered the number. When she answered the computer welcome with Nadine Victor's name, a real human spoke. "Dr. Victor isn't available right now. We're not sure when she'll be back."

"I heard she was hospitalized but was hoping—"

"She's at home."

"That's great! Thanks."

Clutching the package, Libby went to the garage and started her car. On the road, she struggled to keep her speed below her racing pulse. When she parked in front of the Victor house, she glanced at the big window in the house across the street. No snoopy neighbor. She dropped the flash-drive package into her jacket pocket, left her car, and approached the front door.

She lifted her hand to the bell, but something yanked the front door open, and a red-faced fury blocked the entrance. Tina Patrick waved one finger like a damaged metronome. "Deenie's never heard of you. You lied!"

"I'm sorry."

The older woman sneered. "Beat it."

"All I want is—"

"To make trouble." She drew back her head and sniffed. "Deenie's not having visitors. Especially

lying...bitches...like you!" Libby winced.

"Tina." The soft voice belonged to a tall, slender woman who could have posed for a statue of the Egyptian queen Nefertiti. The chiseled planes of her face stood out as if her illness had pared away everything beneath her skin, and she leaned against an inside wall. "What's all the fuss about?"

She doesn't look too good. I should go. But since I'm here... Libby clutched the flash drive.

"Get yourself right back in bed, Deenie. You should rest. It's the one I told you about. The one who said she was your friend." The small eyes narrowed. "She had red hair then."

When the white-haired woman turned slightly, Zanna Archer

166

Libby edged into the door frame. "Dr. Victor, if I could—

"Leave Deenie alone."

"I can explain!"

"I bet you can. She's a good liar, Deenie."

Libby appealed to Nadine Victor. "Please!"

The slender woman eased into the nearest chair.

"You broke into my house."

"You left a key under a rock."

"You stole my mail. Messed with my computer."

"No, I didn't. The people who claimed to be from the Health Department did that. Didn't Mrs. Patrick tell you about them?"

When Nadine Victor's gaze shifted to her neighbor, the woman glared at Libby. "You lied to me. Right in my sitting room."

"You're right. I did abuse your...hospitality." The apology stuck in her throat. "I'm sorry."

Libby turned to Nadine Victor. "Just a few minutes. About Schuyler Pope?" She pulled the flash-drive package from her pocket.

"Sky." Nadine Victor brought a hand to her heart and shook her head. "I'm not talking to the press."

"I'm not—" Libby gritted her teeth. If she told the truth after so many lies, why would Dr. Victor believe her?

The doctor stood, looking even more regal. "Please go."

"I am sorry for your loss, Dr. Victor, and I hope you make a full recov—"

"Get out!" The white-haired woman pushed Libby toward the door.

Door slamming behind her, Libby hurried to her car. Best get out of town before Tina Patrick called the local police.

Chapter 21

Libby spent her first week with O'Malley catching teenaged joyriders. As she filed her last report, she shook her head. Kids never learned.

That night, she awakened with a start. Sweat drenched her body, and her pulse raced. Images from the dream—more like a nightmare—tumbled across her awareness. Dash looking fantastic in a dinner jacket. A flash. Dash gripping his chest. His long legs buckling. Between his spread fingers, a growing stain. Red. Blood red.

A fist squeezed Libby's heart. The images faded, but three words remained. DASH. DANGER. WARN. Unable to sleep, she paced through the apartment and waited for a reasonable time to call.

****

"Honeycutt."

"Dash."

Libby's breathless voice swirled into his ear like a hurricane. He tightened his grip on his phone. "What? Can you tell me again? A little slower?"

"At the…mayor's reception…someone is going to…shoot…you."

She sounded so somber he stifled a howl. "Where did you hear that?"

"I didn't. I—don't laugh at me." When she paused, he envisioned her smoothing the curve of her hair against

169

her cheek. "I had a dream."

Not the kind I've been having about you.

"Please believe me, Dash! I don't—I've never… This felt like more than a dream. A vision. My sister Steffi has ESP, so I decided to warn you in case I have it, too. It was so real. So terrible."

"Thanks, Libby." The concern in her voice made him want to wrap his arms around her and reassure her. "Of course, you realize I protect Alexandros. He's the target."

"Not in what I… I don't know who. I don't know why. I don't even know where exactly, except—any way you can avoid the mayor's reception?"

Don't I wish! "Nope." Alexandros liked showing off his full entourage.

"Then…be careful. Please!"

Dear God, she sniffled. The image of tears shining in her dark eyes made his throat tighten. "Let me—" Before he could tell her he'd be right there, she'd hung up. He threw on some clothes and was waiting for the elevator to the parking lot when his phone rang again. He took a deep breath and was about to utter her name when a deeper, more familiar voice boomed in his ear.

"Honeycutt!"

"Yes, sir."

"Technical run-through at the convention center. Meet me in the lobby in five minutes."

"Yes, sir." He'd have to change out of his T-shirt and sweats, and Libby…he'd call—no. The reception wouldn't run that late. When it was over, he'd go to her apartment so she could see that nothing had happened. She could even give him a physical if she wanted to. Of course, if he suggested that, she might deck him. So no physical. But a slow, sexy kiss would let her know that his heart was in the right place and everything else was in working order. After that? Who knew? Whatever happened, the prospect of seeing Libby again would be an enjoyable end to the day.

****

That evening, Honeycutt stood beside the doorway that joined the mayor's formal dining room and the grand reception hall with its high ceilings and Federalist molding. If Libby were here, she'd be muttering critical comments about every stylishly dressed, slightly sloshed guest. *Is she still worrying about that nightmare?*

He glanced at his watch. Soon—not soon enough—he'd knock on her door. When she answered, he wouldn't say anything. He'd wrap his arms around her and kiss her like—

"Honeycutt!" Surrounded by guests in the center of the reception hall, Alexandros summoned him. "I was telling these good people about the preparations for tomorrow's presentation."

"A team effort, sir, with superb cooperation from Dr. Crenshaw at the convention center and the Summerhaven Police." Honeycutt gestured toward the uniformed officers assigned to every exit.

"But every team needs a good leader." Alexandros scanned his listeners. "Mr. Honeycutt will be happy to tell you about the arrangements." When the other guests ran out of questions, Alexandros reclaimed the center.

"Thank you, Mr. Honeycutt." *Dismissed.*

Soothed by the music of a string quartet, Honeycutt spied Robin Calvert near a back exit. Despite her eccentricities, she and her partner were effective liaisons.

More important, Robin knew Libby. "You're

171

shining tonight, detective."

"Thanks." She twirled a sparkling turquoise curl that peeked from beneath her cap.

He eyed the guests. "Quite a party." Robin's ruby lips curled.

"You disagree?"

"We see so much dirty linen that it's hard to be impressed by appearances." She gestured at the guests. "Tonight, for instance, everyone here looks perfect. Who knows how many have deep, dark secrets?"

"Good point." He lowered his voice. "Speaking of secrets, you and Libby are friends, right?"

Robin shot him a sly smile. "We were at the academy together, and we've worked together. But we're not close."

"I'm not trying to snoop. I wondered... Is she psychic?"

When Robin sputtered, he gave her his pocket handkerchief. "So no intuition."

Robin patted her mouth and returned the stained cloth. "I wouldn't say that. On the job, I think we all use some intuition. But psychic?" Robin shook her head.

"So she doesn't share strange dreams or visions?"

"Maybe with her sister Steffi but not with me." Robin folded her arms. "Why do you ask?"

"She called me this morning to warn me about a bad dream she'd had. I tried to laugh it off, but she was so intense." He brought his hands to his ears. "I can still hear her."

Robin regarded him as if she were a schoolteacher and he was a curious student. "If I were you, I'd take what she said seriously. Be careful. If nothing happens, nothing lost. But if—who knows? Maybe she is psychic."

"Thanks, Robin. And keep sparkling."

Chapter 22

As the evening wore on, Libby paced in her apartment until she could have covered the distance to the mayor's mansion. The image of the red stain spreading across Dash's chest haunted her. "I have to stop it." She checked her firearm, slipped into her shoulder harness, and pulled on her jacket.

She drove up the winding road that led to the mayor's residence constructed on a ridge between Caulfield's Ridge and Thorne Valley. The big brick mansion was officially known as Hodgkins Manor, in honor of the family that donated it to the city after their effort to create a tourist attraction failed. Huge oaks, maples, and evergreens covered the hills surrounding the deforested ridge.

Libby stopped at the gate where the property began and flashed her badge at the single patrol officer on duty. She gestured at the many cars, SUVs, and small buses that occupied a patch of land used for parking during the unsuccessful tourist period. "Busy night."

"Alexandros fans. Want to get a glimpse of their guy." The young officer laughed. "Had to call out four more on patrol so we could check everybody out." He gestured down the tree-laned blacktop. "You can park closer."

"I need the exercise."

After finding a space in the lot, she waved at

theguard and hiked down the road. Glowing windows on the top floor came into view before she reached the premium lot reserved for the media and guests. Libby flashed her badge again, this time at one of the uniformed officers guarding the wide driveway directly in front of an elegant veranda lit by fake gas lampposts. The driveway also separated the house from the grassy, people-covered bank that crested at the forest near the top of a hill.

Media people occupied the flat section of lawn nearest the veranda. Cameras. Cell phones. *Nothing...no one...unusual. Maybe it was a stupid dream. I should leave.*

The Alexandros fans who covered the open hillside ranged from tattooed teens to silver-haired grandparents. Some wore jewelry, fancy shoes, bow ties, and sweeping skirts. Most chose jeans or sweats and gray or black T-shirts. The graphic message on one popular black T-shirt speared Libby's heart. In the center of the shirt, a figure lay on its back in a red pool—a naked human torso with lifted paws, a brushy tail, and a snout.

When she moved through the crowd on the hillside, voices surrounded her. Some were attending their first Alexandros event, but others had followed him from the start. Many spoke about hoping to get a photo—even an autograph—tonight. Hardcore fans assured the newcomers that Alexandros was always good to "his people."

Libby's stomach churned. A creepy bunch, but why would anyone here want to hurt Dash?

When the front door of the mansion opened, the Alexandros admirers swelled like an incoming tide and drew closer to the flat lawn. Libby stayed with them until she stood on the far edge of the drive.

She patted her holster, a comforting but meaningless gesture. If a shooter appeared in the crowd, she couldn't return fire because she might wound an innocent bystander. *Captain Weatherby would love that!*

With a smile for the press, Mayor Dawson brought Alexandros to the center of the porch, where someone gave her a microphone. She addressed the other guests. "Once again, I'd like to thank you all for coming this evening and welcoming our esteemed visitor."

Dash stood by Alexandros's left shoulder. Like the personal guard and PD officers, he monitored the crowd. His gaze passed over Libby but returned. Stopped.

Libby lifted a hand below her shoulder and twitched her lips.

Dash dipped his chin and resumed watching the crowd.

As the fans on the lawn roared, Alexandros silenced them with a wave of his gloved hand and took the mic. "I'd like to thank you, Mayor Dawson, for this warm reception. I've heard many good things about Summerhaven and am delighted that they are all true." He indicated the mayor. "I know I will see you tomorrow at the convention center, your honor, and I hope that many of you" — he gestured at the others on the veranda— "will join us." When his followers on the hill roared, he beamed at them like jolly old Saint Nick. *Rancid jelly in that belly, for sure.*

"As well as my devoted friends and followers. I hope to see you all tomorrow." With a more serious expression, he addressed the invited guests. "I know many of you share my concerns…and those of my people…about the safety of our families, of our communities, of our country itself." He faced the cameras. "Together, we will expose this hidden menace, and we true humans will prevail!" When he clasped the mayor's hand and lifted their arms, his followers roared. The mayor's smile outshone the lamps.

Already sees herself in the governor's mansion.

Libby pressed an arm against her stomach. *Barf city.*

Cars appeared at the edge of the driveway. Alexandros and the mayor posed for pictures with the guests, who sashayed off to their waiting vehicles. Together on the veranda, the mayor and Alexandros approached the press.

Libby scanned the crowd again. *So far, so good. Whoa! Top of the hill.* An almost skeletal figure seemed to peel away from the thick trunk of a tree. *Where did he— Something by his leg. Arm up. Rifle!*

Libby whirled to face the mayor and Alexandros, who stood chatting on the porch. "DASH!" Barreling forward, she launched herself in Dash's direction.

A shot rang out.

Heat sliced into Libby's lower body, and she fell forward, her landing cushioned by the person beneath her. Too soft for Dash. *Where is he? Is he hit?* She lifted her head. *Legs milling around. Cries. Shouts. Thumping. Stomping. Blood-stained shirt?*

"Libby." A familiar voice crooned her name, and a big hand rested on her shoulder.

Electric blue eyes met hers. "You're—"

Dash was looking down at her. He pulled her to her feet and extended a hand to the figure beneath her. "Sir?" Dash dusted off his employer.

Libby clapped her hand across her mouth. "I am so sorry."

When Alexandros lifted his gloved hand, she backed away and would have tripped if Dash hadn't caught her.

"You're bleeding!" Gesturing at Alexandros's forehead, the mayor sent an accusatory glance in Libby's direction before instructing her security chief. "Call 911.

And keep those people—" She pointed at the Alexandrites. "—where they are. Don't let them get out of control."

Libby regarded Dash. "You moved."

"I was stepping in front of Dr. Alexandros to block the shot. But you were faster."

Wetness spread slowly down Libby's thigh. *Urine or blood?* Her fingers found the aching spot on her butt where the bullet had entered. She flinched when she tightened her glutes *Lots of cushion there*. Her gaze went to the tree line. *Gone. One minute, that spot was empty, the next...*

With everyone focused on Alexandros, disappearing was easy. As she hurried down the driveway, Dash called her. She walked faster. *If I hadn't...he would have taken that bullet. Like the dream.* About an hour's drive to the Lassiter Clinic. A bird could fly there more quickly. But damaged tail feathers made flying risky. She'd have to drive.

On the edge of the access road, she paused and lifted one hip at a time. Her left side felt strange. *Duh! You've been shot.* But when she pinched her left thigh, she felt nothing. Her left leg wobbled.

Must get...to...car. Three legs better than hopping or crawling. Cheetah! As her claws came out, her left leg buckled, and she lurched to her left. She reached out with her left arm, which was becoming a front leg, but something kept her from falling.

Dash's deep voice cried, "Ouch!"

Libby drew a deep breath. *Be human. Be Libby.*

Claws retracted. Her bones and muscles made a hasty return to her human base.

Strong arms scooped her up.

"Dash! Thanks for catching me." She rubbed the smooth tips of her fingers. Moved toes on right foot. Left foot, nothing "My left leg's not working." Dash drew her closer.

She wiggled in a half-hearted attempt to get free.

"Relax," he said. "I've got you."

In any other situation, this would have felt wonderful. Not tonight. "I can walk with a little help."

"Nonsense." Dash pressed his forehead against hers. "You're sweating. Could be going into shock." He looked around. "Where's your car?" Libby pointed to the lot.

"I'll take you to the ER."

"No! I have a chemical…imbalance. Need my doctor. Thea Lassiter. Lassiter Clinic."

Dash walked as if he were carrying a pound of feathers, not a full-grown woman. Like his step, his breath was even and unstressed. "Not much of a parking lot. Good thing everyone else is hanging around to look after Alexandros. Use your keys to light up your car."

She pulled them from her inside vest pocket and groaned. "Somebody's blocking me."

"Not a problem." When they reached the car, he set her down facing the front fender. "Lean on the car for a minute." He opened the back door. Then he took off his jacket, his dress shirt, and his vest. "Your phone call spooked me so much I wore protection."

She gasped. "You believed me."

"Guess so. Too bad you believed you." Even in the dim moonlight, impressive muscles moved beneath his white T-shirt. He laid the vest on the seat. "This may be a little uncomfortable, but it will keep stains off your upholstery." He folded the dress shirt, tucked it inside her pants, and pressed it against her butt.

"Hey!"

"You can feel that?"

"No, but I can see where your hand is."

He chuckled. "You're still bleeding. Put your hand where mine is and apply pressure." He wrapped his jacket around her. "This should help you stay warm." He guided her toward the rear seat. "Lie down."

Libby glanced over her shoulder. "We'll be stuck here until the fans—"

"I'll handle it." His hands cradled her face and brought her gaze to his. "Call your doctor." He shut the car door.

While describing the incident to Thea Lassiter, Libby moved so she could see through the windshield. Dash approached the sedan and SUV parked in slants that blocked her car from driving forward into one of the exit paths. "At first, I felt like I'd been kicked by a mule, but now I can't feel any—"

Dropping the phone, she pushed herself up to sitting and looked through the full windshield. Dash held a four-door sedan as if it were a big tin box. His muscles were amazing.

"Libby!" Thea Lassiter's voice cried out from her phone, which Libby retrieved from the floor without taking her eyes off Dash.

"No, I was—I lost some feeling in one leg. Left side." *He picked up a car. Now, he's...SUV. He moved two cars!*

Then Dash wiped his hands on his trousers—that torn pants leg made his dress suit a total disaster. Wearing the widest grin she'd ever seen, he strolled back to her car. Didn't even look as if he'd broken a sweat. Not a Shapeshifter but definitely not a Simple Human.

Dash got in and pushed the driver's seat as far back as it would go.

"See you soon, Thea." She ended the call as Dash pulled onto the road. "Go East on the main highway. In about an hour, we get off at the Winston exit."

"Lie down and rest."

After watching you lift two cars? I don't think...

Libby yawned. Stretching out, she pressed her cheek against the covered car seat. Dash's musky masculine scent, on his vest and jacket, surrounded her. The car felt like a rocking chair. Dash zipped through the radio stations until slow, dreamy music filled the air. He'd need directions when they got to Winston, but she could close her eyes for a minute.

Chapter 23

Honeycutt leaned against the wall that faced the closed door of the treatment room and envisioned instruments extracting the bullet from Libby's body.

Ding! Metal struck metal.

"Got it!" The doctor's cheerful voice belied her gruesome task.

One of Libby's moans carried beyond the door, along with snatches of conversation.

He eyed the small waiting room. Dr. Lassiter seemed pleasant enough, but her clinic didn't look like an emergency facility. If they'd gone to the Summerhaven ER, Libby could be sleeping in her own bed by now while he watched from that barrel chair by the window.

Of course, if they'd gone to the ER, she'd have thrown a fit, and that wouldn't have been good for her.

She'd wanted to walk on one leg.

When the door opened, the doctor, an angular nononsense woman with graying hair, appeared. Behind her, Libby lay on the examining table with her right elbow bent so she could prop up her head. Her bloody jeans lay on the floor.

"Stay there," Dr. Lassiter said to Libby. "I'll get you something to wear home." The doctor turned to Honeycutt. "You can go in."

He stood over Libby. The thin blanket that covered

her lower body nestled around her curves. "What did the doctor say?"

"That the paralysis in my leg should go away in a few days."

Paralysis! His heart skipped a beat. "Any other damage?"

Libby gestured at her left hip. "Stitches."

"Don't touch it." The doctor carried a pair of pale green scrub pants. "No shower or bath until this time tomorrow. When you do shower, cover the wound to keep it dry. Leave the tape on either for a week or until it falls off. Your...friend" —she gestured at Honeycutt— "can help if you have a problem reaching the area."

"I'll manage." Libby waved at the door. "Get out and let me get dressed."

Honeycutt faced the doctor in the hall. "She'll be all right?"

"As long as she doesn't do something stupid like try to pull out her stitches. She'll be on crutches for a while. May need help getting around."

"I'll do what I can." He stretched. "I caught up with her as her leg gave out. I think she would rather have crawled to her car than let me carry her."

The doctor's gaze moved from his feet to his head. "I doubt that. Of course, she does strike me as independent." Dr. Lassiter rolled the bullet in the small metal bowl she'd carried out of the treatment room. "And lucky."

Libby opened the door. Over her own jacket and Tshirt, she still wore his jacket, which almost reached to the knees of the new scrubs. She leaned on her crutches. "Did you tell Dash about the Barestium?"

He turned to the doctor. "What?"

Libby indicated the bowl. "It's a drug. Caused the paralysis."

The doctor stopped her. "Looks like the bullet was treated with Barestium. I haven't seen much of this stuff, so I won't know for sure unless your crime lab sends me a report." She dropped the bullet into a small plastic bag, which she sealed and gave to Libby.

"When I get home, I'll label it." Libby passed the bag to Honeycutt. "Tomorrow, please ask Robin and Zeke to send this to the lab." He nodded.

Libby regarded her doctor. "Works like curare, right?"

"But it's synthetic."

Honeycutt rubbed his jaw. Not something a good old boy would use with a hunting rifle. Did a Shapeshifter have it in for Alexandros?

Libby looked at him. "Thea says if the bullet had hit me higher, it could have been worse."

Once again, he saw Libby hurling herself toward him.

The doctor gave him a thoughtful once-over. "Might have bounced off someone like you." She smiled and Libby chuckled, but Honeycutt didn't join them.

"I wore a vest."

"Smart move." The doctor clapped. "You say you're not feeling any pain, Libby, but as the Barestium wears off, that could change. If anything hurts, use your regular over-the-counter painkiller. Bed rest for three days." She held up three fingers.

Libby pressed her lips together.

"Put a pillow underneath you to lift your derriere. Try to get it above heart level."

"Like when I put my legs up against the wall in yoga?"

"Not that extreme. Tomorrow, I'll have Kim send a report to your captain."

"Thanks. Back less than a week and now this…"

Honeycutt patted her shoulder. "A lot of police were at the mayor's house. They saw what happened." "I knocked Crispin Alexandros on his butt."

He lifted her chin. If only he could kiss away the worry that tightened the corners of her lips. "They saw you save Crispin Alexandros."

Libby looked as if she might throw up.

"So stop worrying." Honeycutt locked his gaze with hers. "Relax and get better."

The corners of Libby's lips turned up.

"Good." That pretty mouth was made for smiles and… He swallowed and stepped back.

Dr. Lassiter pulled a wheelchair from a nearby closet. "Let's get you out to the car. At home, use the crutches as necessary. I'll see you back here in ten days—sooner if the paralysis sticks around more than a day or two, you experience persistent pain or a severe pain, you have anything more than a little bleeding, or you see any infection."

Libby extended fingers as she spoke. "Paralysis. Pain. Bleeding. Infection. Got it."

When she saluted, she listed to her left, and Honeycutt caught her. "Any chance we can borrow that chair?"

"Crutches will do fine." Settling in the chair, Libby rested them across her lap. "My apartment's not that big, and I'm not going anywhere."

Honeycutt turned to Dr. Lassiter. "I know it's late,

and you're not my doctor, but I wonder if you could look at my leg. No bites." He opened his torn trouser leg.

Libby gasped.

Dr. Lassiter studied the injury. "Looks like all you need is a cleanup. Come on in. Any idea how it happened?"

He glanced at Libby, who seemed suddenly fascinated with the indoor-outdoor carpet. "A few."

After Dr. Lassiter cleaned his wounds, he helped Libby sit on the outside edge of the rear passenger seat with both legs dangling. He leaned above her. "Is there someone who can come stay with you? I'm good for tonight, but tomorrow I'm on duty."

"Helping Crispin Alexandros save civilization from evil Shapeshifters." She wiggled her fingers in fake horror.

Honeycutt grinned. "I see your snarkitude has not been damaged. I'll be gone pretty much all day."

"No problem." Libby fumbled in her jacket. "I can—" With a muttered curse, she withdrew her hand. "Ellyn's not here." When she looked up at him, lights glowed in her dark eyes. "Stop worrying. I'm a big girl. I'll manage."

He snorted. "In a few days, yes. But you shouldn't be alone, especially tonight. I'm taking you back to my hotel room. We can stop at your place to pick up clothes and anything else you need." His cheek twitched. "At least you don't have to worry about that cat." Libby's jaw tensed.

"Tomorrow, while I'm working, you should take advantage of hotel services and pamper yourself. Stretch out on that big bed. Order room service. Get a massage. Watch movies. A grateful Alexandros should be happy to pay any extra charges. Most of all, you should sleep. I'll let the concierge know—if the staff has seen the news, I'm sure they'll all be happy to help one of Summerhaven's finest."

"Please! When will you be done?"

"We follow the same routine, but the actual time is hard to say. After Alexandros finishes talking, he signs autographs and poses for selfies with admirers while Tony and his techies break down and load up their equipment. We all meet in the Alexandros suite for a debriefing. He praises what he liked, complains about what he didn't, and tells us how to improve next time."

Libby offered a half-smile. "Sounds like fun."

"A million laughs. But the booze is decent, and the food is good." He touched one of the scratches on his leg. Already scabbing. "After that, I'll check out of the hotel and take you to your apartment. If you like, I can hang around until you're back on both your feet. How does that sound?"

"Like a lot of work for you."

"Everyone else believes you acted to save Alexandros. But I know" –he leaned toward her— "you took that bullet for me."

Libby's eyes widened. "In the dream, I saw it hit…" She rested her palm above his heart.

The heat of her hand burned into his chest, and his heartbeat pounded in his ears. "I'm safe, Libby. Thanks to you." He lifted her chin. Her delicate features disguised how fierce, how fearless…how pigheaded…she could be. He brought his mouth to hers.

When she gave a small breath, he would have drawn back, but the hand on his chest had moved up to his shoulder. The delicious pressure of the kiss deepened into a sweet, slow connection that tickled his groin. Time ceased to exist.

When they separated, they each took a deep breath.

He rubbed his forehead. "I shouldn't have done that…but tonight, when I saw the blood, all I could think was I would never know the…pleasure…of kissing you. I'm sorry—"

"Don't be." Libby pressed a finger against his mouth. "I'm glad you did."

"You sure?"

She gave an enthusiastic nod. "Ever since last week, I've wondered…"

"Me too."

They both laughed.

Her hand stroked his jaw. "Here you're as solid as Montana granite. But here…"

When her pinkie traced the top of his upper lip, he almost jumped out of his skin.

"You're soft…warm…like rose petals." Her gaze met his. "You didn't have to stop."

He chuckled. "Yes, I did…do." He kissed her hand and held it between his own. "For one thing, you're vulnerable."

She scoffed. "I wanted to kiss you, too."

"Also, I'm working tomorrow, and you'll be recovering. We both need sleep." He released her hand.

Her lower lip jutted out in a tempting pout. "Does that mean you won't kiss me again?"

He drew back. "Not tonight." He fingered the car keys. "Next time…maybe you could take the lead." "I could…" She yawned.

"Lie down and close your eyes."

Chapter 24

Libby opened her eyes and drew a sharp breath. *Where am I? Dark. Light seeping in between curtains. Big window on the right. Fan noises. Hotel?* She tried to sit up, but her left leg refused to move. When the events of the previous evening flashed through her mind like an old-fashioned silent film, she groaned, more in frustration than pain, and flopped back onto the mattress. "Easy." A big, warm hand rested on her shoulder.

She turned her head, and her cheek brushed the hand. "Dash?" Silly question. Who else had hands this big? She inhaled. Or such a comforting scent? Even in the darkness, his face had a slight glow. *OMG. We're in bed together.* The Alexandros presentation was tomorrow. *Today!* "I'm sorry. Didn't mean to wake you."

"No problem. Do you need anything? Want help getting to the bathroom?"

"No." Under similar circumstances, Tommy would have complained. Pushing at her numb leg, she rolled as far as she could onto her left side. An expanse of mattress, sheet, and pillows yawned between them. "I thought you were taking me home."

"I said we'd stop there for clothes but decided not to wake you."

She sniffed her T-shirt. "I need a long, hot shower."

"Not till this evening. Doctor's orders, remember?" She opened her mouth, but he continued, "If you want to wash up, I'll help you into the desk chair and wheel you into the bathroom."

"Sounds like heaven!" Libby chuckled. "I can't believe how low my expectations have fallen! These scrubs are clean, but I'm stuck in this—" she tugged at the crew neck of her T-shirt "—till I get home."

"Maybe not." Dash got out of bed and went to the dresser.

Libby lay on her back and focused on the ceiling. Enough light crept in from the hall and the window that she could make out the form of a naked man, especially if the light in Dash's face extended to other, more intimate spots. She pressed a hand to her forehead. *I must be losing my mind. I took a bullet in the butt, am partially paralyzed, and I'm wondering if Dash Honeycutt's...equipment...glows in the dark? Good grief!*

Dash stood by her side of the bed. "Try this." He held up a white T-shirt.

She rolled to her right and propped herself on her elbow. Her eyes made a cautious journey from his bare feet, up those long, long legs—her fingers curled at the damage her claws had inflicted—to the bottom edges of his boxer shorts and the T-shirt that covered pretty much everything. His arms and legs did have a slight glow.

"This will be long on you. If you need help, give a yell." His eyes sparkled with a teasing grin. "I promise not to look."

Libby's face heated. *Not that I have much to look at.*

What if Thea was wrong? What if her leg remained...

"Libby!" Dash's hands rested on her shoulders, and his eyes met hers. "Are you in pain?"

"No. Just worrying."

"Next stop, bathroom." Dash lifted her from the bed and settled her on the office chair.

When he stepped behind the chair, Libby lifted a hand. "Wait." She planted her right foot on the indoor-outdoor carpet. "Let me try something." Dash stood back.

Libby took a deep breath. When she pushed with her working foot, the chair rolled smoothly. "Aha!" She lifted her arms like goal posts and wiggled her fingers. "I'm mobile!" She rolled toward the bathroom.

"Slow down!" Dash followed her. "Don't run into anything."

She paused at the bathroom door. "Too bad we only have one chair. With two, we could race down the hall." She tilted her head and fluttered her eyelashes. "If one of your team members is on this floor, maybe you could borrow—"

"Not now." Although Dash scowled, his glow deepened. "Everyone else on the team is sleeping. And no one on this floor would appreciate the Office Chair 500 at this hour."

"Killjoy."

"And you're an impatient patient." The corners of his lips turned up. "Let's make a deal. Tomorrow, before I check out, I'll find another chair, and we'll have one race. How's that sound?"

"Great. You'd do that?" Libby hugged herself. *He said he would. Of course, he will.*

"Think about the prize." Dash turned on the bathroom light. "Need anything else?"

Libby scanned the room. Towels, washcloths, soap, toothpaste, even a toothbrush still in its wrapper. "Nope."

"Call if you need me." He left the door slightly open.

When Libby pulled off her shirt, bra, and socks, most of the crud went with them. She washed her face, neck, and ears and swiped the soapy washcloth under her arms. Good thing Thea had cleaned everything from the waist down. Feeling like a slightly new woman, she pulled on Dash's T-shirt, which hung like a loose nightgown.

Finished, she turned her chair and scooted into the bedroom. The light on her side of the bed illuminated Dash, lying on his back with his hands laced underneath his head. Strong, steady breathing. *Sleeping?*

She rolled the right side of the chair to her side of the bed. Balancing on her right foot and arm, she used her left hand to push her body out of the chair and toward the bed. Her torso landed on the mattress, but both legs trailed over the side. Sitting up slightly, she grabbed her left thigh. With a grunt, she lifted the leg to the armrest of the chair.

"What are you doing?" Dash's voice rumbled in her ear.

She released the leg and fell back onto the mattress.

"Trying to get back into bed without waking you." He chuckled. "I appreciate the effort." He sat up.

"When my left leg didn't cooperate, I thought I might make it higher like Thea told me to."

He eyed the leg on the armrest. "Ingenious. But looks uncomfortable."

She rubbed the numb thigh. "I can't feel it. Go back to sleep."

"I was resting my eyes. May I help you?" "Sure."

He got out of bed and came to her side. Wrapping one long arm around her shoulders, he slipped his other arm beneath both her legs and arranged her with her head against one pillow. Then, he tucked another pillow beneath her tush. "How's that?"

Libby smiled at him. "Much better. Thanks." She sniffed the T-shirt she was wearing.

"Problem?"

"This shirt doesn't smell like you."

Dash grinned. "That's because it's clean. You need anything?"

A used shirt? Libby shook her head. "I'm good." She reached out and touched his hand. "I don't know what would have happened if you hadn't…"

Dash squeezed her hand and released it.

"Alexandros would have sent someone to check on you."

The words chilled her. Was that why he followed her? Because Alexandros had ordered him? *Don't ask.*

"How's your leg?"

"Healing."

Remembering how her claws had dug into his flesh, Libby clasped her hands. "Good."

Dash's eyes locked on hers. "When were you planning to tell me you are a Shapeshifter?"

Libby pursed her lips. "What?"

Dash stood straight up. "Don't look so surprised." He sounded slightly amused. "I've been scratched by plenty of house cats." He gestured at his leg. "Your claws go deeper."

"Maybe you cut your leg when you lifted those cars."

Dash blinked. "Nice try. You were shifting when I caught you."

Her heart ached. "I didn't mean to hurt you. I'm sorry."

"For scratching me or for lying to me?"

"I never lied…"

"Yes, you did. About your friend."

Libby lay back and studied the ceiling. "I didn't say Ellyn wasn't…and even though she is…that doesn't mean I'm—"

Dash pressed a finger to her lips. "Even if I didn't know what happened last night, I had suspicions." Libby stared up at him.

His finger moved from her lips to the air. "From the moment we met, you've defended Shapeshifters while claiming they don't exist. And something left a fresh pile of gnawed wood particles under Schuyler Pope's bed." *Rats!*

"When I entered the suite, you were in the bathroom…returning to your human?"

She opened her mouth with the intention of denying the charge, but why bother? Dash already had the evidence in his leg. "Yes. I'm a shifter." She met his gaze. "What are you?" When he didn't respond, she pointed at him. "I saw you lift those cars."

Dash's jaw set. "Sometimes under great stress, humans can—"

"Get real. You tossed that SUV around like a Lego structure."

"Pain medicine is making you delusional."

"You did it before I had any medicine." She rested back against the pillows. "And Simple Humans don't glow in the dark."

Dash regarded his hands as if seeing them for the first time. "I guess I could tell you I've been exposed to some chemical, but…it's a stress reaction."

"So you're not human."

"I am. Partly. I'm also part Titan."

Libby's jaw dropped. "Weren't they like gods in Greek mythology?"

"The first Titans were the children of Gaea, the earth goddess, and Uranus, god of the sky."

She eyed Dash's chest. "That's how you moved those cars. But I always thought Titans were huge."

"Centuries of breeding with humans has diluted our powers." He yawned. "Tomorrow, we can talk Titans…and shifters. Now, let's sleep." He patted her cheek and started to move away.

Libby grabbed his arm. "You won't tell anyone about me, will you? Please!"

The corners of his mouth softened, and he stroked her hand. "Your secret is safe with me, and I trust mine is with you."

"Of course."

"Good." He turned off her bedside lamp.

When Dash lay down on his side of the bed, Libby reached out and touched his shoulder. "Dash?"

"What's wrong?" He rolled over, facing her.

"Nothing…but I…like…feeling close to someone." She stroked the stubble on his jaw. *You.*

He slipped his arm under her head, so her cheek rested against his chest. "Better?"

The warmth of his skin permeated the cotton of his T-shirt, and his steady heartbeat thumped in her ear. "Much."

One of his hands cradled her jaw and lifted her head.

His lips brushed hers with the gentleness of a spring breeze. "Sweet dreams."

Chapter 25

Honeycutt grabbed the phone on his nightstand with his free hand and silenced the alarm. Libby's tousled hair curled on his shoulder, and her breath warmed the skin beneath his T-shirt. The soft curves of her upper body nestled against his torso. How long had it been since he'd woken up with a beautiful woman? *Too long*.

After today, they'd have time together. He slid his arm from beneath Libby's head, rolled his shoulder, and got out of bed. He was finishing in the bathroom when his phone rang again. Pulling his T-shirt over his head, he hurried to the nightstand.

"Hello, Handsome." Julianna sounded as if she'd been swilling energy drinks since dawn.

"What's up?"

Libby stirred. So much for letting her sleep in.

"The Boss wants to make sure everyone is up and dressed."

"I'll be in the lobby on time." He ended the call and sat on the edge of the bed to put his shoes on.

Libby moved.

He turned to meet her sleep-dusted gaze. "Sorry about that. Didn't know I'd get a wake-up call."

"Two." She pushed up to sit, and a trace of amusement played around the corners of her mouth. "One of your admirers? 'Good Morning, Handsome'."

Honeycutt smiled at her creditable imitation of

Julianna's husky drawl. "Not an admirer. A coworker."
One of Libby's eyebrows arched.

He put on the shirt he'd left hanging on the back of the bathroom door. "We were together for a while, but it didn't go anywhere. She's ambitious." He stood by the mirror with his tie.

"And you're not?"

His fingers rested on the final fold of the knot. "Like I told you, I'm with Alexandros for information, not a career. Jules moved from secretarial staff to management and is now his executive assistant. Right below Alexandros on the organization chart." He came to Libby's side of the bed, slid one hand under the covers, and wiggled it beneath her.

"What are you doing?"

"Feel anything?"

"No."

He drew back. "I pinched you."

"Damn."

"Roll onto your good side. Let me check your wound."

"You don't need to. I can tell by—" She reached toward her hip but stopped. "I can't feel it, but if you have a hand mirror, I could see—"

"I don't have time to look for a mirror now." He eyed the blemish on her otherwise perfect derriere. "No redness. No swelling. A little dried blood on the dressing, but your doctor said that might happen."

"Scar?"

"Maybe a little dimple."

She swatted him. "Get your hand off my butt and get yours in gear."

He stepped away with a laugh. "Fair's fair. I looked

at yours. Tonight, you can check out mine. How's that?"

Libby rested one hand against her chest. "Be still, my heart."

He drew himself up in mock offense. "Mine's not as pretty as yours...but no one's ever objected." He slipped on a gray jacket with the Alexandros insignia and opened his arms. "What do you think?"

Libby's gaze took a leisurely tour from the top of his head to his polished shoes. "That Alexandros is going to stick you in the farthest corner of the room so the women in the audience will look at him."

That's more like it. Honeycutt grinned.

Libby lifted her index finger. "Remember your promise. Don't tell anyone. Especially not him."

He rested his hands on shoulders that felt like concrete blocks. "Don't worry. I'll keep your secret. You keep mine." Releasing her, he stood. "I'll be back as soon as I can. You—"

"I will be fine." She patted the arm of the desk chair. "I may even do some practice runs."

"That's cheating! You're supposed to stay in bed!"

The laughter that bubbled out of her lit his heart. He touched the upturned tip of her nose. "Doctor's orders."

He stepped back. "See you later."

****

When the door closed, Libby lay against the pillows and swore. No kisses this morning. She eyed the desk chair. *That should be the prize*. When she won, he'd have to kiss her until...what? She had to rest in bed for two more days. By the time she felt better, Dash would be gone.

She glanced at her nightstand and smiled. Dash had

left her phone and the remote within easy reach. She picked up her phone and called Captain Weatherby.

"Hello, Detective. How are you?" He sounded no gruffer than usual.

"Good, sir."

"I got the message from your doctor. I'll pass the word to O'Malley…and to everybody else. They're all worried about you, especially those who worked the reception."

Libby swallowed.

"Take care of yourself."

"I will, sir."

Setting her phone on the nightstand, she settled back against the pillow. Nothing to do but rest. *Thea would be pleased.*

Three ring tones interrupted a wonderful dream that featured Dash. *Steffi.*

Mom and Dad.

Dayzee.

The story's gone viral.

"Let me look at you, honey." In the video call, lines of worry etched Mom's face.

Dad hovered at Mom's shoulder. He'd pushed his glasses up above his forehead, and the wire-rims sent his thinning hair in all directions. He looked like a mad scientist.

Libby threw back her shoulders as if every cell in her body felt as invincible as her spirit. "It's a minor wound."

Her mother's dark eyebrows knitted. "Are you sure?"

"Yes, Mom." Libby swallowed the lie that congealed in her throat. "Doctor Lassiter said that I'll soon be good as new."

"Thank God!" Mom's forehead smoothed. "When I saw the news…I know you love your work—we both do.

We're proud of you, too, but…"

"It's dangerous." Dad spoke in a near-growl.

Libby regarded her parents. "The job can be dangerous, but most of the time, it's not. My partner, Mike, retired without ever shooting anyone…or being shot." *But then there's Oliver Dumire. And me.*

Her mother's gaze slipped from Libby to a spot over her shoulder where one of those generic hotel abstracts hung. "Are you in the hospital?" Mom's voice rose at the end of her question.

"I'm at Ellyn's."

"Of course." Mom gave a little chuckle. "I forgot she moved to Summerhaven right after you did." Mom smiled at her. "Follow your doctor's orders, and if you need anything, call." She looked ready to move the Beartooth Mountains.

"I will, Mom. Thanks for calling. I love you both more than I can say."

One down. Libby's stomach growled. When had she eaten last? Yesterday, she'd been too edgy to think about food. She scanned the menu Dash had left beneath the remote and pressed the Room Service button on the hotel phone.

She'd finished placing her order when Dayzee's ring sounded. Robin would have envied the blue and white stripes in her sister's golden hair. Amazing eyelashes framed eyes almost as blue as Dash's. "Hey, Day, what's up?"

"You tell me. You're the one who got shot."

Libby shrugged. "It's no big deal."

Dayzee leaned into the screen. "That's not how it looked."

"What do the news people say? If it bleeds, it leads?"

"I guess." Dayzee lounged in her chair. "Did you really save Alexandros?"

"I suppose. But if I hadn't, his security people would have."

Dayzee sat up and straightened her blouse. "Like that big blond stud muffin standing beside him?"

Stud muffin! Almost choking on laughter, Libby nodded.

"Do you know him?"

"We worked together for a while."

Dayzee flashed a wicked grin. "Must have been fun."

Back off, Baby Sis. Libby drew a deep breath. "It was work, Day. And he's a big Alexandros supporter."

"Too bad." After a sigh, Dayzee brightened. "He could still be great in the sack."

Libby lay back. "When you get shot, you have more important things on your mind than…"

"I guess that would put a damper on romance." *He did kiss me.*

"What was I thinking?" When her sister threw up her hands, her nails glittered. "I bet you're still getting over your breakup."

Someone knocked and opened the door. "Room Service."

"I gotta go, Day." Libby turned toward the door. "Come on in."

While the waiter wheeled the breakfast cart toward the bed, Dayzee stayed on the line. "Before you hang up, there's something I need to know." Dayzee's mobile features stilled. "Starshine Productions is thinking about doing a documentary on Crispin Alexandros."

Libby wrinkled her nose. "Why?"

"Because he's everywhere these days. He might even run for President."

Libby swallowed a groan as the waiter arranged her tray.

"Since you saved his life, I thought you might have an in…could help me set up an interview with him."

"Sorry, Day, but by the time I'm recovered, he'll be far from here."

Dayzee rolled her eyes. "Worth a try. Hope you're feeling better soon."

"I'll keep you posted."

Dayzee brightened. "Maybe you could send me Studmuffin's number."

Libby blinked. "What?"

"He might be willing to help me, and even if he wasn't…you never know." Dayzee's smile winged across the ether. "He's taken." Libby ended the call.

Two down. One to go. But first…food!

She reached for coffee. *Come on, caffeine. Wake up those toes!* No luck. *Wonder how…or when…the feeling will return.*

Libby eyed the TV remote. *Might as well see what's on.*

She pressed the power button. Vivid images of the Mark V facilities assaulted her eyes. *Next!* Local programming. A blonde reporter, almost as perky as Dayzee but with compressed lips—the gravitas of a genuine TV journalist—faced the camera while people milled about in the space behind her.

When Libby spied the convention center auditorium, the spicy sugar of the French toast turned to sludge in her mouth. Libby changed channels again and again, but local stations and national networks all carried the presentation.

I shouldn't watch this. My breakfast will go down better with that new mystery on my phone. Then, a nap.

"Doctor's orders." Libby aimed the remote at the screen and rested her index finger on the power button.

"Know the enemy." The voice in her brain froze her finger. Where had she heard that? Police training? Not likely. They didn't use words like "enemy." *Ellyn! The morning after...*

Libby's gaze returned to the television screen. *I can't know the enemy if I pretend he doesn't exist.*

Cameras swept the audience, packed mostly with people sporting those ghastly shirts she'd seen at the mayor's house. In the area outside the meeting room, someone on the Alexandros staff probably hawked antishifter paraphernalia.

Jeff Dearborn and the other personal guards surrounded the stage, and Summerhaven police occupied strategic spots. The camera lingered near an entrance where Dash conferred with Robin. When the consultation ended, the camera followed Robin's turquoise curls and bouncing hips instead of staying with Dash.

Libby swore.

The moment Crispin Alexandros entered, the crowd noise grew softer, or the sound technicians lowered it. Accompanied by Mayor Dawson, whose green suit probably cost six months of a detective's salary, the big, white-haired man swaggered toward the lectern. As usual, he looked full of himself.

Libby turned up the volume. Then she returned the remote to the nightstand and poured herself another cup of coffee.

Chapter 26

Standing near the center of the auditorium, Honeycutt scanned the doorways. Alexandros security and Summerhaven police were in place. He glanced at his watch. *Hope you're sleeping.* When his mind replayed the easy rise and fall of Libby's breath, his mouth relaxed.

On the stage, the wide-eyed mayor looked like she'd received a transmission from outer space. Alexandros towered behind her as she lowered the microphone to accommodate her height. "Ladies and gentlemen, residents of Summerhaven, visitors to our fair city, and viewers across this great country, it is my pleasure…it is my honor…to introduce someone who really needs no introduction."

Is that the best you can do?

The usual whoops and shouts from the audience.

The mayor lifted her hand. "Please hold your applause." She rattled off the standard biography and thrust a fist in the air to punctuate each of Alexandros's

"outstanding achievements."

He needs a new list. Honeycutt watched the audience.

As the mayor continued, Alexandros's chest swelled like an overinflated balloon.

Too bad that belly can't lift him up into the stratosphere. Libby would lead the poppers. The image made Honeycutt smile.

"Ladies and gentlemen, may I present Dr. Crispin Alexandros."

"Please! Please!" Alexandros lifted his gloved hands and dipped his chin.

Mr. Modesty. And always with a straight face.

"...her kind remarks." After Alexandros acknowledged the mayor, two of his personal guards hustled her offstage. Alexandros seized the lectern. "I'd like to tell you how happy I am to be here with you today.

"Unfortunately, the truth is that, much as I have enjoyed the charms of your lovely city and the gracious hospitality of your mayor, I stand before you today to speak of a very serious matter...a matter of life and death for those dearest to us and most vulnerable."

He stood silently long enough to let his words sink in, but not so long his followers would start twitching.

"I speak, of course, of our children." Soft mumbles rippled through the audience. On the screen behind him, stock footage of children in playgrounds appeared. "Many of us recall the carefree days of youth." Cheerful music accompanied images of kids playing tag, zipping down sliding boards, and climbing on jungle gyms.

Most of the audience looked as if they recalled those happy days.

Set them up. Then knock them down. On his mic,

Honeycutt ordered staff near the back of the room to watch the people who sat in their seats like solemn lumps.

"But times have changed." The children's movements slowed to a crawl, the music faded, and the playground dissolved into a montage of children coughing and wheezing. "Asthma...allergies...these

207

days, many children struggle simply to breathe." When a chart with a climbing red line popped up, Alexandros quickly ran through the numbers showing a dramatic increase in allergies over the years. Too many statistics, and people would fidget. Several of the grim spectators in the back leaned forward.

Alexandros planted his elbows on the lectern. "Scientists offer various reasons for this alarming trend." He ticked them off on his fingers. Then, he grasped the lectern. "According to my researchers, the cause is far more insidious…and far more dangerous."

A blank screen replaced the coughing children. One by one, the big black words appeared: SHADOW PEOPLE OR SHADOW SLAYERS?

Honeycutt gnashed his teeth. A world of possibilities existed between those extremes, but the Alexandros audience hadn't come to hear a thoughtful lecture. Tension thickened the air. His earpiece picked up a noisy group viewing the broadcast outside the convention center. *Time to attack. Hope Libby's reading or watching a movie. She doesn't need this!*

Alexandros stepped away from the lectern and moved closer to the front of the stage. "Most of you know I've spent a great deal of time…and money…attempting to awaken our society to the problems presented by those who pretend to be human like us but are in fact Shapeshifters."

His tone became less authoritative, more conversational. "I also call them Shadow People because that's how they live. They hide from the light of truth. They also threaten the very existence of *true* human beings like you and me." He slapped his chest.

Someone in the middle of the auditorium leaped up

and shouted, "Yes!" Those around him applauded.

The light in Alexandros's face dimmed. He hated losing the attention of his audience, even for a heartbeat.

"You know it, brother. We all do." Alexandros lifted his arms with his palms up. Then he turned the palms down and brought his hands back to his sides.

Honeycutt alerted the nearest security person to approach the disruptor, but the standing man took the hint from Alexandros and returned to his seat.

"These Shadow People lurk among us anytime, anywhere—in this very auditorium. *They* know." He touched his heart. "But we true humans do not."

More than one person in the audience shot suspicious glances at others sitting nearby. On his wire, Honeycutt relayed to his associates the locations of those who patted possible concealed weapons.

"They hear what we say. They watch what we do. They take what they want when they want it. And, left unchecked, in time they will destroy the laws and beliefs that bind our human society together."

Like humans don't do enough of that on their own.

"I've already called for policies that would allow law-abiding citizens like us to identify these shadow people and bring them to justice. But those who claim to love civil liberties attack me at every turn." He smirked. "They prefer fear and danger to safety. But now…" Holding up one hand, he came to the edge of the stage. "Now the existence of these shadow people has become a matter of"—his deep voice dropped as if he were an old-time radio announcer— "life and death." An alarmed buzz traveled through the audience. *Relax, Honeycutt. It's noise, no action. They'll cool off.*

Most of them, anyway. A few often returned home

from these events and harassed or even threatened possible shifters.

Alexandros drew back and clasped his hands.

"Before I present the research that led to this conclusion, I would be remiss if I failed to note that among the scientists who worked on this project was one of Summerhaven's own. Dr. Schuyler Pope met an untimely end that I believe involved his research." He glanced over his shoulder at Pope's picture on the screen. The audience applauded politely. "Dr. Pope—Sky to those of us who knew and loved him—will be missed not only by his family and friends but by his colleagues and associates at the Crispin Alexandros Research

Laboratories and the Crispin Alexandros Center."

****

"Gimme a break, you sleazeball."

Statistics and graphs flashed on Libby's TV screen, accompanied by an undertone of ominous music that echoed the theme from a horror movie. Credits for the Crispin Alexandros Center and the Crispin Alexandros research labs occupied the bottom corners of the screen. Alexandros's deep voice crooning about shifter DNA markers and human allergies sneaked into her brain and sidetracked her attempts to make sense of the numbers. "Extensive tests show, beyond any doubt, that these shadow people secrete a substance that triggers an allergic response in human beings."

Libby's jaw dropped. *Preposterous* When the camera scanned the audience, her doubt wilted like a dying lily. Almost everyone in the room—even Dash! — gazed at the speaker as if hypnotized. *This can't be happening*. But it was.

Alexandros continued. The shadow people posed a

threat to real human beings, especially children. This problem had one sensible solution. A horizontal word appeared near the top of the screen: Identification. Once identified, all shadow people would be physically marked. "A tattoo, perhaps, or a small brand." *Cute.* Libby sneered.

Letter by letter, a second word descended from the central I: Isolation. "And they would be relocated."

"Like the camps we put the Japanese in during World War II?" A white-haired man in a tweed suit stood up near the back of the room.

Libby pounded the mattress. "You tell him."

The questioner looked like the college professor he was, when he wasn't functioning as the alpha of a wolf pack she'd met in the wilderness area near Caulfield's Ridge. Several other shifters from the small Summerhaven pack sat nearby.

"Good question!" Alexandros gave a hearty chuckle. "These would not be internment camps but functioning communities where these creatures can live and work together."

Creatures. Libby's breath caught in her throat. With a single word, Alexandros reduced her and every other shifter to something less than human.

A skinny woman near the front popped up. "Your plan sounds like it would cost a lot of money." She had a surly mouth. "I don't want my taxes taking care of *those freaks.*"

"You needn't worry about that, my dear." With a smarmy smile, Alexandros explained how the seizure and sale of the shifters' own resources would finance their new lives.

Resisting the temptation to hurl the remote at the

screen, Libby turned off the TV and sank back against her pillow.

How could Dash work with this man? *He wants to find his sister.* She picked at the bedspread. *That's what he says. He could be lying about that. About everything.* He might have Titan ancestors. *I did see him lift those cars.* But he might also be human enough to believe antishifter propaganda. *Human enough to tell Alexandros about me?*

She put her empty coffee cup on the breakfast cart.

Steffi's ring tone sounded.

Libby grabbed her phone.

Her sister's face appeared on the screen. "Libby, how—"

"Recovering."

"Glad to hear it." Steffi put on her best big-sister face. "I can't believe you risked your life to save that *demagogue*."

Fire burned in Libby's cheeks.

"Sawyer's family has bombarded us with messages. He tells them you couldn't help it. Your cop instinct kicked in."

Libby laughed. "What happened is even stranger. I dreamed that Dash got shot. I had to save him."

Steffi cocked her head. "Really?"

"It sounds silly. He's bigger and stronger than me." *He can pick up cars.* "But… in the dream…the bullet hit…the blood spread, and…he…died." Libby drew a deep breath. "I couldn't let that happen."

A smile fluttered across Steffi's lips. "I hope he appreciates you."

"He has his moments."

Steffi sat back. "Was the shooting as bad as it

looked?"

"Probably not." Libby described the coated bullet. "Thea says the paralysis should be gone in a day or two." With a grunt, she moved. "Right now, I'm in Dash's hotel room, and he's offered to stay at my place until I've recovered, which sounded like a good plan..." Libby pretended to find a fascinating detail in the boring white blanket.

"But?"

Her free hand curled into a fist. "Steffi, he knows...about me."

"What? How? You lived with Tommy for two years and never...but after two weeks with this Honeycutt guy, you—"

"I didn't tell him. After...he followed me to my car. When my left leg stopped moving, I started to shift but stumbled. Dash caught me, and I clawed his leg. He promised not to tell anyone. He's been honest with me about other things, and I want to believe he'll keep his word." Libby mentally replayed the concern in Dash's eyes, the gentle warmth of his big hands, the tenderness of that first kiss, his own admission of supernatural ability. *So much I like, so much I want to trust.*

"But I've been watching him on TV today. He fits right in with Alexandros and his followers. Steff, I don't know what to believe."

"Stay safe."
Call OASIS.

Chapter 27

Honeycutt juggled the chilly package in his hands and opened the door to his hotel room. Late afternoon sun peeking around the edges of the closed curtains silhouetted Libby lying in the middle of the bed with her face turned toward the window. Sleeping. *Good.* He closed the door and did his best to tiptoe to the small refrigerator beneath the TV, where he squatted and opened the door.

"What are you doing?"

When Libby's question shattered the silence, he dropped his heels to the floor, stood, and turned. She was up on her elbows watching him.

"I thought you were asleep." "I tried, but..." She waved a hand. *Something's changed.*

The set of her pretty mouth and the tilt of her chin looked as if someone had honed her delicate features into angles. Maybe she'd seemed soft and sexy this morning because that was what he wanted, and this was the real Libby. *Detective Maitland.*

She pointed at the item in his hand. "What's that?"

"Thought you might like a sundae appetizer."

When he showed her the label, delight lit her face for the space of a heartbeat. Then the light in her dark eyes dimmed. "That was nice of you. I'll have to pass." Words as frosty as the package in his hand.

He stared at her. Could this be the same woman

who'd rhapsodized her way through the menu at the dessert place? *What's happened to* my *Libby? Slow down. She's not mine, never will be.* "What's wrong?"

She stretched. "I don't want to gain weight while I'm recuperating."

Makes sense. He placed the rejected treat in the small refrigerator and shut the door. "Robin said they didn't catch the shooter."

"You'd think that with all those cops…so much security…"

"They found the weapon, but no prints…no serial number. Robin assured me they'll get him eventually."

"We always say that." The lines at the corners of her mouth drew down. "One minute he wasn't there, and the next, he was. He moved like a shadow." She glanced toward the window. "Maybe Summerhaven does have a demon portal."

Honeycutt gave a dry chuckle. "Demons don't need guns."

"How would you—"

"I've encountered a few." He rubbed his hands together. "Let's talk about something more pleasant. Tony says I can use his desk chair if we let him watch the race. He's betting on you." Honeycutt grinned and raised his arms like goalposts. "Let the games begin!" Libby sank into the pillows.

He itched to sit beside her. But she looked as if she might bite. "Painkillers?"

"No. I'm stiff. I didn't rest enough to race." She gestured at the television. "Thanks to your boss."

Maintaining distance, Honeycutt sat at the foot of the bed on his side. "You didn't have to watch something else."

215

"True." Libby nodded. "But like every other shifter in this country—this world—I need to know the enemy. If I pretend Alexandros doesn't exist, I won't have any strategy to protect myself or the others when his followers turn on us…like in the old days."

When she gripped her hands and closed her eyes, he reached out to her. "Libby…"

She brushed off his touch. "Please don't." Her gaze washed over him like a chilly rain. "I like you, Dash, but you are one of his people." *One of "his"—no!* "I told you—"

"That you're working for Alexandros because you're trying to find your sister."

The less you know, the better.

"Today, whenever I saw you, you looked positively enthusiastic. You were as entranced with what he was saying as his audience was."

The scorn in her voice was like a slap. Honeycutt stood and drew himself up to his full, human height. "I wouldn't go that far."

"I know what I saw. You flashed those big smiles and nodded until I thought your head might pop off."

"Cut me a break, Libby. We all do what our bosses want. When you're in a meeting and Jack Weatherby introduces a policy you don't like, you don't sit in your chair and grumble, do you?"

"Sometimes, yes."

"You're lucky he hasn't called you out yet."

Libby smiled. "Sometimes he does. He usually ignores me. We must follow orders, whether we like them or not."

"But you don't have to pretend you like them because you have a union, right?"

"I guess."

"I don't have that kind of protection. Everybody who works for Alexandros works at his pleasure. He wants everyone on the traveling team to behave as if we are thrilled by every word he utters. Anyone who doesn't perform enthusiastically enough gets fired."

Libby laced her hands behind her head. "That doesn't sound fair."

"He who owns the business makes the rules."

"And you go along with them."

His foot beat an impatient tattoo. "I do what I have to do."

"You've seen what he calls research." She enclosed the word in huge air quotes.

"Security is my job. I don't pay much attention to anything else." *Except for what I send SUNATNET.*

"That's too bad. If you listened, you'd know how ludicrous his claims are. For example, he provides statistics about shifters and childhood allergies as if they represent absolute truth." She toyed with strands of hair that feathered her cheek. "My parents are scientists. I've seen how real research works. You don't throw out a bunch of numbers and make up a story about them. You experiment. You use a system that other people interested in the problem can repeat. That tests your results.

"From what I heard today, his researchers didn't isolate children to control their exposure to different allergens. He didn't even mention actually working with children. As far as I can tell, he's all paper, no people."

Honeycutt paced to and from the window. "That may be true. But Alexandros does seem to believe what he says. I will agree that he sometimes sounds extreme."

"You think?" Libby lifted warning fingers. "Branding us? Seizing our property? Putting us in camps? I felt like I was watching a history movie."

Honeycutt stopped at the foot of the bed. "Remember: to go through with any of these wild plans, he first must identify shifters. He makes that process sound easy, but he still has no reliable way of doing it. He also has impatient followers. If they knew he was still stuck at Square One, he might lose them, so he does what he can to keep them engaged."

"Engaged? More like enraged. When you're working those meetings, don't you see what's going on? Today, for instance. Most of the people in that auditorium—and who watched the broadcast—accepted what that man—your boss—told them. They didn't just accept—they embraced every word. They left that auditorium looking ready to hunt people like me down, kill us if necessary. That's why shifters have spent centuries convincing Simple Humans we don't exist."

Libby tossed off her covers. "I should go home."

"Do you still want me to stay with you?"

She hugged her right knee. "I don't have much choice...so, yes, I do need your help if you're still willing..."

He smacked his forehead with his hand. She sounded so resigned. The good feelings between them might revive if they spent time without the shadow of Alexandros. *A few days...* "Don't worry. I'll do what you want me to, and I'll keep my distance. This is on my time, not Alexandros's. Is that clear?"

"Yes."

He went to the closet. "After packing, I'll check out online. Then, I'll call for your car. While you're waiting, you sure you don't want to sample that sundae?" He shot her a quick grin.

"Don't tempt me." Her tone was serious, but her mouth relaxed.

"I'll take it with us. In case you want it later." When he packed his bag, he chose a position that hid the erection triggered by her words. Tempting Libby was a challenge he'd cheerfully accept.

****

During the short drive from the hotel to Lovegrove Lane, thoughts about Dash swirled in Libby's awareness. He worked for a terrible person, and he knew it. He claimed he'd taken the job to find his sister. He could be lying. Everything he'd ever told her might be lies.

Still, he'd given her little reason to doubt him. He'd told the truth about his time at the Mark V. He'd helped her when she was wounded. Of course, he might be following his boss's orders. *If so, wouldn't he have dumped me in the ER instead of driving me to the Lassiter Clinic?* And after the clinic, he'd done what he could to make her comfortable. And safe. Snuggling against him, she'd felt warm, protected. She touched her mouth. His kiss had tasted of desire, not duty.

Dash parked her car in the small garage beneath the apartment, came around to the passenger side, and opened the door. "How's your leg feeling?"

"I can wiggle toes." She got out and rested against the rear fender. "I'll try the crutches."

"Not up those stairs." Dash opened the door that led to the stairway. "You'd have to lean on me, and it's too narrow for us to walk side by side. If you curl into a ball, I can carry you." He hugged his elbows. "Or I could use a fireman's carry." He extended his arms out from his shoulders. "The stairs should be wide enough. Or you could wrap your arms around my neck and let me hook both your legs with my arms."

"Piggyback." Libby laughed. "Dad used to do that when we were kids."

"If I carry you against my chest, we'd lean backward. In either the fireman's carry or the piggyback, we'd lean forward. Forward is probably better."

Plastering her body against his. Resting her cheek against his warm nape with wisps of that golden hair and that sexy Dash scent. What could go wrong? *Everything*. "Anything else?"

"Baby steps. You sit and push yourself up. I stand below to spot you. That would take longer...and might be hard on your arms and shoulders. If you get tired, I'd have to climb over you to pull you up, and that would be awkward."

Libby threw back her shoulders and lifted her chin. "I can shift."

Dash's mouth dropped open. Even his teeth were perfect. "Won't that be stressful?"

"I don't think so." "But last night—"

"If I'd finished the shift, I could have limped on three legs to my car. When you showed up, returning to my human was the smart move." She put her phone in one of his big hands. "If something goes wrong, press the emergency—wait." She took the phone and replaced Ellyn's number with Steffi's. "My sister will call for help."

"Carrying you up would be better."

And more beguiling. "Don't be silly. In my new shape, I may be able to make it up the stairs on my own, but even if I can't, I'll be small enough for a comfortable carry."

"Shifting's not necessary."

"I think it is. One misstep on those stairs, and we could both end up at the bottom in a pile of bruises and broken bones."

He planted his feet and squared his broad shoulders. "I won't let that happen."

Are all Titans this arrogant? "That's what an accident is, Dash. Something unexpected that you can't stop. Go wait in the stairwell for about ten minutes. Then come back. Will you stop looking at me like I've lost my mind? I don't normally shift with my clothes on, and I don't want you watching."

"If I come back in, and you're not..." He held up her phone.

"Call Steffi."

Instead of leaving, he approached. One of his knuckles lifted her chin. When his clear blue gaze softened her resistance, she drew her head back. His hand fell away, and a hint of gray clouded his eyes.

"Don't worry." She pointed at the doorway. "Go."

Alone, Libby pulled off the loose clothing. She peeled off the wound dressing. The site was tender. *I can feel it!*

Closing her eyes, she focused. Dash liked cats. Especially domesticated ones with claws that couldn't mutilate his leg.

Libby visualized a short-haired tabby. Steady breathing relaxed her body for the transformation. The muscles in her wounded leg moved slowly, but they did transform, and the foot smoothly became a paw.

Standing beside the car, she stretched. Her left hind leg was weak, but the other three provided good support.

"Libby?" Dash opened the door.

She sat back on her haunches, tilted her head, and meowed.

His grin was like a burst of sunlight. "You did it!" He strolled toward her and stood above her. "You are one beautiful cat. I bet you were a knock-out cheetah, too, but those claws…" He flinched.

Libby stood and stepped forward. When her left hind leg crumpled, she hissed at the spike of pain that shot through her hip. Dragging that leg upstairs would hurt.

"Slow down." Squatting beside her, Dash offered an immense hand, which she sniffed. Her feline sense of smell intensified that musky all-male scent. Without thinking, she licked his palm.

When he picked her up, she nestled in the warm curve of his neck. Almost as comfortable as sleeping against his shoulder. Stroking her fur with one hand, Dash mounted the stairs. Libby purred. A more comfortable trip for them both, but why had she ever thought it less sensual than piggybacking?

"Mission accomplished!" Supporting her body and legs, Dash moved her from his shoulder to her bed. "I'll unpack the car, and you can treat yourself to a cat nap."

If she'd been human, she would have laughed. When he tickled her under the chin, she purred.

Dash reached for the blanket that lay at the foot of the bed. "This will give you a cover when you return to your human. If you need help, yell or yowl." He stroked her head. "Rest."

Libby curled up and closed her eyes.

Chapter 28

Libby opened her eyes and purred. She touched her face. *Paw. Cat.* Closing her eyes, she visualized her human shape. Minutes later, her upper arms stretched beside her ears, and her human legs—both legs! — pushed toward the foot of the bed. She moved her left knee up and down. She flexed and relaxed the left foot, then did the same with both feet because moving felt so wonderful. *The drug wore off like Thea said it would.*

Blinking back tears of joy, she kicked off the thin blanket that had covered her and sat up. Shades darkened the room. *How long did I sleep?*

She checked the date and time on her phone, which Dash must have left on the nightstand. "Oh, no! It's already…"

Her fingers froze on the phone. She glanced at the rumpled blanket. OASIS had wanted to schedule their "visit" ASAP, but she'd assured them that Dash would be so busy helping her he wouldn't have time to contact Alexandros. OASIS agreed to wait till she was on her feet. She hadn't planned to sleep so long. She looked at the phone again. *What has Dash been doing?*

She rolled over to the side of the bed and planted both feet on the floor. When she stood, her left leg buckled slightly, so she grabbed the crutches at the head of the bed. *Thanks again, Dash!*

She thumped to the dresser. Left hip still stiff.

Twinge in the wound site. Standing in front of the mirror, she turned her back and looked over her shoulder at her left buttock. *Cute little dimple, ha! Cops don't have dimples. We have scars.* The skin did pucker.

A knock sounded on the bedroom door. "Libby?" *Dash!*

She held the crutches in front of her as if they could hide her. "I'm not dressed."

"I heard noises."

"I got up, and I need to get dressed." She adjusted her crutches. "Left leg's weak, but I can manage."

"I'll stay here in case you want help."

From a dresser drawer, Libby pulled underwear. In her closet, she found a knit A-line dress that slipped over her head. She brushed the teal skirt. *Good color.* Not that Dash would notice once OASIS…

She opened the bedroom door. Clad in T-shirt and jeans, Dash lounged against the wall in the hall. "You didn't need to wait."

When his eyelids lifted, the shadows in the hall lent a hint of smoke to his blue eyes. "Nothing else to do."

Leaving the door open, she returned to the dresser and tamed her hair.

Dash stood in the doorway. "Does it hurt?"

She eyed the item in her hand. "Brushing my hair?"

"No." Dash laughed. "Shapeshifting."

Libby laughed, too. "Depends on the shape and how well my body knows it. Most shifters don't start until they're teenagers, and for them it's harder because their bones have been human for so long. My sisters and I began when we were babies, so our bones and muscles have always been flexible." She looked at him. "Why did you let me sleep so long? It's—"

Dash moved to the window and opened the shades. "Not quite noon."

"You shouldn't have—"

"We didn't get here until late afternoon, and you needed the rest."

"I suppose." She bent her left knee and circled her ankle.

Dash applauded.

"I can't believe I'm so excited about something so simple. Thea told me I'd be fine, but I was still…scared. Silly me."

"Not at all." Dash touched her cheek and turned her face toward his.

His gentle hand and quiet voice reignited memories of that first kiss. His mouth was so close… *No. OASIS is coming.* She moved away. "While I was sleeping, what did you do?"

"Checked my messages."

"Alexandros keeping track?"

His glance was so sharp it could have sliced an eyelash. "Other than asking about your progress, no."

"What did you tell him?"

His gaze locked on hers. "That you were doing well." No trace of evasion in his posture or his voice.

"What else did you do?"

"Streamed a movie on my phone. Looked at some of your books." He grinned. "We both like mythology and spy thrillers. Exercised. Cooked dinner. Stretched out on the—"

"Back up." Libby stared at him. "You cooked?"

"Don't look so shocked. Since we kids all liked to eat, Mom put us to work as soon as we could reach the table."

"Smart woman. Most of the guys I know think cooking means peeling off the plastic and sticking it in the microwave." A corner of her mouth twisted. "That's what it means to me, too, more often than I'd like to admit."

"You were short on vegetables, so I made a quick run to the produce store near your dessert place. How do you feel about stir fry leftovers for brunch?"

"I'll eat anything. How can I help?"

"Make coffee or tea?"

"Definitely among my kitchen skills." In the hallway, she stopped by the bathroom door. "I need to wash up and put a clean dressing on the wound."

Dash touched his fingers to his forehead in a quick salute. "Yell if you want help."

After cleaning up, Libby entered the front room and gaped. "Looks like a florist's shop!"

Dash emerged from the small kitchen. "Lots of people are thanking you for saving…you know." Libby wrinkled her nose.

"They mean well." He held up a round vase full of carnations. "Your fellow officers sent these."

Libby smiled. "Peppy red. Full of good energy." She read the card attached to a small crystal boat containing orchids and lilies. "Alexandros?"

"He thinks you saved his life."

"If he knew…"

"Some things he never needs to know." *Like my shapeshifting.* Libby tensed.

Dash was at her elbow. "What's wrong?"

"I'm…overwhelmed." Her gaze returned to the flowers. *So many Alexandros supporters.* "When I can drive again, I'll take most of these to the local hospital."

"I can do it." Dash found a pad of paper near the bookcase. "Why don't you make a list of other useful errands? Grocery store? Laundromat?"

I can't let you out of my sight until after OASIS. But I slept so long it could already be too late. "Thanks, but that's not necessary." She gestured at the greenery. "Could you clear the table...put the flowers by the window? Some...friends... are coming...for Game Night."

"What?" Dash stared at her as if she'd announced the running of the bulls.

"We get together every few months, and tonight it's my turn." Libby avoided his gaze. The OASIS cover story had sounded lame when she'd heard it, even weaker in her own voice.

Dash glanced at the bookcases. "You don't have any—"

She gave an unconvincing laugh. "I was in such a hurry to move I left all my games behind. They're bringing some favorites."

Dash gestured at the crutches. "You shouldn't overdo it."

The concern in his voice wrapped around her like velvet. "After sleeping so long, I think I could handle anything. If I do get tired, I'll send them home." *But not before they've...* She glanced at Dash. "How's your leg?"

He rolled up his pants leg.

Libby pursed her lips. "Not even scratch marks." Dash rolled down the fabric. "We heal fast."

One less item to forget...

"How big is this group?"

"Tonight, just two. I should heat the tea water."

Soon, Dash's rice and stir fry adorned Gran's plates. "This looks wonderful. Your mom did a great job."

"Now she teaches grandkids." Dash took the seat beside her and lifted his cup. "Here's to your recovery."

Libby brought her cup to his. "And the people who made it possible—Thea Lassiter and you."

"After what you did, helping you was the least I could do." Dash attacked his food.

Especially if Alexandros ordered you. "Tell me more about being a Titan."

He chewed and swallowed. "Not that much to tell."

"I saw you move two cars."

Dash frowned. "You should have been resting on the backseat."

"I was curious."

"You know curiosity killed the cat."

"But satisfaction brought it back."

Dash groaned. "Our primary functions are to help and heal. We also have special responsibilities because we're Prometheans, descendants of—"

"I know about Prometheus!" She gestured at her bookcase. "He was punished for eternity because he gave fire to humans."

"Not quite eternity, but it must have felt that way. The other gods chained him to a mountain, and an eagle tore out his liver. Since he healed fast, the eagle claimed a fresh liver every day. He existed like that until Herakles released him."

Libby shivered. "I didn't know that part of the story. I'm glad he got free."

"Prometheus also created…what you call Simple Humans."

"Like my mom and dad."

Dash blinked. "They're not shifters?" Libby shook her head.

"But how can that—Shapeshifters inherit their ability from their parents."

"Most do. OASIS—The Organization—"

"I know who they are."

"They call me and my sisters The Three Anomalies."

Dash's eyebrows dipped. "Why?"

"Because we have Simple Human parents and can take any biological shape. Mom and Dad are scientists. OASIS thinks some chemicals they worked with scrambled my mother's eggs. Does Alexandros know you're a Titan?"

"No. He thinks I'm a big, strong human." He rested his hands on the edge of the table. "Do you have any idea how amazing your ability is? Like yesterday, for example. One minute you were there, and five minutes later you were different—but still you." The corners of his generous mouth curved up.

Libby looked deep into those amazing blue eyes. "You could see me?"

"Of course." He brushed a wisp of hair on her forehead. "Fur the color of your hair." He tapped her chin. "Same chin. And eyes."

"So you knew it was me." Lowering her gaze, Libby nibbled a piece of cooked carrot. "But you also knew I was shifting. If you'd seen a cat sitting in the garage, you wouldn't have—"

"They were your eyes, Libby." He lifted her chin and captured her gaze. "Your spirit sings through them." The gentle strength of his voice caressed her heart.

Dash's hand cupped her chin. "I will always know

you."

If only I could believe that, believe you! Libby swallowed the lump in her throat.

Standing, Dash gathered the dirty dishes.

Libby sat back. "That was delicious. You could be a chef."

Dash stopped at the entry to the kitchen area. "I doubt I'll ever need a job. We Prometheans are responsible for human behavior. When not working for Alexandros, I spend half my time trying to keep Simple Humans from wrecking the planet and the other half rescuing them from the fury of my ancestors, Gaea and Uranus."

"Sounds exhausting."

"Right now, I want to help you." He glanced at the kitchen. "Do you have anything to feed your company?" *Rats!* Libby pulled a credit card from her wallet. "Could you pick up chips and pretzels at the gas station on the corner?" *Five to ten minutes away, but still enough time to call Alexandros.* "Nonalcoholic beverage, too."

"While I'm gone, you should rest."

When Libby settled on the sofa with her tablet, Dash clapped a hand on her forehead. She looked up. "What are you doing?"

"Checking for fever. You're too willing to take it easy."

She laughed.

He leveled an index finger at her. "If I come back here, and you have changed or moved anything in this apartment, I will cancel Game Night, got it?"

"Got it." Libby lifted her chin. Dash's handsome face made it easy to believe he was descended from the gods. Of course, the Greek gods in myths did lie and cheat...a lot. Her heart ached. "Kiss me goodbye?" The request slipped out before she could stop it.

Dash stared at her. "What?"

"The other night...you said I should take the lead."

"I know, but..." Instead of leaning toward her, he pulled back. "If I kiss you, I won't leave. And I will chase your friends away." His fingers brushed her lips. "Tonight, after the games..." His words held the depth of a promise.

When he closed the door behind him, something shattered inside Libby.

After the games...

Chapter 29

When the doorbell rang, Libby drew a deep breath. *Let the games begin.*

Dash cocked his head. "Sure you're up to this?"

His tense jaw and clouded gaze chilled her. After tonight, he would never look at her with such concern. "As ready as I'll ever be." *Except for the twinges in my gut.* Libby placed a hand on her heart, which ached as if OASIS had already torn out a chunk. The sooner these agents did their job, the better. "Please let them in."

Moments later, a big bear of a guy wearing a backpack crushed her in a hug. "How ya doing, Libbers?"

Call me that again, and I'll fwow up on your shoes. Libby wrestled free. "Better."

"You were on the front page of our paper." A thin woman with long blonde hair clutched Libby's hands. Leaning in, she whispered, "Stay calm."

Libby pulled away. "Dash, this is Ivan and Flo." *For tonight at least.* "Dash is helping out for a few days."

"The more the merrier!" The big guy pulled game boxes from his backpack and set them on the coffee table.

"What's the quickest?" Dash pointed at a box. "Murder in the Mansion?"

The newcomers exchanged glances. "As good as any." Ivan eyed Libby. "I brought cards, too—if you want to try to win back what you lost last time."

Libby waved off the offer. "I'll pass."

"Where's your spirit of adventure?"

"I took a bullet two days ago. That's all the adventure I want."

Ivan snickered. "Tough cop."

Dash glared at the other man. "I take it you're not in law enforcement."

"Woodworking." Ivan pulled out a business card. "It's a knotty business, but someone's got to do it." His thick eyebrows wiggled.

Everyone groaned at the pun.

Dash stuck the card in a pocket without reading it.

Ivan turned toward Libby's window. "Nice bookcase, Libbers."

Libby fisted her hands behind her back.

"Let's get started." Dash carried the game to the dining room table.

Flo lifted a small cooler. "You know how Ivan likes his brew, Lib."

How many hours had she practiced that annoying giggle?

"Deed I do." The big man pulled two bottles from the cooler. "You into craft brew, Dash?"

Libby came to full alert. *What's in that bottle?*

"Dash likes Irish malt."

"That's my favorite, but I'm always happy to try something new." Dash took the offered bottle.

"You won't regret it." Ivan settled into a chair and opened the game. "My club sends a new variety every month." He opened his bottle and took a healthy swig.

Libby turned toward the kitchen. "You need glasses."

Dash rested a hand on her arm. "I'll get them…along with snacks. You and your friends can set up the game."

Libby slipped into her chair at the table. "Dash has been a terrific help."

Flo shot her a sidewise glance. "You're going to miss him."

You don't know—or care—how much.

"Here we go!" Dash dropped the bags on the table and juggled the glasses.

Libby offered a tight smile as she fisted the hands in her lap. *Why did I do this?*

Flo positioned the game board in the middle of the table. "Let's review the rules."

Libby winced. *First Rule. Protect our own.*

Doubts danced in Libby's mind. The OASIS agents weren't going to hurt anyone. They would fix her mistake. *I should never have told…but I didn't. He saw. He guessed. I should have lied. But he would have known.* Although Dash lounged in his chair and his mouth looked relaxed, his gaze made her want to squirm.

"Earth to Libbers!" Ivan interrupted her reverie. "Who do you want to be?"

"Ivan, do you really need to ask?" Flo's smirk was as annoying as her giggle. "Petunia Pennypacker." She offered Libby a bright pink token. "Isn't that right?"

"Yes."

The game went smoothly. Flo filled any lulls with anecdotes about "mutual" acquaintances. Every lie added a brick to the wall of second thoughts building in Libby's brain.

Dash played like the game really mattered. *They must have played this a lot in his family. If he knew the real game…* After the memory-wipe, what would he see when he looked at her? His deep voice lingered in her awareness. *"I will always know you." And I will never forget you.*

Ivan and Flo seemed blissfully engaged in trying to solve the grisly murder.

Dash leaned toward her and whispered, "I know you did it."

She gaped at him as if he'd torn off her clothes in Summerhaven Plaza. *I had to call. We protect our own.*

Dash sat forward. "Petunia Pennypacker with the carving knife in the greenhouse."

Oh! The game! Libby laughed and offered her hands for cheesy handcuffs. "Guilty." Flo and Ivan applauded.

When Ivan handed Dash another bottle, Libby said, "You might want to ease up on that." He wasn't showing any signs of a drug. Yet.

Dash waved off her warning and took a hearty drink. Ivan and Flo exchanged glances. *Something's wrong.*

Ivan gathered the game materials. "Want to go again?"

"Libby." Flo grabbed her upper arm, and her gaze ranged across the ceiling. "My sister wants to put an apartment over her garage, and I'd like to see a little more of this one."

"Not much to see. Bathroom and bedroom."

Flo's fingers dug deep enough to hurt. "I want to see the rest."

"I'll need my crutches." Flo released her.

"I can show you," Dash said.

"No." Libby stood. "I should move around." If worst came to worst, she might be able to whack the bitch with her crutches. Dash could deck the big guy and toss them both onto Lovegrove Lane.

"While the girls are home decorating—" Ivan pulled a sealed box of playing cards from his pocket. "—feel like a little poker?"

"Sure."

Libby drew in a quick breath. "Be careful."

Dash grinned at her. "I've played before." He looked too cocky. His glass was almost empty, but his voice was clear, his gaze looked sharp, and he moved with swift precision.

When Libby led the other woman into the bedroom, Flo shut the door behind her. "We have a problem."

Libby leaned on her crutches. Although delight with Dash's strength sang in her blood, she kept her tone neutral. "If the drug's not working, I guess you'll have to report this as a failed—"

"No. Now, it's your turn."

Libby blinked. "What?"

The OASIS agent sat on the bed and patted the spot beside her. "Sit, Ms. Anbruzzen."

Libby ignored the order. "Ever since I called you, I've had second thoughts. I'm sorry I wasted your time. You and your partner should leave."

The other woman's thin lips curled in a feral sneer. "Sit."

This time, Libby obeyed.

"You're not canceling a reservation at a restaurant. *You* created a problem, and you need to help us fix it." "I don't know how to mind-wipe."

The other woman lifted her hand. "You and the target have strong mutual attraction."

"He's not a—" *He's not a target. He's Dash.*

"Listen." In terse sentences, the OASIS agent

outlined the plan.

Horrifying images danced in Libby's head.

"Is that clear?" Libby nodded.

"Afterwards, you will use this." The other woman pulled a small package from her purse.

"Drug him." The words rasped against the roof of Libby's mouth.

"You're not going to harm him in any way. This is merely an anesthetic. When he wakes up, he won't even know it happened."

"But he will know something's missing." *I did.* "Be creative. He could have dreamed it all."

Libby glanced at the window where the "cat" escaped.

The agent pushed the drug equipment into Libby's hand and stood. "We will say good night and drive around until you let us know he's ready."

"No." Libby stood and grabbed her crutches. "I should never have called you. Dash made a promise, and he will keep it."

"I understand." The OASIS agent's expression was as cool as her voice. "He's a real hunk. Of course, you want to believe he won't expose you. He might have the best intentions, but there's always the possibility—the likelihood. Even if he's careful, he could let something slip at his workplace."

"Dash would never—"

"OASIS cannot take that chance. We protect our own."

"I know, but…"

"You've had a very stressful time, Elizabeth." The other woman got to her feet and inched toward Libby. Her crisp voice softened to a soothing murmur. "After everything you've been through, you must be exhausted." She caressed the bedspread. "Why don't you lie down for a minute and close your eyes?"

Libby lifted her chin. "No."

The other woman moved her hands in front of Libby. "Relax, Elizabeth. You are tired. So very tired. You've had a long, long day. You need to rest." *No, I don't. I slept well.*

"Take a few deep breaths. Close your eyes. Feel the tension leave your muscles. Lie down. Put your head on the pillow."

Libby covered her ears. "Stop it!"

"Let me take away your worries. Take away your pain."

Libby stiffened. "And my memories." Dash grinning at her cat. Nestling her on his shoulder. Stroking her fur. Gazing into her soul. *"I will always know you."*

She pointed at the other woman. "You'll take those away, too, and then what? You and your partner will gang up on Dash?" She scoffed. "Lots of luck." She thumped toward the bedroom door.

"Libby—"

The OASIS agent reached for her, but Libby wrenched open the door and hobbled toward the front room.

The other woman again tried to grab her.

Libby balanced on her strong side and swung her other crutch at her assailant, who landed on her rump with a thud. *One down.*

"What the—" The male agent's scowl replaced his fake happy-go-lucky demeanor.

"Get out!" Libby bellowed. "Both of you!"

Standing and rubbing her hip, the female agent

regarded her partner. "Ms. Anbruzzen has changed her mind."

The male agent dropped his playing cards and approached Libby. "You should know better than that."

When Dash left his seat and stood beside Libby, his strength surrounded her like a shield. "Libby told you to leave." He opened the apartment door. "Go!"

"Libby's been through so much." The female agent whined. "She needs sleep."

Dash scoffed. "For old friends, you don't know her very well, do you? I met her a few weeks ago, and I can tell this is not her tired face. This is the face of a royally pissed woman...and not merely a woman. An extraordinary Shapeshifter whose dragon could turn you both to toast."

Standing side by side, the agents froze.

"Get out. Now!" Dash's words rolled like thunder, and the shoulder seams of his shirt strained against his expanding muscles.

The unwanted visitors dove for the door and scurried down the steps.

Dash followed them down the stairs. Returning to the apartment, he opened the big front window and tossed the backpack and games into the street, where they landed in a satisfying jumble beneath the streetlight.

"Too bad I couldn't throw them out, too."

"I don't want to hurt them."

"Speak for yourself. I'd happily have pounded them into pulps."

"They were doing their—"

"—what you requested."

Avoiding Dash's accusing eyes, Libby put the top on the cooler. "Don't forget this."

"Leave it. The beer's good once you neutralize the drug." Dash touched his chest. "Immunities." He shut the window and turned toward the sofa.

Libby huddled on the far end. The corners of her mouth drooped, and tears glistened in her eyes. She looked miserable. *Good.* Instead of comforting her, Honeycutt strode to the dining room table and scooped up a small stack of bills. "Either your OASIS friend is a lousy poker player, or he was trying to sucker me along."

"He's not my friend. I've never seen either one of them before tonight. I hope I never see them again."

"Doesn't matter." He pocketed the currency. "I won." Clearing the table, he carried the glasses and trash into the kitchen area. The drinking glasses clinked in the stainless steel sink, and he smashed the trash into a wastebasket badly in need of emptying. *Leave it for her.* He left the kitchen and stood by the breakfast bar.

"I'm so sorry, Dash." Her near-whisper vibrated in his ear.

You should be. He cupped a hand behind one ear. "What?"

She drew a deep breath. "I said, 'I'm…sorry.'" She almost choked on the word.

"I thought you trusted me."

"I did. I do."

"You've got a strange way of showing it."

Libby straightened up. "I shouldn't have…" She looked at him, but he remained silent. "But watching Alexandros…and watching *you* watch Alexandros…I got upset. You looked so…enthralled. That's when I called OASIS. Later, when you came back to the room, being with you felt so good…so right. Especially when you explained why you pretended…I

240

started having second thoughts. But it was too late to cancel."

"You could have warned me."

"I should have. But OASIS works on Simple Humans, and you have so much more power… I thought if whatever they tried didn't work, they'd leave…and everything would go back…" She clasped her hands as if praying. "It's never going to be the way it was, is it?"

"I don't know." He leaned against the breakfast bar and crossed his arms. "Something that woman said really got to you."

"She *ordered* me…to have sex with you…and inject a drug that would knock you out so they could do their thing." Libby shook her head. "When I refused, she tried to mind-wipe me."

He scratched his jaw. "I didn't think OASIS did that to their own."

"Me either…until that night. One minute I was watching your car leave. Next thing, I'm waking up with this horrible headache, and the cat—"

"Your friend."

"Ellyn was gone. At first, I didn't know…I wasn't sure…on the job, date-rape drugs…"

Honeycutt drew back. "Did you think I—"

"No. Because we see it a lot, drugging was my first thought. But you've never lied to me, and I trust you. That night, I must have been too tired to fight the mindwipe. This time, I blocked the attempt because I didn't want to lose any of the memories of our time together. Even this." She sniffled. "You'd probably be happy to forget everything."

He sat beside her. "I wouldn't go that far. I'm surprised OASIS doesn't have more potent drugs for

Titans."

Libby's lips quivered. "They didn't know."

"Why didn't you…"

"We said we'd keep each other's secrets."

He took her hands. "And you did. No wonder they almost jumped out of their shirts." He kissed her fingertips. "As the largest portion of our supernatural population, Shapeshifters sometimes forget the rest of us exist. When OASIS organized, we nonshifters hoped it would take a major role in the larger supernatural community. But OASIS backed off. Like you, we keep a low profile in working with the humans, and we have to deal with our own differences from time to time."

"Do you have some sort of organization?"

"Supernatural Network—SUNATNET for short."

"Do you belong to this group, or do you work for them?"

Careful! "Titans were among the founders, but all Supernaturals—even Shapeshifters— automatically belong. I went to work for Alexandros because I wanted to find my sister, but the more I've learned about his organization, the more I've watched him." *And reported my observations*.

"So you're worried about Alexandros, too?"

"A campaign against Shapeshifters can easily expand to other Supernaturals."

"I wish you'd told me about this earlier. Before I called those…creeps." She covered her face with her hands.

"You called them." He leaned toward her and took her hands in his own. "But you also kicked them out. Efficiently, too. I half-expected you to clobber them with your crutches." Still holding her hands, he smiled at her.

"All I had to do was watch."

"You did more than that." She freed one hand and touched his shoulder. "I thought you were going to bust the ceiling."

"I didn't get anywhere near that big."

"Your shirt looked ready to split into pieces."

"Special elasticized fabric." He tugged at his collar, which spread. "Our tailor claims it can stretch up to five hundred times the normal size."

"Wow!"

"Nobody I know has ever fully tested it."

"I didn't scare the OASIS people off. You did."

"You took the lead."

"What if I hadn't?"

"I'd have pretended to forget…stuck around for another day or two."

"And now?"

The hope in her question stole into his ear. His fingers tingled as if they were holding her beating heart. The wrong word, the wrong move could crush her. "You came through."

"At the hotel…I liked being with you."

"I enjoyed it, too, although being so close was a taste of heaven and a full serving of hell. I'm not spending another night like that."

A tiny wrinkle formed between her eyebrows.

"You're going to sleep on the sofa?"

"This time with a pillow and a blanket."

Her fingers crept like blossoms down his arm. "I'll miss you."

He dropped a light kiss on her lower lip. "Put that pout away before it gets you in big trouble."

"You'd rather stay out here than be with me."

"Don't be ridiculous. I'd rather spend hours stroking and kissing every inch of your gorgeous body." The words made his cock stand at attention.

Libby's face glowed. "I'd like that, too." She glanced at the bulge in his trousers. "I wouldn't mind doing some exploring of my own."

"Maybe when you're fully recovered." *Before we say goodbye*. "Until then, follow your doctor's orders." His hands framed her Valentine-shaped face. "Shut up and kiss me."

Chapter 30

Libby almost ran into the huge Welcome Back, Libby! banner that sagged across the main aisle of the Special Ops unit. The greeting made her heart sing. On a nearby table sat a sheet cake adorned with strawberries arranged in the shape of a heart. The front desk must have alerted her fellow officers of her arrival because they were already standing. Applause filled the air.

Libby blinked away happy tears, and the emotions of the past few weeks landed on her shoulders like a heavy backpack. She surveyed her smiling colleagues. "You shouldn't have. I haven't been gone that long."

"You know us." Tweedledum Chad spoke up. "Any excuse for cake." He gave her a quick hug.

Robin rolled a chair behind her. "Shouldn't you sit down?"

Libby rested her hands on her hips. "I'm ready to work."

"You're a glutton for punishment." Robin's smile softened her tough words. "Especially since you have Honeycutt home health care."

Heat rose on Libby's cheeks, and she focused on the cake. "Dash has been a big help."

Robin leaned in close enough to whisper, "I'll bet!"

Libby faced the other woman, whose turquoise streaks were fading. "He's leaving tomorrow."

Captain Weatherby appeared. "Detective Maitland!

Good to see you. We need to talk." He didn't look happy, but his face wasn't red.

Before entering Weatherby's office, she dipped a finger in the vanilla icing. "Don't wait on me. Have at it!"

The captain shut the door behind her and gestured at the chair directly in front of his desk.

Uh-oh.

He settled behind his desk and rested his forearms on the blotter. "It's good to see you."

Libby reached into her shoulder bag. "Here's my doctor's report." She laid the sealed envelope on the desk.

He didn't touch it.

"Am I still assigned to O'Malley, or can I come back to Special Ops?"

The captain's mouth tightened. "Things aren't that simple."

Libby gripped the armrests. "Sir?"

"The commissioner has looked at homicides reported over the past few weeks." He ticked them off on his fingers. "The Pope homicide. The Caulfield's Ridge homicide. The attempt on Crispin Alexandros. These events have two common elements. A missing perp and—" He pointed at Libby. "—you."

She threw back her shoulders. "You sent me to the Pope crime scene, sir."

"I also ordered you to keep your distance from Crispin Alexandros. Yet you attended the Pope memorial service. As did Alexandros."

"I went to pay my respects." *Hope he hasn't heard about Nadine Victor.* "If I'd known Alexandros would be there, I'd have stayed away. After the service,

Alexandros wanted to meet me, and we exchanged greetings. Robin can attest to that."

The captain's demeanor remained solemn. "That same day, you showed up at a crime scene on Caulfield's Ridge."

"The scanner broadcasted a friend's address. I wanted to make sure she was safe." The captain moved a few papers.

That wasn't too bad. Libby prepared to stand but sat back when Captain Weatherby tapped his desktop.

"And then we have the incident at the mayor's house." The captain regarded her as if she were an alien invader. "What part of keeping your distance from Crispin Alexandros did you not understand?"

Libby studied the hands in her lap. He'd never believe she'd reacted to an intense dream, let alone that she'd wanted to protect someone. "I had to—something didn't sit right with me."

"So when the gun went off, there you were. Slamming Summerhaven's honored guest to the ground. Now, you did protect him. I'll give you that. But Alexandros has bodyguards. He didn't need you. And you had no business being there."

Captain Weatherby sat back as if waiting for an explanation, but Libby remained silent. "Finally, and most egregiously—" He opened a file. "—your conduct has put the department in legal jeopardy."

Libby lifted her chin. "I beg your pardon?"

"A woman in Odenton who saw your picture in TV news coverage is suing us for harassment." *Tina Patrick!*

"She claims you also harassed a sick friend and broke into that friend's house."

Libby opened her mouth, but the captain's gaze

froze her protest in her throat.

"The mayor was not happy about this. Nor was the commissioner. Their accumulated displeasure gathered momentum until it reached its destination." When he pointed at Libby, she flinched. "You are now buried beneath a pile of shit that reaches from here to Caulfield's Ridge." He leaned forward. "What the hell did you think you were doing?"

"I wanted to interview the woman who called
Schuyler Pope the night he was killed."

"You were off that case."

"I know, but after the homicide at Caulfield's Ridge, everybody seemed eager to move on. I didn't harass anyone. I asked some questions. I didn't break into anyone's house, either. The neighbor invited me in, and Dr. Victor keeps her house key under a rock." She met her captain's gaze. "I never said I was with the police."

"Let's be thankful for small favors." He shuffled a few papers. "When you started here, I had reservations." Libby frowned.

"You soon excelled. I thought you had a bright future. But after all this…"

Eyes on the rug, Libby tried to swallow the boulder in her throat. Captain Weatherby's anger passed like summer storms. His disappointment pierced like a polar vortex.

"Now I wonder if Mike spent more time keeping you on track than he let on. Internal Affairs will consider this." He held up the closed folder. "Until they clear you, you're on paid leave."

"But—"

"You know department policy. You may consult your union rep. But you might want to think twice about hiring a lawyer because they can tie these things into a bazillion knots, and no one comes away feeling any better."

Libby glanced toward the outer office, where her colleagues shared cake beneath the goofy banner. *They were so happy to see me. What will they think when they hear this?*

The captain stood. "The commissioner's trying to quash the harassment complaint, and word hasn't gotten out about the investigation. I'll tell the unit that although you want to return, after reviewing your doctor's note, I don't think you're ready."

Libby stood. "Thank you, sir."

"I need your—"

She ran her hand across the ridges of her badge.

"Badge and gun."

She felt as if she were surrendering a piece of her soul.

After forcing down a slice of the too-sweet cake and receiving encouragement from concerned colleagues, Libby hunched over her steering wheel in the parking lot. She couldn't stay here. She couldn't go home and face Dash. He'd planned a big evening. Dinner at the best restaurant in town. Then, dancing in clubs near the university. A celebration of her recovery and return to work. *Ruined.*

She rocked in her seat. *I can't go home, can't face Dash.* She started the car. *I need to get away.*

She drove to the outskirts of Summerhaven, where a big public park encircled most of the Veterans Administration hospital. After parking near the fitness trail, Libby peeled off her jacket, which she left on the backseat. She rolled up her shirtsleeves and stuffed her car keys into her pants pocket. Anxiety propelled her to the one-mile marker, but every thud of her foot seemed to link her more tightly to the Earth, to this god-awful mess. What had Captain Weatherby said? *"Buried beneath a pile of shit that reaches from here to Caulfield's Ridge." How true. I can't dig out. I can't run away. But I can shift.*

She hurried up one of the hills that ringed the trail. Near the entrance to the park and the medical facilities, they'd thinned the surrounding timber, but the farther she went, the deeper the woods became until she discovered the perfect secluded spot. She surveyed the sky. Birds enjoyed true freedom. She checked for intruders. Then, she stripped and left her stacked garments in a mesh of interlocked shrubs at the base of a big maple.

Closing her eyes, she visualized her favorite raptor. Moments later, spreading powerful wings, she left the Earth and her problems behind. Above the river, she relished the air currents that rushed above and beneath her wings, supporting and guiding, but not gripping. *I could fly away and never look back.*

When she rounded a curve of the river, a tall runner, golden hair glinting in the sun, came into view.

Oh, no! It's not. It can't be. She was so busy watching the man that the wind seized her and pushed her toward him. *So much for freedom.* With a flurry of her wings, she stayed aloft, but when she turned her head, his eyes met hers. Dash held out one arm as a perch.

Rejecting his offer, Libby mounted in the air. Higher, higher, as high as she could go!

Dash cupped his hands around his mouth and shouted, "Meet me at Phil's!" His deep voice rumbled in the air.

Libby followed the river and tried to regain her earlier exhilarating freedom. Fat chance. No matter how she tried to escape, the world pulled her back. *Not the world. Dash.*

A short time later, trapped in her human shape and wrapped in human clothes, Libby trudged toward the block building that occupied the flat piece of property across the road from the park entrance. She didn't pause to admire the drawings of ice cream treats on the big front window. The sooner she ended this, the better.

On the inside, Phil, a retired veteran, had done his best to re-create an old-fashioned ice cream parlor. Round, glass-topped tables were scattered across a black-and-white tile floor, and revolving stools upholstered in red leather sat along a Formica-topped counter. On weekday afternoons, business was slow. Chatting with Phil, Dash stood by the ice cream selections. Even in faded red running shorts and a sweaty gray T-shirt, he was sexy as hell.

Chapter 31

When Libby entered the ice cream place, Honeycutt's throat tightened. This morning, she'd been so excited about returning to work she lit up the room. Now she looked like her best friend had died. *Did she?*

"What would you like, mister?" The burly man behind the counter interrupted his musing.

"Small pistachio cone, please." Honeycutt regarded the grim detective. "Libby?" She shook her head.

Red lights flashed in his mind. *What's wrong?*

"Thanks, Phil." He paid the owner and joined Libby.

"Why did you want to meet here?" Brackets tightened the corners of her mouth, and she tucked her arms into her body as if trying to disappear.

"I wondered— Let's talk over there." He indicated a table in the far corner.

"I can't stay."

When she pushed the door open, he caught it. "Are you working?"

"No."

He followed her across the two-lane road onto the paved park path. "Libby. Wait."

She stopped, leaning forward with her shoulders slightly rounded, as warding off an attack.

"Did I interrupt…are you doing a surveillance?"

At this, she did smile. "No. Just flying."

He grinned. "Your hawk is amazing. How does it

252

feel?"

"Powerful. Free. Perfect for getting away." *Getting away? From what? From me?*

She pointed at the ice cream. "It's melting."

He took a big bite. "Sure you don't want some?"

"Maybe a little." She licked the drips and resumed walking.

"What's wrong? Bad news about your friend?"

Libby scoffed. "No. Wherever she is, Ellyn's fine." When he kept up with her, she stopped. "What are you doing so far out of town?"

"I might ask the same question. Why aren't you at work?"

Libby's back stiffened.

Duh! If only he could rewind his words. He tossed the remains of the ice cream into the shrubs and wiped his hands on his running shorts. Libby was ahead of him, but his long strides erased the distance. "Since you don't seem to have any problems moving, I'm guessing your body feels good, so something else must be wrong."

She eyed the cloudless sky. "It's a beautiful day. Could we walk for a while?"

"Sure." When he clasped her hand, her tense fingers relaxed.

For a time, they walked hand in hand, listening to woodpeckers and mockingbirds, watching squirrels and chipmunks. Finally, Libby spoke. "I thought it was going to be a great day." She described her colleagues' welcome. Then the enthusiasm drained from her voice.

As the details of her meeting with Jack Weatherby burned Honeycutt's ears, he ached to stomp into the office and shake her captain until his bones rattled. Too bad that wouldn't help.

"I'm at the bottom of the heap. The End."

"Maybe not." He eyed the glints of green in her dark eyes. "Since you weren't acting in an official capacity, the lawsuit against the department may not go forward. The neighbor could sue you, but you don't have enough money to make it worthwhile. And Internal Affairs—"

Libby stopped and faced him. "No matter what IA decides, I am dead. I've done everything Captain Weatherby says I did. I didn't follow orders, I guess I've been insubordinate. And I didn't think I was harassing anyone, but harassers seldom do."

"You also saved a life. That should count for something."

Libby waved toward the river. "Yesterday's news. Tomorrow, the mayor gets credit for removing a bad apple from the department. Voters love that." "It sucks."

"I agree. I had good intentions but screwed up. Majorly." She continued walking. "The worst part is that all I've ever wanted was to be a cop. I watched cop shows on TV. All the books I read from picture books to criminal justice textbooks involved police. Movies. Games. Even Halloween costumes." She stopped. "The day the commissioner pinned on my badge I knew that was where I was meant to be. Nothing in my life…not even shapeshifting…made me feel so right." She pressed one hand above her left breast.

No badge. Her pain was so intense he could almost touch it. He cupped her chin and lifted it so he could look deep in her eyes. "You're a good cop. You've made a few mistakes. That shouldn't outweigh your record."

"From your lips to the ears of Internal Affairs. But they'll hear what they want to hear…the higher-ups demanding my head on a pike."

"I will not let that happen."

For the first time that afternoon, a full smile blossomed. "Don't worry. They won't really cut off my head. They'll just trample my heart. But life goes on. Thanks for listening to me rant. I'm feeling better."

"Good." When she patted his shoulder, the warmth of her touch streamed straight to his heart. "I know you have friends here, but if you ever want to talk, don't hesitate to call me." *I love the sound of your voice.*

Although they walked in silence, with every curve, his mind churned with possibilities. Alexandros liked Libby. The mayor liked Alexandros. Maybe he would talk to the mayor about Libby. *Won't hurt to ask. I'll call while she's getting ready for dinner.*

When they reached the parking lot, Libby turned to him. "Did you walk all the way from my apartment?"

Dash laughed. "Bus."

"Do you want to ride home with me?"

"Yes. I should stop and pick up my new suit."

"About tonight." Libby leaned against her car. "I don't think you should waste your money on a fancy dinner. My work is a disaster, and tomorrow…you'll be gone."

Her words hung in the air like a spiderweb.

He patted his wallet. "First of all, it's not my money. I won it from that OASIS guy. Second, your recovery is worth celebrating. Third, it will be good for us to get out of the apartment tonight."

She nibbled on her lower lip. "I've never been to Riverden's." The trace of longing that crept into her voice suggested she was on the verge of yielding.

"Then it's time you went." Mirroring her posture, he

stood beside her. "Could you wear that dress you had on the day we met? The one with the flowers. And those strappy sandals? Show off your toenails."

"Too late for a pedicure."

He laughed. "No big deal. The first time I saw you, I wanted to know more about the sexy woman underneath that bulky work jacket."

The trace of a blush colored her cheeks, but she didn't look away.

He rested his hands on her shoulders. "For tonight, let's forget I even know Crispin Alexandros and you're a cop who hates his guts. Let's be two people who care about each other. How's that sound?"

Libby's fingers touched his cheek, and she must have stood on tiptoes. When her lips brushed his, tremors of desire cascaded from his head to his groin.

"Wonderful."

He captured her sweet mouth in a slow, sensuous kiss. *Wonderful, indeed.*

Chapter 32

Libby applied rose color to her lips. Stepping back, she assessed the figure in the full-length mirror on the back of the bedroom door. The pink wrap complimented the color of the flowers that splashed across the skirt. She did a little shimmy of delight. *When was the last time I felt this special? With Tommy, in the beginning? No.*

Even during their best times, she'd held back.

Dash was right. Dressing up for a night out lifted her spirits. *Especially when he talked about making the evening about us. More than like, but not quite love. Not yet. He leaves tomorrow. Maybe never.*

Still, he thought she looked sexy in the dress. *Even at that ghastly crime scene.*

She straightened the bedspread. The prospect of ending the evening in bed with him sent hot tremors up and down her torso. At the same time, a bell tolled in her brain. *Tomorrow…*

She faced her reflection. "It's not fair." Even as she protested, she could hear Dad singing that old song about getting what you need instead of what you want.

When she entered the main living area, Dash stashed his phone in his jacket pocket and smiled at her.

Libby twirled.

"You look great!"

Her cheeks heated. "Thanks." She clasped her hands and surveyed him from shoulders to polished loafers.

"So do you. Nice suit." He did a full turn.

She fingered the sleeve. "Is it that stretchy fabric?"

His deep laugh seemed to wrap around her. "Not on such short notice. Our tailor takes a few weeks."

"If you were wearing burlap sacks, you'd still be the best-looking man in town."

The twitch at the corners of his mouth suggested he was suppressing a smile. "I don't know about that. Some of those university guys look sharp. And let's face it. No way Riverden's would admit anyone in burlap sacks."

"You're probably right." Libby approached the sofa where clean underwear, socks, and shirt lay beside Dash's closed luggage. "You're all ready." Dash nodded.

"What time is your flight?"

"Two-thirty. I thought we'd have the morning together before you—"

"That's one good thing about my situation. Now I can take you to the airport." The words felt like a dull knife slicing into her heart.

Dash checked his watch. "We should get going."

She dangled her keys. "Want to drive?"

"Not tonight. I called Summerhaven Chauffeurs. So we don't need to worry about driving."

She sauntered up to him. "You think of everything." "I try."

When he touched the wrap on her shoulder, her blood simmered.

"Your dress looks nicer with this than it did with that jacket."

She pulled the wrap tighter, which brought his hand closer to her cheek. "The captain called me on a day off, and I'd already dressed. No time to change. I keep the jacket in the car for emergency use." She looked down at her toes. "Should have included sensible shoes."

"I don't know." Dash wrapped an arm around her shoulder. "I liked getting a glimpse of your wild side." Her ear tingled from his warm breath.

When his phone buzzed, he checked the screen. "Our driver awaits." He opened the apartment door and made a slight bow. "After you."

Minutes later, they arrived at an imposing building on the edge of the downtown theater district. The cutstone façade rose to Dash's height, and not even he could peer in the narrow rectangular windows that lined the front. He eyed the broad stone steps leading to the arched entrance. "This place looks more like a church or a museum than a restaurant. You sure this is right? They don't even have a sign."

Libby laughed. "They don't need one."

In the quiet reception area, Dash approached the maître d'. "Honeycutt. Reservation for two."

The lean, bald man moved to consult a computer screen built into his desktop but swung his gaze to Libby.

"Why you—you're Detective Maitland." Libby swallowed. Where was this going?

"I'm a great admirer of Crispin Alexandros. So is the owner." He pressed a button on the desk. Moments later, a gray-haired woman in a dark dress with scarlet accents appeared. After a quick whispered exchange with the man, she displayed a brilliant white smile. "Welcome to Riverden's, Detective Maitland. We are honored to serve you and your companion this evening. Please come this way." She led them through an elegant dining room with discreet alcoves, pristine table settings, comfortable-looking chairs, and soft lighting. In one corner, a small group of musicians played reflective music.

Libby clutched her purse. *We should split the bill.*

In the back of the dining room, the woman stopped.

Like the artwork on the other walls, the painting in front of them depicted a forest paradise.

The woman gestured at what looked like a hall near the end of the back wall. "This way, please."

Libby looked around. "Where are we going?"

"We'd like to seat you at the chef's table."

"We have a reservation."

The woman smiled at Libby. "The chef's table is the best seat in the house."

Libby looked from Dash to the woman. "I appreciate your…but I've never…I was looking forward to eating in the dining room."

"Whatever you wish, Detective. You may find the chef's table more private."

Libby lifted an eyebrow.

Dash's breath brushed her ear. "People are watching you."

Libby tightened her shoulder wrap. "No wonder. We marched through the whole place."

Dash addressed their guide. "Could we have a table for two near the back?"

"Of course." The woman's smile didn't waver. She surveyed the spacious room and led them to a corner spot with a view of the other diners. "Will this do?"

"It's perfect." Libby sank into the chair Dash held for her. "Thank you."

"Thank you for choosing Riverden's. May I recommend our eight-course tasting menu? An appropriate wine accompanies each course."

"Eight courses?" Libby eyed the woman. "Sounds like a lot of food." *And a ton of money. No wonder she recommends it.*

Dash leaned toward her. "I think a tasting menu means samples, not full courses." He regarded the woman in black. "Isn't that how it works?"

The woman beamed at Dash the way women always did. "It's a special order. Not a menu selection." She drew herself up. "And this evening, in tribute to your courage, Detective Maitland, you and your companion dine as Riverden's guests."

"Thanks," Libby whispered.

"Your server will be with you shortly."

As soon as the gray-haired woman left, Libby turned to Dash. "About being guests...does that mean what I think it does?"

Dash grinned. "Sometimes it pays to be a hero."

"But I'm not—"

"Excuse me." A well-dressed young woman with an artful array of platinum curls stood by Libby's shoulder.

"Aren't you the person who saved—"

Dash smiled at Libby. "She's the one."

The young woman pulled out her phone. "Could I get a selfie with you?"

Libby stared at the woman. "Well...sure."

It was the first of many interruptions throughout the long meal. Some diners stopped to shake her hand or speak. Most wanted selfies. Wherever Libby looked, another diner smiled or offered a small wave. "So much for our intimate dinner."

"Enjoy the attention. You've earned it."

"No, I didn't. And once stuff about the investigation leaks, they'll want to tar and feather me."

"All the more reason to eat, drink, and be merry." Dash lifted his wineglass in a salute. "The food is excellent."

"Wine, too." Libby sipped. *Good thing we're not driving.*

While they ate, she talked about growing up in Montana, and Dash shared stories about his family in Pennsylvania. When he cut a morsel of roast lamb, his big hands moved efficiently, with no wasted motion. *Strong but gentle.* Libby touched her cheek. Tonight, when they returned to the apartment, they might finally surrender to the emotions their lengthy kisses hinted at. How would those hands, those lips feel against her skin in the heat of passion? And what about tomorrow at the airport when they said goodbye?

"Earth to Libby."

She took a deep breath. "Sorry."

"If you're tired, we can leave early."

"Oh, no! Not till we have dessert." She gestured at the empty plate in front of her. "This is the best dinner I've ever had."

He took his final bite of the lamb. "Fanciest one I've ever had, that's for sure." He stretched. "Good thing we're near the end."

Libby clasped her hands in her lap. "Can I ask you a personal question?"

"That depends." Dash leaned toward her. "What do you want to know?"

"When we were dealing with…at Game Night…when you got angry, you got bigger."

"Happens sometimes."

She rubbed her hand against her knee. "Like when you get…excited?" She almost choked on the word.

The corners of Dash's lips tipped up, and his shoulders jiggled as if he was trying to prevent an explosion of laughter. "No one's ever complained."

Libby stared at the table. *If I could slink away....*

When her body started to contract, she sat up and eyed her amused companion. "I don't think...people...complain. They might move on. Or hope things improve." *Like with Tommy.*

"Paula!"

Libby gasped. Tommy's voice slammed against her ears as if thinking his name had made him materialize.

One of her ex's hands wrapped around the twiggy arm of a tiny brown-haired woman who smiled at Libby. "I knew it was you! I wanted to thank you for saving him." When she brought a small fist to her chest, it sank between generous breasts.

"You've made your point." Tommy grasped the woman's arm. "Hello, Libby. This is Paula Kingston."

As in Kingston, Inc. "Nice meeting you, Paula. Dash, this is Tommy Maxwell. Tommy, Dash Honeycutt."

The two men exchanged nods.

"Sorry for the interruption." Tommy tried to turn Paula. "Let these people get back to their dinner."

His companion pulled out her phone. "Could I get a selfie with you? Please!"

Tommy's jaw line hardened.

Something inside Libby shriveled. "Of course, you can." She shifted position and indicated a spot beside her. She smiled at the other woman.

Paula's lips had a slight tremor.

"You've got a great smile," Libby said.

The other woman brightened. "You think so?" "Sure

you do, babe." Tommy waved the phone.

"Got it." He grabbed his companion's hand. "Come on."

She continued to face Libby. "Thanks again. How are you feeling?"

"Paula…"

He never used that tone with me. But I had a gun.

"It's nice of you to ask, Paula." Although Libby spoke softly, Tommy avoided her gaze and stepped back. Libby turned to his date. "I'm much better."

"People on the news made it sound awful."

Tommy grabbed his date's arm. "You know how they exaggerate, babe."

Her red mouth twitched. "She's nice. I don't understand those nightmares." *Oh, no!*

Tommy sent a sidewise glance at Libby as if trying to peer beneath her skin.

See my human. Only my human.

"After we… things were crazy. I had trouble sleeping." Tommy rocked back on his heels. "The doctor gave me something that helped."

"Good."

Tommy turned his companion toward the center of the room.

Chapter 33

That Tommy character nearly dragged that cute brunette back to their table. The radiance of Libby's face dimmed. "I thought you'd never been here before." Honeycutt spoke in a quiet voice.

"I haven't." Libby focused on a vegetable course. "He said it was too expensive."

For you? Honeycutt took in the dark eyes, sweet mouth, and shapely body that housed a warrior's heart. Nothing was too good for Libby. "So, he's the one."

"I thought he was." Libby's chin dropped like a slicer cutting off further questions. She finished her serving like a dutiful child.

She didn't want to talk about him, but Tommy now occupied the middle of their table like a giant hippopotamus. If they didn't talk now, he'd waddle along when they left the restaurant and squeeze between them in the car. He could wreck the rest of the evening. *Our last night together. Thanks a lot, Tommy.*

With Libby's work problems and his leaving, didn't they have enough to deal with? *Might be better if we did back off.* Still, the curve of Libby's butterscotch-colored hair against her cheek, the soft swell of her breasts, and the alluring female scent beneath her perfume primed his cock for action.

"Why are you looking at me like that?" She straightened the top of her dress, which offered the barest suggestion of cleavage.

"Thinking about how pretty you look."

Her cheeks turned an enchanting pink. "Thanks."

He looked over her shoulder. "Our dessert approaches."

"None too soon." When the server set an elegant chocolate mousse in front of her, Libby pursed her lips.

"This is almost too beautiful to eat." *Almost. That's my girl. No. Not mine.*

Libby leaned toward him. "What's wrong?"

For a heartbeat, he considered lying. "I'm going to miss you."

She caught her breath. "I'm going to miss you, too. I'd like to stay in touch, but I don't know what I'll be doing. Part of me wants to stick around and fight, but another part thinks I should pack my bags and take the first flight out."

"If you do fight, I bet plenty of people in this town will back you up. Starting with half the patrons in this restaurant."

She gave them an indifferent scan. "Fair-weather fans."

"What about Dr. Crenshaw?"

Her spoon paused midway to her mouth.

"And not just because he thinks you're hot."

Libby's jaw dropped. "What?"

"I saw how he looks at you…how he hovers."

She pointed her mousse-laden spoon at him. "He was a good friend to my grandmother. His wife died six months ago."

"Maybe he doesn't know yet, but—forget it."

She leaned closer. "Are you jealous?"

"A little." He took another taste of dessert. "Mainly,

I wanted to remind you that you have friends in high places."

"I guess." She returned her full spoon to her bowl. "I'm sorry about tonight."

The pain in her voice pierced his heart like a piece of barbed wire. "What?"

Libby pushed her bowl toward the middle of the table. "You planned a wonderful evening, but I don't feel like dancing, and…" Her gaze strayed toward her ex's table.

Dash lifted the full dessert spoon to her mouth. "The food has been fantastic."

When she swallowed, she looked as if she'd tasted heaven.

"And the night's not over."

They dawdled over the delicious mousse and drained the final serving of wine.

"Will there be anything else?"

Libby smiled at their server. "No, thank you. It was a wonderful meal. Please send our compliments to the chef."

Honeycutt slipped most of the cash he'd won from OASIS Ivan under the edge of his plate.

The young server smiled at him. "It has been our pleasure to serve you."

During the short drive to Lovegrove Lane, they sat side by side without touching. He gave their driver the remains of his OASIS winnings. By the time he joined her, Libby was waiting by the stairs. He followed her into the apartment. "If you're tired—"

She spun to face him. "I thought that we—but if you don't want—"

"I do. But we should talk first."

She gave an uneasy laugh. "We've talked a lot."

"That Tommy—"

"Oh, him!" Her attempt to sound breezy landed with a thud.

"Something happened when he showed up."

Libby nibbled on her lower lip. "It's the first time I've seen him since we…."

"Having second thoughts?"

"Good Lord, no!" Libby plopped down on the sofa, and Honeycutt joined her. "I mean, he's a decent Simple Human. But…" She fidgeted.

When he took her hand, she didn't pull away.

Speaking slowly, she described the Dumire encounter. "Tommy watched me change to a pit viper as long as my human."

Honeycutt pursed his lips. "Intimidating."

"Deadly. After I…killed…Dumire, I shifted back to my human. When Tommy looked at me…tonight, I saw it again. Sweaty face, huge eyes, mouth all twisted and moving but nothing coming out—as if he wanted to scream but had forgotten how."

He drew her close. "It's over, Libby."

"For him, yes. But not for me. It was the first time I…I killed." She stared into space as if reliving the moment her fangs pierced Dumire's carotid artery.

He massaged the tension in her hands. "Look at me, Libby. You did what you had to do…what you were trained to do. Protect and defend. You saved an innocent victim as well as yourself."

She gave a half-hearted nod. "I don't think about it much. But when I saw Tommy, it all came rushing back."

"I understand." He kissed her hands. "I'm glad

you're not sorry you broke up."

Libby laughed. "I should have left the first time I tried to tell him about my shifting but couldn't. I kept believing someday I'd be able to. But someday never came." She rested her head on Honeycutt's shoulder. "When you found out I was a shifter, you simply accepted it."

He stroked her cheek. "What if I hadn't guessed?"

She turned and smiled into his eyes. "I would have told you. When the time was right."

He looked at the ceiling and groaned. "Sounds sort of like your Tommy story. You called OASIS on him, too."

"That was different. They cleaned up the mess, and mind-wiping Simple Humans is SOP—standard operating procedure. Once I knew you were more than Simple Human—"

"You still called."

Libby threw up her arms. "But I got rid of them, too. I was wrong. I've already apologized. Are you ever going to let me forget that?" He grinned.

"What's so funny?"

"You're cute when you're feisty. Your cheeks get all rosy, your eyes light up, and you look like you're ready to breathe fire."

She glared at him. "Don't tempt me."

His grin settled into a smile, and his fingers caressed the soft curve of her neck. "I like tempting you."

"One of these days, you could be sorry."

"I'll take my chances." When she lifted her chin, his mouth met hers in a long, sweet kiss. She tasted like wine and chocolate. He drew her into a warm embrace and loosened the wrap that covered her shoulders.

Her lips were inches from his ear. "What are you doing?"

He looked at her. "If you have to ask, I must be doing it wrong."

"Oh."

The word hit his erection like a pin in a balloon. A pinprick for sure. "If you're tired, we can call it a night." He dropped a kiss on the tip of her upturned nose.

"I'm not that tired." She rested a hand on his forearm. "While I was recovering, I thought about when we would…but now when I look at you, all I see is tomorrow."

He held her close. "It will hurt."

Libby's eyes stared deep into his soul. "If you and I… I haven't had much experience, so sex is a big deal to me. I thought I was in love with Tommy…until I wasn't. What I feel for you is different…deeper, but I don't know… Have you been with a lot of…females?"

"I haven't counted." Dash ran a hand through his hair. "The first time was high school."

"That young?"

"We were crazy about each other. Until she went off to college in California—the state—and I went to the University of California in Pennsylvania. We stayed in touch for a year, but after that…" He held out his hand with his palm up and opened his fingers. "Since then, I've been with a few…but nothing memorable. Except for the siren."

"A siren? Really?"

"Most gorgeous creature I've ever seen." He smiled. "With a song like a net that pulled me so close I'd have given her everything she wanted, including my soul.

Good thing my parents chose that moment to call me

home because of Christie and her wolf-man. They broke her spell. You don't ever want to see a disappointed siren." He shuddered. "I will take that image to my grave."

Libby's solemn gaze met his. "Must have been awful."

"Most of it was amazing, and I feel sorry for the siren. It's a horrible way to live. That was my big adventure." He brushed his hands. "And then, Julianna. You know about her."

"That's all?" She sounded surprised or maybe disappointed.

"I've never…with a Shapeshifter."

Libby hooked her arms around his neck. "Until now."

He drew back and regarded her lovely face. "You sure about this?"

Her gaze locked with his. "Yes. I'd rather regret what we did do than what we did not do."

His fingers hovered above her cheekbone. "For almost as long as I've known you, I've thought about how good we'd be together. When you weren't trying to nail me for Schuyler Pope's murder, that is." Libby grimaced.

"Right now, we both have uncertain futures." He rested his hands on her shoulders. "The one thing I know for sure is that I want to be with you. And more than tonight."

Libby swallowed. "Me, too, but—"

"Why don't we start there? We want to be together. We will be together…eventually. If you stay in Summerhaven, I'll join you once I've found my sister. If you decide to leave, I have a cabin on the edge of nowhere and a few acres of woods where you can shift when you get the urge. There are some towns nearby and a couple of cities about an hour away where you could probably find work."

"Sounds great." Libby tilted her head.

"This…cabin…did you and Julianna…?" "Nope. I bought it after we split up."

"Does it have the basic necessities?"

"It's comfortable—and big enough that when…if…we get to the point where we…there's plenty of room for pets or… What do you think?"

Chapter 34

Libby studied the solid jaw and clear gaze of this amazing man who wanted to share a life with her. "Yes!" She brought her mouth to his.

The kiss was a slow, sensuous promise of passion and commitment. Every movement of Dash's tongue in Libby's mouth raised her body temperature until she melted against his broad chest. His strong arms surrounded her. His touch was sure but easy as he found the zipper on the back of her dress and eased the garment to the floor, revealing her pale pink bra and matching bikini panties. When he toyed with her bra strap, she pulled off her sandals and pointed at him. "Your turn."

Smiling, he took off his shoes, then slipped out of his jacket and tossed it on the sofa. He started to pull off his tie, but she covered his hand. "Let me."

"I'm all yours." Dash let his arms hang at his sides. "Please don't tear the shirt in your haste to get me naked."

"You wish." Libby rested her palms on his chest. "I plan to go slow." She unbuttoned the top button. "So slow you'll wish I was doing shirt—" She freed the second button. "—and trousers." She slid the tip of her tongue across her upper lip.

Dash fiddled with his belt. "Do that again with your tongue, and I'll have to kiss you."

Another long kiss made her ache for more.

She opened the shirt and stroked the white T-shirt that covered his chest. "I bet you have dynamite pecs."

He grinned. "Wait till you see the abs."

"Don't tease me like that." Her hand slipped under the cotton shirt and played with his ribs. "Or I may lose control."

"Please do."

She lay the shirt beside his jacket. Then, she gestured at his T-shirt. "You'll have to take that off." Dash pulled off the T-shirt.

"Don't move." Studying every exposed inch from abs to deltoids, she circled him. "You look good with your clothes on." She stopped in front of him and rested her hands on his bare chest. "Spectacular with them off."

He held her at arm's length. "And you've got eyes a man can get lost in, a sweet, sassy mouth, and a body that won't quit."

Libby kissed his chin.

His lips brushed her temple. "You also know who you are but don't feel the need to broadcast it."

She avoided his earnest gaze. "After today, I'm not so sure about that."

He cuddled her. "We all have times when life doesn't go the way we thought it would. Some people get stuck there. But you're not 'some people.' You're Libby—Elizabeth Maitland."

Libby drew back. "Actually, I'm not."

"What?" He looked at her as if she'd crawled out of a hole.

"When I joined the force, I decided to use my grandmother's maiden name. To keep my family safe. My real name is Elizabeth Irene Anbruzzen."

Dash extended a hand. "Pleased to meet you, Ms.

Anbruzzen." When Libby took his hand, he drew her close and kissed her again.

She rested one cheek against his chest. "You feel good. Warm and solid."

"Protection is a primary Titan duty."

She looked up at him. "Knowing you're here makes me feel safer."

While he unhooked her bra, she undid his belt and slipped one hand inside his trousers.

Dash regarded her with a lazy smile. "That feels better than good."

"Just wait." She winked at him. With one hand, she unbuttoned the slacks. Her other hand eased down along the inside of the zipper. "It's a tight squeeze, so I want to be... You are a handful." One by one, her fingers gripped him, and Dash caught his breath.

When her hand relaxed, he groaned.

"Lose the pants."

With a chuckle, Dash stepped out of his trousers and placed them with his other clothes. "Before we go any further, what about birth control?"

"No problem." Libby smiled. "I'm on the—" She slapped her forehead. "I take my pill before breakfast, but I missed the morning after the shooting. I took it that evening when I got home. Since then, I'm back on schedule. Should be good."

Dash retrieved a small package from the inner pocket of his jacket. "Better be on the safe side?"

Her shoulders relaxed. "I suppose."

Dash faced her. "Now, where were we?"

"En route to the bedroom."

A wicked smile played on Dash's mouth. He patted one of her butt cheeks. "You have a gorgeous ass." The pats became slow circles that made her want to melt into his arms.

"Keep that up, and we'll end up doing it here on the rug."

With a laugh, he scooped her up and carried her down the short hallway. He sat on the edge of the bed while she straddled him. He buried his hands in her hair. Her tongue traced the contours of his mouth before a searing kiss left them both breathless.

Libby rubbed her silk-covered center against his cock. "You feel good."

A long finger probed inside her panty leg. "So do you."

Shivers of desire rippled through her. When he moved deeper, she tightened around him.

"And already wet."

His tongue teased her earlobe. In her next breath, he rolled her onto the bed and stripped away the dangling bra and the scanty panties. He turned on the overhead light.

Warmed by the glow in his eyes, Libby lay back.

Dash's long fingers trailed a path from the swell of her breast to the curve of her hip. With every stroke, his power hummed against her skin. "I've seen you as an almost-cheetah, an adorable kitten, and a fierce hawk, and I guess you've been other creatures, including your inquisitive rat. Yet your human body shows no trace of all that shifting. Amazing!"

Libby smiled. "Once, my tiger got nicked by barbed wire." She opened her left leg and pointed to a pale scar on her inner thigh.

"Ouch!" When Dash leaned over her extended leg, his gentle kiss on the soft skin intensified the fire in her belly. As if he tasted the heat, he returned to sitting and drew her close for another round of long, bone-melting kisses that ended in a sweaty tangle of arms and legs.

Dash's long body enveloped her. When his erection poked her, she looked from his cock to his face. "What happened to your shorts? How'd you get them off?"

He flashed a roguish smile, and his breath teased her ear. "Magic!" He waved a hand as if casting a spell.

Libby swatted him on the shoulder. "Titans can't do magic."

"You sure of that?"

Libby swallowed. "Maybe not." Enchantment was certainly a better reason for what was happening than… *Is this how falling in love really feels?* She lay back on the pillows.

Dash propped himself up on one elbow. His fingertips traced a circle around the fullest part of one breast. Tiny kisses fluttered from her earlobe to the curve of her neck.

"Nice."

The circles became smaller and slower as he neared the nipple. He licked the stiff nub.

Libby gasped and offered her other breast.

Dash chuckled and began a second round of circles. "You liked that?"

She stroked the hairs on his chest. "I like everything you do. The more you do, the more I want. And the more I want to make you feel good, too." She kissed the plane between his nipples and rested her ear against his chest. His heartbeat thundered in her ear.

Dash moved down and nuzzled the hollow between her breasts. His kisses seared a trail down her torso to her stomach.

Thank God for all those crunches at the gym!
When he neared her navel, Libby giggled.
Dash lifted his head and looked at her.
"Ticklish."
"Now you tell me. What about this?" His tongue teased her navel.

She threw back her head and laughed. "Still tickles!"
Dash grinned. "Will this get worse the lower I go?" He stroked her inner thigh.

Libby caught her breath as ripples of pleasure radiated across her skin. "No."

"That's more like it." Dash touched his lip. "Maybe it's my mouth…and…" He stuck out his tongue. "One way to tell." He shifted position, and a trail of small kisses sent another wave of heat to her throbbing center. He looked up at her. "You're not laughing."

Libby tried to swallow the breath trapped in her throat. "I want you."

"Not yet." Wherever his fingers moved, they set off sparks beneath her skin. "You have such solid muscles, but you're soft in all the right places. A beautiful combination of silk and steel." He kissed her thigh, and she whimpered.

When he began a leisurely exploration of the territory between her legs, Libby melted against her pillow, and the tingles fused into a current that heightened the longing in her core. Every caress and kiss sent fresh waves of desire, slow at first but building in strength and frequency until she felt as if she were surfing a tsunami.

When Dash entered her, she pulled him closer as if she could draw him inside her. Their coupling renewed the passion in every cell in her body. Her muscles quivered in accordion-like spasms—tightening and releasing with every breath. Her heartbeat battered her ribs. She and Dash were bound together in flesh and spirit racing, racing, racing... Dash's arms held her fast.

Her inner storm subsided, and she sank back into the mattress as Dash collapsed on top of her. A slight move took the pressure off her wound site. "That was amazing." She stroked her lover's sweat-drenched hair.

Dash propped himself up on one elbow and eased to the side of her without breaking their physical contact. "You think?"

She smiled up at him. "Best orgasm I ever had. Maybe the best in human history!"

"Yeah, but..." One of Dash's eyebrows quirked. "You sort of...exploded."

Libby blinked. "I was right here. With you." She wrapped her arms around him. "You felt so good. The perfect fit."

He kissed her forehead and stroked her hair. "I could feel you with me, around me. It was like getting sucked into a tornado."

Libby drew in a breath. "Sounds dangerous."

"Not at all." Dash scratched his chin. "It was incredibly exciting."

She framed his face with her hands. "You sure you're all right?"

His laughter seemed to rise from deep within him. "Absolutely. At first, I was surprised. But when I went with the flow, so to speak, everything was...what was the word you used? Amazing?" He gave an emphatic nod and kissed her.

When they paused to breathe, Libby murmured, "As good as the siren?"

"Way better." He stroked her cheek. "And you weren't trying to steal my soul."

Libby's gaze roamed slowly over the broad planes of his handsome face. "I might have changed state."

Dash nearly sat up. "What?"

She kissed the corners of his eyes. "My sisters and I each have something unusual about our shifting ability. I can change from solid to liquid…in theory, even gas. Although I've never tried to become a gas, you wouldn't believe all the jokes Steffi and Day made about it."

Dash's laughter shook the bed. "Oh, yes, I would! Nothing potentially gross escaped my siblings." He eyed her with respect. "So you can become a blizzard or a hurricane or—"

"Changing state is risky. The first time, I was inside watching snow fall through a window and thinking about how soft and beautiful it looked. Next thing I knew, I was snow…inside the house. Fortunately, Dad was there. He called me back to my human before I melted into the carpet. He thinks I should avoid state shifts unless I'm in a controlled environment. Otherwise, pieces of me might be blown away or absorbed, and I would cease to exist."

"Definitely not a good option. What happened with us…you were you, but you were also…your passion touched every inch of me. I can still feel that connection."

Libby kissed the soft stubble on his chin. "Me, too."

"I should clean up." With a grunt, he left the bed and headed toward the bathroom with the used condom.

Libby sat up. "Do you have more of those?" She crossed her fingers.

Dash paused in the doorway. "Enough to last till morning."

Moments later, when Dash returned to the bed, his arm around her shoulders brought them together skin to skin from hip to heel. He nuzzled her neck and triggered a fresh shimmer of longing in her core.

Libby stroked the blond hairs that covered Dash's belly until she reached his stiff cock. "You're ready so soon?"

"What can I say?" Dash fondled her breasts. "You're a hot shifter, and I'm a horny Titan."

Chapter 35

Bodies entwined, they lay on a bed of rosebuds, violets, and buttercups. The rays of the rising sun caressed the subtle bend of Libby's waist and the curve of her hip, soft and warm beneath his hand. When the hint of a cloud appeared on Libby's torso, Honeycutt tried to brush it off.

"Dash! Dash!" Her cries echoed in his mind. "Dash, wake up!" The dream shattered. With a groan, he squinted at the woman shaking his shoulder. Clad in a short, silky robe with a knotted tie, Libby waved her phone as if she might clobber him with it. "Did you tell Alexandros I got fired?"

Rubbing his eyes, he sat up. "I said you were having problems with the department." He scratched his chin. "Asked if he might put in a few good words for you with the mayor."

She put the phone on the nightstand. "He offered me a job."

Alarms beeping in his brain, Honeycutt sat straighter. When Libby joined him on the bed, the sexy cleavage exposed by the gaping robe made concentration almost impossible.

"He said he's always looking for good security staff."

"True." *But is it right for you?* "What did you tell him?"

"That I appreciated the offer but need to think about it. I'd have to give notice, too, although if I quit, the department will save money. I also reminded him that I don't agree with his ideas."

"Good for you. How did he respond?"

"With one of his big ho-hos." The corners of her pretty mouth turned down. "That man has ruined Santa Claus for me. He said he shared Lyndon Johnson's philosophy about having people who disagree with him inside the tent pissing out—he apologized for the language, made sure I knew he was quoting Johnson— anyway, better inside pissing out than outside pissing in. Of course, that image doesn't work for women."

Honeycutt chuckled and eased the growing tension in his groin by adjusting his position.

"He tried to impress me by talking about his converts." When she tilted her head, her gaze hit him right between the eyes "You're his prime example."

"What did you say?"

"Nothing. I'm not going to blow your cover."

"Thanks."

She paced the room. "My parents might think working for Alexandros isn't as dangerous as police work. Good starting salary, but he didn't say anything about raises or promotions."

"No union. Everything depends on Alexandros."

"Decent benefits and my favorite fringe benefit." Facing him, she linked her arms at his nape.

He placed a hand on her silky hip. "As much as I'd like having you near, I don't think you should base your decision on that." When he nuzzled her neck, her breath tickled his ear.

"Once you find your sister, we can both leave. So

Zanna Archer

what's the problem?"

"New recruits have a six-month probationary period when they all live in a dormitory to build a sense of community and weed out misfits."

Libby's husky laugh stroked his ear. "So for the first six months, we can only spend weekends together."

"A lot will depend on our schedules."

"We'll work it out." She toyed with the stubble on his chin. Then, she rained kisses on his chest and wiggled her hips against him until he thought he might explode. "Getting hot in here." Reaching between them, she unknotted the tie on her robe and opened the flaps. The tips of her breasts grazed his chest, and her belly melted into his. "Much better. Don't you think?"

He opened his mouth to agree, but Libby's fingers meandered to his erection. "Your plane doesn't leave until this afternoon, so we have plenty of time for a prebreakfast appetizer."

He kissed her while her laughter bubbled in his throat.

****

After lunch, as Libby drove toward the airport, Dash talked more about working conditions at the Alexandros Compound. "They'll issue you a phone. Don't use it for personal calls and leave it in your car when you're offCompound. Get in the habit of checking your car for tracking devices whenever you take it out. Alexandros likes being able to contact employees in case of emergency."

"How can you live like that?"

"Like you said, the money and benefits are good.

The actual work itself isn't hard. Many of the employees are true believers who happily satisfy his demands." "I'll have to bite my tongue until it looks like beef jerky."

"I won't let that happen." He gave a warning glance. "No shapeshifting in the Compound."

"No kidding?" Her wide eyes and the exaggerated "oh" of her lips communicated her scorn. "Once I learn how the surveillance system operates—"

"Libby, please don't—"

"What kind of idiot do you think I am?" She pulled into a parking space and turned off the car.

"I don't think you're an idiot, but I know you like a challenge. Are you sure about this? The idea of you being so close to Alexandros is creepy."

"I know. But I'm excited about being with you." When she touched his cheek, he kissed her hand and then found her waiting lips.

The gentle kiss began to deepen, but Dash pulled away. "I have a plane to catch."

"Right. Let's get you checked in, and then…but it won't be goodbye, will it? In a few weeks, we'll be together again."

Libby's sunburst smile struck the shadows in his awareness. Although she seemed committed to being with him, she also had a life in Summerhaven. Once he was gone, she might reconsider.

When they finally stood by the airport security gates, the animation left her features and her voice died.

She hugged him. "Call me when you land." After one last kiss, he entered the line.

Libby waited at the airport until they announced the final boarding call for Dash's plane. As she walked toward her car, a departing jet zoomed above her. Even

though no one could see her and it probably wasn't even
  Zanna Archer

Dash's flight, she waved. When she unlocked the car, she sat in the passenger seat, closed her eyes, and rested one cheek against upholstery that still carried Dash's scent. For a few minutes, he was with her. Then she opened her eyes and sat up. She got behind the wheel. "Soon we'll be together."

****

The next few weeks passed in a storm of activity, punctuated by nightly video chats that ended with Libby snuggling an empty pillow. After accepting the Alexandros offer, she handed in her notice and scoured Summerhaven PD and her other local contacts to find a sublet for her apartment. She packed essentials to take in her car to Dash's cabin and rented a truck that hauled the remainder to a small unit at Summerhaven Storage.

Before the farewell luncheon thrown by her fellow officers, she called her family. Mom and Dad's relief that she was no longer on the force tempered their concern about her new job. Dayzee had no reservations. "You and Studmuffin? Way to go, girl!"

Steffi was less exuberant. "Have you lost your mind?"

Libby laughed. "Don't worry, Steff. If necessary, I can always shift and fly away."

"Are you that hot for Honeycutt? Is that why you're leaving a perfectly decent job?"

"Dash and I…but…" Libby swallowed the bitter lump in her throat. "I've had major problems at work." As she presented her situation, the lines on Steffi's face softened.

"I'm sorry, Lib. I know how much you care about your work and how good you are at it."

"Not good enough. I was going to wait…see how the investigation went, but then Alexandros made the offer. It's a solid job, and Dash and I can find out if we have what it takes to stay together."

Steffi smiled. "Interesting. Tommy's wanting to settle down made you nervous. But with—"

"Dash isn't like Tommy."

"He's Simple Human. Be careful."

"I will." Keeping secrets from Steffi felt strange. "I need to talk to Sawyer because I wondered if OASIS still needs an agent at the Alexandros Compound. Since I'll be there—"

Steffi's chin came up. "Don't even think of it.

Simply being around Alexandros is dangerous enough." "That's why OASIS needs eyes in the Compound. The more they know about what he's doing, the more they can plan a defense or a counterattack."

"I wish you weren't so conscientious." Steffi gave her a frustrated, big-sister eye. "You have the OASIS number. Why don't you call them?"

Knew you'd ask. Libby took a deep breath. *Keep voice and expression steady*. "You know how much they hate dealing with us Anomalies." *Especially when we kick them out*. "If Sawyer could talk with his uncle…"

"I'll pass your request along. But I hope you'll reconsider."

"Don't worry, Steff. I'm—" *I was a cop*. Admitting her failure stung. "I know how to protect myself." *And I have a Titan backup.*

Chapter 36

Libby stretched and rolled over. "This bed is so big I could get lost on it."

"Never fear." Dash moved to face her. "I will always find you." His kiss seemed to massage each of her postorgasmic muscles.

"I missed you."

"Missed you, too."

"Ha!" She pulled back slightly. "You were hanging out at New Orleans hot spots."

"Cut me some slack, darling."

The smooth strokes of his hand on her hip almost erased her scorn.

"I went out with the guys to keep them from teasing me about you. I'd have enjoyed it more if you'd been there."

"Nice save." She kissed his chin. "I was stuck here with the sacred Alexandros manual." She rolled a shoulder. "Damn thing's so thick it could be carved from stone."

"I saw your test scores posted in the main office. Straight As."

She pushed down the small swell of pride. "I don't care about that."

"Says someone who saved her police academy scrapbooks." He held her closer. "And you went into Osborne with some of the other recruits."

"I was trying to get to know them better." She scoffed. "Osborne is no New Orleans. It shuts down at nine." She flopped onto her back. "I didn't realize how much you'd be gone."

"I told you—"

"About Florida and New Orleans." She slapped his shoulder, but when sculpted muscles warmed beneath her touch, she kissed them. "But then you headed for Texas."

"Schedule change. Not my department." He nuzzled her neck.

Sparks of desire shimmered down Libby's spine. "Someone may want to keep us apart."

"Get real." He nibbled on one of her earlobes. "The travel schedule has nothing to do with us and everything to do with what Alexandros wants. I'm sorry I haven't been here much. After California, I won't travel again until March."

Libby snuggled against his broad chest. "I wish we could stay like this forever. But I go back to work in two days."

Dash cradled Libby's head in his hands. "Let's make the most of the time we have." His lips and fingers reawakened the desire in Libby's core.

****

After the other members of the travel team left the meeting room in the Compound headquarters, Honeycutt helped Julianna clear the long table and carry her presentation materials to her office.

"Alaska!" She clasped her manicured hands. "You guys have all the luck."

He stacked the boxes on the chair beside her desk.

"Any chance you can adjust our departure

schedule?"
Zanna Archer

"You have a lot of territory to cover."

"I know, but Harry's wife is due when we're supposed to leave. It's their first kid. He should be here to welcome it."

Julianna smiled at him like a teacher dealing with a difficult student. "Find a replacement."

"No." He wanted to thump a fist on her desk. "My team has been doing this job for so long that we don't need as much prepping time as you schedule."

Julianna tilted her head. "You sure this is all about Harry Kramer? Is Recruit Maitland—"

His face heated. "This has nothing to do with Libby. She understands the demands of my job. And by spring, she'll have a full-time assignment here at the Compound." When Julianna didn't return his smile, anxiety coiled like a snake in his gut. *Does she know something I don't?*

"She is an outstanding recruit in many ways."

The last time Julianna used that cool, measured voice, she was listing her reasons for breaking up with him. "But?"

Julianna looked down at her neat desk. "She has completed assignments with distinction. But she has not established good relationships with her fellow recruits, the very people she may lead."

"She's trying."

"She should try harder. More social activity might keep her from wandering around the Compound on her own."

"She's an investigator at heart. Naturally curious."

Julianna studied her manicure. "You should talk to her."

Me? "As The Boss's assistant, you—"

Julianna straightened the already organized folders on her desk. "She looks at me as if she'd like to boil me in oil. You didn't..." He shrugged.

"That was stupid, Dash."

He ran a hand through his hair. "I never thought she'd be here."

"Well, she is, and we'll manage. Her academic performance is outstanding. But her social interaction is minimal, and as you know, we don't tolerate troublemakers." Julianna pointed at him. "Tell her. The sooner, the better."

Chapter 37

Honeycutt stood on the cabin porch and checked his watch. *She'll be here soon. It's been so long. But then...* His smile faded. *We'll have to talk.*

When Libby's hybrid made a silent stop beside his truck, the sky looked bluer, the autumn leaves, more brilliant, and the air smelled sweeter. A radiant Libby bounced from her car. "Four days!" Stretching out her arms, she spun.

Like Christie and Kinsey on Christmas morning. He bounded down the steps.

Libby threw herself into his arms. "I love this place!"

And I love... Would she feel the same after... *Better get work out of the way.* But when he opened his mouth, she lifted her chin and presented her lips. As the soft kiss and gentle embrace grew longer and more demanding, rising passion buried Julianna's "Tell her." *Not yet.*

Shedding garments, they kissed their way up the steps, into the cabin, through the big front room, and onto the bed. A shared language of moans, sighs, gestures, and laughter communicated desires more clearly than words. *I want this.* Swollen with pleasure, he buried himself in Libby's beautiful body, every inch more welcoming and wonderful than the time before. *I want you.* Spent, they lay entwined in the middle of the bed.

Now. Libby's steady breath warmed his chest.

Always.

Libby lifted her head, and her fingers rubbed the corners of his mouth. "Why so tense?"

"Nothing I want to talk about right now." Forcing a smile, he kissed her fingers.

She started to pull away.

He wrapped his legs more tightly around her. "Dash!"

A long, slow kiss. *Four days!*

A dreamy smile lingered on her face. "I should get my bag."

"No rush." He kissed the delectable curve of her neck.

She pecked at his chin. "I'll be right back."

"Don't go."

She pulled her legs free and met his gaze. "You sound so serious. What's wrong?"

Jack Weatherby said you were stubborn. What an understatement! "Nothing, really." He rolled out of bed and grabbed his socks. "Let's put some clothes on. Then we can talk."

Uncomfortable silence followed as they returned to the front room, recovered their cast-off garments, and dressed more slowly than they'd undressed. Libby chose the big easy chair on one side of the empty fireplace. With her back straight and her hands clasped in her lap, she sat near the edge of the seat with both feet planted on the hardwood floor.

Her wary gaze made him want to hold her close and tell her all that mattered was being together. Instead, he chose the chair opposite hers.

"Well?" Her question shattered the stillness.

"Last week, I was talking with Julianna."

When he uttered the name, Libby tilted her chin. "Strictly business."

Libby's shoulders relaxed, but her eyes narrowed.

He summarized Julianna's concerns. "I don't know what you're doing on these walks, but if you keep poking around, you could be fired."

"If I'm going to work on the Compound, I should know how it fits together. I've tried to be inconspicuous."

As if someone who looked like a breath of springtime could ever be ignored! Dash studied the wooden floor. "You know what's off limits."

"I haven't approached the research labs."

"Smart. What about the Research Quarter?"

"I avoid it, too." She nibbled on her lower lip. "But once…I needed a bathroom. So I stopped at that little coffee shop." "MacMurray's." She nodded.

"It's in the Research Quarter."

"It's on the outer edge of the Quarter." She wiggled. "And I was in a hurry."

"So you used the facilities. What then?"

She rubbed her hands together. "It seemed only fair I should buy something. So I ordered coffee and a cinnamon scone."

"Takeout or eat there?" She drew a deep breath.

"Libby…"

"The place was empty, so I sat down by the front window. I was almost finished when a man came in for coffee and sat at the table next to mine. He wore a research lab ID." She scrunched her eyes shut for a breath. "Ray…no, Ralph…Ralph Jones."

"A researcher."

"We chatted."

"About what?"

"Not his work." She gripped her elbows and leaned forward. "This is just between us, right? You won't report me?"

"No. But I should know in case someone else does. What did you talk about?"

"Schuyler Pope." The name emerged in a whisper, and she held up both hands as if she feared he would pounce on her. "He asked where I was from. When I said, 'Summerhaven,' he started telling me how surprised everyone was about… That was it."

"Have you seen him again?"

She drew herself up as if he'd smacked her. "Of course not."

"And you won't see him again because you will not enter MacMurray's again…or any other facility in the Quarter."

"Not while I'm probationary."

"Even after—it doesn't matter." Standing, he loomed over her but then drew back and smiled. "Once you have an assignment, you'll be too busy to explore."

"I still need to learn as much as I can about what goes on at the Compound."

"No, sweetheart." He patted her shoulder. "Alexandros decides what you need to know. Nothing less. And nothing more."

She drew a deep breath. "I'm not here for myself alone."

"What do you mean?"

"I'm…with OASIS."

Honeycutt clapped his hand to his forehead and swore so loudly the windows rattled. "Do you know—do you have any idea—no, of course you don't because you didn't bother to talk to me before you... You jumped right in without thinking about how your actions could affect anybody else."

"But—"

"No buts. Listen to me, Libby, and, for once, pay attention." He stepped back. "Alexandros thinks I'm here because I want to find my sister."

Libby tilted her head so her chin tipped up. "You're not?"

"I am, but my search for Christie also provides a great cover story."

"You're with SUNATNET!" Libby leaped out of her chair and squeezed his hands so hard he cringed. "That's great! We're a team! Whatever I find out, I'll share with you, and whatever you find out—"

He pulled away. "No."

"What?"

"No." He leaned against the mantel. He felt more exhausted than he had at the end of his first triathlon.

"I don't understand." Her words cracked as if something inside her was disintegrating.

"I'm sorry." He circled the room as he spoke. "This could be bigger than you or me, Libby. Much bigger. Today, Alexandros threatens Shapeshifters. Tomorrow, he could threaten all Supernaturals. Since I've worked here, I've established myself as trustworthy. I haven't learned anything useful until recently. Something new is in the works. Something big. At his rallies and in his broadcasts, Alexandros delivers his standard antishifter message, but he's been spending less time with his researchers, and I think some of his top-level people have left."

"How exciting!" Libby beamed like a demented

angel. "Together—"

"I can't risk working with you. People at the Compound have already noticed you bending the rules. That full-steam-ahead, find-the-truth-no-matter-what attitude—I know it's a big part of who you are, and it's one of the things I love about you." The word slipped out. Maybe Libby wouldn't notice. "But that attitude also got you into trouble in Summerhaven, and it could get you fired here. If you go down, I don't want to go with you." He held out his phone. "Call OASIS and tell them you're out. Then, buckle down and follow the rules."

Libby stared at the phone. "I can't."

"Sure you can."

"You don't understand. Now that Schuyler Pope…"

Honeycutt frowned. "What does he have to do with this?"

"He was spying for OASIS. I'm his replacement."

No! The memory of that mangled body froze his heart. "You need to leave. Now."

"But—"

He grabbed her hands. "If Pope was working for OASIS, then you were right all along. It must have been Alexandros." Releasing her, he circled the room until he faced her again. "At the crime scene, you also said the killer was sending a message." He placed his hands on her shoulders. "You were right about that, too. But the message wasn't to Alexandros. It was from Alexandros to OASIS: This is what happens to your agents. If he discovers…or even suspects… Libby, you're in danger. You must go. Now."

"Dash, relax." Instead of reflecting the horror that gnawed at his soul, Libby offered a faint smile. "Schuyler Pope was smart and cautious. But he was also a civilian." She tapped her chest. "I know how to protect myself. And I thought I could rely on you."

"Always." He put an arm across her shoulders and tried to draw her close.

She pulled away. "Then why don't you trust me?"

"Libby, be reasonable. You saw what the killer—"

"I have a job to do, and I intend to do it, especially if something big is in the works." When Libby locked her jaws, the tip of her chin looked less like the point of a Valentine and more like a small spear aimed at his heart. She threw back her shoulders. "I'm going to find out as much as I can."

"Libby, please—"

"I trusted you, Dash. I admired you. I want to work with you, but you don't..." She started to leave but turned back. "I'll stay out of your way." When she pointed at him, the tip of her index finger struck him like a knife. "You stay out of mine."

The slam that closed the solid front door rattled his bones. Honeycutt sank onto the long wooden bench beside the dining table and rested his head in his hands. *What have I done? What I had to do.* He'd expected

Libby to be upset about the Compound restrictions, but spying for OASIS? What was she thinking? She wasn't thinking. Jack Weatherby's words echoed in his memory: "the first to tackle any new challenges as well as to volunteer for dangerous assignments." Joan of Arc indeed. *And if she's not careful...*

****

For the next few days, Libby handled her assignments with double diligence. She wanted to spend more time with the other female recruits, but their orgasmic raptures every time their trainers quoted

Alexandros made her draw further into her shell. Whenever she saw Dash, she walked the other way.

On the positive side, every Dash sighting renewed her determination. After dark, her rat might be able to access the research facility. Her nose twitched. But once her rat found a way in, she'd have to shift to search, and the ever-present cameras would record her return to her human shape.

If Dash's suspicions were accurate, the existing labs no longer mattered. To find the location for the important action, she'd have to sneak into Alexandros's office. A fly couldn't breathe on those walls without being monitored.

I don't know what I'm looking for. Has OASIS learned anything from that flash drive? Together, Dash and I could have... Walking in one of the "approved" areas, Libby kicked a stone toward the nearest curb. *He said he loved me. He didn't mean to, but I heard it.* She scoffed. *He may love me, but he doesn't trust me, doesn't want to work with me. What kind of love is that? Just hot, sweaty sex. Hot, sweaty, fantastic sex. When I find out about this new project, I'll share the information with him. After I tell OASIS.*

Smiling, she turned a corner and almost collided with Harry Kramer.

"How's it going, Libby?"

Libby looked around. "What are you doing?"

He coughed. "Walking."

Libby tilted her head. "Looks like you're standing around without your buddies."

"They're all busy. Except—Dash is busy but not here. Checking out another lead on his sister."

Libby drew a quick breath. "I hope he finds her."

She eyed the thin man. "I hear you're going to be a dad. Congratulations!"

"Yeah." Harry sounded less than thrilled. "Kid's not even here, and she's already changing my life. Tess says no smoking at home."

"I bet the first time you see that baby smile will be worth all the cigarettes in the world."

He offered a grudging nod. "I sure hope so."

Libby started to leave but turned back to Dash's colleague, who remained in his spot. "You guys should stop following me around."

Harry opened his mouth.

"I noticed that lately, when I'm not in class, someone from your team is always nearby."

"Dash wants to be sure you're—"

Libby held up one hand. "Contrary to what Dash Honeycutt believes, I'm a big girl. I can take care of myself. So please, buzz off." Leaving him on the corner, Libby strode toward the dormitory, an imposing hunk of concrete that looked like a massive doorstop. She greeted the woman at the main desk and checked her mailbox. Empty. Bypassing the elevators, she took the stairs to her room. When she opened the door, something scraped. She bent over, retrieved a folded piece of unlined white paper, and closed the door. Leaning against the door, she opened the paper.

Five words printed in black ink: *Meet me at the cabin*. At the bottom, a huge D.

Staring at the message, Libby slid down the door until her butt hit the floor. She turned the paper over. No distinctive marks. *I must have seen Dash write…sign his name.* She sighed. *I was probably too busy looking at him to notice. He wouldn't call or text me while I'm here at the Compound.* She fingered the page. *Must have come up the back stairs where no one would see him.* She stood and circled the small room. The words almost exploded from the page. *Maybe he found his sister, and she needs help. Something only a woman...* Dash had another sister. *But Kinsey's not here. I am.*

Chapter 38

Near midnight, Honeycutt parked in front of his cabin. The darkness echoed his inner emptiness. From a nearby tree, an owl hooting to his mate mocked his loneliness. Libby had come here two times yet left an indelible impression. From the porch, he surveyed the front lawn where she'd twirled in anticipation of their time together. If he listened hard enough, her laughter still filled the air. *"Four days!"* Before sunset, she'd been gone.

In the bed, her rosy scent clung to the linens. Lying on his back, he replayed the end of their last meeting. Every inhale triggered the memory of an angry statement. Every exhale, a regret.

Libby was so thrilled by the prospect of their working together that she lit up like a Fourth of July sparkler. Why had he shot her down so quickly? She should have talked to him before she volunteered to spy for OASIS. But he hadn't told her about his connection with SUNATNET. *I was too tough on her. But OASIS...the danger...*

He left the Libby-haunted bed and stretched out on the couch, where his feet dangled off an armrest. *I'll see her tomorrow. We'll work it out.*

****

In the morning, he entered his office, and the other members of his team looked up.

"Quick trip." Tony refilled his coffee mug.

Honeycutt logged into his computer.

Harry cracked his knuckles. "Any luck?" "No." He eyed his colleagues. "How's Libby?" The three men exchanged uncomfortable glances.

His hands fisted. "What's wrong?"

Harry brushed the front of his shirt. "She got huffy. Told me…but meant all of us…to buzz off."

Honeycutt stared at each of the men. "And you did?"

"Why not?" Tony put down his coffee cup. "She's not some cute cupcake. She was a police detective."

"And we all have work to do." Ben pointed at papers stacked on his desk.

Harry coughed. "I haven't seen her since—"

Honeycutt was out the door. The recruits were streaming out of the classroom for a morning break. No Libby. He scanned the classroom. No Libby.

The instructor stood by the computer. Shrewd brown eyes matched the tone of his skin.

"Where's Libby Maitland?"

The instructor's lips tightened. "Quit."

Across the street from Alexandros headquarters, Honeycutt paused. *If she realized I was right about the danger of spying for OASIS, quitting would be sensible.* He snorted. *She's too stubborn to be sensible. She'll keep going as long as…* He entered the outer office.

"Morning, Kate. I need to talk to The Boss."

The matronly woman flashed a smile he didn't return. She punched a button on her phone, spoke in a low voice, and looked up. "You can go in."

He opened the door to the inner office. Alexandros sat behind his desk, and Julianna occupied a chair on the other side.

Julianna leaped to her feet.

"Sit down, Julianna." The order rolled out in an almost sleepy voice. Alexandros gestured at Honeycutt. "You sit there." He indicated a chair on the far side of the room.

Honeycutt ignored the order and approached the desk. "Where's Libby Maitland?"

"How should I know?" A trace of amusement flickered across the other man's face. "I don't follow quitters."

Honeycutt clenched his fists. "So she walked in and quit."

Julianna rubbed her palms. "Not quite. One morning, I found her training materials stacked at the front door. The piece of paper on top had a huge 'I quit'." He scowled. "That doesn't sound like Libby."

Alexandros sat back in his chair. "Maybe you don't know her as well as you thought you did."

I know… Honeycutt regarded Julianna. "Do you have the note?"

She shook her head and pointed at a nearby wastebasket.

Alexandros cleared his throat. "You may recall that we were a difficult fit right from the start."

Honeycutt glared at him. "Libby was a great recruit. Top of her class."

Alexandros tilted his head slightly to one side, and his upper lip curled. "Honeycutt, I'm sure this must be hard, but try not to take it too personally. When she didn't get what she wanted here, Miss Maitland no doubt decided to put the whole experience behind her, including…" Alexandros extended a hand in Honeycutt's direction.

Walking out on me? On us? But after that argument... He eyed the sleek, red-haired woman and the bulky, white-haired man. The more sympathy they exuded, the more their story rankled. "When did she leave?"

Julianna and Alexandros conferred over a calendar. "Two days after you," Julianna said.

How convenient. You wanted me out of the way.

Alexandros sat up. "Any luck with your search?"

"No."

"That's too bad." The smarmy voice oozed fake sincerity.

Honeycutt fought the desire to dismiss the Titan's duty to protect humans. *I want to smash him.*

Alexandros turned to Julianna. "First thing tomorrow, have Tony set up security tapes that cover the days before and after Miss Maitland left." *As if I'll find anything.*

The older man's pinched smile and casual demeanor implied no need for urgency. He lifted a sheaf of papers. "Now, we have business…if you don't mind."

For the rest of the day, Honeycutt felt like a sleepwalker. *If she quit, she must have gone somewhere.* He called Libby more times than he could count. No answer. *Not like Libby, unless she's still mad and avoiding me.* He left apologetic and supportive messages at every prompt and texted frequently.

Alone in the cabin, he placed another call. "Hi, Robin. Dash Honeycutt here."

"Good to hear your voice. How's everything going? How's Libby?"

Not in Summerhaven. "That's why I'm calling. I was away on personal business. Just got back. Libby's missing. Alexandros says she quit."

"She wouldn't walk out on you."

"I don't think so, but we had a disagreement before I—I won't bother her. I want to know she's safe."

"I haven't heard from her. Sorry."

"Any chance she could be with that Ellyn person?"

"As far as I know, Ellyn Broderick is still in the wind, but I'll check her house. Of course, her neighbors are so spooked they call us whenever they see a shadow."

"What about her folks in Montana?"

"I think she'd go to her sister Steffi first."

"Do you have Steffi's number?"

"I'll send it to you."

Eternity passed during the silence between call and message. Eyeing the screen, he itched to jump into his truck and head for Libby, but he had only a phone number. *If you are there, I will go. I will tell you how smart you were to get out. How sorry I—*

The phone rang forever before someone answered. Hints of Libby in the female voice squeezed his heart. *Be here! Please.* "Hi. My name is Dash Honeycutt. Could I please speak with Libby?"

The gasp that seemed to vibrate across the miles spoke more loudly than words.

"She's not with you?" He rasped the words. *Where else?*

"No." Now Steffi's voice was crisp. "Last time we talked was about a week ago. Right after you..." He sensed the older sister looking down at him as if he were a mud-covered mongrel.

"Libby and I had an argument, but before we could work things out, I got called away. I just got back, and Libby's gone. Alexandros says she quit. Walked out—

which doesn't feel like Libby. She doesn't answer her phone, and I can't find her." He rubbed the back of his neck and rocked in place. "She was determined to learn everything she could about Alexandros and his plans."

On the other end of the line, Steffi exchanged agitated whispers with a deeper male voice that asked, "Did Libby tell you that?" The man's question held the hint of a snarl.

Honeycutt opened his mouth to reply, but Steffi spoke in a lower voice to her husband. "That's why they argued. You know I didn't want her working for OASIS because of the danger. Not because I think Libby's an incompetent hothead."

Steffi's words hit him like a punch in the belly. "I never said—"

"You didn't have to. You made her cry." Steffi's words cut into him like acid.

"I was afraid that she…" His thoughts spun in tangled circles. "Is there anywhere else she might—"

"No."

A huge hand seemed to squeeze his lungs. He forced himself to breathe.

Silence on the other end of the line for a moment.

"Does Alexandros know about her ability?" Steffi asked.

"Not as far as I—I didn't tell him anything if that's what you're suggesting."

"As a Simple Human, you might inadvertently—"

He sat up. "Wait. You don't…" Despite the urgency of the call, he smiled. *You didn't even tell your sister.*

"I'm not just human. I'm also part Titan."

"Oh." Steffi drew in a sharp breath. "No wonder she felt so safe. With a Titan backing her up."

Until I wasn't. If I'd been here, none of this...

"Alexandros has already killed one OASIS agent. If he discovered that Libby…"

"No. I would sense the loss."

Steffi's quiet assurance eased his frantic heartbeat. "Somehow, he may have learned she's a shifter. He may be using her to help identify…" Images of scalpels and syringes invading Libby's soft skin brought bile to the back of his throat. "I can search some of the Compound, but he has cameras everywhere."

Libby's brother-in-law spoke. "Sounds like you need someone who can have full run of the place without attracting undesirable attention."

"From what I've read and what Libby's told me, Alexandros likes publicity." Steffi's thoughtful voice almost calmed the turmoil in Honeycutt's heart.

Once again, the two speakers on the other end of the line held a private discussion. He caught the two final exchanges: The husband's "You think?" and Steffi's

"I'll call." "We're on it," Libby's brother-in-law announced.

Honeycutt stared at his phone. *I wish I shared your confidence!*

Chapter 39

Details of sites for the Alaska trip flashed across the screen. Honeycutt turned off the computer, eased his aching neck, and yawned. Although he'd gone from avoiding the trace of Libby's scent on the bedroom sheets to craving it, he still spent sleepless nights. *Who am I kidding? I don't care about these travel plans.*

He rubbed his temples. Nothing from Steffi. *I shouldn't be here. I should be… Libby, where are you?*

His phone rang. *Julianna.*

"The Boss wants you. Now." The line went dead. He eyed the phone. When Alexandros said, "Jump!" everyone was supposed to leap as high and fast as hopped-up hares.

At a more tortoise-like pace, Honeycutt stood and straightened the papers on his desk. Before stepping outside, he did several minutes of thoughtful breathing. He sauntered past the other office buildings to headquarters, where he entered Julianna's office.

Once, her gaze would have chilled him. "Took you long enough."

He looked around. "Where's The Boss?"

Julianna gestured at the closed door to the inner office. "Being interviewed."

He folded his arms and leaned against Julianna's doorframe. "You made it sound like an emergency."

"He wants you here when he finishes. He's on a tight

schedule. Flying out this afternoon."

Where? Honeycutt's breath caught in his throat, and he faked a chuckle.

Julianna's forehead wrinkled. "He may be sizing up possible locations for a new Compound."

"Is that what the interview's about?"

"No. Some filmmakers he met in California have a project in Nebraska. Since they were in the neighborhood, give or take a few hundred miles—" She uttered a small laugh. "—they decided to stop here to get a feel for what they could do if they made a documentary about The Boss."

"Good documentaries don't always provide good publicity."

"The Boss knows what he wants and how to get it."

The door to the inner office opened, and Alexandros emerged with a striking woman on either side of him. "Now, ladies, remember: I see everything before you put it in the film. No fancy editing."

"Of course not." The curvaceous platinum-haired beauty beamed at him.

The other woman, a stylish redhead, touched his arm. "Rest assured that we understand the importance of your work and the need to waken a sleeping world!" Her French accent made her words purr.

"Couldn't have put it better myself, Evie!" Alexandros fixed his gaze on Honeycutt. "I'd like you to meet the executive producers of Starshine Productions." When he dropped a gloved hand on each of the women's shoulders, their perfect faces remained so still they could have been marble. He pushed them slightly toward Honeycutt and indicated the blonde. "Marguerite Starshine."

The stunning woman gave a solemn nod.

"And Evie Gree-ant." Alexandros mangled the French pronunciation of her last name.

The redhead's smile didn't reach her eyes.

"Ladies, this is Dash Honeycutt, my travel security chief. Working with you will brighten his day." Alexandros handed off the two women. "Help Margie and Evie break down and pack their equipment. Then, give them a deluxe tour of the Compound."

"How much—"

"Show them anything they want to see. I have nothing to hide."

Since when?

"Ladies, I look forward to seeing you when you return with your full crew. If you have any questions after the tour, don't hesitate to ask my assistant." Alexandros gestured at Julianna. "Now, I must bid you adieu." With a wave, he headed for a car idling near the entrance to the building.

After loading their equipment, Honeycutt looked from one woman to the other. "Since the main office is the heart of the operation, we should start here."

The blonde turned away from the outer door. "I could use some fresh air…and exercise."

As he led them down the main street, the two women drew attention. When they neared the Research Quarter, the blonde pulled a small film camera from her huge bag.

Honeycutt lifted both hands. "Sorry, no photography allowed."

"I trust you'll make an exception for our film crew?" The corners of the blonde's full lips twitched as if she was controlling a laugh.

"Of course, Miss Star—"

She turned big blue eyes on him. "Call me Dayzee." His mouth dropped open. "You're—"

She winked. "Yvette and I want to see everything worth seeing."

"We can start at the far end of the property. Less surveillance and a better place to hide…" He drew the women away from the watching cameras. "This doesn't feel right. Alexandros is never so open with visitors."

The redhead grinned at her associate. "You charmed him."

Honeycutt regarded Libby's sister. "He's an expert at handling media."

Dayzee laughed. "You'd be surprised what people will do to become a star."

"Let's keep moving. Stay close and keep your voices low." They resumed their walk. "If Alexandros had set up a date for you to return with your full company, he would have time to make this the place he wants the world to see." Honeycutt's pace slowed. "Instead, he wants me to show you…" He kicked a curb. "I've looked everywhere. If Libby were here, I'd have found her."

Dayzee pointed a dramatically manicured finger at him. "Unless she doesn't want you to."

As Dayzee's blue-laser gaze seared his brain, he stared at her. "What?"

"You hurt her. Steff said she'd never seen Libby so upset."

"We had a…I love Libby, and I want to find her…not waste time—" He snapped his fingers. "That's it! That's why he told me to give you this tour while he— he never goes away like this without planning. He has a new, secret project, and I think it involves Libby. I'll bet he's on his way there now." He looked over his companions' heads toward the Compound entrance. "If we follow him, we'll find her."

"Will his assistant—"

"No. She may not know where he's going, but she would warn him about us." He regarded the two women. "Once I get on the phone, I want you to walk at a brisk pace to your car. Drive to the first rest stop on the highway. I'll meet you there, and you can follow me to the private airfield." His words flowed faster. "The people there know me, so I should be able to find out where he's headed."

Dayzee squared her shoulders. "See you at the rest stop."

He took out his phone.

Dayzee and Yvette scampered toward the Compound entrance. Good thing they wore practical shoes.

"Hi, Jules, it's Dash. Ms. Starshine got a call about an emergency with their project in Nebraska, so they're cutting the tour short. Since I sent you my recommendations for the Alaska hotels, I'm done for the day. See you tomorrow."

Although aching to sprint, he kept a deliberate stride to his truck and took his time removing the tracker. The half hour that passed between leaving the Compound and entering the rest stop felt like days. Another hour passed before they reached the airfield, where the cooperative staff not only bought his lie about them missing their flight with Alexandros but also arranged a second flight, billed to Alexandros Enterprises, for Honeycutt and his companions.

Onboard, Dayzee and Yvette sat opposite him.

Dayzee took out her phone. "Hey, Steff. We're flying to Minot, North Dakota. Yvette's doing online checks for new or unusual activity in the surrounding area. You should do the same. Sawyer should contact OASIS" –she lowered her voice— "and summon the wolves!"

Listening to Dayzee's confident voice—so like Libby's—Honeycutt experienced the first stirring of hope since he returned to the deserted cabin. *I will find you, Libby. I will always find you.*

****

A dingy white ceiling loomed over her. *Where am I? Dash's note…the cabin…garage…*

"Ah, you're awake."

That fake concern…prime Alexandros. What have you done to my body? When he moved into her limited field of vision, air pushed into her throat. A machine beeped frantically.

"Please relax. My doctors didn't want to bring you back to consciousness too soon, but I didn't want to risk damaging your brain."

Libby released something like a snarl. *Toad!*

"Can't speak but can still sneer. You've spent several days in an induced coma. The Barestium paralyzed your appendages but shouldn't affect your internal organs."

Barestium? When Libby tried, her eyebrows moved. At least, she thought she felt them. *Left leg. Can I wiggle—I can't feel my toes. Like the last time but worse. Both feet.*

"The bullet you took at the mayor's house gave us a good idea of how the drug affected you. You were the target. Not I." His complacent smile would have made

314

her flesh crawl if she could feel it. "Your lungs became compromised, and my doctors inserted a respirator to help you breathe. Hence, the coma."

"My" doctors. Some doctors! When the beeps accelerated, Libby drew a deep breath. The beeps slowed. *Way to go, heart! Glad they didn't screw you up, too.*

"In a day or so, you may be breathing on your own."

He gestured at her arms. "When the paralysis ends, don't even think of shapeshifting." One of his gloved fingers wagged back and forth, and he indicated the monitors. "An attempt will set off alarms in your vital signs. Should we catch you during a shift, we will apply Barestium, which I suspect would cause mental havoc between your human shape and your intended animal."

It didn't affect my cheetah shift, but that was a smaller dose. I haven't regained full strength in my left leg. With the drug everywhere in my body...and the time unconscious...even if I do shift, I'll be weak... But first...body, wake up!

"I'm sure you wonder where you are...and why. Blink once for yes and twice for no. Is that clear?"

"You s...s... s...." The word ended in a long hiss that seemed to drag skin from her throat.

"You won't be able to talk for a while. But you can listen."

To your lies? No thanks. I need earplugs!

"The place doesn't matter. This facility is staffed with dedicated professionals and local followers who are thrilled to serve. They believe their work provides an excellent opportunity to learn more about Shapeshifters, which, of course, it does. Most don't know about the greater vision."

He paced around the room and spoke as he did during his public appearances. "I built my reputation by arousing people's fear of your kind. But it turns out some people who have amassed the wealth to do anything they wish don't want to destroy you. They want to be like you, and they generously reward whoever fulfills that desire." He tapped his chest.

You bloated windbag.

"Schuyler Pope stumbled onto my plan but didn't quite know what he'd found."

Libby blinked. *So you did it. How?*

"When I approached potential clients, I soon realized that basic shapeshifting—becoming merely a wolf or an eagle—would not satisfy. They wanted more because they always want more. They want to be Supershifters." His piggy gaze drilled into Libby's brain.

"Like you. And they are willing to pay billions." Libby's face froze.

Alexandros chuckled. "I didn't even know shifters like you existed until Honeycutt told me."

What? She felt as if a knife pierced her heart. The machines went wild.

"Don't look so shocked, my dear. Honeycutt has been with me every step of the way." He checked his watch. "Right now, he and Julianna are setting up housekeeping on that Pacific island he purchased with a portion of his finder's fee."

No…no…no! If she squeezed her eyes shut and blotted out Alexandros, he would crow louder. *Dash would never… He promised. Said he loved me. No. Said there were things he loved about me. Not the same. He's a Titan. Titans protect and heal. But he's also human.*

"Honeycutt doesn't matter."

He does to me. She gritted her teeth. *Alexandros lies. Dash never...he has always told me the truth. I will not cry.*

"What does matter is that you are here, your DNA provides a useful map, and my people will discover which of your tissues works most efficiently when injected into human subjects." He flashed another vile smile. "Now you're really listening, aren't you?

"Good, good." He rubbed his hands. "We've had some success with your skin. Since it's your largest organ, we are continuing to explore its possibilities."

You want to flay me? Fury made the monitor beeps increase exponentially.

"Calm down. My doctors will take what they need and do their best to alleviate unnecessary pain."

Libby glared at Alexandros. *That's big of you.* She looked at the ceiling, the monitor, the IVs in her arm. *I need to get out. How?*

His phone buzzed. "We'll talk again soon." Libby opened her mouth to scream, but the best she could manage was a tiny grunt. *Stop him. How? Muscles and bones won't move. Protect skin. How? If they can't peel it or cut it, what will they do? Knock me out again and hope it turns human? Might buy time. Time for Dash...* She closed her eyes and visualized his earnest face while his words drowned out the Alexandros lies. *"I will always find you."*

She opened her eyes. Same stupid ceiling. Silent screams filled her brain. *Find me, Dash! Please!* Libby swallowed, breathed more smoothly, and closed her eyes. *Cool down. Protect skin. Can't transform whole body. Can I change only my skin? Steady. Steady. Don't set off monitors. Visualize change moving from toes to crown of head. The outside covering. Something strong. Porcupine quills? Armadillo scales? Too connected to shape. Shells?*

***** Someone squealed.

Libby opened her eyes. At the foot of her bed stood a beefy young man clad in gray hospital scrubs. The jaw at the bottom of his round face had dropped so far that it looked as if it might reach the floor. He pulled out his phone. "Hey, Sam! Get down here. Stat. You gotta see this!"

The next minutes brought fast, no-nonsense steps. "Well, I'll be…" A sweet-faced young woman also wearing scrubs joined the young man. "Looks like a lobster." The young woman reached toward Libby.

When Libby uttered a guttural protest, the young woman hopped back and held up both hands. "I won't touch you."

"How are we supposed to prep this?" With a loose fist, the young man gently tapped the carapace that covered Libby's upper arm. "Call Dr. Miller."

Within minutes, a group surrounded Libby's bed. Standing by the head of the bed, a silver-haired woman in a lab coat confided to a thin, balding man, also in a lab coat, "He won't like this."

Libby stared at the silent, dark-haired woman who stood off to the side of the other doctors. *Nadine Victor?*

"What's the problem?" the loathsome voice boomed. When Alexandros entered the room, the group parted. Most gave him full attention, but Dr. Victor gazed at the floor. Shoulders hunched, she looked uncomfortable. Standing at the foot of the bed, Alexandros cast a cursory glance at Libby's face, then regarded his staff.

The silver-haired doctor spoke up. "We'd planned to gather additional samples this morning, but this isn't skin." She rested a hand on Libby's shoulder. "It's almost armor."

"Nonsense. Ignore the cheap tricks of this shifty Shapeshifter. It's turned its skin to shell." Alexandros regarded the bystanders. "Which provides a visible reminder that these creatures are not human." *More than human.*

"Obviously, it wants to impede our progress, but we're not going to let that happen, now, are we?"

The silver-haired doctor cast a dubious look in Libby's direction. "I guess not."

The balding doctor said, "No."

Alexandros gestured at Nadine Victor, who still looked at the floor. "Dr. Victor? Do you agree?"

She lifted her head and met his gaze. "Yes, sir." She spoke as if programmed to approve.

"Right." When Alexandros slapped Nadine Victor's shoulder, she flinched. "We haven't come so close to give up." His gaze roamed from Libby's encased feet to her eyes. "We may need a few can openers."

You wouldn't dare! Libby swallowed. He would, of course. He'd do anything to get what he wanted.

The male doctor cleared his throat. "Forgive me, sir, but we may not be able to get anything usable from this…shell." He tapped Libby's leg.

"Perhaps we should take a different approach." When Alexandros's gloved fingers touched Libby's elbow, she wished she could pull away. She still felt nothing, but seeing his hand on her body turned her stomach. "Since the shifter has decided to put on a shell, why not treat it like a crustacean? Separate the claw from the body and obtain samples from the tissue beneath." Nadine Victor gasped.

Alexandros smiled. "Don't look so distressed, Dr. Victor. The shifter leaves us little choice."

When the dark-haired woman didn't respond, he pressed her. "Don't you agree?" She nodded.

Alexandros regarded Libby as if she were an untrainable puppy. "Of course, if it decides to cooperate and return to its human skin, we won't need to take such extraordinary measures." When he touched her shell again, vile flavors congealed in Libby's throat.

With a single gesture, he emptied the room and returned to Libby. "My doctors are preparing to declaw you, but that won't be necessary if you turn this stupid shell back into human skin. The choice is yours." He winked.

"Sonuvaitch." Libby's words emerged in an unintelligible growl.

Both eyebrows soaring toward his forehead, Alexandros drew back. "Don't insult my mother. She's a quiet little old lady who has never harmed a soul." *Unlike her monster son.*

Alexandros slammed the door behind him.

Beneath the shell, Libby's mouth managed a small smile. *Gotcha!*

Chapter 40

"This must have been where everybody lived." From a window of the rental car, Dayzee's camera captured a deserted main street. On either side, tall grass rose.

"There's the property!" Honeycutt pointed at a building in the distance.

Dayzee sat up. "Looks like a castle."

Or a prison. "When the county clerk said the survivalists had built a fortress, I thought he was exaggerating, but those walls must be thirty feet high."

Dayzee kept her camera on. "If that's the outside, can you imagine what their underground tunnel network looks like? Too bad they destroyed the plans after they finished the construction."

He glanced at the deserted countryside. "Where are the wolves? You said there would be wolves."

"We travel after dark." Yvette's voice rose over the wheels crunching on the poorly maintained paved road.

"We can't wait. If there's a guard at the entrance, I'll show them my ID. If that doesn't work...can either of you use a gun?"

"Sorry," said Yvette.

Dayzee sank back into her seat. "I played a spy in a Civil War movie, but her weapon was seduction." His serious mouth twisted into a half-smile.

"I could become a mole and burrow under the wall

to let you in," Dayzee offered.

"That will take too long."

"Do you think they'll call the police?" Yvette asked. "With a kidnap victim? I doubt it." *Alexandros wanted her alive, but if she becomes a liability... Every minute counts.* A narrow road encircled the high walls. "No lookouts or cameras."

"Maybe he hasn't had time to install them," Yvette suggested.

He doesn't plan to be here long. Just long enough...Libby, my love, what is he doing to you?

"All that's missing is a moat," Dayzee observed.

He snorted.

Dayzee sat up. "You work for Alexandros security. Why didn't he have you look at this place before he bought it?"

"I handle travel security. And I don't think he told anyone at the Compound about this, except the researchers he needed. He purchased this property as CAP, LLC, not Alexandros Enterprises."

He hit the brakes hard. A huge steel slab covered the entrance. More like a drawbridge than a door or a gate. His growing shoulders pressed against the flexible fabric of his shirt. "I'm going in."

"Wait." Dayzee touched his arm and pointed at a rising dust storm on the northern horizon.

He squinted. "What the—eighteen-wheelers! Looks like your wolves are traveling in style."

As if operating under central command, the convoy kept a distance but surrounded the walled estate. When the trucks stopped, humans and furry black wolves poured out of the trailers and headed for the biggest rig, which stopped beside Honeycutt's rental. A tall man

Shifting into Shadows

with silver-streaked hair stepped out of the truck cab and turned to face the assembly. When a dark-haired woman opened the passenger door, Dayzee scrambled out of the car to hug her while Yvette headed for the man.

Honeycutt got out of the car and pulled on his utility belt.

The dark-haired woman gave him a cool once-over with brown eyes like Libby's. "You must be Dash Honeycutt."

He nodded. "Steffi?" A solemn nod.

She's still pissed at me.

Dayzee hung on her sister's arm. "We've got to get her, Steff."

Steffi offered a faint smile. "We will. Soon, we'll be together."

"But she's—" Honeycutt rested a hand on his heart. "She needs—" Steffi began.

Dayzee clapped. "First, let's find her. Then you guys can argue over custody...although I'm betting Libby will have her own ideas."

"Just like always." Steffi sighed.

He almost laughed.

Yvette approached with the tall man. "Sawyer, this is Dash Honeycutt."

Libby's brother-in-law extended his hand. "Sawyer Montaigne."

"Thanks for being so quick." Honeycutt shook the strong hand.

"We protect our own. Steffi's handling central communications." Sawyer kissed his wife's cheek. "Get the wolves in position." He turned to Honeycutt. "More

323

trucks on the way. Closer packs are running." He patted his hip. "All drivers are armed, and we also have rifles for any wolves who decide to return to their humans." He gestured at the wall. "Any idea what's in there?"

Libby! On the hood of his car, Honeycutt laid out a copy of the mansion blueprint they'd picked up at a historical society. "This is the original house. Nothing about the underground work."

Sawyer eyed the steel obstruction. "Some of the bigger trucks, working together, can plow through that." Honeycutt dropped his utility belt on the ground. "Don't bother." As his growing body sought release, the stretch fabric tore. Below him, the ground trembled and people shouted. He stomped to the wall and looked over it. No activity in the big front yard. In the house, sirens, flashing lights, and moving figures. He gripped the top and bottom edges of the steel barricade and ripped it away from the boulders that held it.

Behind him, a roar went up.

He hurled the steel chunk through the new opening. Shrinking to his human size, he stooped. Shredded fabric littered the ground. He wrapped the belt containing his emergency gear around one bare shoulder.

He joined Libby's brother-in-law, Sawyer, and an armed contingent gathered at the entrance. "Alpha Team, search the top floors of the house. Beta Team, you're with me and Dash." Sawyer regarded him. "Once we have Libby, we'll continue the search because there could be others."

Sawyer addressed Dayzee and Yvette, who were recording the scene. "Stay with Steffi."

"No way!" Dayzee glared at him. She turned to Yvette. "You record the house search and what's

324

happening with the wolves." She eyed Sawyer and
Shifting into Shadows

Honeycutt. "I'm coming with you."

"Don't get in the way." Sawyer waved a finger. "And don't get hurt. If you do, I'll never hear the end of it."

Honeycutt looked at Sawyer and his teams. "Have you finished yapping, or do I have to throw you out of the way so I can get in there?"

"I don't doubt that you could, but you'd look silly." Lips twitching in a smile, Sawyer made room for Honeycutt at his side.

"Go!"

Behind the two leaders, the teams marched from the gaping hole in the wall onto the broad lawn in front of a once-elegant mansion that now looked like a haunted house. The steel barrier had landed in the middle of the lawn like an odd modern sculpture.

A huge garage on one side of the house contained several vans.

"No personal cars," Sawyer observed. "Everyone must be staying here until the end of his project." Honeycutt's fingers curled into fists.

Sawyer touched his arm. "We'll find her. Libby's tough."

"I know." *But Alexandros is a monster.*

Nothing else in the garage. Sawyer and Honeycutt led both teams to the front door. Unlocked, all alarms blaring.

Weapons at the ready, Alpha Team mounted the grand staircase.

Beta Team swept the first floor. Solid, well-used

furnishings. Bookshelves attached to the walls. No humans.

Alpha Team reported by phone. "Dormitory rooms in the attic, three single bedrooms and one big suite on the main floor. Empty."

The basement too was empty. And dark. Shelves containing enough canned goods to stock a supermarket lined every wall. They tried every shelf, but none moved. Concrete floor. Honeycutt played his flashlight around the furnace, over the hot water heater, and… "Under the stairs. A door in the floor." His light captured what looked like more concrete but was a crusty cover. Sticking his flashlight in his utility belt, he pulled on the handle. With a grunt, he pulled harder, and the door came up, revealing narrow metal stairs cemented into a stone floor. More alarms and flashing lights. *They left you there. Alone in the dark.* He clenched his jaw.

While Sawyer divided the two teams into smaller groups to search each corridor, Honeycutt surveyed the twisting paths. *Libby, where are you?*

Chapter 41

Outside the room, alarms sounded, and lights flashed. *Dash!* No longer paralyzed, Libby struggled against the restraints that bound her to the bed but had to lie back and breathe. Although she'd often flexed her fingers, wrists, and ankles, moving her arms and legs had been almost impossible.

Panting and breathless shouts echoed off the corridor walls. Hasty footsteps slapped the stone floor. A dark-haired woman slipped into her room. When Libby struggled, Nadine Victor said, "Be still. I can help." She removed the IV catheter and loosened the restraints on one arm.

"Dr. Victor!" That contemptible Alexandros voice cut through the chaos like a whip.

Nadine Victor drew back as if to avoid his lash. She gestured at Libby. "I was only—"

"I'll handle it." He pushed the doctor into the corridor. "Shelter! Go!"

With a fearful glance at Alexandros, the dark-haired woman disappeared. Libby wiggled her free arm.

"Move along! Move along!" Blocking Libby's doorway, Alexandros shouted at stragglers. "To the Shelter! Together, we will destroy these Shadow People!"

When he returned to Libby, his gaze sent a frost down her spine. "My people have trained for this attack.

They will annihilate your damn shifters." *But not my Titan!*

"And I'll take care of you." Flaunting a syringe, Alexandros lifted one foot.

"Stop!" Libby straightened her unrestrained arm. *Shift! Storm!* Her pointing fingers fused.

With his evil Santa Claus laugh, Alexandros took a step into the room.

The lightning from her fingers streaked toward him. His smile split into a scream.

Libby's human shape became a rising storm cloud that escaped the remaining restraints. Narrowing into a funnel cloud, she swept Alexandros across the walkway and slammed him against the corridor wall. *Good!* His body sagged and slid to the floor.

Be human! Be Libby! She collapsed.

****

Another dead end! Honeycutt's curse should have made the gray walls blush. He and Sawyer retraced their path.

"We'll find her." *Where? When?*

Sawyer pointed toward the corridor on his left. "Let's go that way." With a marker, he slashed a red arrow on the wall. A sudden rumble filled the air.

Thunder! Honeycutt's pulse raced. *Solid, liquid, gas.* "It's Libby! I'm coming!" He bolted in the direction of the resounding boom. The corridor seemed endless, but he ran without stopping. When he rounded the corner into yet another passage, he stumbled over a naked figure crumpled by the wall.

"Libby." Kneeling beside her, he laid his fingers against her neck. Cold, damp skin. Thready pulse. Shallow breaths. "Stay with me, sweetheart." His heart thudded in his chest.

He pulled a knife from his emergency gear, pierced a pulse spot near his collarbone, and held Libby's limp form close. When his blood began to flow, he pressed her lips against the wound. "Drink!" The command rasped against his dry mouth.

At first, she mewed like a confused kitten, but after he rubbed some blood between her lips, she began to suck. "There you go. Take what you need." Tears blurred his vision, and his breathing eased as she drew from his strength.

A panting Sawyer stopped and leaned against the wall on the other side of the corridor. "Are you also some sort of vampire?"

"No. Titan blood can heal." Honeycutt smiled down at the woman in his arms.

Sawyer looked at Libby. "She's wet." He gestured at the doorway. "I'll try to find some towels."

"No. She should absorb any moisture. But she could use a light blanket, and I need some sort of cover." Honeycutt touched a scabby spot on Libby's back. *What did he do to you?* He rested his palm against the wound. *Heal.*

The skin warmed beneath his hand, and Libby's breathing grew more regular. The pulse in her neck was slow but steady, stronger. His lips brushed her temple. *Good work, Libby.*

Minutes later, Sawyer emerged from the room with blanket and sheet. "When she's done sucking, I can apply pressure to your cut."

"Thanks, but it will stop." When he wrapped the blanket loosely around her, Libby stirred. The light in her dark eyes warmed his heart. "Welcome back."

The corners of her lips curved. "You found me," she whispered.

He kissed her forehead. "Always."

The tip of her tongue sampled traces of blood that stained her mouth, and her eyebrows squished together.

"You needed strength." He touched the cut on his shoulder, which was already beginning to mend. "From my heart to yours."

"Thank you." She lifted one arm and displayed a bloody spot. "IV fluid." She gestured at his belt. "Got any solid food?"

"Trail mix." He pulled out a packet and poured a selection in his hand. "Go slow."

Libby touched two fingers to her forehead and chose a piece of dried banana. She chewed slowly and swallowed. "Heaven!"

Sawyer hooted. "You're fussing over dried fruit in front of the man who opened a vein for you."

Libby rested a hand on her lover's chest. "Dash is more than a man."

"I feel like a rat. You wouldn't be here if we hadn't argued."

"Alexandros would have found a way to separate us." She touched his cheek. "You said you would find me, and you did." She took the trail mix and tucked it into a fold of her blanket.

Her fingers on his bare shoulders were warm and steady, not cold and limp. *Thank God*.

"I'm naked because I shifted." She kissed his shoulder. "What happened to your clothes?"

He released her just long enough to wrap the sheet around his body in a makeshift toga. "Got big."

"Humongous," Sawyer muttered.

Libby's eyes widened. "You went full Titan, and I missed it?" She lifted a fist as if she would punch him. Instead, she opened her hand and brought her palm to his chest.

He kissed her fingers. *Warm. Alive. Safe. Mine.*

"Don't worry." Gasping, Dayzee waved her camera. "Yvette and I got everything."

Libby looked over Honeycutt's shoulder. "What are you...how did you...?"

"Sisters to the rescue." Honeycutt kissed Libby's cheek. "Once you've recovered, I'll try to get big again...just for you, but I've never done anything so extreme."

"He could see over a thirty-foot wall," Dayzee contributed.

Libby pursed her lips. "Wow!"

"I don't know if I can repeat..."

"Doesn't matter." She caressed his jaw. "You're my Titan."

In the shadows beside them, Crispin Alexandros struggled to his feet. Grasping a limp arm with his other gloved hand, he leaned against the wall. "Ow!" He exposed a lightly toasted forearm first to Honeycutt, then to Dayzee's camera.

He touched a bloody spot on his white hairline.

"Concussion. Honeycutt, call help. Medical helicopter." Libby tensed. Honeycutt held her closer.

Alexandros stamped his foot. "Now, Honeycutt! I need help."

"You need to be locked up. For a long time." Sawyer's cool voice supplied no comfort.

Alexandros shifted his gaze to Sawyer. "Who...what...you trespassers...you will pay." He tried to wave his damaged arm but moaned and once again cradled that arm close to his burned clothing. "Attacking my people. And for what? For that." When he pointed at Libby, his torn glove slipped, exposing a dark, hairy palm and fingers. Honeycutt and Libby exchanged surprised glances. *Monkey?*

Alexandros returned to Honeycutt. "Unhand that shifter slut and summon help. Now!" He flapped his arms as if he thought he could fly.

Honeycutt glared at the pathetic but contemptible figure. "If you ever insult Ms. Anbruzzen again, I will tear out your tongue, and that will be only the beginning."

"That creature seduced you, Honeycutt. It ordered me to make It more powerful."

"Liar." Libby pinched her lips together and looked away.

Alexandros rocked back and forth. "I pretended to agree. I believed that here with my people, we would find a way to destroy It and defend ourselves against the shifter menace. We must save humanity!"

He turned to Dayzee. "Miss Starshine, you understand. As I told you at the Compound, I want to make our human world safe—" His forehead wrinkled. "Why are you here?"

Dayzee looked up from her camera with a beatific smile. "I go where the story is."

Honeycutt glanced at Sawyer. "I have my arms full, Sawyer, but you can use the rope on my belt to tie him up. Find something in that room to gag him with, too, before I knock his teeth down his lying throat." Alexandros moaned.

Libby buried her face in Honeycutt's shoulder.

Alexandros whimpered and stepped back, dragging one leg slightly.

Honeycutt visualized the damaged cells spinning in that demented brain. He turned to other members of the search party. "Some of you should hold onto him. Make sure he doesn't escape."

"I would never..." But Alexandros kept stepping backward.

Honeycutt kissed Libby's lightly scorched fingertips. "Too bad you couldn't hit him harder."

Sawyer emerged from the room and tossed his associates a jumble of electrical cords and IV lines. "Tie him up."

Alexandros wailed. "Please, don't! I never...all I want...save humans!" His pleas and protests continued while he struggled.

"For heaven's sake, stop whining." Libby wrapped the blanket around herself and stood with one hand gripping Honeycutt's arm. "Let him go."

"What?" Honeycutt and Sawyer spoke in unison. "Let. Him. Go."

Honeycutt stared at her.

Sawyer looked from Alexandros to Libby. "Are you sure?"

Libby's chin descended like a spear. "Do it."

Holding his damaged arm, Alexandros shuffled away, moving backwards as if he feared they might still pursue him.

"I don't get it." Honeycutt shook his head. "We could put him behind bars."

"He won't stay there," Libby said. "He has money and powerful friends, not to mention all his followers. If he didn't jump bail, and the case did go to court...even if we won, we'd lose. Simple Humans would know we exist."

Sawyer scratched his jaw. "Good point."

Honeycutt looked from Libby to her brother-in-law. "So he walks away?"

"The wolves are everywhere," Sawyer said.

Sawyer and Libby exchanged glances.

"We protect our own," she told Honeycutt. "Speaking of protection"—she turned to Sawyer— "the Alexandros people in the shelter are well armed and trained. Without Alexandros, they may not fight, but you should keep the wolves out." She snapped her fingers. "Also, one of the doctors—Nadine Victor—tried to help me. Please talk with her."

"Victor…got it." Sawyer entered a note on his phone. Then he told his phone, "Call Steffi."

Libby stared at her brother-in-law. "She's here, too?"

Sawyer nodded. "We've got her, Steff. A little the worse for wear, but still Libby." He listened, then offered Libby the phone.

Libby grinned. "Big Sister lecture." She listened for a few minutes.

Sawyer turned to Honeycutt. "Steff got a call from your brother-in-law. He said to say, 'Hi'."

Dash's eyes widened. "Josh is *here*?"

"His pack answered the summons."

"I want to see him before he leaves."

"I'll tell Steff."

Libby spoke into the phone. "Everything's good. Great."

When she winked at Honeycutt, every cell in his body lit up.

Libby returned the phone to Sawyer, who spoke quickly "Me again. Please tell everyone to bring their biggest guns and meet me at the entrance." He looked at the phone. "I don't think we'll have any trouble but should be prepared. And Dash wants to talk to Josh Savant. Thanks." He smiled. "Love you, too."

"I'll meet you at the entrance." When Honeycutt spoke, Libby's fingers tightened on his arm.

Sawyer must have noticed. "No. You have more important business here." He whispered into

Honeycutt's ear, patted his shoulder, and left.

Libby kissed Honeycutt's chin. "What did he say?"

"That I shouldn't forget to tell you I love you. Not that I needed a reminder." His lips brushed hers. "I do love you."

She kissed him. "I love you, too."

"I want to catch Josh before he leaves." He swept her up in his arms. Libby felt much lighter than air, with skin taut against her cheekbones.

"Hold on, you two." Dayzee blocked their exit. "You getting back together is a great ending." She held up her camera. "A kiss would make it even better."

The sparkle in Libby's dark eyes flooded the corridor with brightness. "I think we can arrange that, don't you, Dash?"

He no sooner opened his mouth to agree than Libby was kissing him as if her life depended on it, and his longing joined hers.

"Cut!" The voice sounded worlds away. "You can stop now."

Oh, no! He shrugged off Dayzee's hand on his arm and deepened the kiss. Libby—his brave, amazing

Libby—filled his arms and his heart. *We're just getting started.*

Chapter 42

"It's good to finally meet you, Ms. Anbruzzen." The Director of OASIS, a muscular man with silver hair, gripped Libby's hand as she and Dash entered his office. "Although after years of reading Mentor reports, I feel as if I already have." He turned his sharp gaze on Dash. "Together, you and Mr. Honeycutt performed outstanding service to Shapeshifters everywhere." He released Libby's hand and touched his chest. "OASIS thanks you."

Libby dipped her chin. "I'm glad it's almost over."

"I understand SUNATNET operatives demolished the Alexandros operation in North Dakota." Dash flashed a huge smile.

"Indeed, they did, and OASIS agents supplied mindwipes. The Simple Humans have returned to their previous lives with the understanding that their topsecret project ended in failure. OASIS also dismantled the Alexandros main office, destroyed all records, mindwiped all employees, and relocated those who lived on the site."

The director turned to Libby. "On a happier note, Dr. Nadine Victor confirmed your suspicion that Alexandros had coerced her into joining him."

Libby lifted a fist. "I knew it!"

"Alexandros suspected that Schuyler Pope had confided in her, so he had an operative plant the virus on the computer keyboard in her Baltimore office. Although she acquired some immunity from the earlier attack, he threatened her with a fatal dose unless she joined his North Dakota operation."

"Poor woman." Libby regarded Dash. "No wonder she looked so scared."

"You saved her." Dash winked. "Maybe she'll get her nosy neighbor to withdraw that harassment complaint."

Libby laughed.

Dash looked at the director. "What about Alexandros? Did your wolves…"

The older man smiled. "They heeded our Second Rule and would not harm a Simple Human, but they did capture him." The director stepped behind his desk and sat. "OASIS has floated rumors that Alexandros disappeared because he could not face the failure of his research projects. Also, that he absconded with money and is somewhere in the South Pacific. In reality, we took care of him. He won't bother anyone again."

Libby gasped. "You dosed him with X-Ting? I thought OASIS administered the drug only to rogue shifters."

"Alexandros showed his monkey paw to the wolves and claimed to be a shifter. That gave us the authority to act. The X-Ting deleted any shapeshifting ability and halved his intelligence. With a new name, he will remain under our supervision."

The older man pressed his lips together. "Now, on to more unpleasant matters." He held up a document. "You've made serious accusations. Are you sure you want to follow through?"

"Yes." Libby pushed the word from her tight throat

across her dry mouth to her lips.

"Very well." The director indicated two chairs on the right side of the room. "Please be seated."

Dash and Libby sat. When she rubbed the thigh of her slacks, Dash's hand covered hers. "It will be all right." His whisper steadied her.

The director punched a button on his desk. "Enter."

Between two OASIS guards, a scrawny, dark-haired woman in a dress that looked like stitched-together burlap bags entered through the doorway on the left side of the room. The woman charged the director's desk. "What's going on, Mel?"

The silver-haired man stood. "I am the director of OASIS, Miss Broderick, and you will address me with respect. Is that clear?"

The woman recoiled as if slapped. "Yes, Me—s-ssir." Glancing toward Dash and Libby, Ellyn brought her palms together, and a beatific smile replaced her scowl. "Libby!" She started toward Libby.

Leaning against Dash, Libby pointed a finger at the other woman. "Stay where you are." With her other hand, Libby squeezed Dash's fingers as if she could draw upon his strength.

Ellyn pressed her palms to her chest. "It's good to see you."

Libby tilted her head. "You look like hell."

Ellyn tugged at her stained skirt. "I've fallen on…hard…times."

The director addressed Libby. "She left Summerhaven and stayed with a few rogue shifters."

When a trickle of lost memory stirred, Libby drew in a sharp breath. "You said it was your attorney."

"I was with…" Ellyn rolled a shoulder. "I thought they were friends until they stole my money and threatened to expose me. I had to run. I found work but couldn't stay anywhere. So I took my cat shape."

"By then, we'd alerted everyone," the director said. "Found her when she tried to join a clowder."

"But that's all past." The corners of Ellyn's thin lips turned up. "I'm glad that you are—"

Libby scoffed. "No thanks to you."

"I beg your pardon?"

Libby stood and approached her Mentor. "You sold me to Crispin Alexandros."

Ellyn fanned her chin. "After so many years together…how could you believe I" –she brought a hand to her breast— "could do such a terrible thing? If you want to know who deceived you, look there." She pointed at Dash.

Libby watched the other woman's lying eyes. "No, Ellyn, it was you."

Ellyn's lips curled in a familiar smile. "Libby, dear…"

"Don't 'dear' me!"

The director interrupted the exchange with a cough. "Miss Broderick, you've refused legal counsel. Are you certain about that?"

"Of course. This is simply a dreadful misunderstanding."

"It's dreadful all right." Libby addressed the man behind the desk. "When I went to a crime scene at Ellyn's house, I found a cat I sensed was Ellyn and brought her home with me. When she returned to her human, I planned to take her to the police station so she could explain why she shot that man. The next morning, the cat was gone."

"That's what this is about?" Ellyn looked at the OASIS director and lifted her hands. "A missing cat?"

"No," Libby said. "It's about the hole in my memory."

Ellyn smiled. "As a man of the world, your...friend...no doubt seized the opportunity to take advantage of you, poor dear."

The director turned to Dash. "Mr. Honeycutt, SUNATNET confirms that you are a Titan."

Dash leaned forward. "Our mission is to protect and heal. We do not drug others, Supernaturals or humans. Nor do we enter their minds unless invited."

"There you have it." Ellyn brushed her hands as if she'd solved a puzzle. "Libby no doubt opened her mind to him without even being aware of it. He erased her memory of the rape. Perhaps he even let the cat out."

"No." Libby pointed again at her former Mentor. "You mind-wiped me. You also planted a message—a command—in my head...to protect Dash at the mayor's reception."

Ellyn clicked her tongue behind her teeth. "You give me credit for far more power than I ever had."

The director said, "You and the other early Mentors did receive mind-wipe training."

"What?" Libby nearly leapt over the big desk.

"OASIS thought that if you and your sisters forgot you had shapeshifting ability, you could all live happy Simple Human lives." Melvin Sawyer tugged at his collar. "The plan failed."

"That's an understatement." Ellyn smirked. "Steffi nearly fried poor Bev's brain."

"That's what happened to Steffi's first Mentor?"

Libby stared at the director. "You tried to wreck my sister's mind?"

The director's lips twitched. "That happened before my time, but as I've indicated, damaging you was never the intent."

"Even if ordered to mind-wipe…" Ellyn turned to the director but indicated Libby. "Libby's like a daughter to me. I could never hurt her."

"Cut the crap." Libby stepped toward her.

The older woman appealed to the guards. "She's always been hot-tempered. Please don't let her attack."

"Stop trying to make this about me. Or Dash. This is about what you've done." Libby waved a fist.

Ellyn cowered.

The director faced Libby. "I know you're upset, Ms. Anbruzzen." The sympathy in his deep voice softened Libby's mounting rage. "But please sit down."

Dash patted her chair. When she sat beside him, his warm hand on her arm reminded her that no matter what happened today, they'd already won.

From her seat, Libby spoke. "You killed that man at your house. Then, you became a cat, let me take you to my apartment, shifted back to your human shape while Dash and I were gone, mind-wiped me when I got home, planted the information about the attack at the mayor's house, and took off."

"Sounds like an exhausting evening." Ellyn yawned. "Too bad you have no proof."

Libby itched to tear off that slimy smile. "You set me up to be shot."

Ellyn sniggered. "That's absurd. As I've said, you're like a daughter to me. The daughter I never…"

The director shuffled a few papers. "Leave the

personal angle aside for a moment. Miss Broderick has asked a reasonable question. Why would she want you to be shot?"

"Because that's what Alexandros wanted. He told me the bullet was coated with Barestium so he could learn how the drug affected me." Libby looked at Ellyn. "Like you, he claimed that Dash had betrayed me."

Ellyn puffed out her chest and threw back her shoulders. "See? It *was* Honeycutt!"

Libby shook her head. "But Dash didn't know I was a shifter until *after* the shooting."

"Libby, Libby." Ellyn crooned the name as she had when Libby was in her cradle. "When he plundered your mind, he learned everything and shared that information with Alexandros."

Libby and Dash exchanged a glance before Libby addressed the older woman. "It wasn't Dash. It was you." Libby turned to the director. "Even after Dash learned I was a shifter, he didn't know the full range of my ability. Only one person in Summerhaven, besides me, has ever known that." She pointed at Ellyn.

Ellyn folded her arms. "This is ridiculous. You've known me for years, Mel-s-sssir. You can't believe her stories. These Anomalies...they're a whole other breed. Renegades. Rebels."

The director smiled. "I might have agreed with you before my nephew Sawyer mated with Steffi Anbruzzen, and her sister Libby destroyed a major threat."

Libby shuffled her feet. "Forget about me for a minute. Let's talk about Schuyler Pope." "What?" Ellyn asked.

"Pope provided OASIS with information on his Alexandros research," Libby said.

The director gestured at Ellyn. "You were his OASIS contact."

Ellyn rolled her shoulders. "Hardly in a position—"

Libby sat up. "Exactly in a position to kill him when Alexandros wanted him out of the way."

"Libby!" Ellyn opened her mouth and widened her eyes.

Libby brushed the imaginary insect crawling up her arm. "Don't play innocent. When Pope came to Summerhaven, he didn't go to his family. He stayed at a hotel under an alias. He'd found something important that he wanted to give OASIS."

"This is ludicrous." Ellyn appealed to the director, who sat back in his chair.

"The killer didn't break into Pope's room. Which suggests that he trusted the person. So he let you in, you drugged him, and then—" Libby swallowed. "—you butchered him."

Ellyn pressed a fist to her chest. "Did anyone in the Summerhaven Police Department find any evidence of my having been at the hotel on the day he died?"

"No."

"So once again, you have no proof to support your lies." She fingered one of the stringy black locks that had replaced her silver tresses.

Libby's eyes narrowed. "They didn't know exactly what to look for. I think you posed as a housekeeper. No one ever notices the help, but I bet if they look again—"

Ellyn turned to the director. "I can't believe you would allow this…inquisition."

The director spread a few papers on his desk. "Before you became Pope's OASIS contact, we received substantial reports. With you, the information flow thinned. How do you explain that?"

"It's simple. Schuyler was no longer doing significant research. He feared that Alexandros was on to him. That's why he left so abruptly."

The director pulled a spreadsheet from a folder. "We've also reviewed your financial records over the past few years."

Ellyn stiffened. "What?"

"In addition to your OASIS work with the homeless, it looks as if you've been holding down another job."

"Don't sound so surprised." Ellyn studied her mangled fingernails. "It's not as if OASIS pays that well. When I think of the years I devoted to helping this one and her sister Anomalies... The other Mentors came and went, sometimes with alarming speed. But I was there...from the day Libby was born. Even after she graduated from high school, you charged me to stay near her until she finished college. All those years...I could have been making a name...building a solid career with OASIS. I could have been so much more. I could have been a chief investigator, a Board member, maybe even a director. Instead, I was a glorified babysitter. Even now...I babysit homeless shifters and Simple Humans."

The director studied the spreadsheet. "It looks as if you've found a comfortable second income and recently received substantial payments. One shortly after Schuyler Pope died and another after Ms. Anbruzzen was shot."

Ellyn offered a tight smile. "Coincidence."

"What sort of work did you do for this CAP, LLC?"

Dash sat up. "That's the shell company Alexandros used to buy that place in North Dakota."

"Ellyn!" The director's voice bounced off the walls.

"I gave him misinformation. Nothing that would have hurt any real shifters. He paid well, and I needed the money." She moved about the room. "I went to an Alexandros presentation out of curiosity. I'd heard so much about him as our potential enemy, and I thought I might use what I learned to serve my fellow shifters."

Her pace slowed. "Then I heard him. Most of his speech was nonsense, but the audience swallowed it whole, so I stayed behind to meet him." She gave a dramatic pause. "When he shook my hand, I knew he was special."

Those horrible gloves! Libby clenched her own chilled hands.

The older woman seized the floor. "Away from the crowds, Cris was…gracious… charming. The more we talked, the more I wanted to keep the conversation going. At first, I thought I might convince him he was wrong about shifters, but he was already having second thoughts."

"Because he'd learned people would pay to become shifters," Libby interjected. "But they wanted more than simple shifting. That's when you told him about me and my sisters."

"I didn't tell…I merely confirmed rumors he'd already heard."

"Is that when you told him you were a shifter?" the director asked.

"I don't really remember…perhaps… When he asked for my assistance, I was flattered." She hugged herself. "He made me feel important. Do you have any idea—" She thumped the desk.

The director stood and glowered at Ellyn.

She stepped back. "Of course you don't. With your

big desk and your big salary."

Alexandros used you. Pity stole into Libby's heart until Ellyn spun in her direction.

"You know how it feels, Libby. Remember how the Summerhaven police turned on you?"

"They didn't turn on me, Ellyn. But you did." Libby rubbed her temples. "I always thought of you as someone I could count on...almost family."

Ellyn sneered. "You don't get it, do you? You Anomalies can never be a part of the true shifter world."

Dash's hand on Libby's arm kept her from landing a punch.

"As I said earlier, Honeycutt here could have shared the information he gathered from Libby's mind with Alexandros."

Libby stood. "That's not true. Dash never—"

"Oh, Libby, Libby. You poor child. I know how much you've craved a man since Steffi—"

"Shut up, Ellyn. It took me a while, but I know who I am and what I want. I'm sorry you feel I ruined your life. Perhaps I—and OASIS—should not have relied on you so heavily. Stop making these stupid accusations about Dash."

Libby approached the director's desk. "Dash Honeycutt led the rescue effort. He found me. He healed me." She glanced at the spot above Dash's collarbone where his shirt hid a pale scar. *And he loves me as I love him.* "If he had been working with Alexandros, he wouldn't have done any of that. He would have collected a finder's fee and let me die." Libby glared at Ellyn. "As you were doing."

"I knew nothing about the actual operation. I

thought Alexandros would have his people take DNA samples, blood tests, perhaps a few small tissue samples…nothing invasive and certainly nothing…catastrophic." Ellyn's lips trembled, and she turned to the desk. "Believe me, Mel—sir. We've worked together for a long time. You know me."

"I thought I did." The silver-haired man gazed at his desktop. "What about the Simple Human you shot?"

"Self-defense."

"Right," Libby muttered, returning to her chair.

Ellyn focused on the man behind the desk. "He was one of the homeless people I worked with, and I brought him to my house because I wanted to hire him. Old houses always need repairs. Everything was going well until he…he pulled out that garden hand with knives attached to each of the fingers…that horrible, bloody…" She lifted one hand with her fingers curved. "All I could think was that this must have been the last thing poor Schuyler saw."

"Of course, you would think that." Libby stood and approached the director. "The police department put a hold on the details of Schuyler Pope's death. Information on the murder weapon has never been made public." She confronted her former Mentor. "Only the killer would know."

Ellyn glanced from Libby to the director, whose face looked as if it had turned to stone. "The Simple Human must…maybe he said something, and that's why I—"

"No!" Libby cried. "That night—the night I came to your house after I killed Dumire—you'd left a drawer open in your dining room sideboard. I thought that was strange because you're so neat. That's where you hid the

Pope murder weapon, isn't it?" Ellyn shook her

head.

Libby approached the woman she'd once revered. "You hired that homeless man to dispose of it." "No." Ellyn stepped back.

"What happened? Did he refuse when he saw the weapon? Or did you decide to kill him so the police would think he'd murdered Schuyler Pope?"

Ellyn appealed to the director. "I never—"

The director stood. "Both the Summerhaven police and OASIS know you shot this man. Either tell me the truth, or we'll administer a truth serum. The choice is yours."

Ellyn gave a long sigh. "He wanted more money."

"So you killed him." The director's expression was grim.

Ellyn stared at the back wall. "It seemed reasonable at the time. He was a Simple Human, and not a particularly sound one."

"That's irrelevant. You know we do not harm Simple Humans. Schuyler Pope was also Simple Human…and our friend."

Ellyn clasped her hands. "I made a mistake. Who hasn't?" She looked ready to fling herself over the desk. "I've worked for OASIS for almost thirty years. Don't forget how much good I've done for shifters everywhere. I helped those Anomalies develop their ability and learn to function within our culture.

"Becoming involved with Alexandros was a mistake. I knew it almost as soon as…but he was clever. Very clever. When he threatened to expose me—and all the shifters I knew—I had no choice but to go along."

What happened to the flattery and feeling important?

Ellyn's panicked gaze met Libby's. "I never wanted to hurt you."

Libby cringed.

When the director gestured at the two guards who still stood by the side door, they took positions on either side of Ellyn.

"All I ever wanted was a good life. You must understand that." Ellyn collapsed in front of the desk and lifted her hands. "If you cannot show mercy, please allow me to shift to my cat shape before applying the X-

Ting, so I may live out my days in that form." The director gestured for the guards to remove her.

When the door closed, Libby sank back into her chair.

Dash blotted her cheeks with a handkerchief. "She doesn't deserve your tears."

"I trusted her for years. I never knew how much anger and resentment she hid...although I do think she didn't realize Alexandros was going to kill me." "She must have known he could never release you." Libby sighed.

She and Dash stood.

Libby approached the director's desk. "Ellyn appealed for mercy, sir. I hope you can help her."

The silver-haired man placed the papers and spreadsheet in a folder. "I will convey your concerns to the Tribunal, but she has confessed to killing one Simple Human and assisted in an attack on a fellow Shapeshifter." The corners of his mouth turned down. "Not any shifter but one for whom she had a special duty of care. Also, her plea to live as a cat is a ruse. We've learned the hard way that X-Ting affects shifters only in their human shape."

350

Libby caught her breath. "That must be what happened with Oliver Dumire."

"Exactly. Thank you for bringing this matter to my attention." The director looked from Libby to Dash.

"Where are you headed now?"

Libby spoke up. "Steffi and Sawyer's."

The director's mouth split into a wide smile. "The perfect antidote to this meeting. Please send my regards."

Libby gave him a smart salute. When they reached the door, she stopped and turned. "One more thing."

"Yes?" The director's pen tapped the desk as if eager to return to routine tasks.

"It's about our OASIS classification. The Three Anomalies." The last word stuck in Libby's throat.

Chapter 43

"The Three Supershifters!" Dayzee crowed. "I love it!"

Steffi smiled. "How did you come up with it?" "It's what Alexandros called me." "Ugh!" Dayzee held her nose.

Steffi's upper lip curled.

Libby laughed. "Even a slimeball can have one promising idea. Supershifters sounds way better than Anomalies and more accurately describes us." The tilt of Libby's head dared her sisters to challenge her.

Sawyer joined them in the living room. "How did Uncle Mel respond?"

Dash wrapped his arms around Libby's waist and drew her back against his chest. "He looked as if she wanted to rewrite the OASIS Charter." He kissed the crown of her head. "But Libby wore him down." "Of course she did," Steffi observed.

"That's our Libby!" Dayzee chimed in.

"Supershifters." Steffi stared into space. "I could get used to it."

Dayzee hopped from foot to foot. "We need uniforms."

"Too flashy. How about this?" Libby unzipped her jacket to display a T-shirt on which the new designation sparkled. She opened the bag sitting on the coffee table and offered similar shirts to her sisters.

"I love it!" Dayzee grabbed the garment and held it to her chest. "I want to see how it looks. You should try yours on, too, Steff."

"Maybe later."

"Now! Once the twins wake up, you'll be too busy. And we need a picture." Dayzee offered her phone to Yvette. "Would you?"

The other woman smiled. "With pleasure."

Dayzee gestured to Steffi. "Come on, Steff. We also need a slogan." Her eyes narrowed. "Supershifters.

When you need to shape things up." Steffi and Libby groaned.

Steffi followed Dayzee from the room.

Dash checked his watch for the third time that day.

Libby wrapped an arm around his waist. "Stop worrying."

"They should be here by now."

"It's a long drive, and when you have kids, you have to stop a lot."

He ran a hand through his hair. "What if she changed her mind?"

Libby smoothed the misplaced strands. "You talked to Christie. She wants to see you as much as you want to see her."

"I know, but it's been so long." He shook his head. "I still can't believe Josh was one of the wolves who helped us."

"We do protect our own," Libby reminded him. "Good thing he arrived in time to see you go full Titan and told everybody in earshot that you were his brotherin-law. If he'd gotten there after you went into the house, he wouldn't even have known you were there."

Dash laughed. "I'm glad we had a chance to connect before he left. You can't believe how wonderful it was to hear Christie's voice." He gave Libby a sweet smile and then checked the time again.

Libby wagged a finger. "If you look at that watch one more time, I'll throw it in the trash."

Dash unhooked the watch and handed it to her.

Libby stuffed it in one of her pockets.

Dayzee strutted into the living room and struck a pose. "What do you think?"

"Looks great." Libby laughed. "Of course, you'd look terrific in a paper bag."

Steffi stood off to one side with a tolerant smile that counterpointed Dayzee's flamboyance.

"Where do you want us, Yvette?" Dayzee asked.

Yvette gestured at the sofa.

"You'll have to join your sisters." Dash's lips brushed Libby's temple.

Her heart gave a happy hop.

Dash moved away and leaned against the entryway that separated living and dining rooms. His gaze strayed from the trio on the sofa to the front door.

"Day, you and Libby sit in the front. I'll stand in back."

Libby glanced at her older sister. "You're just doing that to show off your boobs."

Dayzee said, "It's to hide that new baby bump, right?"

Steffi lifted her hands and eyes to the ceiling.

The doorbell chimed.

Dash stood straight up. He looked ready to race to the door, but Sawyer went first.

Libby grinned.

Unfamiliar voices floated in from the foyer, but Dash hurried toward them and collided with his tall, blonde sister, who hugged him hard.

Libby winced. *Don't snap those ribs!*

A tall brown-haired man with a baby sleeping in its carrier and a little boy clinging to the man's side entered the living room.

Dash stared at his sister as if he'd just opened a present. "It's great to see you. I missed you so much."

His sister drew back. She was tall enough to look him straight in the eye. "I missed you, too." She reached up and brushed the hair back from his forehead. Her blue eyes sparkled like Dash's. "You already know Josh. Meet your two terrific nephews." She indicated the baby. "Wiley." She turned to the boy. "And this is Giles." She gestured. "Come meet your uncle Dash." The boy inched forward. "Uncle?" Dash smiled at him.

Libby's heart swelled. *That's how he'll smile at our kids.*

The boy looked from Dash to his father and back.

His eyes, as blue as his mother's, narrowed. "Wolf?"

"No," said Dash.

Christie hugged her son. "He's like me, honey. Uncle Dash."

The boy regarded Dash. "Uncle Dash. Dash!" He giggled. "Funny!"

Dash laughed and stooped so he and the boy were almost eye to eye. "I always thought it was a silly name, too. But I am your uncle Dash. And this—" He gestured for Libby to join him. "—will be your aunt Libby someday soon."

"How exciting!" Christie enveloped Libby in a cloud of pine fragrance. "When's the wedding?" Dayzee hovered by Libby's shoulder. "Yeah, when?"

"Beats me." Libby gave Dash a playful smile. "Was that a proposal?"

Dash scratched his chin. "I planned to take you someplace special." He scanned the group that surrounded them. "But I guess there is no place more special than with people we love. So…" Taking Libby's hand, he got down on one knee. "Elizabeth Irene Anbruzzen, I will love you for as long as the sun shines and the stars sing in the night sky. Will you do me the honor of marrying me?"

Tears misted Libby's vision but didn't hide Dash's hopeful smile. "Dashiell Honeycutt, for as long as the sun shines and the stars sing in the night sky, I will love you." She touched her bosom with her free hand and then rested that hand on Dash's solid chest. "From my heart to yours, yes, I will marry you."

Standing, Dash embraced her while everyone else cheered loud enough to wake the baby.

Dash's sister hugged Libby, reached for the wailing baby, and grinned at Dash. "Guess Mom and Dad will have to get used to more Shapeshifters in the family."

"Most of the shifters in this family should now be working on supper," Steffi announced. She turned to her husband. "Sawyer, please check on the twins. You can also show Josh and Giles the playroom. Let's give Dash and his sister some time together."

Smiling, Sawyer led Dash's brother-in-law further into the house.

Dash drew his sister and nephew close. "After we leave here, I'm taking Libby to meet the folks. Why don't you and Josh come along? We could have a real family reunion."

"I'd love to." Christie dug into the diaper bag hooked onto the baby carrier. "But we both have to work." Cooing at the baby, she changed him and offered him a breast. "When we do go back—and we will, I promise—it will be all of us although Mom and Dad never liked Josh. Neither did you."

"I didn't know him."

His sister's solemn gaze speared him. "You didn't try to know him. He's a good husband. A wonderful father. You don't have to love him. You don't even have to like him."

Dash lifted a hand. "Chris. Stop." He locked his gaze on his sister. "Josh helped save the woman I love. Didn't even know her. Just came when called. For that alone, I will always be grateful to him." He smiled. "And seeing you happy with him…I can't tell you how much…joy…it gives me." He touched his chest.

"Good." Christie smiled at him and moved the baby to her shoulder for a solid burp. "I hope it's different with Mom and Dad for you and Libby."

"I'll let you know how things go. And I'll take pictures of you all. Once they learn they have grandchildren, Mom and Dad may be knocking at your door."

"I'd love that!" Putting the baby on the couch beside her, Christie hugged Dash long and hard. Her bright blue gaze was like a cloudless sky.

"No matter what happens with everyone else, Chris, let's be sure we stay in touch." Dash dipped his head until his forehead touched his sister's and held up one hand with his palm out. Christie's palm met his.

"Twin promise," they intoned together.

When Libby coughed, Dash and Christie separated.

"Sorry to interrupt you two, but dinner is served."

Christie stood and picked up Wiley. "Great!"

Dash hooked arms with his two favorite females and entered the big dining room.

****

Following an enjoyable meal, everyone settled into a small screening room with comfortable chairs and a big screen. Yvette and Sawyer stationed themselves with the video equipment in the back of the room. Steffi sat on one side with the twins and a few toys. Dash's younger nephew snuggled on his mother's lap while Giles sat between his father and his uncle Dash. When Libby rested her hand on Dash's thigh, he covered it. Libby leaned toward him. "You feel so solid."

He chuckled. "I do my best." He tilted his head. "When do I get my watch back?"

She grinned. "When I get my ring."

"I saw one I like, but we'll go shopping tomorrow, and you can decide." He kissed the tip of her nose.

Everyone else applauded Dayzee, who stood in the front of the room. "Don't get too excited. This needs a lot of editing." She looked toward the back of the room. "Lights out!" In the darkened room, she sat in the front row.

Crispin Alexandros appeared in close-up.

The remnants of Libby's meal rose in the back of her throat, and she buried her head in Dash's shoulder.

While a chorus of boos bounced off the walls, Dash stroked her cheek.

Libby shook her head and pressed her hands over her ears. "That voice."

Dash held her trembling body close. "Dayzee!"

Dayzee stood. "Stop, Yvette." Dayzee faced the

audience. "It gets better after this."

Libby's fingers dug into Dash's thigh.

He patted her hand. "We all know the Alexandros pitch," he told Dayzee. "Can you skip the interview?"

"I agree." Steffi chimed in. "The less Alexandros, the better."

"Okay." Dayzee looked toward the back. "Please fast forward to the good stuff, Yvette." Her colleague laughed.

While the interview whipped by, Libby sat back in her chair, but Dash kept her hand on his thigh.

Libby watched Dash, Dayzee, and Yvette on their flight to North Dakota. "You look so determined," she whispered to Dash.

"I promised I would find you." His kiss tickled her ear.

After interviewing the county clerk about property, Dash pinpointed their destination on his phone.

"Thank God for GPS!" someone shouted. Everyone else laughed.

When the open sky filled the screen, Dayzee said, "This road rolled on forever. Prairie, prairie, and more prairie. Yvette, can you fast forward to the ghost town?" Dayzee addressed the audience. "Not really part of the story, but interesting."

At last, tall walls appeared, and Sawyer stared up at the steel barrier.

"Watch this," Dash whispered in Libby's ear.

The camera pulled back to show Dash growing and growing until his head was higher than the walls.

Libby gasped.

"Thirty feet!" Dayzee announced.

"Can you do that?" Josh asked Dash's sister.

Christie laughed.

Steffi said, "You'll get an X rating unless you blur some details."

Everyone hooted.

"What's so funny?" young Giles muttered.

"Grown-up stuff," his mother told him.

When Dash pulled the steel away from the huge stones, Libby stared at the man seated beside her. "You look like you just opened a cardboard box. How could you do that?"

Dash squeezed her hand. "I'd have taken that place apart rock by rock to reach you." She kissed his cheek.

The video followed a fruitless search of the elegant, empty mansion. *So that's where they stayed when they weren't...with me.* Libby shivered and closed her eyes.

"Now we're entering the underground tunnels," Dayzee announced. "Terrible lighting and those noisy alarms."

The camera recorded every frustrating movement before a boom sounded.

Wow! Libby sat up. "I was really loud," she whispered to Dash.

Dash grinned. "You were great." He leaned toward his nephew. "That's your aunt Libby. She turned into a thunderstorm."

"No video here." Dayzee laughed. "I was too busy trying to keep up with Dash and Sawyer."

When the camera captured Libby cradled in Dash's arms, Libby cried, "Dayzee, turn it off. Please!"

"But this is the big—"

"I don't care. Please stop."

The screen went black, and the lights came up.

Dayzee stood by the screen. "Libby, I know this was

painful, but it's the big finish. They were hunting all over for you and finally found you."

"I look half-dead."

Dayzee placed her hands on her hips. "You'd just decked Crispin Alexandros. You flattened a monster."

"But nobody saw that part, and I don't want people to see…" Libby gestured at the screen. "Especially Mom and Dad."

Dayzee approached. "Lib, this is great material. It could put Starshine Productions on the map."

"It's not material." Libby stood. "It's my life. And I don't want you to use it."

All the sparkle left Dayzee's face, and she dropped into a nearby chair.

Standing beside Libby, Dash caressed her still-bony shoulder. "It's a dynamite video, Dayzee. You and Yvette did amazing work. You two make a wonderful team, and you were with me all the way to the end." He was using a gentle voice. His jaw tensed. His next words were going to wound. "But even if Libby agreed, you can't show this."

"Don't worry, Dash." Dayzee faked a laugh. "We'll put some pants on you."

He rubbed his forehead. "You have a bigger problem, no pun intended. This video exposes Shapeshifters."

Sawyer spoke up. "Dash is right. OASIS won't allow it."

"Nor will SUNATNET."

"So the big supernatural conglomerates censor us small independent filmmakers." Dayzee pouted. "That's not fair."

Steffi put an arm around her shoulders. "It's a matter

of protection, Day."

Dayzee wiggled loose.

"In addition," Dash said, "this material would raise questions about what happened to Alexandros. Except for what we see here, he has no connection with this place. He used a shell corporation for the purchase, and no one who worked there will remember anything meaningful. OASIS is already floating a story about him swindling wealthy clients and disappearing with the money."

Dayzee sulked.

Libby joined her sister. "I don't want you to use your actual footage. But there's no reason you can't tell the story as a story. Something made up. That's what we've done in the past, isn't it?"

The Shapeshifters in the group murmured agreement.

Dayzee lifted her head. "I'll need a script."

Libby hugged her sister. "You're a good writer. I'll tell you everything that happened, and you can add those scenes. Think of how it will look and sound when my storm slams Alexandros against the wall." She patted her chest. "That's the me I want the world to see."

Dayzee's pout disappeared. "It might work."

"Changing fact into fiction always has," Steffi assured her. "And the story has everything people look for in those big blockbusters. Even a nasty villain."

"I'll give it a try." Dayzee left her chair and approached Sawyer. "But I can't write the script without our videos."

Sawyer held her off. "Leave them with me for now. I'll bring everything to you in California, along with some OASIS agents, who will be responsible for the video until you finish the script. Then they'll destroy the originals."

Dayzee worried her lip. "Couldn't they store it somewhere? In case something happens to my script?"

"We'll see," Sawyer said, "but eventually—"

"Yeah, yeah." Dayzee counted on her fingers. "Re-creating the location. Hiring dynamite actors. It won't be cheap."

"I'll talk to my father about funding from The Montaigne Foundation," Sawyer said.

"That will help, but we'll need a lot to make it look good." Dayzee ran a hand through her hair and mussed her blonde curls.

"Thank you, Day." Libby hugged her.

Dayzee didn't return Libby's smile. "I'm doing this because I love you. Not because of OASIS."

Libby nodded. "I understand. We three have never been comfortable with OASIS. I guess Steffi made her peace with them when she married Sawyer. SUNATNET welcomes all Supernaturals, even us accidental ones."

Sawyer regarded Libby. "Uncle Mel said you turned down a job offer from OASIS. Are you headed to SUNATNET?"

"Oh, no. I had something much better. Even before he proposed." Libby smiled up at Dash. "Dash and I are going into business together."

"Anbruzzen-Honeycutt Associates," Dash intoned.

Dayzee cried, "Aha!"

Libby clapped. "Exactly. AHA! Investigations. Mostly routine investigations, but SUNATNET may be a big client."

Dash ruffled Libby's hair. "They've already given us our first assignment."

"Something exotic?" Dayzee asked.

Libby and Dash looked at each other and laughed.

"We're heading back to Summerhaven to monitor a demon portal that's acting up." Libby looked as if she'd received a party invitation.

"Demons." Steffi frowned. "Sounds dangerous." "Don't worry, Steff." Libby embraced her sister. "My partner is a Titan, and I have promised to keep my worst impulses in check."

Dash dipped his chin. "And I promise to pay more attention to my Supershifter partner's best impulses."

"But first, we have a wedding to plan!" Libby threw her arms around Dash's neck and kissed him.

A word about the author...

People like to quote F. Scott Fitzgerald on there being no second acts in American lives. Born in Baltimore, Maryland, in 1944, I am entering my fifth act. I began to write at age twelve when I received a portable Smith-Corona typewriter for Christmas. (My mother thought I'd make a good secretary. Little did she know!) I was a staff writer with Maryland Public Broadcasting in its infancy (1969-1972) but left to go "back to the land" AKA my hippie days, where I freelanced and did contractual work with MPB to keep us financially afloat. I started writing romances in the late 1980s but put them aside to earn a PhD in English and pursue an academic teaching career (academic writing, not as much fun). }(Upon retiring in 2014, I returned to romance with a renewed sense of purpose and a stronger awareness of the craft. I'm also a sucker for happy endings.

Thank you for purchasing
this publication of The Wild Rose Press, Inc.

For questions or more information
contact us at
info@thewildrosepress.com.

The Wild Rose Press, Inc.
www.thewildrosepress.com

www.ingramcontent.com/pod-product-compliance
Lightning Source LLC
Chambersburg PA
CBHW072307020726
47501CB00002B/427